The Triumph
of the Lions

The Triumph of the Lions

a novel

Stefania Auci

Translated from the Italian by
Katherine Gregor and Howard Curtis

HarperVia

An Imprint of HarperCollins*Publishers*

THE TRIUMPH OF THE LIONS. Copyright © 2021 by Stefania Auci. English translation © 2024 by Katherine Gregor and Howard Curtis. All rights reserved. Printed in the United States of America. No part of this book may be used or reproduced in any manner whatsoever without written permission except in the case of brief quotations embodied in critical articles and reviews. For information, address HarperCollins Publishers, 195 Broadway, New York, NY 10007.

HarperCollins books may be purchased for educational, business, or sales promotional use. For information, please email the Special Markets Department at SPsales@harpercollins.com.

Originally published as chapters 1 to 4 of the original Italian edition, *L'inverno dei Leoni* in Italy in 2021 by Nord.

FIRST HARPERVIA EDITION PUBLISHED IN 2024

Library of Congress Cataloging-in-Publication Data has been applied for.

ISBN 978-0-06-293170-2

24 25 26 27 28 LBC 5 4 3 2 1

To Eleonora and Federico,

for all the tenderness and affection.

I am very proud of you.

I have lived long enough: my way of life
Is fall'n into the sear, the yellow leaf;
And that which should accompany old age,
As honour, love, obedience, troops of friends,
I must not look to have; but, in their stead,
Curses, not loud but deep, mouth-honour, breath,
Which the poor heart would fain deny, and dare not.

—WILLIAM SHAKESPEARE, *MACBETH*, ACT V, SCENE 3

CONTENTS

THE FLORIO FAMILY TREE
1723–1893

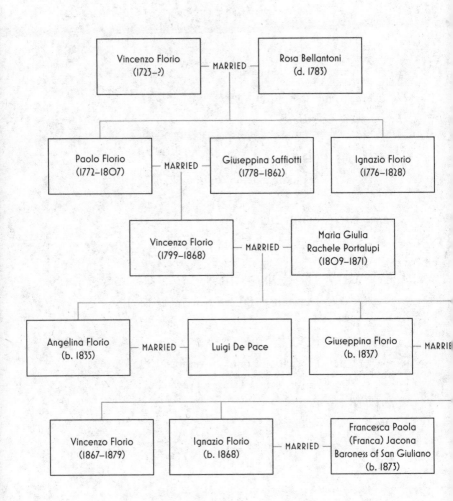

Vincenzo Florio (1723–?) MARRIED Rosa Bellantoni (d. 1783)

Paolo Florio (1772–1807) MARRIED Giuseppina Saffiotti (1778–1862)

Ignazio Florio (1776–1828)

Vincenzo Florio (1799–1868) MARRIED Maria Giulia Rachele Portalupi (1809–1871)

Angelina Florio (b. 1835) MARRIED Luigi De Pace

Giuseppina Florio (b. 1837) MARRIE

Vincenzo Florio (1867–1879)

Ignazio Florio (b. 1868) MARRIED Francesca Paola (Franca) Jacona Baroness of San Giuliano (b. 1873)

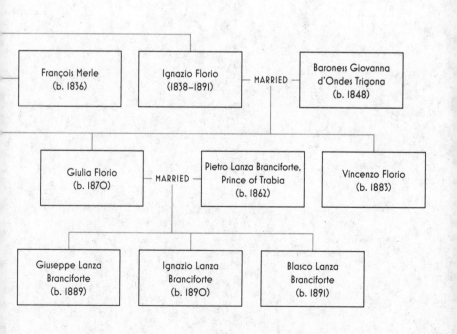

The Florios

1799–1868

ORIGINALLY FROM BAGNARA CALABRA, THE brothers Paolo and Ignazio Florio arrive in Palermo in 1799, determined to make a fortune. They are *aromatari*—dealers in spices—and there's ruthless competition, but their rise immediately seems unstoppable and soon their business expands: they start to trade in sulfur, buy houses and land from penniless Palermo aristocrats, and set up a shipping company. This impetus, fueled by stubborn determination, continues after Vincenzo, Paolo's son, takes over the reins of Casa Florio: in the family winery, marsala—a poor man's wine—is transformed into a nectar fit for a king's table; on Favignana, a revolutionary method for preserving tuna—canned in oil—revamps its consumption. Amid all this, Palermo watches the Florios' success with a blend of admiration, envy, and contempt: these men remain "foreigners," "laborers" whose blood "stinks of sweat." It is precisely a burning desire for social redemption that is at the root of the Florios' ambition and, for better or for worse, marks their public and private lives. Indeed, the men in this family are exceptional, if brittle, individuals and—although they won't admit it—they need equally exceptional women at their sides: like Giuseppina, Paolo's wife, who sacrifices everything—including love—for the sake of her family's stability, or Giulia, the young Milanese who sweeps into Vincenzo's life like a whirlwind and becomes his safe haven, his unassailable rock.

Vincenzo dies in 1868, not even seventy years old, leaving the destiny of Casa Florio in the hands of his only son, the thirty-year-old Ignazio, who, two years earlier, married Baroness Giovanna d'Ondes Trigona, thereby bringing "noble blood" into the Florio family at last. Ignazio has grown up to worship work, aware that the Florios must always look beyond the horizon. He prepares to write a new chapter in the history of his family . . .

PART ONE

Sea

September 1868 to June 1874

Aceddu 'nta l'aggia 'un canta p'amuri, ma pi' raggia.
The caged bird sings not out of love, but anger.
—SICILIAN PROVERB

U'MARI UNN'AVI NÉ CHIESE NÉ taverne—there are no churches or inns at sea—is what old fishermen say. There's nowhere to take shelter, because the sea is the most majestic, elusive element in the world, and human beings can only bow to its will.

Sicilians have always known that the sea respects those who respect it in return. It's generous: it provides fish and salt for nourishment, wind for sails, coral for the jewels of saints and kings. But it's also unpredictable and can snatch back all its gifts at any minute. That's why Sicilians respect it, letting it define their very core—forge their temperament, mark their skin, support them, feed them, and protect them.

The sea is boundless, in constant flux. This is why those who live in Sicily are restless and forever searching for lands beyond the horizon, eager to escape, to look elsewhere for things that, at the end of their lives, they discover have always been at their side.

For Sicilians, the sea is a father. They realize this when they're far away from it, when they can't smell the powerful scent of algae and salt that envelops them as soon as the wind blows and carries it deep into the city's alleys.

For Sicilians, the sea is a mother. Beloved and jealous. Essential. Cruel at times.

For Sicilians, the sea is the shape and border of their soul.

Both bondage and freedom.

At first, it's a whisper, a murmur on a breath of wind. It starts at the heart of the Olivuzza villa, behind closed curtains, in semi-dark rooms. The wind seizes the voice, and it grows stronger, mixed with the tears and sobs of an elderly woman holding a cold hand.

"*Murìu . . .*" the voice says, quivering in disbelief. The word creates a reality, sealing what has just happened, making it irreversible. The whisper reaches the servants' ears, travels to their lips, then once again yields to the wind, which carries it across the garden, toward the city. It bounds from mouth to mouth, adopts tones of surprise, lamentation, anxiety, fear, bitterness.

"*Murìu . . .*" Palermo residents repeat, their eyes turning toward the Olivuzza. *He's dead.* They cannot believe that a man like Vincenzo Florio is dead. Of course, he was old, had been sick for a long time and delegated the management of the Florio business to his son. But even so . . . Vincenzo Florio was the city's titan, a man so formidable that nothing and nobody could stop him. And yet an apoplectic fit struck him down.

Some are glad. Envy and a thirst for revenge have had years to take root in the minds of some people. But it's an empty pleasure. Vincenzo Florio died in peace, in his bed, comforted by the love of his wife and children. And he died wealthy, surrounded by all he was able to obtain, whether by will or luck. As a matter of fact, death seems to have had in store for Vincenzo a compassion he seldom afforded others.

"*Murìu!*"

Full of astonishment, grief, and anger, the voice now pierces the heart of Palermo, soars over the old port of La Cala, and plummets into the surrounding narrow streets. It reaches Via dei Materassai, carried by a breathless servant. There was no need for him to run, because that cry, that "*Murìu!*" has already slipped through the doors and windows and rolled across the floor tiles, all the way to Ignazio's bedroom, where the wife of the new master of Casa Florio is sitting.

When she hears the shouts and sobs from the street, Giovanna d'Ondes Trigona abruptly lifts her head, her long black braid swaying; grasps the arms of her chair; and gives Donna Ciccia—once her governess, now her lady-in-waiting—a quizzical look.

There's a peremptory knock. Donna Ciccia instinctively shields the head of the newborn—Ignazziddu, Giovanna's second child—in her arms and goes to open the door. She abruptly halts the servant on the threshold and asks curtly, "What is it?"

"*Muriu!* Don Vincenzo, just now." Still panting, the servant looks at Giovanna. "Signora, your husband sends word that you must get ready and prepare the house for relatives coming to call."

"He's dead . . . ?" Giovanna says, more shocked than aggrieved. She can't feel sorrow for a man she never loved, a man who, on the contrary, filled her with so much fear that she could hardly speak in his presence. It's true that he'd gotten worse in the past few days— another reason why they didn't celebrate Ignazziddu's birth—but she hadn't expected such a sudden end. She struggles to her feet. The birth was painful, and she feels drained even just standing. "Is my husband there?"

The servant nods. "Yes, *Donna* Giovanna."

Donna Ciccia blushes, tucks in a lock of hair that's escaped her bonnet, and turns to look at her. Giovanna opens her mouth to speak but can't. She reaches out her arms, picks up the baby, and holds him to her breast.

Donna Giovanna Florio. That's what they'll call her from now on. Not "Baroness," as she's entitled to by birth, a title that played such an important role in her being admitted to this household of wealthy merchants. Being a Trigona is no longer of consequence, nor is belonging to one of Palermo's oldest families. What counts now is the fact that she's *the mistress of the house*.

Donna Ciccia goes to her and takes the baby from her arms. "You must wear mourning clothes," she murmurs. "The first visitors will shortly be here to express their condolences." There's a new deference in her voice, a tone Giovanna has never heard before. The mark of an irreversible change.

She has a specific role now and must prove that she's up to the task.

She can feel her breath retreat to her chest and blood drain from her face. She grasps the hem of her robe and squeezes it. "Give instructions for all the mirrors to be covered and half open the front door," she says in a steady voice. "Then come and help me."

Giovanna heads to her dressing room, past the four-poster bed. Her hands are shaking and she feels cold. There's only one thought in her mind.

I am Donna *Giovanna Florio*.

The house is empty.

Nothing but shadows.

Shadows that stretch over walnut and mahogany furniture, beyond doors left ajar, between the folds of thick curtains.

There's silence. Not peace. It's a stifling absence of sound, an oppressive stillness that takes your breath away, discouraging movement.

The residents of the house are asleep. All except one: Ignazio wanders the rooms of Via dei Materassai in darkness, in his bed jacket and slippers. The insomnia he suffered when he was young has returned.

He hasn't slept for three nights. Not since his father died.

His eyes grow moist and he rubs them hard. He can't cry, he mustn't; tears are for women. And yet he feels a crushing sense of alienation, abandonment, and solitude. He can taste suffering in his mouth and swallows it, holding it inside. He paces from one room to another, stops by a window, and looks out. Via dei Materassai is engulfed by a darkness interrupted by only a few fragments of light from the streetlamps. The windows of the other houses are like hollow eyes.

Every breath has weight, shape, and a taste—a bitter taste. Oh, how bitter.

Ignazio is thirty years old. His father entrusted him with the management of the Marsala winery a long time ago and recently invested him with power of attorney over the business. Two years ago, he married Giovanna, who has borne him Vincenzo and Ignazio, male heirs to guarantee the future of Casa Florio. He is rich, respected, and powerful.

But nothing can erase the solitude of his grief.

Its emptiness.

The walls, objects, and furnishings are silent reminders of days when his family was still whole, intact. When there was firm order to the world and time flowed to the rhythm of shared work. An equilibrium shattered into a thousand pieces, leaving a crater with him at its center, and nothing but rubble and desolation all around.

He keeps walking down corridors to his father's study. He briefly considers entering but realizes he can't, not tonight, when memories are so vivid, they seem made of flesh. So he continues past the door and climbs the stairs to the room where his father would entertain business associates during informal meetings or else retire to be alone and think. It's a small room clad in timber and paintings. Ignazio stands motionless in the doorway, eyes downcast. A beam of white light floods in through the open windows, illuminating the quilted leather armchair and the coffee table on which a newspaper lies. The paper his father was reading the night before the stroke that reduced him to immobility. Though months have passed, nobody's had the courage to throw it away. On a corner of the table lay his pince-nez and box of snuff. It's all here, as though he were coming back any time now.

Ignazio almost perceives his fragrance, a cologne redolent of sage, lemon, and sea air, his breathing, a kind of labored murmur, and, finally, his heavy tread. He pictures him again reading letters and documents with that faint smile that gave his face an amused expression, then looking up and muttering some comment or other.

Ignazio is devoured by grief. How can he carry on without him? He's had months to worry about it and prepare, but now he doesn't know how to. He feels as though he's about to drown, just like that time when, as a child in Arenella, he went under and his father dived in, saving him. He remembers gasping for air, seawater burning his windpipe . . . the way the tears he's trying to repress burn him now. But he must resist. Because now he's the head of the family and he must take care of Casa Florio, but also of his mother, who's alone. And, naturally, also of Giovanna, Vincenzo, Ignazziddu . . .

He gulps a mouthful of air and dries his eyes. He's afraid he'll forget what his father looked like, that he'll no longer remember his hands or his scent. But no one must know this. No one must see the emotion in his eyes. He's not a son who's lost his father. He's the new owner of a fortunate, fast-expanding enterprise.

Still, he admits it in this painfully lonely moment: he wishes he could reach out and find his father's hand, ask him for advice, work beside him in silence, as they did so many times.

Himself a father now, he wishes he could go back to just being a son.

"Ignazio!"

His mother calls in a whisper. She saw his shadow cross the light that seeps from under the door to where Vincenzino and Ignazziddu sleep. She's sitting in an armchair, rocking the youngest baby in her arms, a baby born into this world just as his grandfather was departing it.

Giulia wears a black velvet robe, her gray hair in a braid. In the lamplight, Ignazio sees her hands, numb from the arthritis, and her hunched back. She's been plagued by pain in her bones for years, but always managed to carry herself upright. Now, though, she appears almost crumpled, much older than fifty-nine, as though she's suddenly shouldered the whole world's weariness. This is partly because her eyes—so calm and simultaneously alive with curiosity—have become dull, lifeless.

"*Maman* . . . What are you doing here? Why didn't you call the wet nurse?"

Giulia looks at him silently, then goes back to rocking the baby. A tear forms on her eyelashes. "He would have been happy about this child, about your having two boys. Your wife has done very well: at twenty she's already given you two heirs."

Ignazio feels his heart crack open again. He sits down opposite his mother, in the armchair next to the cradle. "I know." He squeezes her hand. "What upsets me most is that he won't see him grow."

Giulia swallows air. "He could have lived long, only he never paced himself, never. He never once took a day off. Even on feast days he worked . . . here," she says, touching her temple. "He couldn't stop. In the end, that's what took him away from me." She sighs, then seizes her son's hand. "*Swear.* Swear to me that you will never put work before your family."

Giulia has a strong grip, a desperate energy that stems from the awareness that time only takes and never gives back; if anything, it burns memories and turns them to ash. Ignazio places his hand over hers, feeling the bones under her papery skin. The crack in his heart widens. "Yes, of course."

Giulia shakes her head, rejecting his mechanical reply. Ignazziddu gurgles in her arms. "No. You have to think of your wife and these little ones—*'sti picciriddi.*" Using a typically Sicilian gesture, she juts her chin toward the little bed where Vincenzino, nearly two, is asleep. A Sicilian gesture from a Milanese who came to the island when she was barely twenty. "You don't know, you can't possibly remember, but your father didn't really *see* your sisters, Angelina and Peppina, grow. He barely even kept up with you, and then only because you were the boy he wanted." Her voice drops, quivering with concealed tears. "Don't make the same mistake. Of the things we can miss out on, the childhoods of our children are among the most painful."

He nods, covers his face with his hands. Years of stern looks surface in his memory. Only as an adult did he learn to discern pride and affection in his father's dark eyes. Vincenzo Florio wasn't a man of words but of looks, for better or worse. A man incapable of showing affection. Ignazio doesn't remember hugs. Perhaps the odd pat. And yet Ignazio loved him.

"And don't neglect your wife . . . Giovanna—poor darling—

loves you and is always trying to get your attention." Giulia glares at him with a mixture of reproach and regret. She sighs. "You married her, so surely you must feel something for her."

He removes his hands as though to dismiss an annoying thought. "Yes," he mutters. He adds nothing else and lowers his head to escape his mother's eyes, which have always seen into the depths of his soul.

That sorrow belongs only to him.

Giulia gets up and, taking slow steps, lays Ignazziddu back in the cradle. The baby turns his little head with a contented sigh and falls asleep.

Ignazio waits for her by the door, places his hand on her shoulder, and walks her to her room. "I'm glad you decided to come and stay here, at least for a few days. I couldn't bear to think of you on your own."

She nods. "The Olivuzza house is too big without him." *Empty. Forever.*

Ignazio feels his breath congeal.

Giulia goes into the room her son and daughter-in-law have given her, the same room where, many years earlier, her mother-in-law, Giuseppina Saffiotti Florio, lived. A stern woman who'd lost her husband when she was still young, she had raised her son, Vincenzo, with her brother-in-law, Ignazio, and for a long time opposed Giulia joining the family, regarding her as a bad lot and a social climber. Now Giulia, too, is a widow. She stands in the middle of the room as her son shuts the door. Her eyes come to rest on the double bed.

Ignazio doesn't hear her words. Nor can he ever understand her grief, which differs from his own: more visceral, more acute, without hope.

Because she and Vincenzo chose each other, wanted and loved each other, in spite of everything and everyone.

"How can I live without you, my love?"

⌒

The door scrapes the floor ever so slightly and closes without a sound. Next to her, the mattress buckles under Ignazio's weight, his body emitting a warmth that mingles with her own.

Giovanna slows her breathing and feigns the sleep that evaporated the moment her husband got up. She knows that Ignazio suffers from insomnia, and she, a light sleeper, often remains awake without moving. Moreover, she thinks Ignazio is much more affected by his father's death than he cares to admit.

Her eyes are wide open in the darkness. She remembers clearly the first time she saw Vincenzo Florio: a large man with a furrowed brow and heavy breathing. He looked at her the way one values livestock at the market.

Uneasy, all she could do was cast down her eyes and stare at the floor in the hall in the Villa delle Terre Rosse, just outside the walls of Palermo.

He turned to his wife and, in what must have been intended to be a whisper but echoed across the hall, remarked, "Isn't she too skinny?"

Giovanna suddenly raised her head. Was she really to be chided for spending her life trying not to become her mother, who was so fat she was practically shapeless? Were they perhaps implying that she couldn't make a good wife? Wounded by this accusation of inadequacy, she looked to Ignazio, hoping he'd say something in her defense.

But he remained indifferent, a faint, detached smile on his lips.

It was her father, Gioacchino d'Ondes, Count of Gallitano, who reassured Vincenzo. "She's a healthy girl," he stated proudly. "And she'll provide your house with strong sons."

That's right, her ability to give birth was the only thing that truly interested Don Vincenzo, not whether she was fat or thin or whether Ignazio was in love with her.

And yet, despite it all, she entered the Florio household with a heart brimming with love for that husband of hers, who was so measured and self-controlled.

Yes, she was thrilled because she'd immediately fallen in love with him, from the moment she'd first seen him at the Casino delle Dame e dei Cavalieri, before she was seventeen, and later she'd been conquered by his calming influence on her, by his strength, which seemed to emanate directly from an unshakable belief in his superiority, and by the calmness of his words.

Desire came later, after they had shared intimacy. But it was desire that tricked her, making her believe that their marriage was different from those that other people had described to her and that it might contain affection or at least respect. Everybody had warned her, from her mother with her vague allusions that Giovanna would have to make "sacrifices" and "tolerate" her husband, to the priest who, on her wedding day, had told her that "patience is a wife's principal asset."

Even more so when you marry a Florio, his eyes had added.

She was patient, putting herself last, obeying, forever seeking a nod of approval or at least acknowledgment. For two years, she lived with Donna Giulia's polite composure and Don Vincenzo's cutting looks, always at a disadvantage because of her dowry, which wasn't very generous, and her education, which was far inferior to that of her sisters-in-law, and lost in a house and a family that had turned out to be foreign to her. She appealed to her aristocratic pride, her Trigona blood, and above all, to what she felt, because in the middle of that house and family, there was Ignazio.

With tenacity and determination, she waited for him to notice her, to really look at her. But all she obtained was affectionate politeness, a lukewarm, elusive attitude.

Hearing him snore behind her, she turns to examine his profile in the dark. She's given him two sons. She loves him, albeit in a blind, foolish way, she knows.

She also knows it's not enough.

The truth, Giovanna thinks, *is that you get accustomed to everything*. And for too long she's made do with crumbs. But now she wants more. Now she wants really to be his wife.

᷈

On the morning of September 21, 1868, the notary Giuseppe Quattrocchi reads out the last will and testament of Vincenzo Florio, tradesman. Wearing a dark, English-tailored suit and black wool crepe tie, Ignazio listens to the sections of the will, divided according to Casa Florio's areas of interest. On the table are numerous files, each carefully stacked. The notary's secretary picks them up and checks the list of assets. A string of locations, names, and numbers.

Ignazio is impassive. No one can see his clasped hands tremble beneath the table.

He's always known they managed an extensive business network, but only now does he *truly* begin to realize just how complex and multifaceted it is. Until a few days ago, he handled only a few sectors, the Marsala winery in particular. He enjoyed spending the grape-harvesting season at the processing plant, waiting to see the sun set behind the Aegadian Islands, beyond the Stagnone Lagoon.

Now, instead, a mountain of papers, money, contracts, and obligations grows before his eyes. He'll have to scale it and reach its summit. But that still won't be enough: he'll have to tame it. The Florios must *always* look ahead. It was what his grandfather Paolo and his uncle Ignazio did when they left Bagnara for Palermo. It was what his father did when he set up the Marsala winery, took over the management of the *tonnara* on Favignana, and obstinately insisted—against everybody's advice—on the Oretea Foundry, which now employs and feeds dozens of men. There's never been any doubt that he would follow in their footsteps. He's the man of the house, the heir, the one who will have to carry on the family name and consolidate its power and wealth.

In a single gesture, Ignazio lifts his joined hands, which have finally stopped trembling, and puts them on the table. Then he glances at his ring finger. Below the wedding band, he wears the hammered gold ring his father gave him on his wedding day two years ago: it had belonged to the uncle he's named after and, before that, to his great-grandmother Rosa Bellantoni. Never before has it weighed so heavily.

The notary has continued reading. He has now reached the bequests to Ignazio's mother and sisters. Ignazio listens, nods, then signs the documents accepting the inheritance.

At last he stands and looks around. He knows everyone is expecting him to say a few words and he neither wants nor is able to disappoint them. "Thank you for coming. My father was an extraordinary man: he didn't have an easy temper, but he was loyal toward everyone and bold in his ventures." He pauses, searching for the right words. His back is straight, his voice steadfast. "I trust that you will continue to work for Casa Florio with the same commitment you afforded him. I intend to continue his work and ensure that our enterprises go from strength to strength. But I'm not forgetting that Casa Florio is first and foremost a resource for many people and provides them with bread, work, and dignity. I promise I'll take particular care of them . . . of you. Together, we will make this company the heart of Palermo and the whole of Sicily." He indicates the files in front of him and places his hands on them.

Some nod. Worry lines relax and tense expressions soften.

At least for now they don't need further assurances, Ignazio thinks, feeling the stiffness in his shoulders ebbing away. *But it'll be different as early as tomorrow.*

All those present rise to their feet and approach him. They all express their condolences again; some ask for an appointment. Ignazio thanks them and motions to his secretary to set up meetings.

The last to come up to Ignazio is Vincenzo Giachery, together with Giuseppe Orlando. They are family friends even before being employees and advisors of Casa Florio. Vincenzo is the brother of Carlo Giachery, Ignazio's father's right-hand man as well as the architect of Villa dei Quattro Pizzi, who died three years ago. Another sorrow Vincenzo bore impassively, withdrawing into himself. Giuseppe, on the other hand, is a skilled mechanical engineer and expert in merchant seafaring, a former Garibaldi supporter, now a quiet official and good father.

"Don Ignazio," Giachery says without beating about the bush. "We need to talk. It's about the steamships."

"I know."

No, not tomorrow: today, Ignazio thinks, tight-lipped. *There's no time, I haven't had any and now will never have any.*

He looks at the two men and holds his breath for a second before exhaling. He follows them out of the room. Servants are handing hats and gloves to the relatives who came for the funeral and the reading of the will. He greets his sister Angelina and her husband, Luigi De Pace, and shakes hands with Augusto Merle, the father-in-law of his sister Giuseppina, who's lived in Marseille for years.

The three men head to Vincenzo's study. At the door, Ignazio hesitates, just as he did the night before, as though he were facing a wall. He's been to this room on countless occasions, but only while his father was alive and called the shots at Casa Florio.

What right does he have to enter it now? Everyone says he's the heir, but isn't he rather an impostor? Who is he without his father?

Ignazio closes his eyes and, for an extended moment, imagines opening the door and seeing him sitting there, in his leather armchair. He sees him lift his head, his gray hair tousled, his brow furrowed, a quizzical look in his eyes, a sheet of paper clasped in his hand . . .

Instead, it's Vincenzo Giachery's hand that comes to rest on his shoulder. "Courage," he says under his breath.

No, not today: now, Ignazio thinks, trying to banish the dread that oppresses him. From him, death has taken a father; from them, a guide. *Now, not later*, because the moment has come to prove that he'll be a worthy successor to his father. That his life—dedicated to Casa Florio since the moment of his birth—is not useless. That the fragility of grief doesn't belong to him and that, even if he feels it, he must conceal it. He's the one who must reassure them. The time when he can rely on their support and comfort is already over for him. Indeed, it seems it never even began.

So he steps through that wall, walks into the room, and takes possession of it. The study returns to being what it is: a place of work, paneled in dark wood, with solid furniture, two leather armchairs, and a large mahogany desk heaped with documents, papers, and account reports.

He sits behind *that* desk, in *that* armchair. For a moment, his eyes home in on the inkwell and the tray where lie a paper knife, seals, a ruler, and a few sheets of blotting paper. There's a fingerprint on one of them.

"So." He takes a deep breath. On the blotter, he sees notes of condolence, Francesco Crispi's on top. *I must write to him right away, too*, he thinks. Crispi and his father met when Garibaldi's followers arrived in Palermo, and a relationship of frankness and mutual trust began immediately and grew stronger over the years. He was the Florios' lawyer and now seems on his way to a brilliant political career: he has recently been elected to the Maglie college and that of Castelvetrano. "We must first and foremost reassure everyone. They must continue to trust us as they have been doing up to now."

"And what's your view of government subsidies? Rumor has it the government is reluctant to renew them, and it would be dangerous for Casa Florio to be without that support. The Mediterranean is swarming with companies that would sink one another with cannon fire just to obtain an extra route."

Immediately on the front line, Ignazio thinks. Here it is, the prickliest question.

"I know that perfectly well and haven't the slightest intention of letting anyone step in front of me. I'm considering contacting the general manager of Mail Services, Barbavara: I think it would be appropriate to assure him that we have specific ideas regarding the merger of our Piroscafi Postali with Genoa's Accossato and Peirano, which, as you know, together with Rubattino, owns over half the national steam tonnage. This move would undoubtedly improve transportation in general and our fleet in particular. But, above all, I plan to protest the suppression of the Livorno section: this is highly disadvantageous to us, because it severs the direct connection between Sicily and central Italy. I'll ask our intermediary at the ministry, Cavalier Scibona, to deliver him the letter and support our cause."

In a huff, Orlando rubs his thighs. "Scibona is a lackey—a *spicciafacenne*—his only advantage is that he's already inside the ministry. But he's always been and always will be no more than a pen pusher, so I'm not sure how much weight he carries. We need someone higher up."

Ignazio nods slowly and raises his eyebrows. "That's why I want to speak to the manager of Mail Services in person," he says. "He'll be able to apply pressure when need be . . . Even though . . ." He picks up a paper knife and twirls it. "The problem stems from the source: the government has decided to cut expenditure. Roads and railroads are being built in northern Italy, and trade with Sicily is of little interest to them. It's up to us to give them an incentive to justify the subsidies to transportation, and so make the routes profitable."

Giachery puts his elbows on the desk and Ignazio stares at him: in the dim light, his gaunt face, with his dark hair splashed with gray, eerily resembles his deceased brother's. *It's like being at a ghosts' reunion, with me as the only man alive*, Ignazio thinks. *Ghosts that refuse to leave.* "What do you think, Don Vincenzo?" he asks. "Why aren't you saying anything?"

The man shrugs his shoulders and gives him a sideways glance. "Because you've already made your decision. Nothing is going to make you change your mind."

These words snatch a laugh from him—the first in many days.

It's to his credit. "Exactly. It's a matter of making it sound attractive. Make it so that Barbavara understands it's best for him to be amenable to Casa Florio and our interests."

Giachery spreads his arms. With a hint of a smile, he replies, "And so it is."

Ignazio leans back in his armchair and peers into the distance. The letter he's going to write is already taking shape in his mind. It's not a responsibility to delegate to his secretary: he will handle it himself.

"Besides, we have to watch our backs from competition in our own backyard," Giuseppe Orlando says. "A little bird told me that the shipping magnate Pietro Tagliavia means to build a fleet made up exclusively of steamers in order to trade with the eastern Mediterranean." He stifles a yawn with his fist. These have been trying days for everyone, and they're tired. "When the French canal opens in Suez, it'll be much easier and quicker to go to the Indies—"

"That's another thing we need to talk about," Ignazio says, interrupting him. "The spice trade brought much wealth to my father, but it's no longer as important as it once was. We must now concentrate on the fact that people want to travel fast and without sacrificing comfort. In other words, they want to feel modern. That's what we must guarantee them, by servicing the Mediterranean routes with steamships faster than those of our competitors."

The two men look at each other in alarm. Give up the spice trade, one of the Florios' principal activities? They're advanced in age and have seen many things happen. They know that such a radical departure could have disastrous consequences.

Ignazio stands and walks to the wall, where there's a large map of the world. He spreads his fingers over the Mediterranean. "It's the steamships that will bring us wealth. Them and the winery.

Our main objective will be to protect and nurture those two businesses. If we don't receive support from the government, we'll have to earn it for ourselves, fighting tooth and nail. We'll have to count our friends, but above all know our enemies and how to combat them, and always keep our eyes open, because no one will forgive us errors." He looks at them, speaking calmly and firmly. "We must expand the transportation network. That's why we need powerful men like Barbavara on our side."

The two men exchange tense glances but don't dare speak. Ignazio notices and takes a step toward them. "Trust me," he murmurs. "My father always looked ahead, beyond the horizon. I want to do the same."

After a few seconds, Giachery nods, gets up, and proffers his hand. "You are Don Ignazio Florio. You know what to do." These words contain everything Ignazio can hope for, at least for now. Acknowledgment, trust, and support.

Orlando also stands up and heads to the door. "Will you come by the bank tomorrow?"

"I intend to do so right away," Ignazio replies, indicating a bundle of papers on the desk. "We must close my father's management and open mine."

Orlando merely nods.

The door closes behind the two men.

Ignazio rests his forehead on the jamb. *You've tackled the first hurdle*, he tells himself. *Now the others will come, one at a time.*

The papers on the desk are looking at him, prodding him. He sits back down and ignores them. *Wait a little longer*, he implores, wiping his face with his hand. Then he grabs the notes and telegrams of condolence. They come from all over Europe: he recognizes the signatures and is proud that so many important people knew and respected his father. There's even a telegram from the tsar's court, a mark of the esteem built up over years.

Then, among the last messages, he finds an envelope with a French stamp. It's from Marseille.

He knows this handwriting. He opens the envelope slowly, as though afraid of it.

I have heard of your loss.
 I am sincerely aggrieved for you. I can imagine how much
you must be suffering.
 I embrace you.

No signature. There's no need for one.

He turns the Amalfi paper card over: there are two names printed on the back. One has been crossed out with a firm stroke of the pen.

Ignazio's face darkens with a bitterness that has nothing to do with his father's death. It's a sorrow in addition to another sorrow. A recollection that tastes of regret, of longing for a life never lived, only dreamed of. One of those desires you carry within you all your life even though you know you can never fulfill it.

No.

He stacks the cards up in a corner. He'll see to them later. The one that's unsigned, however, he puts in the pocket of his jacket, over his heart.

❧

Giovanna, in robe and slippers, leans slightly out the window. The Palermo weather is teasing, with a cold humidity that cuts to your bones in the morning and a still-summery heat by midday.

She looks at the traffic of carriages and hears greetings exchanged on the doorstep. With difficulty, she withdraws, collapses into the armchair with a grimace of pain, then looks around. The door leading to Ignazio's bedroom is partially cloaked by a heavy curtain of green brocade; she sees the gilded, embossed canopy and a tortoise-shell and mother-of-pearl headboard with the figure of Christ on the cross. On the feathered mahogany nightstand with brass inlays lies one of her mother-in-law's wedding gifts: a silver toiletry set with floral patterns, made in England.

Everything is refined, luxurious.

But beyond the walls, there's the Castellammare district, the old Merchants' Lodge, full of storerooms, shops, and workers' huts. A world now beneath the Florios' rank. She tried telling Ignazio more than once, but he wouldn't listen to her. "We'll be fine here," he replied. "We'll leave the Olivuzza to my parents, they're elderly and need clean air and peace. What is it you don't like here, anyway? My mother gave us this house, which is much more convenient for us, and closer to Piazza Marina and the Casa Florio offices. I've even just had gas lighting installed. What else do you need?"

Giovanna purses her small mouth and gives an angry huff. She can't understand why Ignazio insists on living here while the Olivuzza remains in her mother-in-law's hands, especially now that she's on her own. She detests living in such close quarters with everyone, on this working-class street. She can't open the curtains without the neighbor opposite immediately stepping out onto her balcony, as though trying to push her way into Giovanna's room. On occasion, she's even heard the neighbor comment out loud on what she could see, for the benefit of the entire neighborhood.

She misses the open air in Terre Rosse, the wide country near the church of San Francesco di Paola, where her parents have their small villa, a building with some pretense at elegance and a little garden. That was where Giovanna grew up. On Via dei Materassai, with its houses all crammed together and its strong odor of soap and cooking, she can't breathe, all the air is sucked into the narrow alleys. There is neither privacy nor discretion.

She doesn't care that the stairs are made of marble, or that the ceilings are covered in frescoes, or that the furniture comes from the four corners of the earth. She doesn't want to live here, in a house of parvenu merchants. It may have been good enough for her father-in-law, but by marrying her, Ignazio has become a member of Palermo's aristocracy and needs a residence to match his new rank.

After all, isn't that why he married me? she wonders, angrily closing the flaps of her robe. *For the noble blood I brought as a dowry, to wash off the dust on his shoes and the epithet "laborer," which my father-in-law never managed to shake off! He wanted Baroness Giovanna d'Ondes Trigona at his side. Well, he got her.*

An embittered thought, followed by an even more bitter consideration.

But then why isn't all this enough for him?

The door opens and Ignazio walks in. "Oh, you're awake," he says, approaching her. "Good morning."

"I've just gotten up and I'm waiting for Donna Ciccia to get me ready." She takes his hand and kisses it. "How did it go?"

Ignazio sits on the armrest of the chair and puts his arm around her. "Unnerving." He can't tell her any more than that: it's pointless, she wouldn't understand. She can't even imagine what it means to bear the whole responsibility for Casa Florio. He strokes her face. "You're pale . . ."

She nods. "I can't breathe here. I'd like to go to the country."

But Ignazio is no longer listening. He's already abruptly back on his feet, heading to the dressing room. "I came up to change my jacket. It's warm again. Now that I've accepted the inheritance, I have to visit the bank's main office to check the list of creditors and promissory notes. Moreover—"

"You need a valet," she says, interrupting.

He stops, hands in midair. "Excuse me?"

"A valet to assist and dress you." Giovanna makes a broad gesture that takes in the city outside the window. "My parents have *un valletto* and *na cammarera pa' mugghiere*—a lady's maid."

Ignazio's lips tense only slightly, but Giovanna immediately senses that he's very annoyed. She bows her head and bites her lip, waiting for a reprimand.

"You know I'd prefer it if you spoke Italian," Ignazio says abruptly. "A Sicilian word every now and then is all right, but never when others are present. It's not becoming. Always remember who you are . . ." He slips on a light jacket, removes the card from the pocket of the other one, places it in a drawer in the wardrobe, and locks it.

It's not the first time they've had this conversation. As soon as they were married, he brought home a kind of tutor to teach her enough French and German to enable her to hold a little conversation with their foreign guests and business associates. If they traveled together, she had to be able to understand people and make herself understood, he explained. And she obeyed, as a good wife should.

She has always obeyed, until now.

Giovanna's humiliation turns to irritation. Ignazio doesn't even notice: he gives her a light, absent-minded kiss on the forehead and leaves.

She leaps to her feet, ignoring the sudden dizziness, and goes into the dressing room. She touches her belly, still swollen and shapeless after the pregnancy. She still has postpartum bleeding, and the midwife says it's because she's so thin. She's told her off and said she should eat more: red meat, pasta dishes, meat broth . . . They've even threatened to make her drink the blood of freshly slaughtered animals unless she builds up her strength. Of course, she doesn't have to struggle to breastfeed, since she immediately got a wet nurse for the baby, a peasant woman who's come from the Olivuzza specially to feed *u' picciriddu*, the little one. But eating properly is a duty for a woman who's just given birth.

The very thought of it makes Giovanna sick to her stomach. Food makes her nauseated. The only things she's able to swallow are segments of orange and tangerine.

At that very moment, Donna Ciccia comes in carrying a small plate of fruit and looks at her reproachfully. "*Ancora accussì siti?* Still here? It's time to get ready." She taps on a basin filled with water. "Your mother-in-law's expecting you."

Outside the front door, Ignazio is met not only by heat that's unusual for this late-summer day, but by a man who approaches and kisses his hand.

"*Assabbinirìca*, my respects, Don Ignazio," he mutters. "Please forgive me. My name's Saro Motisi and I'd like to speak to you. That's why I was on my way to the bank."

"I'm on my way there, too," Ignazio replies with a smile, trying to mask his irritation. It's a short journey from Via dei Materassai to Banco Florio, and he's been hoping to make it alone, in order to think. Instead, this small wine trader from the Tribunali district gets into step beside him, determined to follow him.

"You must forgive me," he repeats, trying hard to speak Italian. "I have documents pending, promissory notes that expire next week, but I've had some difficulties and I received more promissory notes, everyone here wants money . . ."

Ignazio puts a hand on his arm. "We'll see what we can do, Signor Motisi," he says. "Go to the bank; I'll be there shortly. If you can provide guarantees, I'm sure we can consider a deferral of your payment."

Motisi stops and practically bows to the ground. "Yes, of course, you know we're always reliable . . . and besides, it's a matter of a very small sum . . ."

But Ignazio is no longer listening. He slows down and lets Motisi walk away, then stops to look at Piano San Giacomo, which is filled with a light that makes the basalt almost blindingly white. Time hasn't altered the appearance of the square, which he crossed with his father on countless occasions. And yet many small things have changed over the years: the cobblestones, once always puddled by mud, are now clean; the gathering of beggars outside the church of Santa Maria la Nova has gone; there's now a small workshop where there used to be a fruit-and-vegetable store and, a little farther on, someone has opened a store vending earthenware goods. And yet the spirit of the place is still the same: chaotic, cheerful, filled with voices and accents. This is his street, and these are his people. People who are now coming toward him, kissing his hand, and expressing their condolences, eyes downcast.

How can Giovanna not like this district? he wonders. It's so full of life, it's one of the beating hearts of Palermo. Ignazio feels it within his own; it's as though he owns its every stone, front door, sunbeam, and patch of shade. He's walked from his home to the bank hundreds of times and knows every single person who now emerges from their houses to greet him.

He knows them, yes, but now there's something different about them, too: because now he is *u' patruni*, the master.

He briefly savors the melancholy of loneliness. He knows that, from this moment on, there will be no rest, no salvation for him. He doesn't just bear responsibility for his family on his shoulders; the lives of so many people who trust him, his abilities, and his economic power depend on Banco Florio.

Responsibility, he tells himself. A word his father often used. He instilled it into Ignazio's soul, sowed it like a seed, and let it germinate in the darkness of his consciousness. Now it's growing and becoming an awe-inspiring tree. He knows the roots of this tree will end up stifling *his* wishes and dreams in the name of something greater. His family. The Florio name.

He knows it and hopes he won't suffer too much. Won't suffer anymore.

"Good morning, Donna Giovanna."

The wet nurse greets her with a nod. She's breastfeeding the baby. Giovanna looks at her son suckling at that white, swollen, lusty breast.

She compares it to her own, squeezed into the corset she has put on over her shift, insisting her maid tighten the laces so hard it takes her breath away. She thinks she would never want a breast like that. She finds it repulsive.

"Come, Giovanna." Giulia is sitting in the armchair with Vincenzino in her arms. She motions to the armchair where Ignazio sat last night.

"*Comu siti*, Donna Giulia?" She's not afraid to use dialect with her. Giulia has always been kind to her. She's reserved, of course, but has never told her off and occasionally even extended the odd small courtesy toward her. Giovanna, though, has never been able fully to decipher if her kindness is sincere or if it comes from some strange, private empathy. Is it so obvious that Ignazio doesn't really care for her, that all he feels is mild affection?

Giulia doesn't reply immediately. "How am I?" she finally says. "Like someone whose arm has been severed." She pats her grandson's head and kisses his blond hair.

Giovanna doesn't know what to do. Should she squeeze her hand, say a comforting word, because that's what you do with family members? But she can't, and not because she doesn't feel sorry for Giulia, not at all.

The grief she sees in her is overwhelming. She finds the intensity of her loss frightening. She would never have thought that a man as hard as Vincenzo Florio could inspire such attachment in a woman, especially one as mild-mannered and patient as Giulia. *"Poor soul, he couldn't continue like that,"* Giovanna murmurs, and that's the truth, however painful.

Giulia swallows a clump of tears. "I know. I could see it. You know, in the last few days, when you were about to have Ignazziddu and he was slipping away—" Her voice breaks. "When I saw that he couldn't speak and didn't look at me anymore, I prayed for God to take him. I'd rather he died than watch him continue to suffer."

Giovanna crosses herself to hide her embarrassment, then says, "He's with God now, just think of that. He did many good deeds . . ."

Giulia smiles bitterly. "If only that were true . . . He did many things, not all of them good. Especially to me." She looks up, and

Giovanna is taken aback by the power in her eyes. It's almost a fire. "You know that for a long time we . . . we lived in sin. That our children were born out of wedlock."

Embarrassed again, Giovanna nods. When Ignazio's proposal arrived, her mother turned up her nose for that very reason: for all his money, the man had been born a bastard. Giulia and Vincenzo had married only after his birth.

"I remember once . . ." Giulia's voice softens and her face seems to relax. "In the beginning, when he'd already made up his mind to have me and I . . . I didn't know how to resist him, one day I dropped by the *aromateria* downstairs. I had to buy spices, and he'd heard my voice from his office and came to serve me behind the counter. Strange, because he hadn't served anybody for years. He wanted to give me some threads of saffron, saying they were an omen of luck and peace: I refused, but he put them into my hand and forced me to accept them. People in the *putìa* were staring at him in amazement, because Vincenzo Florio never gave anything away . . ." She sighs. "But I wasn't like everybody else. He wanted *me* and no other woman. And after he took me, he took my entire life. And I gave it to him joyfully and never cared about what others thought of me, about the fact they regarded me as a piece of trash. Because he was everything to me." She holds the baby tight to her chest and he wriggles out. "And now you think I can do without the man I loved more than myself just because God took him away?"

Vincenzino starts to whine, reaching out for the toys scattered around the room, then begins to cough. Giulia lets him go. "I've told you all this because Ignazio no longer heeds me. There was a time when I was everything to him, but then his father took him under his wing . . . and Ignazio became *his*." She sighs again. "And now, without Vincenzo, I'm not worth anything anymore."

Giovanna protests faintly, but Giulia silences her with a wave. "Of course, I'm his mother and he loves me," she says, dropping her voice, "but . . . Now you're here, his wife and the mistress of everything. You can help me. You must speak to him, you must tell him that I want to go and live at Quattro Pizzi. I already know that he doesn't want me to, that he thinks it's better for me to stay here, but I . . . I don't want to. That was our home and there I intend to stay, with him and our memories. Will you do it?"

Giovanna would like to reply that Ignazio seldom listens to her, but she's dumbfounded by this request. If her mother-in-law left the house on Via dei Materassai, then perhaps she could persuade Ignazio to move to the Olivuzza. She could sort out the garden and the house and enhance the French-style decor with furniture more to her taste.

It's an unhoped-for gift that Giulia is giving her. And not the only one. She is also entrusting her with her home.

Giovanna merely nods and squeezes her mother-in-law's hand. "I'll speak to him." She already knows how to do it. Because even though it's true that her husband doesn't listen to her, there's one thing he can't resist: the prestige linked to his family's name. In that respect, Ignazio is exactly like his father, controlled by an ambition that eats away at him from within.

And nothing can be as prestigious as what she has in mind for the Olivuzza.

Silent, invisible armed men are minding the security of the extensive grounds, the villa, and its residents. Being a Florio also means watching your back: something Vincenzo already knew but, in his case, he protected himself simply by resorting to friends and a series of favors done and returned. When Ignazio relocated to the Olivuzza in the fall of 1869, though, someone pointed out to him, quietly and discreetly, that he needed something more for the family's "peace of mind." Because Palermo is a lively city where commerce—the trade in citrus fruits in particular—promises wealth, it has attracted to its outskirts workers, carters, peasants, and young men who dream of a life away from the serfdom of agricultural labor, but also smugglers and thieves, bandits both opportunistic and professional. And these men have created an increasingly tight network of "particular" relations, so much so that they've become unreachable to the law. In addition, there's no need to involve the "Piedmontese" police from up north when you can sort things out yourself. Has a wrong been done? It can be put right by sabotaging a certain consignment of lemons about to be shipped to America. An offense received? It can be remedied by setting *that* house on fire. A disagreement? A gunshot is fired into the back of whoever didn't show "respect."

So it became obvious how you should protect yourself: all you had to do was contact certain "men of honor" who would be "delighted" to provide protection in exchange for appropriate favors or a "token" sum of money. It was an almost accepted practice to which everybody—aristocrats and commoners alike—resorted.

It's before the eyes of these "men of honor" that a streamlined modern carriage pulls up outside the oldest group of buildings making up the Olivuzza villa. Nobody has stopped it or searched it because Don Ignazio has decreed that guests are sacred and mustn't be importuned. And this is a very important guest.

A man with piercing eyes and a wide forehead over which fall locks of curly hair gets out of the carriage. His movements are graceful, although he cannot hide a certain unease.

Ignazio is standing by the entrance to the building, waiting for him. He shakes hands with him and simply says, "Come in."

The man follows him through a vestibule, then a series of tastefully furnished rooms and salons. Giovanna's touch is evident in the color combinations of the furnishings, the furniture purchased in Paris and England, the damask couches, and the large Persian rugs. She's had the interior of the villa renovated, choosing every piece of furniture and decoration.

The two men go to the study. The guest pauses by the door, studies the room, and notices a large oil painting of the Florios' Marsala winery, its tall white walls bathed in the fading light. The painter, whoever he is, managed to capture on canvas the dimness as well as the deep green coastal waters.

"Charming," he mutters. "The artist?"

"Antonino Leto," Ignazio says, coming closer. "Do you like it? It depicts my Marsala holdings. Leto delivered the painting just a few weeks ago. He made me wait but the result is splendid and gives me a sense of peace. The sea, in particular, is painted wonderfully. I haven't yet decided whether to leave it here in my study or move it somewhere else. But let's sit down."

He indicates the armchairs and takes a seat. He stares at the man for a few seconds, and a smile appears, barely concealed by his thick, dark beard.

Uneasy, the guest starts fidgeting. "What's the matter, Don Ignazio? Is anything wrong? The work on your father's mausoleum in Santa Maria di Gesù is on schedule. We had difficulty digging the crypt in the rock, but now we're working quickly, and I know that De Lisi has finished the sketch for the sculpture."

"That's not why I asked you here." Ignazio steeples his fingers before his face. "I have a proposition for you."

Giuseppe Damiani Almeyda, professor of ornamental drawing and elementary architecture at the Royal University of Palermo, leans back in his armchair, intrigued. He opens his hands, then joins them in his lap. "For me? How can I help you?" His Neapolitan accent is faintly disguised by a foreign inflection, inherited from his Portuguese mother, the beautiful Maria Carolina Almeyda, goddaughter of Queen Maria Carolina Augusta of Bourbon.

"You're an engineer of the Palermo municipality, not just an architect I hold in high esteem. And you're an educated man: you know and appreciate the past but aren't afraid of the future. On the contrary."

Damiani Almeyda raises his hand to his mustache. He's wary now. Compliments never cease to alarm him. He hasn't known this placid-looking young man for long, but he knows very well that he's powerful, and not just for his wealth. He's also intelligent, very intelligent, but it's the kind of intelligence you need to beware. "What do you wish to ask of me, Don Ignazio?"

"A project."

"For what?"

"For a foundry."

Almeyda's eyes widen, picturing a tuff warehouse covered in soot and crowded with workmen. "The Oretea?"

Ignazio gives a slight laugh. "I don't have any others for now."

There's a pause while the two men study each other. Damiani Almeyda leans forward, hands folded in his lap. "Tell me, what exactly do you need?"

Ignazio stands up and takes a few steps across the carpet that covers almost the entire floor. It's from Qazvin, and he chose it not so much because it's extremely elegant but because of the extraordinary attention given in that part of Persia to the knotting, the quality of the wool, the natural dyes. "You know that my father championed the foundry with a determination that was exceptional even for him, who never lacked willpower. Everyone said the project would be a loss, but he insisted, even ignoring the advice of friends like Benjamin Ingham, God rest his soul."

He stops by the glass wall, recalling Ingham's funeral and his father, stony-faced, caressing the coffin. Ben Ingham had been his friend and his rival, a mentor and an opponent. They were bound by a friendship that was unusual as well as strong, a feeling Ignazio unfortunately hasn't experienced.

Ignazio rouses himself and taps the knuckles of one hand against the palm of the other. "The situation has changed. Nowadays, the foundry has to contend with factories up north, which are much more competitive. It's one of the—the gifts the Kingdom of Italy has given us: enterprises that produce what we produce. I can't blame them: Sicily isn't the kingdom's priority and does nothing to warrant being so. To get anything done here, we have to scheme, threaten, circumvent, or pray to the saints in heaven. And sometimes even they can't help. It's those with a stronger card in hand who win, and what little there is goes wrong. And that makes me furious: there's capital in Palermo and it must be shrewdly invested or else we'll all end up crushed by the competition. The factories in the north will grow and become wealthy, while here we'll continue to cultivate grain, grind sumac, and extract sulfur. No point in beating about the bush: we can't compete now. And that's what we must fix. At all costs."

He turns and Damiani Almeyda holds his breath. This quiet, mild-mannered young man has given way to a surprisingly hard businessman.

"So how can I help you?" he asks, feeling practically compelled to.

"If you wish, you can help me change this situation. Meanwhile, I'm asking if you're willing to bring the foundry into the present and turn it into a modern building. You could start with the façade." Ignazio starts pacing up and down and Damiani Almeyda follows him with his eyes. "You know what the Oretea looks like, don't you? It's little more than a warehouse, a *malaseno* with two planks of timber for a roof. It must become a modern plant, starting from its exterior, like in Marseille, where I saw mechanical workshops for ship repairs not far from the basin and the harbor. The foundry works predominantly with steamers in a state of repair, and we must factor that in."

"So you would like a plan for—"

"For the façade in the first place, then for the renovation of the interior." He doesn't add anything else: it's not yet time to share his idea of building houses for the workers or rethinking the rooms for the foundry's offices, as is common in Britain and France. He is a master, a good master, and he'll take care of his people, the workers and their families. There's much to be done before that, however.

They talk for a long time, as the room fills with a golden autumnal glow. They discuss what Ignazio would like for his factory and how Damiani Almeyda imagines it: full of light, with large rooms for the workers and a high ceiling to allow the heat to disperse . . . They listen to each other, acknowledging and understanding each other. They share the same vision, they want the same future for Palermo.

From this moment on, the destiny of Giuseppe Damiani Almeyda—who will erect the Teatro Politeama, renovate the Palazzo Pretorio, and build Palermo's Historical Archives—will be inextricably bound to that of the Florios.

And it's for the Florios that he will realize his masterpiece, on Favignana.

It's evening. A huge log smolders in the fireplace and a scent of resin wafts through the air. Absorbed in her thoughts, Giulia has a weary smile on her lips. How strange to be in this room again, where Vincenzo died almost a year and a half ago now.

It's Christmas Eve 1869. Ignazio and Giovanna have asked her to come and spend it at the Olivuzza with them, partly because, as Ignazio said, at Quattro Pizzi there are too many stairs and it's too cold. Not even halfway through dinner, however, Giulia gave Giovanna a look and the latter understood, the way a woman can see in another the weariness of living when it's trapped in deep furrows and heavy eyelids. Giovanna nodded and motioned to the housekeeper to help Giulia get up from her chair and go to her room.

Ignazio followed her with an expression that hovered between concern and sadness.

He must have thought, Giulia now thinks, *that there was too much laughter, too much noise, and too much food for me. The truth is I couldn't care less. I just want to be here, where he was.*

She looks up at the window, at the darkness surrounding the grounds of the Olivuzza.

She doesn't feel entirely at ease in this villa. She recalls that it originally belonged to the Buteras, one of Palermo's oldest aristocratic families, and that it was a Russian noblewoman, Princess Varvara Petrovna Shakhovskaya, Prince Butera-Radalì's second wife, who expanded and enriched it. Tsarina Alexandra, the wife of Tsar Nicholas I, actually spent a whole winter here. Obsessed with the need to show off the family's wealth, Vincenzo spared no expense or work to snap up the property. And now it's up to

Ignazio and his wife to enlarge and embellish it. Ignazio has recently also acquired some neighboring houses, making the complex even grander.

It's their home now.

Palermo—her Palermo, with its cobbled streets and dark alleys—is far away, beyond the dusty road that separates the aristocratic estates from the vegetable gardens. Since the city walls were pulled down following the Unification, Palermo has been spreading toward the mountains. New houses are devouring the fields, Italian-style gardens usurp vegetable patches and citrus groves; two- and three-story buildings with identical square epistyles and brown wooden shutters are springing up along new roads leading to the countryside. Via dei Materassai, Castellammare, and La Kalsa belong to another world, another life. The city is changing, perhaps without even realizing it.

She sighs again. The air stagnates in her chest, which hurts. Vincenzo wouldn't have approved of certain eccentricities. But Vincenzo is dead.

And she can feel her own life ebbing away and does nothing to hold on to it.

The servants are clearing the table. Efficient hands collect the silverware, placing it within baskets that are then carried to the kitchens. The trays with sweets and *cassatas* are covered with linen cloths. The crystal glasses and silver samovars are emptied and stowed away in the sideboards after being dried and polished. The lights are dimmed or turned off. The scent of bay leaves and viburnum wilting in Chinese ceramic *cachepots* lingers in the air, as well as the more persistent smells of face powder and men's cologne.

"Giovannina! Giovannina!"

Giovanna is giving orders for marsala wine to be served in the salon overlooking the garden—everyone calls it the green salon because of the color of the tapestry—when her mother's petulant voice makes her turn. Ignazio has insisted on inviting Giovanna's parents, as well as Angelina and Luigi De Pace, his sister and brother-in-law, for lunch on Saint Stephen's Day.

His sister Giuseppina's father-in-law and husband, Augusto and François Merle, are also here this morning, while Giuseppina herself has remained in Marseille: her son, Louis Auguste, is as sickly as his little cousin Vincenzo and she didn't feel like getting him on a steamship and making him endure a sea voyage in the winter. But Ignazio wanted to show the world that the Florios are a close-knit family, so the result was obtained anyway.

Giovanna watches her mother totter toward her, leaning on the two sticks she uses for walking. Her gray hair is arranged in a high bun that emphasizes the roundness of her face. Everything about her is round: from her fingers, into which rings seem to disappear, to her breasts only just contained in her dress, to her petticoats—almost unnecessary since there is much, too much, flesh to hold them up.

Eleonora d'Ondes Trigona, the sister of Romualdo Trigona, Prince of Sant'Elia, is a middle-aged woman who isn't aging well, partly because she's full of aches and pains and doesn't look after herself as she should. Her face is flushed, and she pants and perspires even after these few steps.

Giovanna remains motionless, waiting for her mother to join her, then they set off together along the garden paths.

"*Maronna santa,* I'm so tired. Come, let's sit down," Eleonora suddenly says.

Giovanna takes a few steps ahead, waits for her mother to sit on the stone bench outside the aviary, then sits beside her, in the corner, while the children, accompanied by their nannies, roam around the garden and tease the parrots in their cage, making them flit about.

Not far from them, the men of the household smoke cigars and converse in hushed tones.

There are grease stains on her mother's skirt. *I'm sure she ate before coming for lunch,* Giovanna thinks with a mixture of shock and annoyance. *How could she, a princess, let herself go like this?*

"So you're pregnant and haven't said anything to me? It's from Donna Ciccia that I have to hear it? And now even your mother-in-law's told me . . . I find it hurtful."

Giovanna doesn't reply, just stares at her slim fingers and notices that her wedding ring is almost slipping off. Then she examines the diamond and the emerald Ignazio gifted her during the four years they've been married. For Christmas, he gave her a gold bangle with a flower of precious stones, made especially for her. "I wanted to be sure. Besides, you know how it is, Mamma: it's bad luck to tell too soon."

Eleonora grabs her hand and touches her belly. *"Quannu nasci?"*

Giovanna withdraws, pulling her hand away, and shakes her head. "How do I know? In May or June." She smooths her dress. She's had to loosen her corset because it was pressing uncomfortably on her stomach. Her belly is growing faster than with her previous pregnancies and Donna Ciccia—*the wretched woman couldn't keep her mouth shut!*—says this might be because she's expecting a girl.

"Now you'd better watch out, so your husband doesn't go running after other women's skirts. You've had two children, you're no longer fresh as a daisy. You must keep an eye on him."

"I know. My husband has no skirts to look at." Giovanna is curt. Ignazio is dependable, he would never betray her with another woman, especially not now that she's pregnant. And if he did, she wouldn't want to know.

Mind your own business, she thinks, filled with resentment. *When was the last time your husband could bear to even look at you?*

For some days now, everything's been irritating her, and her mother is no exception.

Eleonora appears to notice. A glint of sorrow flashes across her eyes. "Are you eating?"

"Yes."

"If you don't eat, you'll fade away. A cat that eats well has a glossy coat."

A cat that eats well! As though she were a pet! "I told you *I am eating*!"

The nannies turn to look in her direction and Giovanna realizes she's raised her voice. She feels herself blush and tears of annoyance sting her eyelids. "You see why one can't say a word to you? Because you start screaming like a fishwife."

Her voice is quavering, and she hates herself for it: because everything about her—her throat, her guts, her entire body—reminds her of what it meant to be this woman's daughter. The sister of a prince, who always spoke too loudly, always had her hands full of food, and always kept her mouth open because she had trouble breathing. She remembers the looks relatives would give her and her father: mocking or embarrassed glances at seeing a princess in that state. If only she'd had a brother to pour her heart out to, ask for comfort, share her sorrow with. But no: the shame of this mother fell entirely on her.

She stifles a sob and leaps to her feet. Her mother tries to stop her, calling her to come back, apologizing.

Her steps take her into the dense part of the grounds. She clings to a pear tree and breaks into loud sobs; a handful of dried leaves falls on her hair. Splinters of wood get stuck under her fingernails.

Part of her knows it's the baby making her so brittle, so nervous and out of control. But another, deeper side of her, buried in the pit of her stomach, is seething, trying to rid itself of memories and humiliations.

She bends forward, sticks two fingers down her throat to make herself vomit. She retches once, then again. The food dredges the anger out from her body, purifying and liberating her, never mind that she has a sour taste in her mouth and the mucous membranes in her throat burn. She instinctively holds her dress back so as not to soil it. She learned to do this when she was younger, watching her mother stuff herself and grow increasingly fat, while she herself ate less and less, as though wanting to vanish from the eyes of the world.

At one stage, she started fainting. Disconcerted, her mother forced her to stay in bed and brought her pasta, meat, cakes, and sweets, obliging her to eat, to swallow. Giovanna would obey, then vomit everything. The doctor decreed that her stomach had become only slightly larger than a teacup and that she would never be able to eat normally. She clung to the diagnosis with all her strength, bringing it up, with a faintly apologetic smile, whenever anybody remarked on her poor appetite.

It took Ignazio to challenge her: after the first few months of marriage, he grew tired of having to insist that his wife eat "a little bit more" and took her to a famous doctor in Rome. After a long interview and an even longer consultation, the luminary bluntly declared that Giovanna had to "get over that little-girl fussiness" and that a child would make her body work again "as nature intended."

She simply nodded and Ignazio, reassured, smiled at the thought of that child, who would put everything right. And it turned out the doctor was right, at least to some extent: during her pregnancies, her condition improved, partly because, out of love for the creature she was expecting, she would refrain from vomiting.

But today, sadness clouds her thoughts and casts a shadow over her soul.

She coughs again and feels bile rising in her throat: she has nothing left to heave out. She feels better: free, light. Too light. She sways.

A hand comes to rest on her shoulder. A strong, gentle grip that turns into an embrace. "Is it the baby? Did you vomit?"

Ignazio holds her up, her back against his chest. Ignazio is strong, his body solid. Giovanna seems to disappear in his arms.

She yields to that embrace, welcoming the warmth and sense of well-being the contact produces. "It's nausea," she says, downplaying the situation, breathing through her mouth. "I ate too much."

He takes a handkerchief from his pocket, dabs the perspiration on her forehead, and wipes her lips without further comment. He won't tell her that he followed her because he heard her arguing with her mother, nor that he saw her stick two fingers down her throat. Or that it's not the first time he's seen her do so. He doesn't understand, but doesn't ask, can't ask: it's women's stuff. Besides, the doctor in Rome was very clear: it all boiled down to a few bad habits, and natural female hysteria had done the rest.

He holds and reassures her.

He realized a long time ago how frail Giovanna is and how very frightened she is of not living up to the name she now carries. But he's also learned to appreciate her tenacity and responsiveness. Without that feral courage, that petulance, that resilience, she would never be able to keep up with him, never be able to accept that she wasn't the focus of his thoughts. Because he belongs to Casa Florio and no one else, just like his father. He has never hidden that from her.

"Come," he says.

Giovanna steps away. "I'm fine," she declares, but her pallor betrays her.

"It's not true," he replies very softly. He caresses her face, then lifts her hand and kisses her fingertips. "Remember what you are."

Insecure? Giovanna thinks. *Hysterical?* She wants to ask him, but Ignazio places a finger over her lips and leans forward. She sees a shadow briefly drift across his eyes. A flash of awareness. Of regret.

"You're my wife," he finally says, and lightly kisses her mouth.

Giovanna grabs him by the cuffs of his jacket and pulls him toward her. This is what he can give her, and with this, at least for now, she must make do.

Back home, Giovanna and Ignazio find their guests about to leave. The atmosphere seems calm once again. While Ignazio says goodbye to Augusto Merle and the De Paces, Eleonora approaches Giovanna and, with some difficulty, hugs her, followed by her husband, who, contrary to his formal and usually detached manner, takes his daughter's hand, kisses it tenderly, and whispers, "Take care of yourself."

Giovanna and Ignazio are left alone on the threshold. He runs his hand down her back and lets it linger on her waist. "Would you like to rest for a while?"

"Yes, I would."

He takes his pocket watch out. "I'm going to do some work in the study. I'll join you for dinner if you feel like having something." Then he kisses her on the forehead and walks away.

Giovanna takes Giulia's arm and helps her up the stairs to the oldest part of the villa. They walk into one of the children's rooms. Vincenzino had a little temperature and Giovanna asked the nanny to take him to bed. And here he is, half-asleep under the blankets. Ignazziddu is sitting on the floor, barefoot, playing with toy soldiers. "I'll stay here," Giulia says to Giovanna. "You go and rest." She hesitates, then adds, "I didn't realize your mother didn't know you were pregnant until it was too late . . ."

Giovanna grimaces. "I hadn't actually told her yet."

"I'm sorry." Giulia puts a hand on her daughter-in-law's face and looks at her with sadness. "My mother was like that, too, always nit-picking, telling me off . . ." She lifts Giovanna's chin and forces her to look into her eyes. "Mothers are imperfect creatures. They sometimes feel like our worst enemies, but they're not. The truth is, they often don't know how to love us. They're convinced they can improve us and spare us their suffering . . . not realizing that every woman already demands a lot of herself and needs to experience her own pain."

She has said this very, very softly, with a note of regret that's filled Giovanna's eyes with tears. It's true, she and her mother love each other, but they're incurably different: Eleonora is excessive, impulsive; she herself is discreet, simple. They've been clashing all their lives because her mother wanted an ally, wanted to make her exactly like her. So Giovanna grew up feeling constantly . . . defective. A thought that has never entirely abandoned her.

She walks to her bedroom, head down. Donna Ciccia is there, waiting for her, busy embroidering a baby garment. *"Fimmina sarà,"* she has told her adamantly. It'll be a girl. She's sure of it because she's counted the days of the moon and because some things she senses in her fingertips, through her skin.

Giovanna feels both fear and affection for this woman with her rough, stern features. She doesn't like it that Donna Ciccia does "that stuff" because it makes her feel uncomfortable and gives her a sense that she's losing even the little control she thinks she still has over her own life. In addition, her confessor has warned her over and over again that you must keep away from superstition because the future is written in a book only God can read. At the same time, she's always been able to rely on Donna Ciccia. As a child, if Giovanna ever hurt herself, she would comfort her; when, as an adolescent, she refused to eat, she would feed her in patient silence. It was she who explained the monthly blood and taught her what happens between a man and a woman. She helped her during the birth of her two sons. She hugged Giovanna when she confessed that she was afraid she'd lost Ignazio's affection. More than her real mother, more than a blood relative, Donna Ciccia has always given her what she really needed. Moreover, she owes her fondness for embroidery to her. She began as a little girl, fashioning short stitch squares, and now they decorate tablecloths and sheets together, as well as the odd tapestry.

Over time, Donna Ciccia has even managed to make her eat a little more; at mealtimes, she stares at her with a blend of harshness and affection until Giovanna eats at least a few mouthfuls. Then, when they sit embroidering opposite each other, immersed in a comfortable silence made up of complicity and habit, Donna Ciccia sets next to her a tray with a plate of orange or lemon segments and a small sugar bowl and every now and then Giovanna dips a segment into the sugar and eats.

While helping her change, she speaks to her directly, as ever. "You look pale . . . I saw you eat about as much as Vincenzino does when he's ill. You must be careful, or the little one won't grow. You might even do some harm."

"Sitting and eating a full plate isn't for me. On the contrary. Tell them I won't eat tonight. *Un c'ha fazzu, sugnu troppu stanca.* I can't, I'm really tired."

"Every man and woman has to eat, Donna Giovanna." Donna Ciccia sighs. She takes her wrists, squeezes them, and obliges Giovanna to look her in the face. "You must stop all these childish tantrums; you're married now. You have a husband who respects you; not many women can say that. You have two children who are jewels. I've told you so many times: making a fuss about eating will anger the Lord."

Giovanna nods without making eye contact. She knows she's right, that she shouldn't anger the Lord, but she can't help it. "He doesn't understand how I feel," she says, so softly that Donna Ciccia, who's helping to remove her skirt, has to crane her head closer to hear. "My husband is the best in the world. But . . ." She stops because that *but* conceals a sorrow that never leaves her, a shadow filled with restless ghosts she's unable to give voice to. A solitude as cold as a pane of glass.

Donna Ciccia lifts her eyes to the sky and folds the dress. "I've told you, you have everything and you're still not happy. A husband is a man: he can't understand women's things and doesn't care anyway. You must concentrate on your business: to be a wife and think of your children. You're married to an important man: you can't expect him to constantly pay you attention."

"You're right," Giovanna replies with a sigh.

Donna Ciccia looks at her, unconvinced but resigned. "Shall I call the maid to help you wash and ready you for bed?"

"No, thank you, I'll do it myself."

"As you wish," Donna Ciccia mutters, then leaves to inform the kitchen staff that the mistress won't be dining.

Exhausted, Giovanna leans against the doorjamb. The image the gilded mirror reflects is that of a frail woman practically disappearing into her shift. Today she wore a dress made for her in Paris, cream silk with Valenciennes lace trimmings around the neckline and at the wrists, as well as a pearl necklace and earrings with diamond-framed flower patterns. A wedding present from Ignazio.

The whole family complimented her. Ignazio merely glanced and nodded approvingly before resuming his conversation with Augusto.

As though she had merely done her duty.

That word—*duty*—haunts her. It's her *duty* to eat because she has to be strong and bear children. It's her *duty* to be impeccable, because she has to live up to the family that has accepted her. It's her *duty* to speak proper Italian and know foreign languages.

And, in private, it's her *duty* to remain in the shadows and put up with everything, because that's how a good wife acts, because that's what marriage means: pleasing your husband and silently obeying him. She did so immediately, right from their wedding night. She was docile and compliant, following her mother's embarrassed recommendations: to keep her eyes shut and grit her teeth if it hurt. To pray if she was afraid.

But he was passionate and careful in a way that still makes her blush when she remembers. Her nightgown and prayer book ended up in a corner of the bed, while he took possession of her body and bestowed on her sensations she'd never imagined.

And so it was at first, but after Vincenzino was born, Ignazio wanted her less and less, and without passion. As though *she* had become a *duty*, a chore to perform, and not a companion with whom to share his bed, body, and soul.

For a while, she thought there was another woman. But after Ignazziddu was born, she realized that Ignazio's interest in her was in inverse proportion to his involvement in the family business. She did have a rival, and its name was Casa Florio.

In addition, she has already borne him two sons, the bloodline is secured, so she . . .

She has tried telling Donna Ciccia, but the latter has merely shrugged. "Better work than another woman. Besides, your mother-in-law, poor thing, was very patient. It was Casa Florio first, then her and the children."

Only, she is not Giulia. She wants her husband.

Ignazio isn't dining either. He has a cup of black tea brought to him and continues reading the files on the progress of the *aromateria* on Via dei Materassai. It's no longer as profitable as it used to be, and he's considered getting rid of it on several occasions, but in the end, tradition and sentimental value have had the upper hand. Moreover, he's slightly superstitious: the shop belonged to his father and, before him, to his grandfather and the uncle he never knew. The few lights left are puddles of white in the blackness. It's a piece of their history, like the ring he wears below his wedding band.

He turns out the light and leaves the study, yawning. Maybe he'll be able to sleep.

The servants glide silently from room to room, snuffing out the candles, placing screens in front of fireplaces as logs burn out and collapse quietly into the ashes. Doors are closed.

The night watch monitors the premises. Ignazio can't see it, but almost hears the footsteps of the men patrolling up and down the garden. He'll never get used to this "necessary" surveillance: as a child, he would run around the whole of Palermo, from Via dei Materassai to Arenella, without the slightest care. But everything's changed now.

Wealth attracts troubles.

He takes off his jacket and loosens his tie as he climbs the stairs. He walks past his mother's bedroom but doesn't stop; she's bound to be asleep. He's noticed that she's increasingly weary and frail. He'll try to persuade her to stay at the Olivuzza.

He goes to the nursery. He enters Ignazziddu's room and approaches the bed. His son is asleep, a hand next to his mouth. He has Giovanna's delicate features and strong coloring, he's lively and enjoys showing off. Then Ignazio goes into Vincenzino's room, where the boy is asleep with his mouth open and arms up. He has his father's slightly wavy hair and a slender body that seems to disappear beneath the blankets. He pats him and slips out, wondering whether the new baby will be a boy or a girl. *I'd like it to be a little girl*, he tells himself with a smile.

Finally, he retraces his steps and enters his bedroom, where Leonardo, known as Nanài, the valet Giovanna persuaded him to take on, is slumbering on a stool, mouth agape. He shakes him. "Nanài . . ."

The man is short and stout, with a thick mane of jet-black hair. He leaps to his feet. "Don Ignazio, I—"

Ignazio stops him. *"Vattinni a dormiri. Ancora ma firu a canciarimi sulo."* He can still change his own clothes, he says, encouraging him with a complicit smile to go to sleep. He speaks dialect with the servants so that they don't feel uneasy. A small act of consideration.

The valet bows. "I'm so sorry, signore. I was waiting for you but . . ." He's mortified.

"It's fine. Now go to bed; we have to get up at five tomorrow morning."

The valet shuffles out the door, still muttering apologies.

Ignazio stretches his arms over his head and yawns again. He closes the damask curtains over the windows, drops his jacket on the chair, kicks off his shoes, removes his waistcoat, collapses on the bed, and closes his eyes.

Aided by his fatigue, a memory surfaces. It's so powerful that it snatches him away from the present, erasing everything around him. He feels as though he's slipping into his twenty-year-old body, no longer feeling the exhaustion and weight of his responsibilities.

Marseille.

An acacia tree and a blanket spread on the ground. The perfume of freshly cut hay, the chirrup of cicadas, the warmth of the sun. The late-summer light filtered through the leaves, the wind singing in the branches. His head resting on a woman's body. A hand stroking his hair.

He's reading a book. He takes the hand and kisses it.

Someone knocks at the door.

Ignazio abruptly opens his eyes. The sun, the warmth, and the cicadas vanish. He's back at the Olivuzza, in his bedroom, at the end of a feast day that has tired him more than a day's work.

He sits up. "Come in."

Giovanna.

Wrapped in a lace robe, hair in a braid, she looks even younger than twenty-one. Despite her apparent fragility, she's a strong woman who honors him with her dedication and has brought him new, noble blood.

Giovanna is the certainty that he's made the right decision, a life without rebellion, appropriate to what the Florios represent: a new aristocracy based on money. On power. On social standing.

And she's the mother of his children.

That's what you must think about, he tells himself, *not about what you can no longer have—could never have had.*

She stops in the middle of the room. "You look pleased. Every-thing went well, didn't it?"

He nods, distant, still a prisoner of that memory, unable to mask it.

Giovanna comes closer and takes his head in her hands. "What's the matter?" Her tone is earnest. "I came to tell you about your mother. I'm worried: she's eating less and less and has difficulty walking. It's not good. Is that what's wrong?"

Ignazio shakes his head. He puts a hand behind her neck, pulls her toward him, and kisses her forehead. A tender gesture. "Just thinking."

"About work?" Giovanna insists, stepping away to look at him.

Ignazio is calm as ever. "Of course."

He can't add anything else because he's racked with guilt. This woman loves him with her whole being and desperately wants to be loved back. Only, a part of him is still—always—enmeshed in memory. A memory that runs in his blood. A stone heart beating next to one made of flesh.

He puts a hand on her breast and seeks her lips. It's only a tepid kiss, but it warms him and becomes desire. "Giovanna . . ." he whispers. She welcomes him, holds him, calls him by his name.

But Ignazio is suddenly startled. "Can we still do this? I mean the baby . . ."

She smiles and removes his shirt.

They make love hastily, searching for each other under their skin, pursuing each other.

Afterward, for Ignazio, comes a dark, dreamless sleep.

Afterward, for Giovanna, comes the sadness of a love that lasted only a few moments, as well as the feeling that she will never be able to reach Ignazio in his world of shadows.

On Epiphany, the family gathers again in the dining hall, filled with the voices of adults exchanging good wishes and children receiving gifts. After lunch, candied and dried fruit, as well as liqueurs, are set on the table.

Too much noise, Ignazio thinks. He wants to talk business with François, his brother-in-law, and it's impossible here. He ushers him to the study, and once the door closes behind them, the silence makes them both heave a sigh of relief.

"Les repas di famigghia peuvent être très bruyants!" François says. He speaks fast, mixing Italian, French, and Sicilian. He's a good-looking man with a curled mustache and pale, kind eyes. Ignazio is fond of him, partly because he genuinely loves Giuseppina. "As you know, I came here partly on business. I had a consignment to shuttle to Palermo for my father's store and some debts to collect that—by the way, may I leave some promissory notes in your bank, for safekeeping?"

"Of course." Ignazio pours him a glass of marsala wine and fills his own. "I wanted to ask you if there's any news concerning the leasing of those warehouses in Marseille harbor."

François opens his hands, and a drop of liqueur falls on his finger. "I've found two. Both suitable, although the larger one is *un peu plus loin*."

Ignazio nods. Having a warehouse close to the harbor would mean substantial savings in time and money.

"As soon as I return to Marseille, I'll convey all the details to your agents." François sighs. "I want to leave as soon as possible; I'm worried about *mon petit*, about Louis. I'd like him to be attended to by a good doctor. Do you have good doctors here? I thought Vincenzino looked a little frail . . ."

"He is, unfortunately. He frequently has fevers that weaken him. And now he's getting over a cold that's left him wheezing . . ."

"Oh, no, poor thing! Luckily, Josephine, *ta sœur*, isn't alone with Louis. She's staying with Camille Martin Clermont."

Ignazio doesn't look up from his glass.

"I imagine you've heard that her name isn't Darbon anymore, but Clermont. She remarried—an admiral, a good man."

François's voice suddenly feels very distant. "Yes," Ignazio murmurs. "I think it was in early 1868."

"That's right. She was widowed when she was just a little over twenty. She didn't have children, and now it seems they can't have any. She's suffered a great deal but perhaps she's resigned herself now . . ." He shrugs and finishes his marsala. "Life can be very unfair. But happiness isn't for this Earth." There's a shade of sadness in his voice. Or perhaps an indirect reproach to his brother-in-law?

Ignazio's fingers tighten around the cut-crystal glass. He forces himself to look up with a detached expression. He even manages to nod.

That's when François surprises him. His face softens and the sadness—or reproach?—dissolves. "When I told her I was coming to Palermo, she asked me to send her regards."

Ignazio takes a deep breath. "I understand," he murmurs.

Only, he wishes he didn't understand, know, or remember.

He massages the back of his neck, which feels stiff, then looks down. A breath unable to escape his lips is weighing on his chest, a clump of breath and thoughts that refuses to go away.

He, the owner of almost fifty ships, a foundry, a winery, a bank, and dozens of properties, doesn't want anyone to look him in the face. Not right now.

But then he lifts his head again and looks at François. "Tell her I also send my regards."

He has no right to ask for anything. Only the duty to live in the present.

February 1872 has brought a cold spell to a mild winter. Ignazio notices it almost by chance when he exits the carriage outside the cemetery of Santa Maria di Gesù, at the foot of Monte Grifone. His breath condenses into a small cloud of vapor.

Palermo, in the distance. Around him, greenery and silence. Gray daylight filters through the clouds. Both the sound of rain trapped in the branches of the recently planted cypresses and the dripping from the leaves of the surrounding orange trees briefly distract him from the dark thoughts that accompanied his journey here.

Over the years, the void left by his father's death has slowly closed, like a wound that refused to heal, leaving behind deeply rooted pain. Ignazio thought he'd learned to live with it, found peace in resignation and work. He's kept talking to his father in his head, continued performing the small rituals they would perform together, like reading the *Giornale di Sicilia* right after lunch. And he's kept up some of his habits, like having morning coffee in his office all alone.

And yet . . .

One November night of the previous year, his mother went to bed, and he said good night with an absent-minded kiss on her forehead.

The following morning, Giulia didn't wake up.

She had died in her sleep. Her kind heart had stopped beating, and she'd departed in the same manner as she had lived: silently.

Beneath the mask of sorrow, Ignazio was angry. He couldn't forgive her: she'd been unfair: denying him the chance to say goodbye, to prepare himself to let her go. He could no longer thank her for all she'd done for him: for the kindness she'd taught him, the calmness she'd passed on to him, the respect toward others she'd always shown. His dedication to work, his spirit of sacrifice, and his determination came from his father. Everything else, starting with the ability to weather all life's storms—everything that really made him into a man—had been a gift from Giulia. And—only then did he realize it—her gift had also been that exclusive, silent, unshakable love she'd had for his father.

Then, as the days went by, he understood. His mother had passed away on the same day Vincenzo had died. All that was left of her was a ghost waiting to dissolve in the light of day. An empty shell. Then, at last, that light had come and, with it, peace. Because his father may have been the sea, but she was the rock, and a rock cannot exist without the sea.

Now he pictures them in a place that doesn't exist but looks very much like Villa dei Quattro Pizzi. His father is gazing out to sea and his mother is leaning on his arm. She lifts her head, with that faint smile on her lips; his father looks at her and rests his forehead on the top of her head. They don't speak. They're close to each other, and that's enough.

He feels a lump in his throat. He doesn't know if it's a childhood memory his mind is offering him as a consolation. He doesn't want to know, he tells himself, while walking the last few meters that lead to the tomb he's had built for his parents. *It doesn't matter: wherever they are, they're together, in peace.*

Here's the chapel. An imposing edifice surrounded by other colossal tombs belonging to Palermo's noblest and oldest families. In Santa Maria di Gesù, the city of the dead is a reflection of the living.

Outside the gate, he finds Giuseppe Damiani Almeyda and Vincenzo Giachery. They're talking and, in the silence, their words echo amid the chirping of birds in the cypress trees. They don't immediately notice his presence.

"The recent houses he bought were all acquired in the name of Piroscafi Postali. Do you know what he intends to do with them?" Damiani Almeyda pulls up his collar to shield himself from the humidity.

"He doesn't even look at the spices anymore. He did tell us straight after his father's death, but—"

Ignazio raises his voice very slightly. "And I explained why: times have changed."

Startled, the two men turn abruptly.

Ignazio is thinking about the Marsala winery and about the

liqueur-like wine he produces, which reaches the whole of Europe. About his steamships, which carry goods and people across the Mediterranean and beyond, to Asia and America. "Some are rich, others want to feel rich," he adds.

Damiani Almeyda shrugs his shoulders. "You're right about that. People nowadays aspire to feel rich even if they're not."

"It's always been that way. Folk love to act like royalty." Giachery leans on the stick he's been using for some time because of a painful hip. "First, it was the aristocrats who wanted to continue presenting themselves as rich even if they'd sold the nails from their walls. Now it's the petits bourgeois who think they're being clever." He glances around: plaques with pretentious names alternate with silent, expectant ones. Middle-class families associate themselves with those of ancient lineage, luxurious tombs stand next to sober ones not from choice but lack of funds. Death has finally stricken the hunger for wealth from those who had to sell even their doornails to survive, as Giachery said, while the new tombs of middle-class families legitimize riches earned from hard work, here in Santa Maria di Gesù, as in other cemeteries in the city, starting with the largest one, Santa Maria dei Rotoli.

"And the more time goes by, the more obvious this change will be. It's already apparent in other parts of Europe. As though some people want to prove they own the world when they don't have a penny to their name." Damiani Almeyda descends the steps that separate the chapel from the crypt, where Giulia has recently been buried. He takes a bunch of keys from his pocket, weighs them in his hand, then gives them to Ignazio. "Here. They're yours."

He takes them and holds them tight. They're large, made of iron, heavy. Just like his father's inheritance.

He's outside the door to the crypt now. The key turns. On the ground, there are marks of plaster and footprints.

Beyond the short corridor, there's a large white sarcophagus of carved marble. On the panels, his father, Vincenzo Florio, is depicted as a demigod, a kind of toga over his middle-class clothes. His mother is in a recess behind the sarcophagus. As discreet in death as in life.

While the other two men linger behind, Ignazio strokes the sarcophagus with his gloved hand. The cold stone is silent and yet, deep in his heart, he feels his father's, his parents' presence. A gentle warmth spreads through his chest.

He's doing his best. He's trying hard. But he misses the expression in their eyes, even after time has passed. You never entirely stop being someone's child, just as it's impossible not to be a parent once you've had a child.

He closes his eyes, immersed in memories, from Villa dei Quattro Pizzi to the large citrus grove in Villa ai Colli di San Lorenzo, where he would chase after his sisters; from twirling around the dragon tree outside the porch to dance lessons with his mother, so clumsy she kept treading on his toes, and yet so happy to have that contact with him. She always laughed, her head thrown back, while the dance master huffed and Angelina and Giuseppina rolled their eyes, annoyed by the complicity between mother and son. And his father placing a hand on his shoulder and speaking to him softly, telling him how to operate among the sharks of politics . . .

Then, all of a sudden, a face framed by a mane of blond curls appears before him.

Ignazio has never been able to tell anybody about her. Only his sister Giuseppina knows. And—from the way he acted and what he said—François, too.

He corrects himself: *No. Someone else knew.*

His mother. She asked him if he really wanted to marry Giovanna, and he replied yes, that he couldn't do otherwise.

Not only did you know, Mamma, but you understood all my sorrow.

It's a wound that will never stop hurting because it's been the hardest sacrifice, the price imposed so that his father would consider him a true Florio. A price levied in silence, without a single word uttered on the subject.

Only now does he become aware of another thread that binds him to his mother. Both renounced an important part of themselves to enable Casa Florio not only to keep going, but above all to prosper. His mother sacrificed her love and her dignity so that Vincenzo would be free to devote himself to work, body and soul. And he, Ignazio, went beyond that by giving up the woman he loved so that the Florios could expand their business where his father had been unable to reach: at first into the salons of Palermo's aristocracy, then into the court of the Savoys. Because Sicilian nobility, with their Arab, Norman, and French blood, were convinced they were the descendants of the gods of Mount Olympus, and because of that, the Florios had to aim for that Mount Olympus. And so it had been.

And yet there are days—and nights—when all that is not enough, he thinks.

That's when recollections of Marseille blossom again, memories of the happiest season of his life: he sees himself again as a twenty-year-old, remembers the colors and sounds of a small country house, the scent of roses, of soap rubbed on a woman's body, naked, like his own, in the same tub.

The true curse of happiness is not being aware of it while living it. The moment you realize you were happy, all you're left with is an echo.

He looks at his mother's plaque, Giulia Rachele Florio, née Portalupi. A woman who knew everything, who mediated inconspicuously, who loved, asking for nothing in return, and who was always one step behind.

His daughter, who was born in June 1870, was named after her. Giulia Florio. His little *stidduzza* is now a year and a half old.

He hears footsteps and turns.

Giachery has a kind smile that radiates words of comfort, even though they remain unsaid.

Ignazio immediately hides his thoughts behind a placid countenance. Nobody must see. "It's a job well done," he murmurs. "Of course, the workers could have cleaned the steps better . . ." He kisses his fingertips, with which he touches Giulia's plaque, then crosses himself. Giachery follows his example.

Damiani Almeyda has been waiting for them on the threshold, his hands behind his back. They head for the exit and enter the carriage.

Ignazio breaks the silence hovering over them. "I hope you'll forgive me for dragging you all the way here, but I wanted to see the chapel after my mother was buried."

"Are you happy with it?" Damiani Almeyda asks.

"Very much so." He interlaces his fingers over his crossed legs and peers out the window. The sky is growing wider, patches of blue bleeding through the frayed clouds. "But there was something else I wanted to discuss with you. I'm considering taking control of one of my father's enterprises again."

Giachery frowns. "Which one? After all, your father was an experimenter, and it was hard to keep up with all his ideas."

"You're right. I'm talking about the textile factory, the one he wanted to start in Marsala, next to the winery. But then nothing came of it . . ." Ignazio looks at him closely. "I've heard that Morvillo, the lawyer, is looking for partners for his small cotton plant, here in Palermo. He's the former director of education on the city council and he's an intelligent man. I also like him because he has progressive notions about the workers . . . Try to feel out his intentions, but don't give away too much, you're good at that."

Giachery nods. "He wants to manufacture the cotton we produce here. I expect he doesn't have a penny. The competition from Naples is too strong."

"Of course, it's insane that cotton made in Sicily should be sent to Naples or even up to the Veneto to be spun, then come back here to be sold. The price gets disproportionately inflated, so that it's necessary to beg for British or American cloth. If we can turn the situation to our advantage, why not do so?"

"Very well. I will."

Damiani Almeyda watches Ignazio but doesn't comment. He wonders for the umpteenth time about this man he finds disorienting and fascinating. He's certainly in no way less so than his father, and yet he couldn't be more different. He has an intimate, deep-seated strength and a ruthless determination cloaked within his affability.

Of one thing Damiani Almeyda is certain, however: there is sometimes much more to fear from politeness than from cruelty.

"Yes, stewed vegetables with butter and just a little pepper, and rabbit *à la Provençale*." Giovanna is dictating while Donna Ciccia transcribes, her tongue between her lips. "As for the wine, an Alicante will go well." She wants Ignazio, on his return, to find a calm atmosphere and everything managed in every detail.

Donna Ciccia folds the paper and hands it to the maid so she can take it to the kitchen, then turns her attention to Giovanna. She nods, satisfied, at the black dress with mauve trimmings. It's only three months since Giulia's death and they're still in strict mourning.

"You look lovely."

Giovanna gives a faint smile. She knows she's anything but beautiful, but this white lie helps her feel better.

Donna Ciccia squeezes her shoulder. "To think that you were once scared of everything. And now you've become an excellent mistress of the house. You can even choose the right wine."

"Ma . . . mamamama . . ."

It's little Giulia, the youngest child. The nanny hands her to Giovanna, who smiles and pecks her cheeks. The little girl grabs one of her fingers and puts it in her mouth. "You're so gorgeous, my sweetheart," she says, rubbing her nose against that of the child, who tries to seize a lock of her hair. "You're my life."

Donna Ciccia's heart feels lighter as she watches the scene. She has prayed to God—and not only Him—for so long that her *picciridda* should have some peace of mind. Her *little one*, yes, not her *mistress*, because she's been like a mother to her, raised her, and always been by her side. *How she's changed since she was first married*, she thinks as she folds the shift left lying at the foot of the bed. She was always anxious and insecure, seeking refuge in starvation, as though wanting to vanish from the world. As though she couldn't allow herself to exist. Now, however, she's comfortable in her role as mother and wife. She's even put on a little meat, which makes her look more feminine. Donna Ciccia doesn't know if her *picciridda* has really found peace of mind or if she's become resigned. Of course, her relationship with Ignazio can't be compared to that of the other couple she knew well—Giovanna's parents—which never progressed beyond mutual indifference. Still, the gap between

Ignazio's calm and Giovanna's ardor could, in the long run, have proved unbridgeable. She saw that right away but could only hope it wouldn't happen. And so she silently watched over Giovanna, listened to her, comforted her, and dried her tears, just like a mother.

Giovanna gives Giulia one last kiss and hands her back to the nanny. "Tell Vincenzino and Ignazziddu to start working, because the music teacher will be here soon. I'll join them shortly."

She goes out the door, while Donna Ciccia turns and starts to tidy up the corsets, trying to conceal a grimace. The two boys in Casa Florio are lively, as children should be, but while Vincenzino heeds reproaches and always apologizes, Ignazziddu seems indifferent even to being slapped. "Temperamental," she can't help herself whispering.

"What did you say?" Giovanna asks.

"I was thinking about Master Ignazziddu. He's like quicksilver."

"My husband says it's because he's still young."

"You need to straighten the tree while it's still young," Ciccia says.

"He'll get his head straight as he grows up, you'll see," Giovanna replies, opening her jewelry box to choose some earrings. A few of her jewels—topazes, pearls, and emeralds—used to belong to Giulia, although most were bequeathed to her sisters-in-law. In any case, she doesn't particularly like them: she finds the cut old-fashioned and the settings chunky. Besides, they're not appropriate for mourning. Finally, she picks a pair made of onyx and pearls. "I wonder what my mother-in-law would have said. From what I've heard, Giuseppina and Angelina were far more restless than Ignazio when they were children." She sighs. "At the end, it was hard to talk to her, though. She was always at the window, staring into the street, as though waiting for someone . . ."

"It was him calling her," Donna Ciccia says with a shudder, crossing herself. "On one of her last evenings, she asked me to leave the light on, because her husband would be coming. I thought she was losing her mind . . . But when we found her dead, I got a little frightened."

Giovanna purses her lips. She doesn't like to talk about such things.

She sits down at a small table and takes the letters Donna Ciccia left there for her. They're mainly dinner or party invitations—issued purely out of courtesy, given the mourning of a close relative—but there's no shortage of condolence cards. *They keep coming*, she thinks, waving one, while Donna Ciccia organizes the work basket for the embroidery of a tapestry they're about to complete.

One of Vincenzo's business associates, who was traveling and has only just heard the news; a cousin who lives in Calabria and whose name she can hardly remember; a supplier who apologizes profusely for the delay, but he's been very ill and—

And then.

A note on Amalfi paper with a French stamp, addressed to Ignazio. Giovanna turns it over, wondering how it ended up here. She notices in particular the delicate handwriting, so different from the heavy, angular writing on the other messages of condolence.

She's about to put it aside, but then she looks it over again.

She briefly hesitates, sets aside the other envelopes, picks up one of her hairpins, and uses it in lieu of a paper knife. *Ignazio won't mind if I . . .*

> *Your mother, too, has left you: I know how attached you were to her and can imagine how difficult it must be for you not to be able to mourn her as you would wish. My heart grieves for you.*
> *Your sorrow is my sorrow, you know that.*
> *C.*

Giovanna feels her breath shatter like glass. No tradesman, no relative, no friend would write a sentence like that. She corrects herself: *No man.* Not in that tone. Not in that elegant script. Not on such fine paper.

Your sorrow is my sorrow, you know that.

Only a woman would write such a sentence.

And only to a man she knows well.

Only to a man she *loves.*

Giovanna shakes her head brusquely. Sentences, looks, gestures. Memories crowd her mind. Words that suddenly take on a new meaning.

No.

She lifts her head abruptly and is startled by her own image in the mirror. Her eyes are huge, empty, and dark, as though night has fallen over them.

She looks at Donna Ciccia, who's still fiddling with threads and linen cloths and hasn't noticed anything.

Then she stares at the envelope again. She wants to know, she has to.

The stamp is almost illegible. She tilts the paper toward the light from the window. *Marseille.* The message comes from Marseille. Is it possible it's a woman Giuseppina and François know? For a moment, she considers writing to Giuseppina, but immediately thinks better of it.

What would you ask her? a wicked voice inside says in a tone somewhat similar to that of her mother. *You'd only make a fool of yourself.*

She looks at the card and sniffs it. A faint scent of flowers. Carnations, perhaps. Or perhaps it's her imagination. She doesn't know.

She has pins and needles in her hands, her stomach churns and contracts with a life of its own, and the feeling that plagued her existence for such a long time returns. Away with food, away with emotions.

She closes her eyes and waits until the rising impulse to vomit subsides.

The fears, *those nameless fears*, now resurface and attack her.

She drops the card into her lap, an ivory patch on her black skirt. It almost feels as if it gives off an evil energy.

My heart grieves for you.

"You tend to the children, Donna Ciccia," she says firmly. "I need to answer these notes. I'll join you later." She gets up, hides the card in the palm of her hand, and, almost unconsciously, crumples it.

Ignoring Donna Ciccia's reply, she walks through the communicating door into her husband's bedroom.

She looks around frantically, blood pumping in her ears. In a flash, she remembers another morning, another bereavement. She flings the wardrobe doors open.

Alerted by the sound of her footsteps, Nanài, the valet, appears at the door. *"Chi ci fu?"* he ventures timidly, upset at seeing the mistress rummaging through her husband's clothes.

She turns on him. "Get out! *Vattinni!*" she hisses.

Evidently scared, the man steps out the door. Giovanna seems possessed by a demon.

She wedges her hands between shirts, pushes away robes, feels trousers . . .

She suddenly stops, feeling dizzy, and puts her hands to her temples.

She's above this. But how can you stop yourself, how can you restrain yourself if the man for whose sake you changed your way of being, the man who taught you about love, and for whom you've learned to eat . . . if someone else occupies this man's heart?

She closes her eyes and tries to think. No, her husband's world isn't here, among these items. *He comes into this room only to change his clothes and sleep. He spends most of his time in the study. That's where he keeps* truly *important things.*

Giovanna starts running as she's never run in her life. She rushes downstairs and storms toward the study. Drawn by the disturbance, the children appear at the nursery door and watch her, bewildered: their mother has never appeared so desperate. Vincenzino coughs and gives Ignazziddu a puzzled look, but the younger boy shrugs.

Giovanna opens the door to the study. It's the first time she's set foot here: this is a place of business, of blunt words, leather walls, and cigar smoke. For a moment, she watches as the heavy wooden furniture emerges from the half-light, the low bookcase behind the desk, the oriental lamp on top of the cabinet. She approaches the desk and starts opening the drawers at random. She finds pencils, pens, nibs, logs filled with numbers. She leafs through them in vain. Then she bends down and opens the last drawer. It has a double compartment.

That's where she finds it. The rosewood-and-ebony box with the metal handle. Ignazio used to keep it in his closet on Via dei Materassai. Once she asked him what was in it and he replied, laconically, "Memories."

Her hands are shaking. The box is smooth, heavy, warm to the touch. She places it on the desk and a ray of sunlight falls on it, illuminating the veining of the wood.

She opens it.

Immediately, a fragrance washes over her, similar to the one she thought she caught on the condolence card. Then, under a frayed copy of *La Princesse de Clèves* by Madame de La Fayette, she discovers a stack of letters. She tips the contents onto the leather blotter and, with a mixture of curiosity and revulsion, plunges her hands in. The paper is heavyweight and refined, and the handwriting is that of a woman. Many of the letters aren't even open, while others are practically in shreds. They all carry the Marseille postmark and date back a few years. Suddenly a faded blue satin ribbon appears.

At the bottom of the box, there's a note similar to the one that unleashed this storm, and it now ends up on top of the stack of envelopes on the desk. She scrutinizes the date and reads it. It's a message about her father-in-law's death.

The frenzy rises once again, taking possession of her. "Who is this woman?" she cries aloud without even realizing it. She grabs an envelope and tries to open it.

"What are you doing?"

Ignazio's voice is like ice water in her face. Giovanna lifts her head and sees him standing by the door, holding his overcoat. Instinctively, she drops the envelope.

Ignazio's eyes travel from his wife's face to the open box, then to the papers scattered on the desk. "I asked what you're doing," he says again, white as a sheet, his voice hoarse, almost metallic.

He shuts the door, puts his overcoat on a chair, and walks to the desk. He slowly reaches out for the crumpled note and smooths it with an almost loving gesture. But his face is cold and emotionless. This makes Giovanna even angrier. "What are these?" she hisses, waving the envelope in her hand.

"Give it to me," Ignazio says, his eyes still on the note.

It's a whisper with the weight of a command. Giovanna shakes her head and clutches it to her chest. Red blotches appear on her pale face, oddly contrasting with her black dress. "What are they?" she repeats, now in earnest.

"Things that don't concern you."

"They're letters from a woman. Who is she?"

Ignazio looks up at her and Giovanna's heart skips a beat.

Ignazio—*her* Ignazio—has never lost control. He's always dismissed every setback with a shrug of the shoulders or a detached smile. This ashen-faced man with a clenched jaw and half-closed eyes burning with anger is not her husband. He's a stranger, an individual in the grip of a wrath that's as icy as it is irrepressible.

Giovanna's thoughts are in a muddle, cruel, frightened, contradictory. *How stupid I've been! Why did I want to know? Because I'm his wife and he owed me that. Couldn't I have torn this note to shreds and forgotten about it? No, I should have lied to him, to my husband . . . But everything would have stayed as before! What can I do to placate him now? I have a right to know, though, after all the years I've been sacrificing myself for his sake! And what if he now chooses this other woman? No, that's not possible, there are Vincenzino and Ignazziddu . . .*

She shakes her head, as though to silence the voices that are tearing her apart.

"Why?" she finally asks. She drops the envelope and leans against the desk, bending toward him. It's the only question she can—she wants to—ask him. "Why didn't you tell me there was another woman?" she continues, her voice now tearful. "Is that why you've never really wanted me? Because you were thinking only about this Frenchwoman?"

"Since I married you, there's been no other woman."

His voice is once again steady and controlled. The expression on his face has resumed its usual detachment. Only his lips are slightly twisted as he picks up the envelopes, stacks them, and puts them back into the box.

But the tenderness of his manner, the care with which he rolls up the blue ribbon with his fingers, with which he picks up the book, doesn't escape Giovanna. She doesn't hold back. "Is she so much better than me?"

"It's in the past. It's nothing to do with you," Ignazio replies without looking at her. Then he takes a bunch of keys from his trouser pocket. He uses one of them—a small, dark key—to lock the box. He holds it against him and heads to the door. "It's not your business. And never set foot in my study again. Never again."

⌒

Sand and salt under his shoes. The wind is very hot and strong, the light so blindingly white that he's forced to squint. The air smells of oregano and sea.

Ignazio crouches and grabs a handful of sand and soil, letting it run between his fingers. It's actually crumbled tuff: a pale rock that traps the remains of shells and sea animals and represents the true heart of Favignana.

His island.

It's truly mine, he tells himself, smiling, and resumes his walk to the edge of the Bue Marino cliffs, where he can look out and see the dry land and the sea. Below him, workers are cutting blocks of tuff that will then be dragged to the shore and loaded onto ships heading to Trapani. A fine dust rises in the air before being pushed down to the ground by gusts of wind: it's residue from the extraction of tuff from caves dozens of meters deep, an industry which, in addition to fishing, is essential for the island's residents not only as a source of income but also because you need tuff to build houses.

It's truly his: a few months earlier, he bought the Aegadian Islands from the Marqueses Giuseppe Carlo and Francesco Rusconi and their mother, the Marquise Teresa Pallavicini: Favignana, Marettimo,

Levanzo, and Formica—the latter halfway between Levanzo and Trapani. Ignazio told everyone that this 2,700,000-lire investment ensured the possibility of bolstering his tuna enterprise; that he could use the prisoners in Forte Santa Caterina as a workforce and that, moreover, there was tuff to sell. Basically, he had carried out a detailed examination of every characteristic of the islands, estimated their true potential, and decided to buy them. He also took advantage of the fact that the previous management had been running at a loss, and thereby bargained down the price.

He doesn't need to justify it to himself now, however.

Just as, almost seventy years ago, his namesake uncle immediately loved the tuna plant at Arenella, so did Ignazio fall in love with Favignana: he loves it more than his business, than social standing, than many things his life is filled with. The work-related stress—the difficulties in extracting sulfur, the increase in customs duty—is distant; so is his family. Giovanna's eyes, so sad and serious, are little more than a faint memory.

This is where he wants to build himself a house, just like his father did in Arenella. But it's not the right time yet: there's a lease on the *tonnara* in the name of a *gabellotto*, Vincenzo Drago. He must wait another three years—until 1877—before he takes full possession of the plant and the island.

Beneath him, the sea is roaring, rumbling, clamoring. The wind, a capricious föhn, is changing, he can feel it, then this stretch of sea will also suddenly find peace. It will calm down, the same way he did the very moment he stepped on this island.

He closes his eyes and lets the light permeate his eyelids.

He recalls the first time he came here, when he was just fourteen and his father, who was then running the *tonnara*, asked him to join him. With the stench of rotting tuna saturating the air and the sun blazing on the walls of the houses, Vincenzo rolled up his shirtsleeves, sat down on a large rock, and started talking to the fishermen in dialect, discussing the best spot for lowering the nets and the direction the wind would take during the *mattanza*. Ignazio is different than his father: he's at once cordial and detached. What the men on Favignana see in him, however, is an inner strength, which, far from being expressed in an arrogant attitude, surrounds him with an aura of quiet self-confidence. They noticed it that very morning when Ignazio came to the *tonnara* without warning. The *mattanza* ended a couple of weeks ago, the summer is in full swing, and while work is in progress to complete the canning of the fish, the tuna fishermen are taking care of the boats and nets.

Ignazio spent a long time listening to them, never interrupting, not even when the conversation was confusing, the dialect incomprehensible. Above all, he looked them in the eye and understood all their concerns, their fear for the future, marred by clouds of uncertainty, be it because of competition on the part of Spanish tuna fishing or because of the taxes established by the "Piedmontese." He made no promises and yet his mere presence reassured everybody.

"Are you pleased?"

The voice that awakens him from his thoughts belongs to Gaetano Caruso, one of his most trusted colleagues, the son of one of the administrators who worked with his father. They also spoke for a long time, especially about what Ignazio wants to create on Favignana, about his ideas on how to modernize the plant, and the contracts he wished to stipulate.

"Yes, very much. The men who work here are good, respectful people," he replies, rubbing his hands. There is still a dusting of tuff on his skin.

"That's because you know how to handle them. You make them

feel safe because you respect them and they can sense it. You don't just order them about, as others do."

Caruso sits down next to him. His face is thin, his features sharp, and he has a goatee he keeps worrying. But right now his arms remain crossed, unlike Ignazio, who's looking at the sea with his hands in his pockets, letting the wind buffet him.

"A long time ago, when I was a *picciriddu*, my tutor had me translate a passage from Livy where he mentions Menenius Agrippa's fable. Do you know it?"

"No, Don Ignazio," Caruso replies.

"At the time, the plebs wanted the same rights as the patricians, so they left Rome in protest. Menenius Agrippa convinced them to return by telling them a fable: the limbs suddenly stopping working because they were envious of the fact that the stomach was idle, just waiting to be fed. But this way the entire body grew weak, so the limbs had to make peace with the stomach." He gives a barely perceptible smile. "Our workers have to feel a part of something. My father also used to say that. Wages can't be the only thing they aspire to. I must above all show them that every one of them is important, and I can only do that if I look them in the face, one by one."

Caruso nods. "It's not always easy."

"It is here. These are fishermen, simple people who understand the value of work . . . In the city, on the other hand, workers make demands and look for reasons not to work, or else work less, and they keep asking and asking—only to then criticize whatever's granted them. It's a constant battle." His expression darkens as he thinks about the workers in the Oretea and those in the textile factory he started with Morvillo, the lawyer, which is struggling to be productive.

He turns away from the Mediterranean. Nearby, a buggy waits for them.

Caruso watches Ignazio get into the vehicle, which, like everything on the island, is blanketed in a veil of tuff dust, and then, trying to make him smile, says, "People here consider you a prince, you know? I wouldn't be surprised if the king—"

"I'm an industrialist, Signor Caruso," interrupts Ignazio. "My title is my capital. A title that generates more power and respect than any other."

As the buggy speeds him away from Bue Marino, a part of his soul sings with the same voice as the wind. No, he has no wish to be made prince or count or marquis of the Aegadian Islands. It's owning them that makes him, quite simply, happy.

PART TWO

Tonnara

June 1877 to September 1881

Fa' beni e scordatillo; fa' mali e pensaci.
Do good and forget it; do ill and remember it.
—SICILIAN PROVERB

C IURMA, SARPATU, CHIUMMO, CÀMMARA, COPPU, *bastardedda, panaticu, rimiggiu.*

Words in a dialect that some on the butterfly-shaped island of Favignana still speak, words that echo the sound of time and labor.

In winter, the black ships have been caulked and the nets mended and reinforced. On the feast day of the Holy Cross in May, anchors are dropped following coordinates established by the *rais*, who finds them according to the direction of the winds and sea currents; the Holy Crucifix, the Madonna of the Rosary, the Sacred Heart, and Francis of Paola, patron saint of sailors and fishermen, are invoked. The *rais* is the lord of the *tonnara*, the head of the tuna catchers, fishermen who board the boats when they're barely more than adolescents, and leave only when they're claimed by old age, death, or the sea.

The *rais* reads the wind and the waters, commands the removal of the *tonnara*.

The anchors are dropped to the bottom, as well as a chain and ashlars of tuff from the Favignana quarries, to ensure that the *isula*—the body of the *tonnara*—is stable: because when the tuna come in and struggle with all their strength to stay alive, the nets will be torn and the cables yanked.

The *isula* is divided into rooms: the tuna are ushered to the entrance, the *vucca 'a nassa*, through a *custa*, a wide, long net that bars their way. It has doors made from hand-drawn nets, a *punenti* chamber, and a *levanti* chamber that communicates with the *granni* chamber and the *urdunaru*. There are no nets at the end. The only room with nets on five sides is the *coppu*, the death room. After the *punenti* chamber, the tuna go into the *bastardedda*, the antechamber to the *coppu*. When the door—also made of fishing nets—is finally lifted, the tuna, driven crazy by the increasingly tight mesh, dive into the death chamber in search of a way out.

The day before, the fishermen pray, invoking Christ's name and imploring for the fishing to be bountiful enough to support the family and yield a bonus.

On the day of the fishing, long ships take position in pairs on the sides of the *quadratu*, the surfacing part of the death chamber, with the help of *parascarmi*, smaller boats, and the *vasceddi*, long and imposing with their black hulls, and close off the *quadratu*. They are always in pairs, one windward, the other downwind.

Prior to the *mattanza*, more prayers are said. Songs that bring together Saint Peter and curses against the avaricious enemy sea are intoned.

Then the men start to pull on *u' coppu*, the bottom of the death chamber. They use all the strength of their arms, the water spray adding to their sweat, the tuna thrashing about because they lack room and water. The nets—heavy, drenched, and strained by the animals—are secured to the insides of the ships. Groups of fishermen with strong, muscular bodies whose task is to harpoon the tuna and take them aboard with the *spetta*, a long, deadly hook, lean out of the boats.

The signal comes. Poles and harpoons built by the fishermen appear. They strike the tuna, which now fill the surface of the water, banging powerfully against the ships and colliding with one another. The sea turns red, the water becomes blood. The animals sound and their lament drowns out the shouts of the *tonnaroti*, who beckon and call one another. The tuna try to find a way to wriggle out, but the fishermen lance them, heave them onto the boat with the strength of their arms, and grab them by their fins, while the harpoons tear through their flesh, eyes, and mouths. They're still alive when they reach the bottoms of the boats but will be dead by the time they reach the harbor, and their blood will be washed away with bucketfuls of sea water.

There is respect for the tuna in the *mattanza*, but no pity.

By the time the carriage comes to a halt near the Oretea Foundry at five thirty on a dull gray morning in June 1877, the gates are already open. High-pitched cries and curses echo beneath the metal vaults designed by Damiani Almeyda. The voices rise to the sloping metal roof, decorated with small spirals, and penetrate the thick glass windows. The architect has refined the thick, coarse lines of the original foundry and improved its features.

Sitting on the ground or leaning against the walls, groups of men and boys in work clothes are chatting and arguing. Some bite into pieces of bread.

They've no intention of going in, Ignazio realizes.

All of a sudden, a stout man with a crooked nose and stringy gray hair materializes by the gate. He opens his arms and shouts, "What is this? Is it true you want to work for someone who steals your money and bleeds you dry?"

His voice echoes all the way to the end of the street, silencing everybody.

Ignazio knows him. He's a welder: one of those who, until two days ago, worked on ship repairs and who, since yesterday, has refused to go into the foundry because they heard that they will no longer be receiving a small sum—hazard pay—as compensation. The workers cried oppression and anger spread like a wildfire. At one stage, even the police intervened. On the evening of the second day, the foundry's managers agreed that only Ignazio's presence could resolve the situation and begged him to come to the foundry the following morning as the gates opened.

"They answer to no one!" the welder roars. "They know the tool wagon we have is no use, and they also know we're constantly at their beck and call! We're always here, always available, never complaining!"

A chorus of "*Veru è!* Right!" rises from the crowd, drowning the man's voice. Some rush to the gates and shut them, then hammer at the foundry walls. Within a handful of seconds, the street is throbbing with commotion, with fierce cries. The tension smells of sweat and iron. Dozens of workers punch the walls, shouting that they won't let themselves be robbed, that this job is their families' livelihood, because it's true that they "actually climb slippery walls" in order to do their work and never complain, but now . . .

That's when Ignazio decides to exit his carriage.

He emerges calmly, head high, hat in hand, and walks, unperturbed, toward the entrance.

It's a child who first notices his arrival. He pulls on his father's sleeve. "*Papà, Papà!* It's the boss! Don Ignazio's here!"

The man turns to look, eyes wide open, removes his cap, and holds it to his chest. "Don Ignazio, my respects," he says, greeting him, his cheeks flushed with embarrassment.

The clamor subsides as suddenly as it started. The crowd parts to let him through. The welder lowers his arms and stands aside, as though sapped of all his power. The gates open, albeit just a little.

A few workers remove their caps and stare with a blend of respect and fear. Others take a step back, while others again look down at the ground.

Ignazio returns their greetings with a nod but doesn't say a word.

Some looks, however, are anything but cowed. He feels them on his back, senses their resentment, smells their anger. It has a pungent odor, like gunpowder. These hungry eyes trail him to the door of the administration office, where a man with a graying goatee and a receding hairline awaits him. He's Wilhelm Theis, the manager of the foundry. A small, thin man who looks even slighter next to Ignazio's solid frame.

He closes the door behind them and double locks it. The two men pace silently down a narrow corridor that's still dark and climb the stairs to the offices where some ten employees in jackets and black neckties, starched collars, and percale sleeve stockings are getting ready to start work. Ignazio passes the row of tidy desks, greets the employees, and inquires after their families.

Meanwhile, he keeps an eye on what's outside the window that looks down on the inside of the foundry. From there he has a view of the entire plant. The workers are trickling in: he can see their tired faces and notices several hands gesturing in the direction of the offices.

He doesn't hide. *Let them see me*, he thinks. *Let them all know I'm here.*

Somebody behind him coughs.

"So, Signor Theis. As I understand it, the men are not happy with the new ship-working conditions."

Theis approaches the desk. It's where he, as the manager, usually sits when Ignazio isn't here. But not today. Today, the boss is here.

"Don Ignazio, the abolition of hazard pay on the steamships has triggered a discontent none of us expected—at least not as violent as this. There's no end of grumbling and protesting, and now they're even involving that printed rag of theirs . . ."

"*Il Povero*? Are you surprised? Half the editors are employed at the foundry. I expect them to protest."

"But they're exaggerating. The workers, the welders, and the mechanics in particular are complaining that work on the ships has become too grueling and dangerous, and not worthwhile without that compensation. We resisted for two days, suppressed the protests partly thanks to the police, but now . . ."

Ignazio listens without turning. He rubs his dark beard and thinks. There have been some arrests, and he knows it: it was he who asked the prefect—confidentially, of course—for order to be maintained around the foundry. Just as he knows that it's now his duty to restore calm and harmony.

The tension he senses in the air is like dense steam. It clings not only to the workers but also to the office clerks. It seeps through the white walls of the offices, and the soot-covered walls of the plant, until you can hardly breathe.

Supervisors in uniform push the workers toward their stations. Someone says a word too many, a young man is given a shove, and he reacts. A supervisor strikes him, and others intervene to placate the row.

The hiss of the water pumped through the pipes to cool down the presses announces that the foundry is about to restart in full.

The office door opens with a clink of glass, followed by the thud of a stick. Then comes the clang of mallets forging metal.

"Forgive me for being late," says Vincenzo Giachery, the administrator of the foundry. "My leg refused to move properly this morning."

Ignazio goes to him and offers him his chair. "It's my fault, Don Vincenzo."

"Not at all." Giachery's eyes light up and a smile appears on his face marked by the years. "You share your father's handicap: people immediately do what you tell them to," he says, sighing as he sits down.

Ignazio smiles in return. He strokes the polished surface of the desk, which his father used for years in the *aromateria* on Via dei Materassai and didn't want to part with. He sits down, hands open on the table. "My father and your brother Carlo, peace be with them, were from the same mold. Birds of a feather."

Giachery nods. He crosses his hands on the pommel of his stick and jerks his chin at the plant beyond the window. "What shall we do?"

Theis opens his arms with a disgusted expression. "They're just peasants. Loafers who can't even speak properly. We can't even really call them workmen. These people should be taught a good lesson. Make them understand that we're not at their beck and call!"

Ignazio crosses his hands and rests his chin on them. "They're our workmen, Signor Theis. They may be peasants, but they work here in the foundry and on the ships. We need them. Especially the Genoese mechanics and—"

"They're well paid, Don Ignazio," Theis says, interrupting him and wriggling on his chair. "But if we think of the work they're able to do . . ."

Giachery clears his throat, requesting attention. He speaks cautiously, looking down at the floor so as not to upset the nervous engineer. "Listen: this plant produces a little of everything, from cutlery to boilers. You know that better than anyone else, Signor Theis. I work with these people and listen to them. It's unfair of you to call them peasants. They're simple people who work themselves to the bone for wages that are much lower than those of a French, let alone a German, workman. It's true that they're ignorant and have little desire to learn new things, but they do care about putting food on their tables." Only then does he lift his head to look at Ignazio: it's him he now addresses. "They know that the work on the ships is dangerous and they're afraid, but they also know that if they give up, others are ready to take their places. We're in Palermo, gentlemen, where a two-lira wage at the Oretea Foundry makes you rich. There are people who would give anything just to work here. But this wouldn't be good for us because they'd be totally untrained workers. Moreover, you know how hard it is to persuade someone from Livorno, let alone a German, to come here and teach others his skills. Just consider how much we'd have to pay him."

Ignazio turns his wedding band, then touches his uncle Ignazio's ring. "So, if I understand you correctly, Don Vincenzo, you urge caution."

Giachery makes a gesture with his hand. "Caution, of course. And, even better, the carrot and the stick." He leans forward and tells him in confidence, "I've known you since you wore short trousers: workers listen to you, just like the *tonnaroti* on Favignana. Talk to them."

Ignazio sighs and drums his fingers on the wood. He seems to hesitate, although he knows Giachery is right. For too long he's judged the workmen to have no humility, no wish to improve, and no gratitude. Their lives are very different from those of the *tonnaroti*, but they have the same pride and need to be treated with respect. And now it's up to him to find the right balance between these needs and the necessity to remain competitive—even if he can't achieve this in a short time. "It's essential to lower our costs," he says as though thinking aloud. "It's true that the foundry is doing well, but we've had some tall orders and we need to hire more staff. There are more than seven hundred workers here." He speaks softly and there is no uncertainty in his tone. "We cannot afford to pay hazard pay. And, above all, going back on our decision would create a dangerous precedent."

His last word is accompanied by the drum of hammers folding the huge panels of the dome for the new theater, the Politeama.

The foundry is one of the pillars of Casa Florio, but it will not be able to compete with the factories in northern Italy or Germany for long. It's not by chance that their only government commission is the port in Messina, while the steel factories in the north have contracts to build railroads and careening bays. Production costs are too high and transporting goods and raw materials is inconvenient. The only way to continue working is to keep wages low and count every lira.

Maybe, after a while, they'll be able to introduce changes into the production cycle and think about raising wages. But not for now. Innovations involve investments and the training of new workers. No, the thing that matters right now is to keep up with those industrialists in the north who have been working with metal for decades.

For a few seconds, the deafening sound of metal on metal echoes through the office. Then, suddenly, the bell. It tolls three times. An alert.

Startled, Theis turns and goes to the window. With difficulty, Giachery does the same.

The workmen are gathering in the yards. They've abandoned their hammers and pliers and blocked the presses; only a few have stayed behind to monitor the pressure machines and vent them.

They're all agitated and there's no one able to calm them down, not even the supervisor armed with a wooden stick. In fact, the younger men confront him, surrounding him and snatching the stick from his hands. Two others take him by the arms and restrain him.

One blow, then another. It's a beating.

A supervisor comes running from inside the warehouse, immediately followed by others. The sound of his whistle pierces the commotion, drowning out the cries.

The wounded supervisor is on the ground, moaning, a rivulet of blood trickling from his mouth. The workmen turn toward the other supervisors, who now stand in front of them, sticks raised. But there are only a few of them, and the human tide seems to swallow them, submerge them, suffocate them.

"What's happening?" Theis yells. "Should we call the police?"

"They're killing one another!" Ignazio runs out of the room, down the stairs, and through the door that separates the offices from the plant. His heart is in his throat. He's certain that if he doesn't do anything, there will be a disaster.

As soon as he steps into the yard, he yells, "Stop! Stop immediately!" Then he lunges at a workman who's kicking a supervisor. He grabs him by the shoulders and the man swears, then frees himself, ready to punch, but suddenly recognizes him. His arms fall to his sides and he steps back, swaying, eyes staring. "Don Ignazio!"

The name echoes from mouth to mouth; a murmur that's like a prayer. Fists loosen, arms drop. Clubs and sticks fall to the ground, and the supervisors step away, holding up the wounded man.

"What's happening here?" Ignazio says. Then he looks around and into the eyes of the men in front of him, one by one, waiting.

A mechanic comes forward. He looks only a couple of years older than Ignazio, with a broad build, arms covered in scratches and burns, and a face black with soot. "Excuse us, *Vossignoria*," he says. "But we can't work like this. They're always beating us with their sticks." His voice isn't loud and yet his words ripple.

"What happened? Who was it?" Ignazio asks, in the same calm tone. Then he studies the man more attentively and goes closer to him. They are the same height and have the same dark eyes. In the silence that's been created around them, Ignazio murmurs, "You're Alfio Filippello, aren't you? The chief mechanic, right?"

Reassured, the man nods. "Yes, *Vossignoria*." He can't help smiling. This is the Oretea Foundry: a place where the master knows who his workers are. He knows them, is like a father to them all.

"Tell me—*cùntami*," Ignazio says, encouragingly, in dialect so that the others may understand and trust him.

Alfio seeks support from his fellow workers, who just nod at him shyly to continue. "You know we all have families. Of course, the wages are a great help, plus the money you give us when we work on the steamers. But this way, we have nowhere else to go. We'd have to bring our own things and you wouldn't even pay us for the day . . . This morning, a boy broke his shoulder while carrying tools. They beat us with sticks if we don't work, and we're always inspected when we leave to see if we're taking things." He shakes his head and opens his hands. "*Principale*, we're not getting anywhere like this."

Ignazio crosses his arms and ponders what he's heard. These are poor people who really need even the pittance they earn by working on the steamships. A young man with an injured shoulder, offensive searches, violence and abuse of power on the part of the supervisors, money problems . . . "How do you know this boy hurt himself?"

A young boy, ragged and dirty from the coal, appears from behind Alfio. He can't be more than ten years old. "Don Ignazio—I saw it," he says. His voice is trembling, but his expression is earnest and already hardened by the exacting work. "I carry the box of nails for him, and I saw him: he fell because he was loaded down with things. His name's Mimmo Giacalone."

So he fell from the scaffolding because he was loaded down with tools, Ignazio thinks, beginning to understand why there is so much animosity. "And where is he now?" he asks.

"At home."

"And now what do you intend to do?"

The welder shakes his head. "We can't work like this. They treat us very badly, and not just these wretches, with all due respect." He indicates the supervisors who have come to stand next to Ignazio. "Some of the office people also treat us like dirt."

Ignazio lifts his head and stifles the curse about to fly from his lips. That's the problem: these men can put up with a great deal, but they can't be deprived of their dignity. That's the reason for all this anger, all this resentment.

Above him, the foundry's bookkeepers and office workers are watching the scene with both terror and contempt. Theis is clinging to the window railing. He looks shaken and seems to be trembling.

"I'll speak to the supervisors, I'll tell them to treat you with respect," Ignazio says in a loud voice so that everyone can hear him. He takes a step toward the men and embraces them all with his eyes. He wants them to be sure of his words and to trust him. "But you all have to get back to work."

The workmen exchange puzzled, fearful glances. Alfio leans his head back and listens to the murmuring of his companions. A drop of sweat draws a pale line on his soot-covered forehead.

"We can't, Don Ignazio," he finally replies. His tone is almost apologetic but with a firmness that leaves no room for argument. "It's not us that turned off the furnaces, it's them," he adds, indicating the supervisors. "It's them that should go. We're not animals. We're people just like them!" His voice changes, filling with anger. "We work all day long and then these—these bastards insult us, shut the door in our faces if we're late and don't let us in, then dock our day's wages! They break our bones with their sticks!"

Theis had told him that the workmen were complaining, but failed to specify how they were treated by the supervisors and what happened if they were late.

As though rallied by these words, the other workers crowd around Alfio. Their voices drown out his, and arms rise like a forest of fists.

The supervisors slither away toward the stairs.

Ignazio watches the men but doesn't move. He lets the murmuring die down, then looks at Alfio and says in a low voice, "You're my people." He takes a couple of steps toward the crowd, now silent again. "You are my people!" he repeats, more loudly. Then he turns, grabs Alfio's fists, covered in black dust, and lifts them in front of the workers. "The foundry is your home. If someone's wronged you, I assure you he'll pay for it. Do you really want to strike? Do you really want your home to come to a standstill and for there not to be any more bread and work?" He opens his arms and indicates the warehouse. "Have I not taken care of you? Do I not make sure that your children learn to read and write? Mimmo Giacalone . . . the young man who was hurt. He'll be taken care of by the Benefit Society I created for you . . ." He steps back and looks around. "*I did it! For you!* And if he's not a member, then I will personally make sure that he receives treatment. We're all part of this factory. I'm here with you . . . If need be, I'd take off this jacket and get down to work here, shoulder to shoulder, just so that we can continue. The Oretea isn't just the Florios: It's people! It's you!"

It's almost evening by the time Ignazio leaves the foundry. He waited until the workers left, said goodbye to them at the gates, and kept his eye on the inspections, which were much less aggressive this time. He had a gesture, a word, or a handshake for everyone.

They said goodbye to him with a "Long live Florio!" that echoed all the way to the port.

After his speech, the men returned to work. The grumbling and protesting haven't stopped but at least they've been allayed by the thought that the workers' arguments will be heard because *u' principale*—the boss—has promised it in person. And they trust Ignazio Florio.

He has spared no effort. He visited every department, listened to every complaint, and promised more equality. He asked Giachery for his advice and sought information about the health of the injured worker. His father's old friend took leave with a tap on his back. "It's always a matter of knowing how to fool people, and nobody's better at that than you," he said as he climbed into the carriage.

Ignazio left Theis and the supervisors till last.

He assembled them in his office and sat behind his desk. No one dared breathe. Theis glanced around nervously, avoiding Ignazio's probing, coldly angry gaze.

"Is it necessary to aggravate the situation?" Ignazio asked. His detached tone made more than one head drop. "Inspections can be carried out without humiliation. There's no need to beat the workers like this, just as you can show a little tolerance for tardiness, as you already do among yourselves."

Breaking the icy silence in the room, Theis burst out in exasperation, "With all due respect, Don Ignazio, you don't understand. First, it's five minutes, then ten . . . and soon enough they'll expect to take tools home with them, and heaven knows what they'll do with them. You can see how they're arguing now over the reduction of the hazard pay . . ."

"Let them, they won't achieve anything anyway. I'm not prepared to negotiate on the wages. But anything that can be done to keep them calm without spending a penny must be done immediately."

"It's important to be strict."

"Being strict is one thing, abusing power is another." He formed his hands into a pyramid in front of his face and narrowed his eyes. "You heard what I said and what they told me: the problem isn't just the hazard pay. It's mainly the way they're treated: like rabid dogs. And I promised them that wouldn't happen anymore. So now we're going to ease the inspections and be more lenient when workers are late, at least for the next few weeks, until everyone cools down. We won't fine anyone for the disturbances, and you'll tell the supervisors to go easy with the sticks, because they're not herding a flock of sheep. After what happened today, it'll only take this much"—he squeezes his thumb and index finger together—"to trigger a strike, and God only knows what that could lead to. The Florios have one maxim, and only one: nobody must *ever* humiliate the workers. They are the backbone of the foundry."

No one had the courage to reply.

Ignazio turned to Theis. "I depend on you to guarantee this never occurs again."

Theis coughed to clear his throat. He could imagine very clearly the consequences if he disobeyed that order. "It shall be as you say."

Only now, in the carriage taking him back to the Olivuzza, can Ignazio relax. The afternoon rain and the tramontana wind have swept the sky clean, turning it as clear as glass. Outside the window, Palermo is plunged in the evanescent beauty of a sunset still fragrant with sun.

The city walls are vanishing, demolished in favor of new districts, a sign of a new era being ushered in to take the place of a past not everybody may care to remember. People are moving, leaving their old houses in the city center and looking for larger, more comfortable apartments. Wide, tree-lined roads lead toward the countryside, where before there were only paths winding between citrus groves. The carriage drives past Palazzo Steri, a place his father knew well because that's where the customs offices were based. It has since been restructured by Damiani Almeyda. Work is now underway to clear the square and create a garden. Here, just a stone's throw from the large residence of the Lanza di Trabia family, there's the De Paces' palazzo, overlooking the sea. It's where his sister lives.

All that's left of the imposing Castello a Mare are bits of stone covered in weeds: the fortress was bombarded by order of Garibaldi, since the place where it stood had been strategic for access to the city. Best do away with it to avoid needless risks, the general decided. The Piedmontese did the rest. And now the last rays of the sun climb over those ruins, slipping through the sails and funnels of ships moored at the Cala. On the other side, the yellow tuff of the churches and palazzos seems to emanate heat, attenuating the darkness with a mellow luminosity that smells of summer.

Ignazio lets himself be whisked away to when he was twenty.

For him, each of these places connects to an image, a feeling. La Cala partly reminds him of all the times he waited with his father for the steamships to arrive. Past Porta Felice, he sees the Casino delle Dame e dei Cavalieri, where he met Giovanna . . .

But there are places where Palermo seems to want to rid itself of its past, as well as Ignazio's, all at once: to make room for the theater now towering over the ruins of the bastion of San Vito and Porta Maqueda, the churches of San Giuliano, San Francesco delle Stimmate, and Sant'Agata have been knocked down and an entire district gutted. Everything changes and it is right that it should be so.

He rubs the bridge of his nose. What he likes about June is the warmth that isn't yet smothering, the burst of nature in the garden of the Olivuzza, the fragrance of blooming yuccas, roses, plumerias, and jasmine. He may have enough time for a stroll down the alleys before dinner is served. If there is one thing he loves about this villa, it's this garden. But it's not the only one: he now prefers the Olivuzza to Villa dei Quattro Pizzi, his childhood home, where the aroma of the sea ruled supreme and would intoxicate him; he even prefers it to the house on Via dei Materassai, where Vincenzo and Ignazio were born.

Yes, Vincenzino. He has a fever once again and Giovanna spent the night at his bedside.

He hasn't had news of him all day.

No news is good news, they say. *Yes, that must be right.*

The evening has cast its veil over the trees of the Olivuzza by the time Ignazio's vehicle stops by the large olive tree next to the carriage entrance. The watchmen, like ghosts, move beyond the hedges, approaching to make sure there is no danger. Ignazio sees and motions them to leave.

Everything is quiet at home. Lights and laughter pour out from the large window overlooking the garden.

"*Papà!*"

He barely has time to step on the ground before two little arms hug his legs. It's his daughter, Giulia. *"Stidduzza!"*

The little girl laughs, takes his hand, and kisses it, looking up at him. Her cheeks are flushed and she's full of energy: the picture of health. Together, they head home. Giulia tells him what she did that day, from homework with her teacher to racing with Pegaso, the little poodle she was given a few days ago as a seventh-birthday present.

He listens to her and looks at her hair, dark and glossy like Giovanna's. Giulia's eyes are soft and gentle, but her gestures are confident and there is no uncertainty in her step. She is a Florio.

Together, they walk through the rooms to the green salon. There, Vincenzino is sitting in an armchair, absorbed in a book, with the governess next to him. Giulia sits down on the couch, where a half-undressed china doll is lying.

Ignazio goes to his son. "How are you?"

"I'm well, thank you." The boy looks up. His eyes are shiny, but the fever seems to have subsided. He brushes a lock of hair from his forehead and closes the book. "I ate the beef broth, like the doctor said, then I did some schoolwork. *Maman* said we're going to Naples soon. Is that true?"

"To Naples or France. We'll see." Ignazio studies his face. He has elegant features and a keen intelligence concealed beneath a calm temperament; he already seems very mature at the age of ten. He looks a lot like him. He turns to the governess, who is standing next to the child. "And my wife?"

A shadow of annoyance drifts over the woman's face. "Donna Giovanna is upstairs with Master Ignazziddu."

From her pursed lips, Ignazio senses that his son must have been up to more mischief. "What has your brother done?" he asks the elder boy.

Vincenzo shrugs. "He made the tutor angry because he didn't want to work anymore. When we were left alone in the room, he took the books and threw them out the window." He bites his lip. There's remorse on his little face for tattling. In his eyes, it's tantamount to betrayal.

Ignazio nods. Vincenzino is as responsible as his little brother is a real daredevil. And to think that he's only a year younger. He should be sensible, but instead . . .

Ignazio leaves the room and climbs the stairs, which are lit by two large metal chandeliers fixed to the walls, forged at the Oretea, just like the lamp that illuminates the landing. There, he meets Nanài. "I'll come and change for dinner shortly," he tells him. Then he slowly walks down the corridor to Ignazziddu's room.

He hears Giovanna's voice, stern and hard. "As soon as your father comes home, we're going to tell him what you did! *Accussì, uno pigghia e jecca i libbra, picchì 'un voli sturiari?* Throwing books out, just because you don't want to study?"

Standing on the doorstep, Ignazio huffs. Will he ever make Giovanna understand that she mustn't speak dialect, especially with the children? He marches in, and without even a greeting, addresses Ignazio directly. "I hear you behaved very badly today. Where are the books?"

Giovanna is in a corner. She looks at him and steps back.

The little boy sits on the bed, holding a pillow to his chest, like a shield against the world. He is sullen, his curls tousled, flashes of anger playing in his eyes. He digs his fingers into the bedspread. "I only asked to play for a while so I could rest, but he wouldn't hear of it and just kept talking and talking. So I got tired of listening."

"And you decided to throw the books out of the window? Bad, very bad. There is a time for play and a time for work. You'd better get used to that."

"No! When I say I'm tired, I'm tired!" He slaps the bed several times. "I studied all morning and even had to help Vincenzo because he didn't understand some things in French!" he yells. "Besides, the tutor's here for me. When I tell him that I want to stop, he *must* obey me!"

Ignazio goes closer. Ignazziddu instinctively pulls away on the bed and clutches the pillow to his chest. His anger turns to anxiety and then fear.

His father snatches the pillow away. "Don't you dare speak to me like that ever again." He moves even closer. His voice is deep, like a slap. "And you will never again speak that way to people who work for us. Is that clear?"

The child is almost panting, anger and fear in his eyes. True, his father has never hit him, but perhaps he knows even worse ways to punish him.

He nods as a sign that he understands, but his lips somehow can't utter the answer and Ignazio notices. "Tomorrow you will apologize to your tutor and to your brother. You've been disrespectful to both." He straightens up and looks at his wife. Giovanna has remained still, arms crossed. He stretches his hand to her, and she comes to him. "Let's go," he says. "He won't have dinner tonight. Maybe an empty stomach will help him understand how one should behave."

He turns out the lights while Giovanna waits for him outside the room. The last thing he sees as he is about to close the door is his son's fierce but powerless expression.

Ignazio and Giovanna walk down the stairs side by side, without touching. Suddenly, Giovanna puts a hand on his arm. "But . . . no food?" she asks faintly.

"That's right."

"He's still very young. *Un picciriddu . . .*"

"No, Giovanna. No! He has to understand that he can't do whatever he likes. You have to work—money doesn't grow on trees."

Ignazio must be truly angry to have used that tone of voice, but he really wants his son to understand that earning money involves work and commitment and sacrifice. Giovanna recoils and drops her head, defeated.

He stops and rubs his temples with his fingers. "Forgive me," he mutters. "I didn't wish to be rude to you."

"What happened?"

"Unrest at the foundry. Nothing for you to worry about." He takes her by the arm and gives her the first kind look of the whole day. "Let's have dinner; I have some papers to go over afterward."

‿

After a dinner eaten in suffocating silence, Ignazio stands up and leans over Giovanna to say goodbye with a kiss to her forehead. But she looks into his eyes, takes his hand, and simply says, "Come."

Maybe it's Giovanna's perfume, with its fruity notes, the same she wore back when he met her at the Casino delle Dame e dei Cavalieri; maybe it's her expression: a blend of affection, apprehension, and loneliness. Or maybe it's Ignazio's remorse at having been so harsh with both his son and his wife earlier . . . But he doesn't feel like rejecting her invitation.

And so, guided only by the moonlight, they reach the top of the small hill on which stands a little temple in neoclassical style. Holding hands, they turn to look at the villa and the surrounding buildings, bought and refurbished over the years. The deep silence is broken only by the wind caressing the foliage of the trees.

Now they're sitting on a bench, breathing the night air.

Giovanna's eyes are closed, and her hands are in her lap. Ignazio looks at her: she is the part of his life that holds no surprises, his traveling companion, the mother of his children. That's no trifle, but it's a long way from happiness. Their only real argument was five years ago. They've never mentioned it since, but Ignazio is aware of its consequences. It's as though Giovanna gave up any romantic illusion, and the love she feels for him has turned to stone: visible, tangible, but inert. The torment has never stopped gnawing away at her, that's for sure. He's sensed it in some of her resentful glances, in some of her rather cutting replies, in the lack of affectionate gestures, in a harshness that vanishes only when the children are present. But he can't blame her for anything: she's attentive and caring, as a wife as well as a mother. He doesn't even have the right to expect anything of her, and yet, at this moment, he feels painfully nostalgic for the young woman he married, who no longer exists: for her sweetness and the unshakable trust she put in him. For her patience.

So he tries to take whatever's left, and does so in his own way. Because the sense of guilt he feels toward her is his measure of regret for what he's lost.

He takes her face in his hands and kisses her. After a brief moment of surprise, she responds to his kiss with an abandonment and a gentleness he finds moving.

"Do you want to stay in my room tonight?" he asks in one breath.

She nods, embraces him, and, after such a long time, smiles.

☙

Days of waiting, of whispers, softly spoken confirmations, of letters leaving for Rome. Ignazio has become even more taciturn and spends less and less time at home. Giovanna watches him and worries but asks no questions.

A cool, golden dawn arrives. The sea lapping the cliffs of Foro Italico, the favorite walk of Palermo residents, sounds like a caress. By the time he reaches the offices of Piroscafi Postali, on Piazza Marina, not far from Palazzo Steri, Ignazio has breathed in all the beauty of the city, and his eyes have taken possession of the empty streets, used only by the odd factory worker or carter, or servant women with baskets of fruit and vegetables heading to Vucciria to buy meat for their masters.

Ignazio's office is on the first floor and overlooks Cassaro, almost opposite Vicaria. Nearby, there are the square white walls of Santa Maria dell'Ammiraglio and what remains of Porta Calcina. Behind the building, the monumental Porta Felice, with its baroque arches, spreads like a stage curtain to reveal the sea. He walks into his office. There's a smell of cigars and ink. Ignazio looks at the naval maps on the walls, next to pictures of his steamships. He looks but can't see. He waits.

There's a knock on the door. It's an errand boy. A wiry, prematurely bald young man. He bows and hands him a portfolio of documents. "From the notary, Don Ignazio. They've just arrived: Signor Quattrocchi kept them in his office because they finished late with the receivers last night and he wanted to make sure you got everything without intermediaries."

Ignazio thanks him and dismisses him with a coin, then sits at his desk and pats the spine of the portfolio. It's thick and carries the seals of the notary Giuseppe Quattrocchi, who now draws up all the Florio deeds. The accompanying envelope contains a card on which only one word is written: *Congratulations.*

The cover also simply says: *TRINACRIA, JUNE 1877.*

Every other thought is instantly obliterated.

He opens the portfolio, scans the names, a litany redolent of distant times and places: *Peloro, Ortigia, Enna, Solunto, Simeto, Himera, Segesta, Pachino, Selinunte, Taormina, Lilibeo, Drepano, Panormus* . . .

He leans back in his chair. There it is, his masterpiece, which will allow the Florios' fleet to make a definite leap forward. Thirteen steamships, some of them manufactured in Livorno, all of them built recently. He picks up the deed of the private sale and reads it. Giuseppe Orlando was present on behalf of Piroscafi Postali; he is the company's director and it's with him that Ignazio drew up the plan of action. The satisfaction he feels is almost physical and grows with every page.

Thirteen steamships. All his.

He has been after Pietro Tagliavia and his shipping company, Trinacria, for two years. It was created with many hopes, large ambitions, and a financial base that proved to be as unstable as clay.

Less than six years after beginning to trade, Tagliavia was up to his neck in debt and the banks couldn't—and wouldn't—save him.

Ignazio remembers well the day that distinguished-looking man, his face ravaged by worry, requested a "discreet and private" meeting with him and Orlando. He remembers the quiet dignity and pride with which he spoke about his enterprise.

"Not a sale, Don Ignazio," he said, "but a merger. A solution that would allow me to remove myself from this difficult situation the banks have put me in, not realizing that it's the coal crisis that's eating us alive."

Ignazio agreed. "True. The hike in coal and iron prices is hitting us hard. Even Raffaele Rubattino is having a hard time in Genoa."

"Except that he's up north, so the government gives him money."

Tagliavia gave him a meaningful look. "You have the subsidies from the mail concessions, much more than I do because you hold more routes. The ministry has rightly taken your resources into account and favored you, leaving nothing but crumbs to the rest of us. I have mail concessions to the east, but that's a trifle. Ship owners like Rubattino get bailed out by banks intervening. Only you are solid enough . . . Besides, you have powerful friends. With respect, I'm the one losing my shirt here: I have the Banco di Sicilia snapping at my heels, threatening to suspend my overdraft."

Ignazio immediately liked the idea, and not only because it would allow him to eliminate a competitor. He was aware how much Trinacria's debts amounted to and knew he could easily handle them. Moreover, Trinacria's steamships were new, efficient, and not in need of constant repair like his own *Elettrico* and *Archimede*: junk that he chose not to dispose of only because it remained useful for the local routes.

He asked to see the accounts ledger and debt report for the Livorno shipyard, where the latest steamer, the *Ortigia*, was currently being built. Then, at that point, Tagliavia and Trinacria's administrators disappeared. Ignazio didn't contact them or ask for any more meetings, partly because the government had decided to help the company and prevent its collapse.

It wasn't the Florios who were in dire financial straits or being threatened by the banks. The Florios didn't go begging cap in hand.

Then, in February of last year, disaster struck. The Palermo trade tribunal declared Trinacria bankrupt, and its entire staff was dismissed. The city plunged into chaos, with protests in the squares and strong intervention on the part of the police.

That was when Ignazio decided to pounce.

One of the administrators in charge of handling the bankruptcy paperwork was Giovanni Laganà, who had worked for the Florio shipping company more than once as an advisor of the Maritime Transport Bank. He was a man who knew how to spot those individuals who dictated the rules of the game and act accordingly. This made him as valuable as he was dangerous.

It took only a few well-chosen words to make the receivers realize that nobody else would be able to buy these steamships, not on such short notice.

And that's how the private negotiations commenced.

His calm face lights up with pride. Not only has he purchased ships in better condition than his own, he's also taken over the mail transportation concession Trinacria eventually agreed with the Kingdom of Italy—*all* the mail transportation concessions, in fact. And that means receiving money from Rome. A lot of money.

There's a knock on the door.

"Come in," he says, closing the portfolio with some regret. He loves these moments of solitude he manages to snatch in the morning, precious moments to clear his head or relish his successes.

"I knew I'd find you here, holding the dossier in your hands." Giuseppe Orlando takes a couple of steps forward and sits down opposite him. In the timber-clad room, his imposing frame, in a pale linen suit, seems to bring light.

"Thirteen practically new steamships," Ignazio says, slapping the portfolio. "What could be better?"

"True. And fuel and land equipment at a price you would never have gotten at market. Better materials than ours."

Ignazio opens his arms, then looks at him sideways. "And, naturally, thanks to Barbavara, who gave you a helping hand at the postal ministry."

"Evidently." Orlando crosses his hands on his lap. "I felt sorry for Tagliavia, poor wretch. He tried till the very end . . ." He looks down, embarrassed perhaps. "Too many people were involved in Trinacria, starting with his relatives. This bankruptcy has them all on their knees."

"You've done a good job. Good for us and way too good for him." Ignazio stands up and places a hand on his shoulder. He has no such scruples. "Others would have made mincemeat out of him."

"Of course, I know that, and we must always be thankful to the receivers, who were very . . . well disposed toward your company."

Ignazio purses his lips; his beard quivers, disguising a faint smile. "I'll express my gratitude to them in due course. Meanwhile, we must try to increase the social capital. We're no longer an enterprise with four walnut shells, and we need capital to meet what I have in mind."

Orlando squints. "What are you thinking of?"

Ignazio opens the portfolio and points at the names of the ships. "Rubattino is tackling the French and has even received a subsidy of half a million for a line to Tunis. We must get going with the Adriatic Line: they won't dare cancel the Bari route, not after putting pressure on the government by stressing that it's a port essential to the eastern Mediterranean. But we can't stop at the Adriatic: I want to take our ships as far as Constantinople, Odessa, and then . . ."

Ignazio knows that now's the time to look far beyond the Mediterranean. He's thinking about the Genoese and French ships that carry dozens, hundreds of men and women with bundles on their shoulders and a desperate hope in their hearts: that of leaving poverty behind.

❧

Summer has taken possession of the city. Like a bully, with a ruthless sun and insidious heat that smells of dry grass and infiltrates the rooms, only just shielded by the shutters. Cicadas are chirping from the trees in the grounds of the Olivuzza. The air is still: there's only an occasional puff of wind stirring the cheesewood bushes and jasmine hedges.

Ignazio left early, while everybody was still asleep. Giovanna listened to his footsteps in the bedroom, the sound of drawers being opened and closed, the valet's bustling. As often happens, she's let him go to face a day filled with papers, accounts, and business without his even saying goodbye. In the early days of their marriage, she hoped he would let her into that part of his life. But by now there's no more point in asking why. She has her own, different, duties.

And so now, after breakfast, as the children are playing in the garden while waiting for the tutors, Giovanna sits down next to Donna Ciccia and arranges the small portable writing desk on her lap.

"So it's confirmed. There will be fifty-two people this evening." She raises an eyebrow and scans the list. It's officially a dinner like so many others, but in actual fact, it's the social sealing of the merger between Trinacria and the Florios' Piroscafi Postali, and anyone who's anyone in Palermo will attend. "Not a single one has declined the invitation. We'll even serve the *gelo di mellone* made with Siracusa's best watermelons. The *monsù* is arranging it in French porcelain bowls and will decorate it with jasmine."

Donna Ciccia pulls a face. "He may be a good cook, but knowing him, he'll probably have stripped an entire espalier of jasmine just to pull out four petals."

They both laugh.

For some time now, Giovanna has learned to derive satisfaction from social life. Dinners, receptions, teas, and even "conversations" hosted in their salons at least twice a week allow her to be the lady of the house, and therefore the perfect wife for Ignazio. Thanks to her, he's realized that the Florios' wealth isn't just composed of numbers, ships, wine, and sulfur: in order to be accepted, they have had to change their lifestyle, open their home, receive friends and acquaintances, invite painters and writers. Aristocrats have had to stop viewing them as *pirocchi arrinisciuti*, "jumped-up lice," and for that they've had to go beyond money, beyond the power the Florios have in Palermo.

First Vincenzo and then Ignazio thought that marriage with a d'Ondes Trigona would be sufficient to clean their blood. And for a while, she, too, hoped it would all be that simple. Then she realized that her noble lineage was only a key to carry out the change in the best possible manner. And so she got down to work with patience and determination: on the one hand she read, studied, and learned foreign languages, as Ignazio had asked her to, and on the other hand she grew the value of the house by furnishing it with pieces by Gabriele Capello and the Levera brothers, suppliers of furnishings to the king. She acquired porcelain from Limoges and Sèvres, rugs from Isfahan, a painting by a great seventeenth-century artist, Pietro Novelli, as well as works by contemporary painters such as Francesco Lojacono and Antonino Leto, one of her favorites. She's hosted luncheons, dinners, and parties; formed and strengthened bonds of friendship; kept secrets; listened to complaints and gossip. She has ensured that an invitation to Casa Florio is regarded as a privilege.

Palermo residents like to feel a cut above other people, especially among their peers, and go out of their way to make sure that nobody forgets it. It's a game of mirrors, she thinks as she scans the list. And there it was, the difference between the Palermo aristocracy and the Florios: on the one hand, the certainty—expressed, underlined, and reiterated—of being superior to others by lineage, education, and elegance. On the other hand, there were the facts, in their indisputable concreteness: from parties to charity works, from the purchase of an ornament to that of the Aegadian Islands, the Florios *proved* they were superior. Giovanna took it upon herself to build a bridge between two such different worlds and, through grace and tenacity, succeeded. The evidence lies before her, in this list of the cream of Palermo aristocracy.

She tries not to dwell too often on the thought that this has also saved her from dying of loneliness and despair.

Giovanna looks through other notes: next Sunday, their home will host an English-style tea party, with a small orchestra playing under the little temple at the top of the hill, and tables set in the gardens so that the guests can stroll and enjoy its coolness. There will be candied fruit, cakes, various blends of tea from India and Japan, and brandy for the men. She's expecting almost eighty people, both adults and children.

It'll be lovely, she thinks, already picturing the layout of the tables under the trees, the little ones laughing and the grown-ups chatting.

Donna Ciccia takes a piece of short stitch embroidery from the basket. Giovanna gazes, wishing she could do the same, but other, less happy chores await her in a leather portfolio. She picks it up, takes out some papers, and frowns. Here, in these papers, the city of aristocrats and parties disappears, erased by the poor, the grindingly poor part of the city, which relies on the charity of the rich in order to survive. It's up to her to attend to it, try to work out whose need is greater, and do her best.

She leafs through the requests for subsidy. There's a letter from the Congregazione delle Dame del Giardinello, asking her for help with the dowry of a "destitute" young protégée of theirs and layettes for the newborn babies of a few families in need; another request comes from the wives of some sailors from the Florios' steamers: they would like a schoolmaster for their sons, so they can "at least learn to read and sign their names," they conclude.

Only boys exist, she thinks with a hint of bitterness. Palermo folk don't care if their daughters can write or add up. They want to keep them *stritte dintra i falara*, "imprisoned in their aprons." The fact that they're asking for some basic learning for their sons is already a lot.

She looks at Giulia, who's sitting on the lawn, playing with a doll. She's seven years old and very clever. Recently she has started studying with her brothers, and Ignazio ordered that she learn French and German, as befitting an aristocrat's daughter. Her brothers, on the other hand, are already studying geography and mathematics, and have started taking violin lessons because they have to receive the best instruction, like all European families. Families they've encountered during summer stays across Italy, like the one planned shortly in Recoaro, a health spa in the Veneto. The Florios began staying there after discovering that it was a favorite haunt of various members of Palermo's aristocracy, as well as many northern industrialists and politicians. Ignazio has formed valuable alliances there, sealed not with champagne but a glass of limpid water drawn from the Lelia spring.

Giovanna looks down at the papers once again and examines the accounts. Strangely enough, it was her father-in-law who started the tradition of giving to the Palermo poor. He said back then that he was doing it because, born to a working-class family, he knew what it meant to work for a wretched crust of bread. But forked aristocratic tongues claimed he did it to erase his origins with money and be forgiven for marrying his mistress. In other words, another way to purchase social respectability.

She stares at the long list of petitions and an idea she has been mulling over for some time comes to mind again: to set up an affordable kitchen for the local people, *gentuzza* who can't afford to eat, women constantly pregnant who then watch their children starve to death because they have so little milk. She would have to work out how and where, estimate what it would cost . . .

It's at this moment that Vincenzino suddenly feels unwell.

He was playing with Ignazziddu and lost the ball. His brother egged him on, shouting at him to fetch it before it fell into the small lake. So he ran and grabbed the leather ball seconds before it ended up in the water.

Then a pang in his chest radiated to his throat, like a vise. Vincenzino's legs buckled, and he began to pant. Now he's coughing, little coughs that quickly turn to convulsions. He drops the ball.

The nanny goes to him and taps him on the back, but it's no use. The child's face turns first red, then purple. Ignazziddu, who's followed him and picked up the ball, stops a short distance from him. He takes a step back. "Vincenzo, what's the matter?"

He sees his brother's hand grab the nanny's apron and twist the fabric, hears the hiss of air sucked into his windpipe, insufficient air that seems to escape him. He sees him fall to his knees, the terror of suffocating to death on his face.

"Maman!" Ignazziddu shouts. "Mamma!"

Giovanna suddenly looks up, hears the panic in her son's voice, and immediately sees Vincenzo lying on the ground and the nanny grabbing him and shaking him. "Donna Ciccia!" she yells. "Help! Call somebody! A doctor! Help!"

She leaps to her feet and runs to him. The papers in her lap fly away. "The collar! Take off his collar!" she screams, but then unbuttons it herself. She does so in such a rush that she scratches the skin at his throat. Vincenzino arches his body, gasping for air.

Donna Ciccia comes running, followed by Nanài, who lifts the child in his arms and heads to the salon. "Inside, inside!" he shouts. "I've sent for the doctor!" He grabs Giovanna by the elbow and forces her to her feet, while the nanny drags the by now weeping Giulia away.

Ignazziddu is left alone, immersed in the sunlight, holding the ball.

With small, uncertain steps, he follows his mother and the servants but remains outside the French window, watching them. It's not the first time this has happened: every so often, it's as though the air uselessly trapped in Vincenzo's lungs refuses to reach his throat.

He looks at him with both fear and guilt. It was he who made him run, it's true . . . *No, Vincenzo's always been sick. It's not my fault*, he keeps telling himself, his little nose pressed against the glass, anxiety in his stomach. Around him, there's blinding light and the chirping of cicadas.

His brother's face is regaining its color. His mother is wetting his forehead with a handkerchief, her hand on his chest to calm him down. She comforts him and kisses his fear-filled eyes.

Vincenzo bursts into tears. Giovanna hugs him and cries with him. Donna Ciccia comforts them both, then gets up, walks out of the salon, and returns with the doctor.

Through the glass, Ignazziddu hears the voices and watches the gestures. He'd like to go in and ask his brother to forgive him because a part of him still blames himself, telling him it was his fault Vincenzo nearly choked. He would like to hug him, to promise him he'll never again suggest games that make him run, that he'll be careful.

Anything, as long as he doesn't feel the way he's feeling now.

He can't know or imagine that one day this fear will visit him again.

⌒

Winter 1878–1879 was one of the harshest in living memory. Giovanna ordered the Olivuzza's servants to keep the fires burning all the time so that Vincenzino wouldn't get cold. The health of Casa Florio's firstborn was still uncertain. Ignazziddu was chomping at the bit, like a bull. Giulia was constantly restless. Vincenzo, on the other hand, was always still and silent.

Gripped by fear, Giovanna kept an eye on her son's every step, rushing to him at the slightest cough and eating with him to make sure he wasn't wasting away. In addition, she prayed a great deal. Rosaries, orations, and supplications every day, so that God might watch over her child and grant him the health that seemed to escape him.

Even now that spring is here, the sun has a honey-colored light but it's not warming; even the wind, usually steeped in heat, is a chilly breeze that makes you shiver, carrying no fragrance of flowers or new grass. *Let's wait for the air to get milder*, she thinks. Only then will she spend more time outdoors with her children. Vincenzo will be able to go as far as the aviary in the middle of the grounds, or else play with the hoop . . . And perhaps she'll even take him to Monte Pellegrino in the carriage, as she's promised him so often. But above all, they'll be able to travel: to spend their vacation in Naples, for instance, as Ignazio suggested. Naples is cooler than Palermo in the summer and the air in the villas outside the city is healthier. They could even go back to Recoaro . . .

But it's too early to be thinking about the summer. May has only just started.

Giovanna walks through the rooms and halls, her dress rustling on the oriental rugs. She calls the servants and tells them to close the trunks and pick up the children's toys. They're about to leave, and she feels a strange excitement in her heart, an impatience as effervescent as champagne.

She's finally going to see the house she's heard so much about, on that island her husband is so much in love with.

A house worthy of princes, created for a family that doesn't have ancient nobility, but is wealthier than any other. Not only in Palermo, but in the whole of Italy.

By the time they reach Favignana, the afternoon is softening into a sunset that bathes the sea in molten copper, illuminating the small tuff houses. The air feels warmer here and the wind doesn't have those insistent chilly undertones the wind in Palermo has.

While waiting to disembark, Giovanna talks to Vincenzino and makes him put on a thick jacket; behind him stand Giulia and the nanny. Ignazziddu, on the other hand, has already run down the gangplank, trying to catch his father's attention. He's eleven years old now but is struggling to let go of some of his childish impulses. Ignazio chides him with a glare, then motions him to stand next to him but keep quiet.

Gaetano Caruso, the administrator of the Favignana and Formica *tonnaras*, is waiting for them on the jetty at the foot of the gangplank.

Ignazio takes a moment to study the building that stands just outside the village, at the foot of the mountain, before stepping on land. There are warehouses of golden tuff so light it almost looks white. Wide entrances that open onto the sea, with iron gates branded by an F on the fronton: F like Favignana, or föhn, the westerly wind that beats the sails of the fishermen's boats and makes the sea beneath the coast froth.

F like Florio.

Below him, the sea seeks the jetty, glides over its surface, wets the patina, slippery with algae, that covers its edges.

Ignazio disembarks and takes a few steps on dry land, followed by his son; he peers into the deep green water at the fish swimming amid meadows of seagrass, then lifts his head, studying the line of houses before finally looking up at the mountain and at Forte di Santa Caterina, where so many years earlier patriots were held prisoner and which is now one of the harshest jails in the kingdom.

"At last . . ." he murmurs, taking a deep breath. Here, the smell of the sea is different than any other place in the Mediterranean: a mixture of oregano and sand, salty fish and stubble.

"Don Ignazio . . ." Gaetano Caruso has followed him, somewhat puzzled by his silence.

Ignazio turns abruptly and looks at the man, his high forehead, his thick handlebar mustache, his goatee. "Thank you for your welcome."

"It's my duty," Caruso replies with a nod. "I've had the house prepared to receive you as best I could. You'll find dinner ready and the bedrooms arranged for the night. I've also had the guest rooms readied, since I was told there would be guests."

"Thank you. You really didn't have to go to all this trouble: you're an administrator, not a butler."

Words of politeness. Even though Caruso is mainly in charge of the tuna plant, his job obviously also entails organizing his master's stay on the island. He leads the way and Ignazio walks beside him. They're trailed by Giovanna and the children with Donna Ciccia and the nanny, as well as an entourage of servants and carts laden with trunks and suitcases.

Giovanna has walked off the boat cautiously, always holding her son's hand. Only at the end, once she reaches dry land, does she look at the plant. So this is it, the famous *tonnara*, in which her husband invested a sizable portion of the family's capital with a fierce determination that reminds her of her father-in-law. After taking possession, Ignazio commissioned the trusted Giuseppe Damiani Almeyda to renovate it. The plans for the new family *palazzo*, built after demolishing the old Forte di San Leonardo that stood near the harbor, are also his.

And that's not all.

Giovanna encourages her son to keep going, then searches for Donna Ciccia and Giulia. Head down, she walks along the jetty, trudging up the rise, holding up her dress with one hand to prevent it from getting soiled. She slows down almost to a halt and, at the end of the street, sees a few low, narrow buildings. They are the so-called *Pretti*, where the utility rooms, barns, and warehouses are located.

The servants, hired on the island, are standing at the top of the rise, waiting, their faces baking in the sun, uniforms askew and gloves worn as best they can be. *It'll take effort to make them into real servants*, she thinks, concealing her irritation. Fortunately, her lady's maid, the *monsù*, and a couple of members of the domestic staff have preceded their arrival and begun training. *At least as much as they could*, Giovanna thinks, studying them more closely. Soon they will be joined by a few friends, including Damiani Almeyda and Antonino Leto. Then her parents will arrive, as well as her Trigona cousins, and she wouldn't like to be embarrassed. *I wonder if it might be worth summoning the servants from Palermo here.*

She turns to ask Donna Ciccia's advice and her breath suddenly catches in her chest.

Palazzo Florio stands before her. She's seen the plans and Almeyda's drawings, but Vincenzino's poor health and her family responsibilities have prevented her from coming to Favignana and following the building works. Of course, she's pictured it from what her husband has tried so often to describe. But now she's surprised by how beautiful it is. Elegant. Strong. Almost like a castle.

It's a solid cube made of tuff and brick. The windows are framed by pointed arches; on the right, there's a small tower with a sloping roof. Upon the balconies, spirals alternate with the infinity symbol in a series of lines, compact areas, and empty spaces. There's a merlon cornice on the roof. The iron gates were manufactured in the Oretea, and there's the Florio crest on the frontons: a lion drinking from a stream into which sink the roots of a cinchona tree.

It's magnificent, severe, and powerful.

She looks at the *palazzo*, then at her husband, who's still talking to Gaetano Caruso, his back to her. This building looks like Ignazio. *No*, she corrects herself, this building *is* Ignazio. A monolith that brings together smooth lines and sharp corners, the lightness of iron and the heft of tuff. Strength and elegance.

She wants to run to him, she takes a step, lets go of her son's hand, but no, she can't, she mustn't. That's never been the way they communicate.

Ignazio lets his wife and the servants sort out the house. They'll be staying here for a few weeks, until the *mattanza* is over and the tuna—gutted, cut to pieces, and boiled—are ready to be processed and canned.

He doesn't go into the house. He releases his son to his mother's side with a pat that's more like a slap and goes into the garden, where the bushes and pittosporum hedges struggle to take root in a soil bloated with salt.

Caruso follows him, his hands behind his back. "The *tonnara* has been lowered successfully," he explains. "We expect to carry out the first slaughter sometime between tomorrow and the end of the week."

Ignazio listens and nods. "Did *u' rais* say how much we're likely to fish?"

"He's not sure yet, but he says there's a large shoal coming, and he expects an equally big one next week. But he always ends up praying to Christ and the Blessed Virgin to give us a good year."

They laugh, but then Ignazio's expression darkens. "You realize I'm not sure whether to wish myself an abundant catch or not?"

They reach the rear of the house, where Almeyda designed a large veranda overlooking the garden, dominated by a projecting wrought-iron roof. He looks at the second floor, where the windows are framed by neo-Gothic arches. Those are the family's apartments. On the top floor are the guest rooms. It will be nice to stay there and watch the sea while the boats, loaded with fish, return to the harbor.

Caruso frowns. "That's right," he admits with sorrow. "Competition from Spain has become fierce in the past year."

"The Spanish, the Portuguese . . . They're owners in name, but practically speaking it's the Genoese who manage their plants; so if they sell more, they earn more, and they don't have to pay the taxes we in Italy are forced to pay." Ignazio looks up at the sky. "Instead of thinking of us, all Rome is concerned with is its own pockets. The taxes hurt us . . . It doesn't occur to them that there are families here whose livelihood depends on this," he adds with a hiss like a razor's edge, unable to hide his anger, indicating the sea.

"What can we do?" Caruso asks anxiously. He's not used to Ignazio speaking with such candor.

Ignazio straightens and looks at the *tonnara*. "Nothing much here. But there . . ." he points north. "That's where we have to go."

Caruso understands. "Rome?"

"Not right away and not directly. We need to shake up the cold dead blood clotting the ministries' veins. They have to see things from many points of view. We must lead them to where we want, but without their realizing that it's us who are doing so."

Caruso frowns. "Yes, but in order to get to the people in Rome . . ." he murmurs, then stops because he knows this wouldn't be the first time Ignazio has found interlocutors to *fit* their requirements. It's about proving that some roads can be traveled *differently*. Or that other avenues can open.

"As I said, we're not the only ones interested in fishing tuna. There are many *tonnaras*. Think of the nearest ones: Bonagia, San Vito, Scopello . . . They all suffer the same problem: a tax system that penalizes those who own fishing plants in Italy. In other words, we're not the only ones harmed by this situation. But my name cannot be mentioned. You understand why, don't you?"

Of course Gaetano Caruso understands. He's been working with the Florios for some time and sees how their power goes hand in hand with their wealth. Only, power makes enemies. And some enemies are like worms. It only takes a crack, a weakness, for larvae to settle in and turn a healthy body into rotting meat.

"I'll start by meeting people in Trapani and Palermo, journalists in particular," Ignazio resumes, moving his head closer to Caruso's. "As I was saying, we mustn't be the ones to highlight the flaws in this state of affairs, it must be others, and who better than newspapers that specialize in commerce and seafaring? They'll help us draw attention to this situation because, in the end, what's important is that people start talking and that the government feels pressure. Rome knows that the southern vote has sway, that upsetting the owners of salt and fish-preserving plants could prove a politically detrimental move." He pauses and looks at the sea. "Yes, the papers will mention it first. They can't be accused of acting out of interest or personal envy. When a newspaper says something, it means there's general discontent, and the ministries will have to take it into account."

Caruso is about to reply when a voice interrupts him from behind. "I beg your pardon, the signora is asking when you would like dinner." A servant in livery, one of those who traveled with them from Palermo, has stopped a few steps away, waiting for an answer.

Ignazio rolls his eyes, refraining from swearing. "At the same time as in Palermo, obviously. Tell her I'll come in to change shortly." Then he turns to Caruso. "You'll come for dinner, won't you?"

"I'd be honored."

"Good." He heads into the garden. "Now, if you'll excuse me. I'll see you later."

Left alone, Ignazio crosses the village, heading toward the *tonnara*. He doesn't want to go home, not yet.

He walks with his hands in his pockets. His only company, the sound of waves penetrating the alleys, catches up with him and envelops him. He passes the private chapel, still under construction, along the seafront. Cliffs alternate with lines of sand and dry seagrass.

To his left, just a few fishermen's huts. Children are playing, running barefoot. There's the odd woman standing on her doorstep, the others are making dinner: he glimpses their figures through shabby curtains that partition living quarters from the street. He can smell food and hear chairs and benches scraping on the floor.

"*Assabbinirìca*—my respects—Don Ignazio," an old fisherman sitting not far from the entrance to the *tonnara* greets him. He's repairing nets, threading the string through the mesh, then lifting it to the light to uncover any more holes. His eyes are narrow slits, his lined skin as hardened as leather. Ignazio recognizes him. He's a former *tonnaroto*, now too advanced in years to be on boats. His son and son-in-law have taken his place.

"*Assabbinirìca* to you, Master Filippo."

He keeps walking and reaches the plant.

The clean lines of the buildings are what he wanted and what Damiani Almeyda provided. The half-Neapolitan, half-Portuguese architect has given the *tonnara* a modern façade that's nevertheless reminiscent of the rigorous solemnity of a Grecian temple.

A temple on the sea, Ignazio thinks. He keeps skirting the surrounding wall and takes a dirt road that leads to Forte di Santa Caterina. As he expected, the prisoners have turned out to be invaluable for hard labor in the plant. It's a steep climb but he doesn't walk to the top. He stops halfway up to look at the harbor and the island, then down at his shoes, powdered with a film of tuff dust. He can't help smiling.

When he was fourteen, he was conquered by the mellow luminosity of this rock, which seemed to trap the sun. Now, at forty, he knows he acted not on the wave of emotion, but on the basis of practicality: in order to strengthen the power of the Florios.

But now, alone at last, he can drop the final barrier.

So Ignazio shouts.

It's a liberating shout, one with the wind. A shout of possession, as though the entire island has permeated him, become *his* flesh, and the sea *his* blood. As though the circle of life is taking shape before him, an ouroboros only he can see, revealing to him the true meaning of his purpose on this earth.

A shout that erases his nostalgia for the past and his uncertainty about the future and grants him the happiness of an eternal present.

Tomorrow, when he gets up, he'll see the sun blend in with the stone in the quarry, he'll feel the salty wind brush through the curtains, and observe the hard-won green of the shrubs on the mountain.

That is why he keeps still now, in the company of the wind and the sea, never minding that they're waiting for him and he'll be late for dinner. He knows now that this island, which sweats salt and sand, is his true home.

After dinner, Giovanna is the first to retire to her bedroom on the second floor. It's decorated with furniture from Palermo, carved in neo-Gothic style specially for the *palazzo*.

Lost in thought and ever the insomniac, Ignazio wished her good night before heading to his study, located right next to the dressing room and overlooking the plant on the other side of the harbor.

Giovanna hopes that on this island her husband may find some rest.

Favignana is work, of course. Or rather, also work, she corrects herself with a smile, looking at herself in the mirror while gathering her hair into a braid. There will be an opportunity to spend time together and talk. To try to be a couple, at least for a few days.

She snuffs out the candle. Through the window, which has been left ajar, she hears the lapping of the waves against the jetty and the breath of wind amid the alleys of the village. Giovanna gently slips into slumber, then wakes with a start when Ignazio walks into her room. His waistcoat is unbuttoned and his tie loosened. But there's no weariness on his face; rather a kind of cheerfulness she's not used to, and which gives her a warm pleasure.

He removes his jacket. "Do you like the house?"

She nods. "It's beautiful. Did you leave Nanài in Palermo?" she adds, indicating his clothes.

Ignazio shrugs and hums a song. "I don't need Leonardo," he says. "It's less formal here," he adds, flopping on the bed and kicking off his shoes.

These words are enough for Giovanna to realize that he's happy; that he feels free here. And different perhaps.

She joins him, rests her head on his large shoulders, and hugs him from behind.

Ignazio is surprised. He caresses and kisses his wife awkwardly. They're like two feral cats, jealous of their own vital space, who seldom indulge in touching each other.

"Tomorrow, I'll take you on a tour of the island in a cart. I want to show you how beautiful it is." Ignazio turns, smiling at her with his eyes, and strokes her cheek.

He's looking at her, not at a ghost or at work or whatever else.

At her. Giovanna.

A tremor deep inside her makes her gut tighten, rises past her stomach to her chest, and dilates her ribs, forcing her to take a deep breath. She can feel blood turn her face red, as though for the first time in a long time she's realized she's alive.

All her life she's been waiting for a moment like this—fragile, intense, precious—and now she fears she may not be ready. Her eyes moisten.

"What's the matter?" Ignazio asks, confused. "Are you unwell?"

"Yes, no—it's nothing," she replies, her lips quivering.

"Won't you come for a walk with me?"

She nods, unable to speak. She runs her fingers through her hair, as though trying to loosen her braid. Then she moves closer, taking the hand Ignazio has set on the blanket and lifting it to her chest, and huddles against him.

When you're happy, there's no need to talk.

The morning sun is only slightly veiled by a handful of low clouds. Beyond the sea, you can make out the Trapani coast and the chunky outline of Erice. Next to the coast, the water carries an unusual glare, a blinding white that hurts your eyes and forces you to look away.

"It's the saltworks," Ignazio tells Giovanna, who's sitting next to him, when he sees her squinting. "Basins of salt water evaporate and leave behind a crust of salt. This crust is harvested, dried out, and sold. It's thanks to these saltworks that we produce the brine we use for the tuna." He lifts his arm and indicates a faint spot beyond the village. "Over there, you have the bay where the Romans defeated the Carthaginians in a naval battle. The 'Battle of the Aegates' was important because it put an end to the First Punic War. Even nowadays, fishermen sometimes come back home with a fragment of an amphora . . ." His eyes sparkle; he looks like a happy child.

Sheltering under her parasol, Giovanna studies the landscape: it's rugged, dry, and dusty, so different from the mainland that it makes her feel uneasy. And yet everything's suddenly much clearer to her. It's as though the island is finally handing her the keys to her husband's heart. She can see its secret beauty and sense its silence. "You really wanted this island, didn't you?" she murmurs.

"Yes. You can't imagine how much."

They keep silent for a little while. The only sound to fill the clear air is that of the wheels of their small convoy on the dirt roads: a couple of buggies, a few horses, and even a donkey allocated to Donna Ciccia, who every now and then shrieks with fear.

Ignazio looks at his wife. Even though her face is partly shielded by the hat, he notices a few wrinkles at the base of her nose and on her forehead in particular. Marks of tiredness, perhaps, or else tension. No matter.

No doubt I've gotten old, too, he thinks. He's never worried about it, not even when, in the morning, he sometimes discovers a new gray hair on his head or in his beard.

He almost shrugs at the thought.

I wonder what she's like now.

A sentence that flits through his mind, a thought that strikes like a thunderbolt.

She.

He pictures wrinkles on that face frozen in his memory, hair fading from copper-blond to gray, once luminous blue eyes darkened by circles and heavy lids.

I wonder what it would have been like to grow old together.

Where do these thoughts and questions come from? Which part

of his soul has dropped its defenses to the point of allowing these thoughts to fill his mind? He pushes them back angrily; he won't permit sorrow to take over.

He looks down, afraid Giovanna might read his mind, but the image still pursues him, stalks him, jabs him with the sharp darts of regret.

He grinds his teeth. *I mustn't think about it*, he commands himself. As a distraction, he calls to Caruso, who's riding not far behind them. "So, have the letters from Palermo arrived?"

"Were you expecting something in particular? No, the mail is coming tomorrow."

"Only a couple of reports, and the figures for the closure of the weaving plant."

Caruso scoffs. "Pearls before swine, Don Ignazio. You offered them homes, schooling, and even an oven, and they threw it all back in your face."

"Yes." He pulls on the reins of the buggy. Next to him, Giovanna cocks her head to hear better. "It hasn't been a success," he admits in spite of himself. He doesn't want to use the word *failure*, but that's what it is.

He turns to his wife, and she stares at him expectantly.

"Morvillo, the lawyer, and I set up a weaving plant with homes for the workers next to it, as well as shops, and a school. We'd even thought of nannies to look after the babies and allow the mothers to work . . ."

Giovanna listens to him, frowning and trying to conceal her surprise. Ignazio has never been this talkative about his business. Is Favignana producing another miracle?

"But nothing came of it!" Ignazio continues angrily. "The men decided it wasn't worth working hard to obtain something more, that what they had was enough, even though they were struggling to make ends meet. And the women dug their heels in: they didn't want to leave their children with nannies and sent only the boys to school. There was no arguing against leaving their daughters shut up at home in the most total ignorance. 'Twas always thus and so it had to be. We fixed the price of bread at ten *centesimi* less than in the city, but no one wanted to pay, so we had to close down the oven . . . But the worst thing was the way the workers treated the looms and machinery. Instead of learning how to use them, they damaged them, then abandoned them as though they would fix themselves. They were only interested in pilfering whatever they could. Some even stole fabrics and sold them . . . These people are dirt!"

Giovanna touches his hand lightly, then rests hers on his knee. A gesture of encouragement, an unspoken word of affection.

"Don't worry, Don Ignazio! It'll be different here on Favignana." Caruso is optimistic, cheerful even. "Just don't expect from these people what they can't give. They're used to working on boats, hunched over in the sun, like their fathers did and their sons will. Besides, thanks to the performance bonus, it's in their best interest to be more productive."

"As a matter of fact, I don't expect anything more from them. Just honesty and commitment, which will be rewarded with a little extra money."

The small convoy of carts and horses keeps advancing across the northeastern plain of the island. Giovanna waits for Caruso to ride away, then takes Ignazio's hand.

He puts his other hand over hers without looking at her.

"You did a good thing," she says awkwardly. "It's those rabid dogs who didn't understand."

But he purses his lips in a grimace, unable to conceal his irritation. "I'd pictured a modern factory, like in England, where the workers and their families have the possibility of improving their conditions. I was clearly too optimistic. I'll make sure I don't do anything like that again."

Giovanna leans on his shoulder, and he doesn't push her away.

They can hear their children's voices from the buggy behind them. Even the usually quiet Vincenzino is shouting impatiently.

"Will it be much longer?" Giovanna asks.

"Only a few more minutes. The cove is truly extraordinary. There's a hole in the rocks, like a well that opens onto the sea. I wanted you to see it."

He has actually now driven them all around the island, Giovanna thinks with a smile that softens her frowning face under the parasol. He has revealed to her the radiant beauty of Cala Rossa and promised to show her the sunset over the bay of Marasolo, at the foot of the mountain, near the fishermen's houses.

Ignazio wishes he could stay on Favignana forever, she realizes. This place gives him peace of mind and fulfillment. She can tell by his relaxed face, his patience toward their children, and his prolonged contact with her. But it's impossible for them to stay here. So Giovanna takes these feelings and hides them in a corner of her bosom, so that she can pull them out when dark days come, when the thought of those damned letters comes back to snap at her flesh, when she wonders for the umpteenth time who that woman was. When she and Ignazio are distant even while they sleep in the same bed.

In nomine Patris et Filii et Spiritus Sancti.

The timber grazes the coarse plaster with a hiss. The scent of white lilies can't cover the smell of dust and mortar.

Giovanna and Ignazio cling to each other. A drop runs down Giovanna's pale lips. A tear, quickly followed by another.

She doesn't wipe it away.

Ignazio is stone-like. It looks as if he's not even breathing and, in truth, he doesn't want to breathe. Anything not to feel this torture. He wouldn't feel such acute pain if his flesh were being torn off in shreds with bare hands. His breath scratches his windpipe, pushing to come out, so he opens his mouth slightly, just to enable the passage of that little air—*damnation!*—that will keep him alive.

Giovanna sways and he holds her up just as she's about to collapse. She disengages herself, reaches out, and bursts into sobs. "No, no, wait!" she screams. It's an animal cry. "Don't take him away from me! Don't put him in there! It's cold, he's all alone, *figghiu di lu me cori, anima mia . . .*" She frees herself from her husband's grip and pushes away the men about to close the burial recess. She clings to the coffin, hammers it with her fists, scratches at it. "Vincenzo! My Vincenzino, my life! Wake up my dear heart! Vincenzino!"

Behind her, Donna Ciccia breaks into floods of tears, echoed by Ignazziddu and Giulia, her hand held by the nanny, who then, her own eyes moist, drags the little girl out of the funeral chapel.

Ignazio steps forward, tears Giovanna away from the coffin, and forces her back on her feet. "Stop it, for God's sake!" he hisses.

But she seems out of her mind: she keeps reaching out to the coffin, surrounded by garlands of white fabric flowers. She manages to wriggle away. She sinks her nails into the coffin so deeply that she scratches the wood.

"Stop it, Giovanna!" Ignazio grabs her by the arms and shakes her violently. He's overwhelmed with grief and cannot shoulder his wife's despair on top of that. It would take just one more gram to crush him. "He's dead—do you understand?" he shouts in her face. "Dead!"

But she yells more loudly. "You're all wrong! He's sick, yes, but he's not dead . . . He can't be dead! Let him out, he's probably still breathing!" She repeats the last sentence, searching around, as though seeking confirmation in the eyes of those present.

Ignazio puts his arms around her and holds her so tight that he even stops her sobs from shaking her. Her hat with the black veil slides to the ground. "He had a fever, Giovanna," he whispers. "He had such a strong fever, it wore him down as if he were a candle. You held him and took care of him till the end, but then God took him away. It was fate."

She doesn't listen. She's now just weeping, exhausted. All that's left to a mother who's lost a child are tears and the desire to die.

Donna Ciccia comes up to her and takes her by the arm. "Come with me," she says, gently prizing her away from Ignazio. Then she motions to Giulia's nanny, who has come back in to fetch Ignazziddu. "Let's get some air," she murmurs, and the two women drag Giovanna out among the cypresses that stand around the Florio chapel in the cemetery of Santa Maria di Gesù. It's a mild September, in contrast to all this despair.

Ignazio bites his lip and looks at the door to the chapel. Incredible, how there's still so much life out there, while his son—*he was only a child!*—has no more life in him.

Then he turns to the waiting men. He takes a deep breath and hisses, "Close it."

There's the sound of light footsteps behind him.

Ignazziddu is on the threshold, holding a horseshoe: he and Vincenzo found it together during a day trip to Monte Pellegrino to visit the shrine of Saint Rosalia, the *Santuzza*. His brother told him it would bring him luck.

He should have kept it instead, he now thinks.

His fists in his pockets, he looks at his father's eyes, which are glistening with tears. He feels a sense of emptiness mixed with another, deeper sense. An unfamiliar one.

It's the sense of guilt the living reserve for the dead. It's an adult emotion, and yet Ignazziddu feels it acutely, devastatingly.

It's a drop of poison. He's alive, while his brother is dead, killed by an illness that ravaged his lungs in just a few days.

His father motions him to join him and he obeys. Together they watch the builders at work.

The bricks are laid in a row, one on top of the other. Slowly, Vincenzino's coffin disappears, until all that's left is a small empty space.

Only then does Ignazio motion the men to stop. He reaches out, touches a corner of the coffin, and closes his eyes.

Vincenzino will be twelve years old forever. He won't grow up. He won't travel. He won't learn anything anymore.

Ignazio won't see him become a man. He won't take him to Piazza Marina. He won't be able to rejoice at his wedding or at the birth of a grandchild.

What will remain of Vincenzino are the scores abandoned on the music stand, the exercise books left open on the desk, the clothes hanging in the closet, including that musketeer costume he liked so much. He had actually worn it to the most recent fancy-dress party, when Ignazio hired a photographer to immortalize his children dressed as a noblewoman and gentlemen.

His son will always be twelve years old to him, and for all his enterprises, all his power, all his wealth, there's nothing he can do.

When they return to the Olivuzza, Donna Ciccia helps Giovanna out of the carriage. The younger woman staggers, but then runs to the stairs. She's beside herself: she rushes through the door a tearful servant has just opened, and starts to roam about the rooms, calling Vincenzino as though he were hiding and only waiting for his mother to return before showing himself.

Suddenly, Giovanna collapses to the floor, outside the door to her son's room. She doesn't have the courage to open it. She presses her forehead against the timber and reaches out to the handle, but the strength fails her. That's where Donna Ciccia finds her. She gently hoists her up and takes her to her bedroom.

Giovanna looks around, lost. Grief has taken away the strength to speak and aged her ten years.

On the threshold, Ignazio watches Donna Ciccia pour a concoction of water, black cherries, white poppy syrup, and laudanum into a glass. She lifts Giovanna's head and helps her drink. Giovanna obeys, silent tears streaming from her eyes.

It takes only a few seconds for the sedative to take effect. Giovanna falls into a merciful sleep, still muttering something. Donna Ciccia sits in the armchair by the bed and crosses her hands, clutching a black rosary and looking at Ignazio as though to say: *I shan't move from here.* Besides, she knows that Vincenzino's soul is still here, even though his toys have disappeared and his violin's been hidden. Donna Ciccia knows that it will endure in these rooms, fostered by his mother's memories, a shadow among shadows, just as she knows she'll hear him walking down the corridors of the *palazzo.* She'll pray that his sad spirit may find peace.

Ignazio goes to the bed, bends over his wife, and, holding his breath, kisses her forehead. Then, after one final glance, he leaves the room and heads down the corridor.

I must go to my study. I must think about work. I must think about Casa Florio.

He walks past Giulia's room and hears her sobbing and the nanny attempting to comfort her.

A voice suddenly calls him, and he turns. It's Ignazziddu, standing still in the middle of the corridor. He heard his father walk past and has rushed out of his room. "Papà . . ." he murmurs, crying.

Ignazio clenches his fists but doesn't go to him. He stares down at an arabesque pattern on the rug. "Boys don't cry. *Stop it.*"

His voice is a blade of ice.

"What will I do without him?" The little boy wipes his tears and snot away with the sleeve of his black smock. He reaches out to Ignazio with his arms. "I can't bear thinking about it, Papà!"

"But that's how it is. He's dead and you must accept it." He says this harshly, with anger.

Why did it have to happen?

He looks down at his hands. They're shaking.

The void he feels spreads, reviving the sorrow of so many other bereavements: his father, his mother, and even his grandmother. But that's not what ravages him inside. *No parent should survive their own child*, he thinks. *It's not in the natural order of things.*

And yet maybe not all is lost. Keeping his eyes downcast, he speaks to Ignazziddu in a voice hoarse with grief. "He's not here anymore. It's you now, and you'll have to live up to the name you carry."

He ignores his son's outstretched arms and walks away toward the study.

The little boy remains alone, in the middle of the carpet, a tear running down the curve of his cheek. What did his father mean just now? What was he trying to say? Who is he now? What has he become?

In the corridor, everything is silent.

⌒

Time has no consideration for grief. It seizes it, grinds it, molds it as the days go by, transforming it into a ghost that's more visible, more cumbersome than a body of flesh and blood. Then grief plunges into one's breath so that every gulp of air is a reminder of how hard it is to be alive.

That is what Ignazio thinks as he shuts himself away in his office on Piazza Marina. He prefers to stay away from the Olivuzza, from his wife's stony face and his children's sad, silent expressions. Among the notes of condolence, there's a telegram from the education minister, Francesco Paolo Perez, a friend of his from Palermo, who's championing the interests of Piroscafi Postali with Alfredo Baccarini, the public works minister, and keeping him updated on recent events.

In fact, the public works minister hasn't yet decided what to do with the Ionian-Adriatic shipping route: it was first assigned to the Florios, then suspended while awaiting a general reshuffle of the subsidized trading routes. A reshuffle that has not been realized, and now Ignazio is worried because others, like Austrian Lloyds, are coming forward and offering passengers and traders very convenient services. Even the French from the Valery maritime company and the powerful Transatlantique aren't just standing idly by. It's no longer with cannons that you fight in the

Mediterranean, it's with reduced tariffs and subsidies for transportation firms.

Ignazio writes a draft response to the telegram. *In my extreme grief, I have never forgotten my important duties* . . . He must pluck up the courage to continue.

Work, like time, waits for no man.

"May I come in?" There's a lock of dark hair and an embarrassed patter of feet behind the half-open door.

Ignazio doesn't reply; maybe he didn't hear.

"Don Ignazio . . ."

Ignazio looks up.

The door opens and a well-dressed man with graying whiskers walks into the office.

"Don Giovanni!" Ignazio exclaims, getting to his feet. "Do come in."

Giovanni Laganà is the former liquidator of Trinacria and current director of Piroscafi Postali. He has known and respected Ignazio Florio for many years. Now he stares at him, unable to conceal his surprise. The man before him is extremely pale, has lost weight, and, above all, is permeated with a tiredness that has nothing to do with physical exertion. He walks up to him. "I chose not to come and see you at your home. I didn't want to force your wife to endure the umpteenth condolence visit."

Ignazio hugs him. "Thank you," he mutters. "You, at least, understand."

They sit down at opposite sides of the desk. Giovanni Laganà has narrow eyes and confident gestures. "How are you?"

Ignazio shrugs. "I am."

Giovanni squeezes his arm. "At least you have another son. All is not lost."

Ignazio looks down at the floor. "Let's talk about something else, please."

Giovanni nods, as though to say that everyone is entitled to choose his own escape from suffering. Then, with a sigh, he extracts documents from the briefcase he has brought. He hands them to Ignazio, who quickly scans them. His lifeless face suddenly becomes animated. He frowns. "Are these rumors or are the negotiations as advanced as they seem?"

Laganà's thin lips become even thinner. "What do you think?"

"That the French from Valery are pulling the rug from under our feet, and that the Austrians from Lloyds want to do the same." He puts the papers on the desk and starts to pace up and down the room. "Where did you hear about this?"

"From one of our agents in Marseille. One of his in-laws works at Transatlantique. And we also have many friends confirming the rumors about Lloyds." He pauses and drums his fingers on the papers. "I didn't want to tell you now, with everything that's happened, but . . ."

Ignazio dismisses the protestation with a wave. "In Rome they don't know what's happening here. Actually, not just in Palermo, but also in Genoa, Naples, and Livorno. All the ports are in dire straits. If the government indulges in passivity while Paris and Vienna act and conquer the best routes, we won't know where to go." He leans against the doorjamb, arms crossed, frowning and shaking his head, lost in thought.

Laganà watches him and feels a sense of relief in spite of himself. *He's back*, he thinks. *Grief hasn't broken him, not totally.*

"I've been waiting for an answer with regard to the concession of the American routes," Ignazio resumes. "Piroscafi is struggling to guarantee the service, you know that better than me. We barely cover our expenses, and then only because the Oretea takes care of the repairs. We'll soon be forced to increase the tariffs on our charters in order to recoup the costs, and then there'll be a *débâcle*, because the foreign ships that operate on the same route have much lower tariffs and many more routes." He massages the line between his eyebrows. "They keep talking about how the market must be free, but the French receive subsidies far greater than the Italian ones and merge with one another." He slaps the wall. "Don't they understand in Rome that they're just doing harm like this?"

"Apparently, they don't wish to understand."

Ignazio bursts into an embittered laugh. "They subsidize my line from Ancona, which is no longer of use, but won't give me others for America. And then what does the government ask of me? A subsidized service to the Greek islands, where no one goes and all you can find are olives and goats. Tell me, what's the point?" He moves away from the wall and points at the secret documents from Marseille. "While these people are building new lines to America, what do we do? Zara? Corfu?"

He sits back down at his desk and rests his chin on his hands, fingers interlaced. His breathing is heavy, his eyes closed: a sign that he's thinking.

"True wealth comes from transoceanic voyages, from the wretched people who go off to work in America. I proposed two weekly journeys, but what can I do against the competition from the British, who offer three a week? No, I'm not going to keep still and wait for them to take away all that my father and I have built, while in Rome they chatter about commissions and evaluating op-portunities . . . *Asses!*"

"The one consolation is that Rubattino thinks as you do. You and he are the largest ship owners in Italy. Do you remember what he told me when I went to see him in Genoa? 'The French are making mincemeat out of us, and there's not the slightest reaction from Rome.' He complained about the commission for the reshuffling of the trade routes, which he considers yet another device for wasting time. And he concluded that we had to take measures ourselves, otherwise . . ."

Ignazio opens his eyes. "Yes, yes, admirable words, but meanwhile he and I are still here, doing sweet nothing. The only thing to do would be to establish a single powerful company involving Genoa and Palermo. We must go to Minister Baccarini, Giovanni. I'll reach him myself; I'll ask Francesco Paolo Perez to speak to him, to tell him to stop fooling around, because while he sleeps others get ahead. We must target America and become strong enough to prevent the French and the Austrians from taking journeys and goods away from our ports. Something has to change, and as true as I am a Florio, something's going to change."

"What do you mean, they've canceled the Palermo-Messina route? Dozens of letters, applications, and meetings to increase the shipping routes and reach New York . . . and that's the answer?"

Giovanni Laganà takes a step back, surprised by the anger seeping out of Ignazio. It's December 1880 and they've spent over a year desperately trying to protect Piroscafi Postali from the transportation crisis. The company is struggling, trailing behind the French and the Austrians. Ignazio has spared no effort: he's exhausted all his power, used all his political contacts, made promises and threats. But it seems he's only wasted his time. And that's one of the things that infuriate him the most.

"Excuse me?" Laganà murmurs, approaching the desk.

"Read," Ignazio mutters, throwing him the telegram that's just arrived from Rome. He's so angry, he can't say anything else.

Laganà quickly scans it. "According to them, the route is no longer needed because there's now a railroad to link the two cities, and the train will make more journeys than we can ensure with our ships." *That's reasonable*, he thinks, but doesn't say it. He just glances at Ignazio.

"Obviously, I can see for myself that they're right," he says, as though reading Laganà's mind. He mutters an insult. "But this way they're driving us to bankruptcy. The dividends that can be shared among the partners are very low . . . and now that's something else I'm going to have to explain, on top of the news Giuseppe Orlando keeps bringing from France."

"The merger between Valery and Transatlantique? Unfortunately, the board of directors is in agreement."

"It's now just a matter of paperwork. The Valery company practically no longer exists. It's just a matter of days before it's official. Orlando has intimated it in a telegram." Ignazio's fist lands on the desk. Vincenzino's portrait, in a heavy silver frame, jumps and falls. Ignazio straightens it, then continues in a more controlled tone. "Rubattino is still stalling while we're working like galley slaves. You look for help from those who would give it to you, and they slam the door in your face. Meanwhile, the French are establishing more routes and superseding ours."

Laganà takes a deep, slow breath that hisses through his teeth. "Are you sure? I mean, is it a done deal?"

Ignazio rubs his temples. Anger makes his head feel squeezed and his stomach burn. "Yes. I've personally written to Roussier, our French representative. He's confirmed everything. Transatlantique's next step, after the merger, will be to create a route to Cagliari, then to other Italian ports. So Rubattino should be acting, and what does he do instead? He snivels. *Picchiulia.*" He gives the desk another blow, hitting a stack of papers, which fly off. "He's the largest Genoese ship owner, and he, too, is being shafted by the French. He should speak up, do something, ask Rome for his position to be protected . . . But no, nothing! He's doing nothing! I can't bear this waste of time, this chaos!"

Giovanni Laganà picks a handful of papers up from the floor and smiles. "The more time passes, the more you're like your father."

Ignazio pauses and looks up. There are now spatters of gray in his hair and beard. He seems more annoyed than perplexed by this remark. He looks at Laganà quizzically.

"Your voice," Laganà explains, "your . . . gestures. I'm not sure. I didn't know him very well, but you remind me of him. You don't have the same anger, but you have the same way of expressing outrage . . . and demonstrating it."

"My father would have already gone to Rome and punched the living daylights out of them," Ignazio grumbles. "But that's not my style."

His office is paneled with walnut wainscoting on which hang maps and the company's certificates of merit. The light coming in through the windows overlooking Piazza Marina seems to travel through the shiny texture of the timber, then slide over the bookcases on either side of the door. Leather armchairs and lamps made of Bohemian crystal are arranged around the huge desk.

It's an office worthy of an important shipping company. And he is a ship owner—the most important ship owner in Italy—and wants to be treated like one.

He rubs the bridge of his nose and thinks. Laganà waits in silence.

Ignazio slowly walks to the window and looks out. *Caution*, he tells himself, taking a deep breath. *Caution and focus.*

It's a windy day, as is customary for Palermo's winters. Ignazio examines the square, the buildings with their tuff fronts, the traffic of carts and passersby. Then he lifts his gaze toward the Vicaria, beyond San Giuseppe dei Napoletani, and follows the Cassaro as far as he can. Finally, he takes the gold watch from his waistcoat and looks at the time. "Very well. If our venerable ministers won't listen to us, they'll dance to a different tune."

He has spoken so softly that Laganà has barely heard him. "What do you mean?"

He cocks his head. "The company's general assembly is scheduled for late January. Shortly before that, the royal family will visit Palermo, and I plan to request a meeting with the king." His face is in the shade, chiseled by the light of day pouring in through the window. "I'll speak with him. And if that's still not enough . . ." He starts pacing up and down the room. "Some time ago, when we encountered difficulties with our *tonnaras* because the government wasn't protecting local production, I performed a particular maneuver that yielded good results. It's time to deploy it again, but on a larger scale."

Laganà sits down and adjusts his jacket. "Excuse me, Ignazio, I'm not following you."

"Back then, I asked a few friends to mention the issue in the newspapers. It was essential to highlight the fact that the *tonnaras'* situation was untenable, that fishing had to be protected with an appropriate tax policy. They wrote about this and other things, and managed in that way to give the entire issue a nationwide profile. In other words, these articles made a lot of noise, as I wanted them to. And now I can say it was a kind of dress rehearsal."

Laganà opens his mouth, then closes it again. "So . . ."

 ⌒

The Savoys arrive in Palermo on January 4, 1881. The city is all decked out: Damiani Almeyda has designed a "pavilion for the royal landing," and a small army of workers has swept the streets, arranged the flower beds, and repaired the lampposts that gangs of street urchins enjoy throwing stones at. On the balconies of the Cassaro, Christmas decorations have given way to Italian flags; soldiers parade between ranks of crowds, and people cheer, shout, and wave paper stars with the pictures of King Umberto I and Queen Margherita, as well as banners praising the royal couple.

Palermo is glowing with its own light, like a woman who has rediscovered her beauty after a period of neglect and is choosing an outfit for a much-awaited party.

It couldn't be otherwise.

The city is growing, expanding, stretching toward the strip of plain leading to the sea. A new generation of architects is planning streets, gardens, villas, rethinking public spaces, looking beyond the island's boundaries, toward the mainland. Modernity has arrived, demolishing alleys and narrow streets, pushing poor people into slums, and forcing even the most conservative aristocrats to alter their habits and lifestyle in favor of those from the Continent.

The smells are changing. No more stench of fish, rotting algae, and garbage. Now there's the fragrance of pomelias, magnolias, and jasmine. Even the scent of the sea is milder, drowned by the aromas of coffee and chocolate wafting from elegant, fashionable establishments overlooking the streets of the new city.

Palermo is no longer looking just at itself, but competing with London, Vienna, and Paris. It wants to show off wide boulevards and get rid of that old-fashioned Baroque chunkiness. Even inside .

people's homes, furniture is acquiring new designs with a hint of the exotic, brocade vanishes to make room for Chinese and Indian silks. The *palazzi* of the aristocracy fill with Japanese porcelain and carved ivory alongside Sicilian crafts: fonts made of silver and coral, hard stone tables, wax Nativity scenes. It becomes a competition to see who owns the most beautiful, the most sought-after objects.

Palermo's soul, composed of sea and stone, steeped in salt water, is slowly and irreversibly changing. And many things in this strange metamorphosis carry the stamp of the Florios, or are linked to them, starting with the buildings. For the past seven years, the city has been home to a very elegant theater, the Politeama, designed by Damiani Almeyda. Enthusiastic about Classicism, he decided on a double row of pillars and Pompeii-style paintings on the external walls. But there's a touch of the modern amid all these nods to the past: the roof. Manufactured in the Oretea, it's a shell of metal and shiny bronze panels, which gleams in the sun. A little farther down the same street, work is underway on another theater, the Massimo. They are actually running behind schedule: the first stone was laid in 1875, more than six years ago, and nobody knows when the final one will be. Giovan Battista Basile, the architect who designed it, has in mind a temple to music so imposing and elegant that it will rival the Opéra Garnier in Paris.

Perhaps it's a little too much for this city, Ignazio thinks, sitting next to his wife in the carriage. He drops the curtain and looks down at his crossed fingers. *Palermo is growing more beautiful, but what it might actually need is a dose of pragmatism.*

The vehicle jolts on the calcareous stone. Feeling cold, Giovanna pulls the rug over her and lets out a sigh. Ignazio notices and gives her gloved hand a squeeze. "It'll be fine."

"I hope so," she replies, her voice uncertain with tension.

"I met him in Rome a few years ago. He's a hard but not unreasonable man. As for his wife, she's a princess of royal blood and acts like one." He lifts her chin. "You're no less."

Giovanna nods, but her anxiety doesn't abate. When her husband is once again engrossed in his thoughts, she examines her dress in the half-light of the carriage interior and touches the bodice. It's a style created in Paris, from thick silk, pale gray to match the cloak trimmed with fox fur. Fifteen months have passed since her son's death, so the mourning period is over, but she still wears mainly black, as well as understated jewelry: pearl earrings, an onyx ring, and a mother-of-pearl cameo with Vincenzino's face carved on it, pinned to her heart.

Ignazio doesn't want to relinquish all outward presentation of bereavement either and still wears a black tie. "He was flesh of his flesh," Donna Ciccia said to Giovanna a few days ago, "and he had his father's name. There's no more Vincenzo in Casa Florio. That's why he's unable to let him go."

True, Giovanna thinks. *But Ignazziddu and Giulia are here, and he mustn't forget about them. And yet there are days when he ignores them completely . . .*

The carriage stops with a jolt in the courtyard of the Royal Palace.

Out of habit, Giovanna puts a hand on her stomach and presses it. For years now she has controlled her impulse to vomit, but right now she feels frail. Frightened.

Then she looks into Ignazio's eyes. Another action ruled by habit: she does this whenever she wants to be reassured, as though certain that he can somehow transfer his calmness to her.

She looks at him and almost doesn't recognize him.

His pensive expression has been replaced by a direct, confident look. There's a faint smile on his lips, although it doesn't include his eyes. His back is straight, his gestures slow but authoritative.

Ignazio gets out of the carriage and gives her a hand to help her. He has an iron grip and almost hurts her.

That's when she understands.

Ignazio is ready for battle.

⌒

The couple parts. Giovanna follows the queen's ladies-in-waiting, while Ignazio is let into the study, covered in red brocade, that has been made available for the king's private meetings. He gives him a furtive glance: his shoulders are slightly hunched, his hands squat, his hair graying at the temples and in the large mustache that covers his mouth. Umberto is a man whose gestures are solid, his expression that of someone who's used to understanding what cannot be expressed in words.

"Take a seat," he says, indicating an armchair.

Ignazio sits down immediately after the king does.

The king takes a cigar from a box brought by an attendant, offers one to his guest, then lights it and takes a puff. He keeps his eyes on Ignazio, as though trying to match the man before him to the opinion he has formed of him over the years. "So," he finally says, "tell me."

Ignazio stares at his hands, as though searching for words to say something that's actually crystal-clear. "First and foremost, I wish to thank Your Majesty for granting me this audience. I know you will understand why my wife and I haven't joined the city of Palermo in celebrating your arrival."

Umberto gives a faint, joyless smile. His eyes slide down to

Ignazio's black tie. "I know you've lost a son. You have my deepest sympathies."

"Thank you, Your Majesty."

Umberto nods.

Ignazio crosses his hands on his lap. "I'm here as a citizen, as the owner of one of Italy's largest shipping companies, and—"

"One of?" the king says, interrupting him with a hint of impatience. "Just say the largest. You needn't be modest with me."

Ignazio isn't thrown by this. He knows that the king is direct, if not abrupt. A leftover from the military education he received from a very young age. "Thank you for your esteem." He puts his cigar in the ashtray. "Then you will know that I'm here to explain the reasons for the malaise affecting Italian seafaring."

"A parliamentary commission is currently working on it. I am fully aware of the reasons."

"Forgive me, Your Majesty, but perhaps you're not fully aware of them, since the government has taken no stance, nor any measures to protect it."

"Then lower your rental fees." Irritated, the king fidgets in his chair. The ash from his cigar spills all over the floor. "From north to south, all I do is meet people who complain that the government is doing either too much or the wrong thing. Everybody seems to think they could do a better job! I'd really like to see them try!"

Ignazio waits a few seconds before replying. "Your Majesty, the problem isn't *who* does what, but *how* they do it." He speaks calmly, softly. "There are dozens of ship owners struggling to survive. If Italian seafaring is overtaken by the French and the Austrians, not only will we lose all negotiating power, we'll also become the slaves of a foreign country where transportation and tariffs are concerned." He pauses, as though to allow the king time to grasp the implications of what he's just said. "Obviously, that would be a blow to me and my company, but that's not all: the economy of the whole of Sicily would be in danger of collapsing. Enterprises in the north can send their goods by train, whereas those who work here in Sicily have no other routes but the sea."

"It's certainly not you who's going to solve the situation in Sicily with your boats and your *tonnaras*." The king's voice is so argumentative that Ignazio feels a rush of anger. "Your tariffs are expensive beyond decency. Is it surprising that many people would rather transport their goods by train than by ship?" Umberto puts down his cigar, rings the bell, and asks the attendant to serve a liqueur.

Ignazio raises a finger. "With your permission . . . I've brought you a few bottles of the best marsala from my winery, as a gift. I would be honored if Your Majesty would kindly try it."

The attendant's eyes shift to the king, who nods.

Ignazio waits until he's alone with the king again, then resumes. "The problem isn't just the charter and the tariffs. All over Europe, protectionist policies are being invoked . . . Sooner or later, excise duty will be applied to our goods, and then we truly will be on our knees. If I may say so, Your Majesty, the problem is something else." Ignazio leans toward the king. "It's vitally important to understand that in Italy, the north and the south have different needs, and that's precisely why they must work together. And what my business has to offer would be useful to the whole of Italy. This is why I, in Palermo, and Rubattino, in Genoa, are thinking of acting along the same lines: it's only by joining forces that we can take on our adversaries." He straightens up and catches his breath. "If Italy wishes to keep its power in the Mediterranean, it must be equal to the situation. And that's only possible with government help."

The king scrutinizes him suspiciously. "I know only too well who your lawyer is, just as I know about your ploys to acquire Rubattino. And do you really think I'm not aware of the personal relationships you maintain with various ministers?"

"Crispi may be a lawyer, but he's first and foremost a friend of the family. As for . . . personal relationships, these are acquaintances based on mutual esteem. You know what they say here? For every great government, one enemy is too many and a hundred friends too few."

The attendant brings in a silver tray with a bottle of marsala and two crystal glasses. The liqueur has a fiery amber glow to it.

Umberto takes small sips, then makes a less-than-aristocratic click of the tongue. "Excellent." He lifts his eyes to Ignazio. "In effect, what is it you're asking of me, Signor Florio?"

"That no obstacle be placed in the way of our merger with Rubattino. That the subsidized tariffs and concessions for our mail service be reconfirmed. That our company be given precedence in government transportation."

"You're asking a lot. You southerners do nothing but ask."

"Perhaps that's how others conduct themselves, Your Majesty, but that's not the case with me or my family. My father and I have always fought for Casa Florio and now all I ask is what's rightfully needed to protect my business and my people."

Ignazio waits for his wife at the bottom of the marble staircase of the Royal Palace. He looks tense. Giovanna walks down very slowly, leaning on the balustrade. Now that the stress is over, she feels exhausted. Ignazio urges her on with a brusque gesture, helps her into the carriage, then gets in and gives the order to set off.

Giovanna arranges the rug over her legs and touches the cameo with Vincenzino's portrait. "It was the first thing the queen noticed. She said, 'I can't begin to imagine how you've felt.' She seemed genuinely moved."

She searches for her husband's eyes, but Ignazio just nods absent-mindedly, and when Giovanna tries to take his hand, he shakes her off.

"And the ladies did nothing except admire how I was dressed," she continues. "Imagine, they were ogling the fur on my cloak and one of them asked another in a whisper how much she thought it had cost." She pauses and sighs. "I feel sorry for the queen, though. She was wearing a beautiful pearl necklace, and you know what they say, don't you? That the king gives her a necklace whenever he cheats on her. As a matter of fact, she had a dismayed expression that broke my heart."

Ignazio turns abruptly and gives her an annoyed look. "I spent the last hour trying to make the king understand the disastrous situation of seafaring and came up against a wall . . . and you're talking to me about frocks and gossip?"

"I just felt deeply sorry for her, that's all," Giovanna retorts, offended. "And everybody knows that the king—"

"These things have nothing to do with men," Ignazio snaps back. "It's the queen's fault. A woman, whether she's a scullery maid or a queen, needs to know how to keep her husband. Besides, theirs was an arranged marriage: she should have expected him to take a mistress, and more than one at that. In cases like these, the wives should just keep quiet and bear it."

Silence falls over the carriage.

Giovanna feels cold. Then, from her guts, there is a surge of heat. No, she won't keep quiet. She *knows* how the queen feels. For years now, she's been carrying the memory of those letters . . . He has dismissed Giovanna, pushed her into the darkest corner of his consciousness, buried her under her daily duties, and even under her grief over Vincenzino's death, but her obsession to know who *that woman* was has never left her. Jealousy has been her life's companion, as menacing as a feral cat with hungry yellow eyes, an animal always lying in ambush, ready to bite. This sudden realization terrifies her. "That's how it works for men, is it? To do as they please while their wives stay at home, nice and quiet, with their mouths shut?"

Ignazio looks at her, surprised. "What are you talking about?" he asks bluntly, waving a hand as though to shoo her words away. "What's this fixation?"

"Fixation? A woman puts her heart and soul into a marriage and doesn't have the right to feel humiliated when betrayal slaps her in the face? She has to stay in her place, silent, and perhaps even thankful . . . Don't you think a woman has pride? That she has a heart that can ache?"

Ignazio stares at her, dumbfounded. This is not the Giovanna he knows, the Giovanna who's always reserved, decorous, and accommodating. Has the meeting with the queen frayed her nerves?

Then he sees her eyes brim with tears, and he understands.

She's not talking about the queen, but about what happened between them.

He joins his hands in front of his face, in a gesture both tired and exasperated. "Stop it, Giovanna . . ."

"Why? Isn't it so?" she replies, grabbing the hem of her cloak and holding it tight.

"Some things happen, that's all. If someone is the way he is, you can't change him, let alone change his past." He says this calmly, softly, to placate her.

But she lowers her head and whispers, "No, no, no . . ." She grits her teeth and pushes back her tears, then lifts her head again and looks Ignazio straight in the face. In the faint light of the streetlamps, her eyes are so shiny, they look as if they're made of onyx. "I know," she says. "But you can't ask me to forget. It hurts me, do you understand? Every time I think of those letters you kept, my breath catches in my chest. It hurts to know you've never been mine."

Ignazio recoils, annoyed. "I told you it was an old story. Besides, how long has it been? Nine, ten years? Are you still mulling over something you cannot change?" He can't think of a worse waste of energy.

Giovanna sits back and the darkness inside the carriage seems to absorb her. "You've never understood what it means to feel the way I do. Another woman would have gotten used to it, stopped thinking about it, because one can't live like this. But not me. You're right inside here." She beats her chest. "And you can't run away."

Her voice weakens until it's just a cloud of breath in the cold carriage. She drops her chin to her chest and closes her eyes. It's as though she has just unloaded a burden from her heart, only to replace it with the even heavier burden of awareness. Because from now on, this unrequited love—a feeling that wounds those who bear it but is of no consequence to the object of their affections—can never again be concealed beneath a veil of serenity and resignation. It will always be there, between them, in all its concreteness.

Perhaps for the first time in his life, Ignazio doesn't know what to say. He's angry with himself for not having realized his wife's state of mind, whereas in business, he picks up on every shade, every intention, every hint. He tries to persuade himself it was just an outburst, one of those women's things that come and go, like a summer thunderstorm. Only when the carriage stops outside the Olivuzza and Giovanna gets out, leaning on the coachman who has opened the door, leaving Ignazio alone in the dark, does he understand how she truly feels.

He watches his wife walk away, her head pulled into her shoulders.

Shame constricts his throat.

○~

On February 9, 1881, the *Giornale di Sicilia* prints the first part of a long, detailed inquiry into the conditions of Italian seafaring in general, and in particular in Palermo.

Incendiary words, aimed with precision, first trigger indignation, then anxiety, and finally panic. The ultimate recipient: the Italian government.

In his office, Laganà closes the newspaper and smiles with admiration. Ignazio could not have done more or better. Admittedly, the *Giornale di Sicilia* is practically owned by his family, but the data put forward by the journalists is irrefutable.

It's time to force Raffaele Rubattino's hand. He writes a note to Giuseppe Orlando, who is now the manager of the Naples office of Piroscafi Postali. He's known the Genoese Rubattino the longest and knows how to handle him.

Merger.

The union between the two shipping companies must be celebrated at the earliest opportunity, almost as though it were a shotgun wedding. That's what Laganà writes to Orlando. He adds that Rubattino must stop stalling like a groom with cold feet, because if he doesn't accept the inevitable, and quickly, his ships will vanish from the Mediterranean. In addition, he reminds him of the disaster averted in January of the previous year, when Rubattino tried to agree on a tariff with the French. It took all Ignazio's calm not to hurl abuse at the Genoese, and to explain how, if that agreement had gone through, they would both—he and Rubattino—have become slaves of Transatlantique.

What Laganà doesn't say is that Piroscafi Postali also needs this merger, not only to maintain its dominance over the sea, but also to protect those who work for the company: the Oretea Foundry, the workers in the careening bay, the carriers and the trading agents scattered throughout the Mediterranean. If Piroscafi Postali missed this opportunity and the port of Palermo turned into a peripheral port of call, then not only the city would suffer, but the entire island.

"Stupid Genoese. I can't wait to be in front of the notary," Laganà mutters, signing the note. Then he summons an errand boy to have it dispatched immediately.

But Ignazio and he will have to wait until June before things really get underway: first with the board of directors of Piroscafi Postali, who approve of the merger, and then—at last!—with Rubattino's consent, obtained after laborious, exhausting negotiations.

All they need is for the government to give its blessing, like a celebrant.

And so Ignazio goes to Rome.

He is received by Prime Minister Agostino Depretis, as well as by the director of public works, Baccarini. They both desperately try to explain to Ignazio what he's known for a long time: that, given the importance of the two companies, a draft bill must be submitted to Parliament, because ordinary ministerial clearance is not sufficient; that a lot of public money is being invested, starting with that given to the subsidized navigation routes of both shipping companies, and so caution must be exercised . . .

Ignazio nods and juts out his chin as if to say: yes, obviously. But, later, back at his hotel, what he reads in the evening papers takes away his appetite and his sleep.

From Genoa to Venice, small carriers and owners of sailing ships are protesting: they're crying disaster, accusing the Ministry of Public Works of favoring magnates and not caring about seafaring. Two Genoese ship owners, Giovanni Battista Lavarello and Erasmo Piaggio, have even presented a petition to Parliament, in which they express their "legitimate concern at the creation of a giant anonymous shareholding company, whose shares, currently owned by Italians, could in time be owned in part by foreigners."

No, the merger won't be simple.

⌒

On July 4, 1881, the debate takes place in the Chamber of Deputies. The draft law is passed on July 15, and is then sent to the Senate, where it is voted on the same day. Everyone's in a rush, a big rush, to put this nuisance behind them.

Ignazio is in a private room at the Senate, waiting. If he's tense, he certainly doesn't show it. He asks for tea, and they serve it to him in an elegant porcelain set. Who could ever go against him, the personal friend of ministers and senators? Even so, his hands are trembling slightly from the pressure. He accepts a cigar and enjoys the silence that reigns in the corridors of power.

Minister Baccarini comes to update him on what is happening in the chamber. Amid the cigar smoke and the aroma of freshly served coffee, the minister smiles, cocks his head, and murmurs, "Don't worry, Signor Florio. Navigation with sailing ships is a thing of the past, even though some don't realize that their time is up. Steam is the future. Steam and iron. You will be the standard bearer of this new era, one of the men to take Italy to the New World."

"My father was sure of it," Ignazio says, "and I'm sure of it, too, even more so than you. Twelve years have passed since the opening of the Suez Canal, and naturally, it's through there that the most valuable trade passes. Continuing to use sailing ships is ridiculous. We need large steamships to travel across the oceans."

"And so you have them. That's why the government will support you."

Shortly afterward, the votes are counted. The bill is passed. Ignazio feels his breath escape from his rib cage and the pressure release.

"All we need now is your and Rubattino's signatures before the notary," says Orlando, who has just come in and slapped him on the shoulder.

Francesco Paolo Perez also arrives, followed by a clerk carrying a bottle of champagne and glasses. "Success at last!" he says, hugging him.

Ignazio allows himself a satisfied smile.

But the pride he feels is such that it seems to be running through his veins instead of blood. He has saved Piroscafi Postali from a fate of progressive impoverishment, shielded his people, the Oretea's workers and the seamen, from a future of misery, as well as guaranteeing the port of Palermo years of prosperity. And he, the owner of almost a hundred ships, both steamers and liners, will effectively become one of the lords of the Mediterranean.

And yet this is not the only thing to make him proud. It's also knowing that politics, if handled correctly, can always help him. And never mind if a king is unwilling to do so.

It's also the awareness that the economic power of the Florios can affect the fate of Italy.

Something his father, for all his ambition, couldn't even imagine.

❧

The heat that swept over Palermo at the end of August 1881 has taken hold of the Olivuzza, growing dense in the bedrooms, making the air practically unbreathable. Through the windows overlooking the garden, the city looks like a contour wrapped in the fine dust borne on the sirocco. You can make out the domes of the churches and the roofs of the houses, but they are hazy, remote.

Donna Ciccia is in the green salon, organizing her work basket and gathering embroidery threads into small bundles.

Giovanna opens the door and stops on the threshold. There's boredom and annoyance in her eyes. Her forehead is a stormy sky, her hands full of electricity.

Donna Ciccia immediately detects her bad mood. "What's happened? Why do you look like that?"

Giovanna shrugs and collapses into an armchair.

"What's wrong?" Donna Ciccia insists, irked by her silence.

"My husband has left me alone for more than a month, and now he's writing to tell me that he's not coming back this month."

"Maria santa!" she scoffs. "What's all this? Is it a little girl like Giulia I have here or a married woman?"

Giovanna raises her hand to her lips, as though to stop more words. Then she speaks quickly. "He writes that from Genoa he wants to go to Marseille, to his sister's." Her voice is a hiss. "In recent years, we've always traveled together in the summer, and now he's going on his own. True, it was for the business at first, but he's never been away so long, never!"

Donna Ciccia raises her eyes to heaven. "Don Ignazio hasn't seen his sister for years. Surely he's entitled to some time with her."

"We're a family," Giovanna retorts, slapping the arm of her chair. "Shouldn't a man take his children to meet their aunt?"

Donna Ciccia crosses her arms over her ample bosom. "You've been married so many years and you still don't know your husband? He's a saint, not like some husbands who run after skirts. Please, get these thoughts out of your mind and work on the tablecloth." She takes a linen tablecloth embroidered in Sicilian-style threadwork, gets up, and hands it to her. Giovanna seizes it, not noticing the needle, and pricks her finger. She lifts it to her mouth and mutters, "There are things one can't even imagine . . ." then looks away because she doesn't want her anguish out in the open.

Donna Ciccia looks at her quizzically but doesn't have the courage to ask what's distressing her.

This marriage seems to her as fragile as crystal, and if it's not breaking, it's because Giovanna's feelings on one hand and Ignazio's respect for her on the other make up an unusual suit of armor that shields it from life's attacks. But Giovanna has suffered too much and for too long—in body and mind—and Donna Ciccia now fears that it will take just a quiver to make her crumble. Ignazio's attitude, however, has never—*never!*—given her a moment's uncertainty. That's why she can't even imagine that he might have been unfaithful to Giovanna under any circumstances.

However, it's a notion that has again gotten a grip on Giovanna since she read the destination of Ignazio's trip: Marseille. Her obsession has reawakened, glaring at her with its yellow eyes. She tries to push it away, telling herself that Giuseppina, François, and little Louis Auguste are there. But maybe *she's* there, too . . .

She shakes her head, trying to dismiss the memory of the quarrel she and Ignazio had just a couple of months ago, after the audience with the king. Just like after the discovery of the letters, they never mentioned it again, letting the waves of the sea of habit smooth any asperity. But she still kept dwelling on it. Sometimes she would convince herself that her jealousy made no sense, and that Ignazio was probably right: she was always fretting over something she couldn't change. Only, all it would take was a slightly abrupt gesture or stern look for her wound to reopen. And then she would go back to hating that woman who'd had everything from Ignazio, even the most precious gift you could possibly impart a lost love: regret. Whereas all she herself was left with was the emptiness of unrequited affection.

And yet that terrible evening made her realize something else, too. She'd read it in his eyes, his gestures, and even in his harshness toward her. There was nothing more important for Ignazio than Casa Florio. *More important than me, or even his children.* No loved ones were of consequence in comparison with business. Even that woman couldn't be more important. And so, for some time now, whenever jealousy has loomed, she has clung to this certainty.

She picks up the work basket. Her dark hair, gathered into a tight bun, follows the jerky movements of her head. "I know my husband very well," she says, avoiding looking at Donna Ciccia, and starts embroidering.

Marseille is dustier, dirtier, and more chaotic than he remembered it. But memory, a deceitful guardian of happiness, knows how to freeze the images of some places into an everlasting present, an impossible—and precisely for that reason even more real—reality.

So Ignazio thinks, with a hint of bitterness that darkens his thoughts and leaves a sour aftertaste in his mouth.

Marseille has too many recollections for him.

Now, in late September 1881, the air is saturated by humidity, and the wind blowing from the sea already has something of the chill of fall about it. Here the Mediterranean has different smells, and the water seems darker, as though it weren't the same sea that laps around Sicily.

The streets around the harbor are crowded with carts and barrows. Large horse-drawn wagons carry loads of coal to the steamships moored between the old port—now not large enough—and the new piers. Ignazio remembers their being built, fifteen years ago.

He slowly gets off the steamer, having traveled incognito on a French vessel, like an ordinary passenger. He has trimmed his beard, worn traveling clothes, and his natural reserve has done the rest. He wanted to assess the quality of the service provided by his competitors and the result is satisfactory: excellent overall, but in no way better than that of his own company, at least in first class.

A carriage awaits him not far from the pier. Next to the horses stands François Merle, his brother-in-law. "May I hug you or should I bow before the most powerful man in the Mediterranean?"

"I will grant you that liberty, but I did expect a red carpet outside the carriage."

François laughs and opens his arms, and Ignazio gratefully welcomes the embrace.

"*Comu si*?—How are you?" François asks in a Sicilian that smacks of French as he opens the door.

"Tired. But since I was in Genoa, I really wanted to come and visit you all. I haven't seen my sister in years, and whatever had to be done has now been done."

"It can't have been easy."

"I'll tell you all about it."

The inside of the carriage has seen better days, but Ignazio doesn't appear to notice. He's drawn by the city, studies the changes, the buildings erected in a style that became widespread during the reign of Napoleon III.

"How long are you staying?" François asks.

"A few days. Then I'll go straight back to Palermo." He turns to look at his brother-in-law. "Tomorrow I'm going to Place de la Bourse. They're not expecting me." He laughs. "I want to see the state of my branch."

"You mean the branch of your company Navigazione Generale Italiana." François rubs his thighs impatiently. "Go on, tell me how things went in Genoa."

"Well, if we want to be precise, we should add the joint Florio and Rubattino companies. Since the vote in Rome, it's been plain sailing. We signed the deed before a notary at the house of Senator Orsini, who also acted as witness. Crispi was also with me."

A corner of François's mouth lifts in a smile. "So you brought the entire cavalry."

"Prevention's better than cure."

They laugh. "Are you pleased?"

"Pretty much. Of course, we've had to involve the banks . . ." A furrow appears between his eyebrows. "But we couldn't help it. Credito Mobiliare was Rubattino's bank, and he was heavily in debt to them. We had to include that in the deed at the last minute."

"If you'd waited a little longer, you could have seized it painlessly."

Ignazio shakes his head. "Yes, but then I would have taken over a bankrupt company, which would have made it much harder to be assigned the subsidized lines—assuming Rubattino would have gone bankrupt, and nobody wanted that. Too many people work there."

The carriage slows down because a cart has overturned across the roadway, its goods strewn all over the ground. François lets go of the curtain and swears in French.

Ignazio stifles a yawn, suddenly feeling the weight of these erratic days. He misses the gentle rocking of the steamship, and dry land is making him lethargic.

"Now the company owns everything it needs: the Oretea, the steamers, the buildings . . . But it's what I wanted."

The carriage resumes its journey. "And how did they react to this in Palermo? I mean it's a peculiar city . . ."

Ignazio shrugs. "How can they react? They found out and nobody cared, starting with my workers. Not even a line or comment in the papers. It's as though this didn't concern them. Even though there are more than eighty steamers!" His voice conceals a whiff of resentment, diluted by pragmatism. "All they care about is having pennies in their pockets, never mind what else may happen."

François is about to respond, but the carriage slows down. *"Oh, je crois que nous sommes arrivés!"* he says, jumping off before the vehicle comes to a halt. Ignazio looks up and nods. It's a two-story house, elegant but not flashy, with delicate lines and wrought-iron balconies. Just as he remembered it.

He hears a little cry from a window. *"Fratuzzu!* Brother!"

Ignazio barely has time to get out before Giuseppina appears and gives him such an energetic hug that he almost stumbles.

It's her and, at the same time, a new person: a little more filled out, with hair thinning at the temples, just like the grandmother she was named after. But her eyes are still expressive and kind, and her enveloping embrace hasn't changed.

She looks at him and strokes his face. "My flesh and blood! *Sangu meo!* How long has it been?" She takes his face in her hands and kisses it twice, three times.

Ignazio feels a warmth at the base of his breastbone. His sister's embrace suggests homecoming, peace, shreds of life that eddy, then fall into place. "Too long," he says, holding her tight.

A little boy with straight fair hair appears on the doorstep. His body already speaks of adolescence, but there's still a childish grimace on his face. Louis Auguste, François and Giuseppina's son—his nephew.

His memory immediately switches to Vincenzino. He would have been slightly younger, and perhaps would have shared the same gawky appearance, the same impatient expression.

Don't think about it, he tells himself.

"Come in, come in!" Giuseppina drags him by the sleeve up the stairs to a drawing room furnished in navy-blue damask, with velvet armchairs and mahogany coffee tables. It's not a luxurious room, but neat and full of exotic features, such as ivory statuettes in the corners and a Chinese vase on a table covered with an oriental cloth.

"What a lovely place."

"We do what we can," François says, opening his arms.

"I'm telling you it's lovely and I like it . . . Why are you always making a fuss?" Ignazio replies, laughing. He sinks into the couch and motions to his sister to join him.

Giuseppina, too, laughs and sits down next to him. "Tell me, how's Giovanna?"

"She's well. But what with this paperwork, notaries, negotiations, and lawyers, I've hardly seen her. She's in Palermo, looking after the house and the *picciriddi*. Last time I had a letter from her she was rather . . ." He pauses, searching for the right word. "Resentful."

Giuseppina tilts her head forward. "She must have been very upset about your coming here without her."

He toys with his uncle's ring beneath his wedding band, feeling awkward. "In this particular case, I couldn't help it. It wasn't a matter I could delegate. Laganà and Orlando have been wonderful, but the people in Rome wanted to see me and talk to me, and the signature on the Genoa deed had to be mine. And once I was in Genoa, it wasn't convenient for me to return home and travel back out."

"You're right," his sister says.

François sits down in an armchair opposite his brother-in-law. Louis Auguste remains standing by the door.

"Come here, you," Ignazio says with a wave.

The boy hesitates, looks at his mother, then approaches reluctantly.

"He does speak Italian, but only a little," Giuseppina says, almost apologizing for him.

"Naturally: he lives in Marseille," Ignazio replies, smiling and giving a pat to Louis Auguste, who then runs away. "You should come visit us more often."

"It's not as easy as that," François says. "I can travel, of course. But close the house and come to Palermo . . . It's not straightforward for your sister."

He says this with eyes downcast, staring at the rug, and Ignazio understands the real reason. There are too many differences by now, and it's not just a matter of having a well-furnished house or being wealthy. Their worlds are different.

Ignazio slaps his thigh. "Anyway, as I said, I'd be really glad if you came," he says to Giuseppina. "You have a home and a family expecting you." He turns to his brother-in-law. "When will the baggage be delivered? I brought presents and I'd like to give them to you."

"Oh." François fidgets in his chair. "In the afternoon, I think. But I can go and hurry things on, if you like."

"No, no need." Ignazio sits back on the couch.

Giuseppina grabs his hand and kisses it. "I'm delighted you're here." She says this softly, and in her words there's a trace of the intimate bond that connected them for years.

He nods in agreement, his eyes closed. What he doesn't say is that, after so many stressful weeks, he can breathe freely and no longer feels the tension that prevented him from falling asleep.

He can stop being Don Ignazio Florio for the time being, and simply be Ignazio.

∼

"A party?"

It was the morning after his arrival, and at breakfast Giuseppina told him she would be happy to take him along. "More of an informal gathering of merchants and representatives of the army and navy," she explained, looking over the rim of the teacup from which she was sipping. "Just for some fun and a bit of a gossip."

"After all, they're the ones who protect our trade lines and our stores abroad," François said, pouring him coffee. "It's to everyone's advantage to maintain informal relations."

"Yes, I understand. Only I wouldn't like my presence to be misunderstood. You know what it's like: I'm currently French seafaring's main competitor. People see what they want to see and

163

often see wrongly. I wouldn't wish my attendance to cause you trouble."

"Fear not. You're here unofficially. No one will say anything, and you're hardly an *ingénu*."

And so, this evening, he's in the carriage with Giuseppina and François.

His sister is wearing a pale blue dress with a trick of the drapery concealing her now heavier frame. Around her neck, there's the pearl necklace Ignazio brought her from Genoa. François looked at the gift with astonishment and even blushed once he'd seen his own gift: a gold pocket watch with his initials engraved inside.

"Tu es vraiment élégante, ma chère," Ignazio says to her, smiling. "France agrees with you."

"Yes, it's my home now," she replies, squeezing François's hand and giving him a loving look. "But you're a flatterer and a liar. I'm sure this dress wouldn't bear comparison with any of Giovanna's."

The three of them laugh, then Ignazio turns to the carriage curtain, lifts it, and pretends to be interested in the city's buildings. Giuseppina's not wrong: Giovanna takes great care of herself; she has elegant clothes and jewels. But she doesn't have an ounce of his sister's peace of mind. His wife plays a role. Giuseppina doesn't. And the bitterest thing for him is his knowledge of his own responsibility for this playacting. It was he who decided that their lives should become a performance in which the characters have ended up indistinguishable from those who play them.

The Merles' carriage slows to a halt. Other carriages are waiting ahead. Giuseppina sighs, and François squeezes her hand. Finally, an attendant in livery opens their door and helps them get down. Ignazio looks with interest at the imposing, square-based building overlooking the sea, not far from the old port of Marseille. Fort Ganteaume is a construction that suggests impeccably shiny uniforms and military rigor. And yet this evening, with torches lodged in the ground and the notes of a small orchestra tuning their instruments in the background, it seems to have lost its customary severity in favor of a frivolous costume.

"It reminds me of Castello a Mare in Palermo," Ignazio says to François.

"It was about to end the same way, believe it or not. But then people realized that it would be madness to knock it down. It's too important to the city's defenses." He taps Ignazio on the sleeve. "Come. I'll introduce you to a few officers. Never mind the merchants for now, or they'll mob you with questions about commercial charters . . ."

The courtyard has been decorated with screened chandeliers and cornucopia-shaped baskets brimming with flowers, forming cascades of leaves and petals. Attendants and waiters in livery lead the guests to the hall, from where the final sounds of tuning waft.

Ignazio spends a few minutes conversing in French with a group of officers in dress uniforms. He feels their inquisitive eyes on him. Maybe they're surprised that the new master of Italian seafaring is such an affable, polite person. Others, though, study him with evident hostility. One of them, an elderly admiral with a large handlebar mustache, scrutinizes him resentfully.

"Do you not realize the damage your merger will cause France?"

"That's right: What have you come here for?" says another officer, a prominent scar running down his cheek.

"He's come to visit his sister and nephew," François intervenes, calmly but firmly. "You know, man does not live on trade alone. And Signor Florio is my guest."

The admiral purses his lips. "To each, the misfortunes he deserves," he remarks venomously.

François smiles. "One can always do better, but I can't complain."

While everybody laughs, a waiter serves champagne. The women move beneath the arches that surround the courtyard, some pointing to the weapons room, which has been converted into a ballroom. The orchestra has finally started to play, drowning out the bustle of the guests.

François turns, locates his wife, and quickly walks over to her, followed by Ignazio. They go in, Giuseppina holding both by the arm.

"What's the matter?" she asks her brother, noticing the furrow between his eyebrows.

"Well, I certainly didn't expect to be paraded in triumph, but . . ."

Giuseppina's smile dispels his annoyance. *"Un fare u' santo fora da chiesa,"* she whispers in Sicilian dialect, with a hint of French accent that makes him laugh.

Don't act the saint outside church. It was an expression their grandmother typically used when referring to sudden mood changes she didn't like.

Large mirrors have been brought into the hall and, alternating with drapery as they are, give the impression that the room is much larger than it is. Irises, carnations, roses, and honeysuckles bunched in bronze vases decorate the corners, and there are garlands of flowers wrapped around the pillars on which oil lamps floodlight the hall.

A few couples have already taken their positions at the center of the ballroom. François lifts his wife's hand and bows. She nods, squeezes his fingers, then removes her arm from her brother's. "You will excuse us, won't you?"

Her last words are practically a breath. Her husband takes her to the middle of the room, where, with a laugh, they launch into a contredanse.

Ignazio feels a pang of envy, because what he sees in the faces of Giuseppina and François is the pure pleasure of being together. Theirs is a joyous complicity, far removed from his relationship with Giovanna. A relationship firmly determined to keep up impeccable social appearances, but without joy, abandonment, or lightness. And yet here and now he wishes she were at his side, to fill with one of her smiles the emptiness he feels inside and chase away—even if just for an evening—the sadness that shrouds his every thought.

He takes another coupe of champagne and looks around warily, aware that he's the object of everyone's curiosity. He observes the officers strapped into their dress uniforms, the merchants talking too loudly, the local ship owners glancing in his direction.

It all washes over him, nothing touches him.

And that's when it happens.

The curly hair, blond with a hint of red. The long white neck. The powder-pale pink dress. The elbow-length white gloves. The feather fan.

Ignazio suddenly feels cold. Because—in just a second—he has realized that the oblivion under which he has concealed his memories is paper-thin, that it takes only a moment to tear. And there, beneath it, is his soul: naked, exposed, fragile.

He can't hear anything anymore, except for dull, cavernous background noise. Everything's hazy.

All he can focus on are her slightly cocked head and her lips mouthing inaudible words, as though about to open into a smile—a smile that doesn't, however, materialize.

And yet she actually used to laugh with him.

And weep.

His father once told him that life's most useful rule was also its simplest: listen to your head, not your heart. Heeding passion over what your reason commanded inevitably led to errors. He meant in business, but Ignazio has applied this rule not just in his management of Casa Florio, but equally in private. Control and detachment have always been his most loyal allies, whether in closing a deal or in raising his children.

But now, for the first time perhaps, Ignazio listens to his heart, obeys his instinct for self-preservation, lets himself be transported by fear.

He must leave. Right away.

He'll say he suddenly felt unwell and chose to go home; his sister won't mind. *She mustn't see me*, he thinks; because he doesn't want to—cannot—meet her and speak to her. He retreats to the back of the room. *Let it all end this way.*

Too late.

Camille Clermont, the widow Darbon, *née* Martin, says goodbye to the woman with whom she's been speaking and turns to another guest, a matron bundled up in a burgundy outfit.

And sees him.

Her fan slips out of her hand. For a moment, the feathers flutter before landing on the floor.

She stares at him, lips parted, apparently more in fear than disbelief. Then she blushes violently, so much so that the elderly woman goes closer to her, squeezes her arm, and asks if she's feeling well. She rouses herself, bends down to pick up her fan, grips it hard, and gives an apologetic smile.

With that smile imprinted in his eyes, Ignazio turns and strides quickly to the ballroom door.

Fool, fool, fool.

How could it have failed to occur to him? Camille is married to an admiral or something. He should have remembered. He should never have come here. Naturally, after all these years, Giuseppina couldn't have known or suspected that he . . .

He's practically running. He'll go back home in the carriage, then send it back. *Yes, that's right,* he thinks, *I'll do that.*

As gently as possible, he dodges a couple of merchants trying to involve him in conversation, then stops a waiter and asks him to take a message to the Merles, telling them not to rush back home.

He reaches the portico, panting as though he's been sprinting, then walks across the courtyard.

He's fleeing. He, Ignazio Florio, the most powerful man in the Mediterranean. He who has never trembled before anyone. He keeps telling himself that he's doing the most logical, rational thing, because a war with memory is a war that ends only in defeat. Allowing this ghost to take shape would mean a disruption of the reality he has painstakingly built in his own image. It would mean erasing everything he has valued.

"Ignazio!"

He stops.

I mustn't turn.

Footsteps.

I mustn't see her.

He shuts his eyes. It's her voice.

"Ignazio."

The swish of fabric on the cobblestones.

She's here now, before him.

Her face is gaunter. There are small lines around her blue eyes. Her lips, once full, seem thinner, and there are threads of silver in her blond hair. But her expression—lively, intense, intelligent—is unaltered.

"Camille."

She opens her mouth to speak but closes it again.

"I didn't know you were here."

She says nothing, lifts her gloved hand, lets her fingers hover in midair for a few seconds, then lowers her hand and squeezes her fan to her chest until the feathers creak. "You're looking well," she finally murmurs.

"Well?" he replies, opening his arms and smiling bitterly. "I've grown old, I've put on weight. Whereas you . . . you're just like you were."

She cocks her head, and a smile appears on her lips, a smile Ignazio remembers so well it hurts him. "Liar. I've grown old, too." Only she says it indulgently, as though the passing of time were a gift to accept with gratitude. She takes a step forward. The hem of her dress brushes against the tips of her shoes. "I've been following you from a distance, you know? I've been reading the papers . . . And naturally, I talk about you to Giuseppina." She pauses. "I heard about your son. *Toutes mes condoléances.*"

The thought of Vincenzino is a blow.

He has a family, a wife. Why is he speaking to this woman after more than twenty years?

Because I've loved her above everything else in the world.

Ignazio takes a step back, but in doing so, he smells Camille's perfume, that aroma of fresh, persistent carnation that he's always associated with her.

Everything starts spinning, like a free fall into the past.

"Camille? What's the matter?" The matron in burgundy appears in the portico. She looks at them both, puzzled, then approaches gingerly. "I was worried you might be unwell. I couldn't find you anywhere . . ."

Camille shakes her head, blushes, and quickly moves her hands. The feathers in her fan flutter nervously.

He knows she's looking for an excuse. Strange how he still knows her gestures.

"I saw this old friend of mine and we started talking," Camille finally says with a faint smile. "Madame Brun, allow me to present Monsieur Florio, my friend Giuseppina Merle's brother. Madame Brun is the wife of Admiral Brun, a comrade-in-arms of my husband's."

Ignazio bows and kisses the woman's hand.

This old friend of mine.

The woman points to the ballroom. "Shall we go back in? *Il fait tellement froid . . .*"

Only now does Ignazio notice that Camille is shivering. He instinctively offers her his arm.

"Yes," he replies confidently. "Let's go back in."

It's Camille who hesitates now, but then her fingers slide over Ignazio's sleeve and curl around it. As though they've found their rightful, their natural place.

They walk into the ballroom side by side. It's very warm and the air is stuffy with the smell of sweat, along with the scent of flowers and the guests' eau de cologne.

The small orchestra strikes up a waltz.

Ignazio squeezes Camille's wrist and looks at her.

In the sparkle of her eyes, he finds something he's forgotten: the need to feel alive, as well as the serenity of not having to prove anything to anyone.

"Come."

"But—"

"Come." Ignazio's tone allows no contradiction. It's the voice of a man used to commanding.

Fascinated and confused, Camille follows him, eyes downcast.

Ignazio's hold is confident. He spreads one hand over Camille's back and with the other holds up her hand. Their bodies keep the conventional distance.

She smiles faintly. "On second thoughts, you've changed," she murmurs. "Years ago, you'd never have had such courage."

"I was barely older than a boy." *And I was in awe*, he wants to add.

"You didn't have all the responsibilities you have now. You've had a full life. Many rewards. A good marriage." She pauses as he twirls her then puts his arm around her waist. Their bodies recognize each other and communicate.

She lowers her head. "But you've also had truly difficult moments, *n'est-ce-pas*? And I didn't . . . The only thing I could do was write to you, but I didn't have the courage to do so when your son . . ."

A thought crosses Ignazio's mind. Giovanna. Their row.

Anger squeezes his diaphragm and almost makes him stumble.

"Yes, I received your notes. They were of great comfort to me."

Ignazio feels that his defenses are weak, that the past is overtaking the present. Every single sentence, every instant, every drop of feeling he shared with this woman is resurfacing with an impetus that could destroy everything.

Another twirl. He takes her back in his arms, but this time holds her closer. Now their bodies touch.

"Ignazio." Camile tries to stand back, but he stops her, his eyes closed tight as though he were in pain, and he might well be—she can feel it because she seems to be experiencing the same tension, the same fear.

His breath caresses her ear. "Don't speak."

Through the barrier of clothes, a rivulet of sweat forms between his shoulder blades and slides down his back.

The waltz reaches its final bars. They spin faster and faster, closer and closer, and at the end, Camille throws her head back, her dress whirling around her legs. Her eyes are closed, and her face expresses an abandonment he remembers as typical of other moments, and which makes him quiver.

A tear, first caught up in her eyelashes, runs down her cheek. Nobody can see it. Nobody except him.

The music ends.

They finish up in the midst of the crowd, in a tight embrace.

Then the bustle of the ballroom. Reality.

They abruptly step back from each other. But their eyes stay together, unable to part.

Ignazio rouses himself first. "Come. I'll take you back to Madame Brun."

He takes his leave with a formal kiss on the hands of both women, then walks away.

Camille can't stop looking at him.

How different Marseille is from Palermo, Ignazio thinks. He's quickly gotten accustomed to the dust and chaos and started to appreciate the city's modernity, richness, and vitality. There's a blend of ethnicities, voices, and languages, a blend that forms and unravels, spreading over streets and alleys, transforming the port and the surrounding area into a crucible of faces and smells. "The city has changed a lot over the years," he says.

François nods. "The money from the colonies and the desire to renovate have revolutionized the port. There's talk of enlarging it further, even after the new bays are built." He sighs. "This city has what Palermo lacks."

"The desire and energy to change," Ignazio says, nodding in return.

The Marseille Stock Exchange is imposing, with large pillars and a façade that suggests a Greek temple, situated near the Canebière, the city's biggest trading street.

Everything is in order in the company's office. Someone must have seen him at the party the night before, because the offices are spotless and all the employees are present and correct. Ignazio speaks to them, meets the manager, and briefly outlines the impending changes to their lines now that Florio and Rubattino are one and the same.

But a part of his thoughts is trapped in the memory of what happened yesterday.

As he discusses new itineraries the office will have to manage—there are going to be lines from Marseille to America—his brother-in-law comes up to him. "I must go: one of my men has just come to tell me there are problems at customs. They're claiming there are some transportation taxes we haven't paid."

"Things like that happen all over the world. Constant red tape." Ignazio squeezes his arm. "Go ahead."

François rolls his eyes. "Luckily, I don't have far to go. I'll leave you the carriage, so you can go home if you like."

"I'll send it back to you as soon as I've finished."

"Please do. This promises to be a day full of problems."

Ignazio watches him walk away nervously, then stays to talk to the employees and ask their names. He has cakes and liqueurs brought from a neighboring *pâtisserie*. He knows that people are more loquacious and carefree over food. And he listens to them.

By the time he leaves the office, amid warm goodbyes and wide smiles, it's shortly after noon.

As soon as the doors close behind him, he realizes that—for the first time in ages—he has no other commitments for the rest of the day. He feels disconcerted, almost confused. Around him, there's a to-ing and fro-ing of bicycles, horses, carriages, men in bowler hats, maids with shopping baskets, elegant women with parasols. Everybody seems to have something to do, somewhere to be . . .

What about me? Ignazio wonders. *Where can I go?* He remembers François eulogizing Café Turc, on the Canebière, with its large fountain and mirrors that reflect the patrons. Or else he could take a walk to the harbor . . .

Or I could go to see her.

"No," he murmurs, shaking his head. "Let's not do anything stupid." He takes a few steps forward, stops, then turns back, lifting a hand to his mouth.

A passerby gives him a puzzled look.

Enough, he thinks.

He walks to the carriage waiting for him, asks to be driven home, and sits with his fingers intertwined, his eyes looking at the city without seeing it. No strange ideas: Giuseppina will be happy to spend a whole afternoon with him, he tells himself.

But no sooner is he out of the carriage than he asks the coachman if he knows where Madame Louise Brun and Madame Camille Clermont live, then inquires whether Madame Merle has a trusted florist, implying that he wishes to send the two women flowers. The coachman—slim, with deep scars on his face—replies that yes, of course, he knows where the two ladies live, since they're friends of

Madame Merle. And, after giving Ignazio the address, he tells him there's a florist next door, one of the largest in Marseille . . . perhaps he wishes to be driven there?

Ignazio shakes his head—no, he'll walk—and thanks him with a coin.

The carriage sets off to pick up François. For a moment, the wheels echo on the cobblestones.

Ignazio looks up at the balcony of Giuseppina's house. The shutters are closed, perhaps against the sun. There's no one at the windows.

He puts a hand on the front door and reaches for the bell. Then he pulls it back.

He walks away.

ᴐ

He doesn't know the city well, but he's capable of finding his way back to the Canebière. There, he gets into a carriage and gives the coachman Camille's address.

The Clermont home is on a quiet little street not far from Fort Ganteaume, in a district of white two- or three-story buildings that gleam in the sun. From the large number of men in uniform and flags peeping out of windows, Ignazio realizes it's an area where military men and their families must live.

He gets out of the carriage, which clatters away.

He approaches the door. Part of him is hoping that Camille isn't at home. Another part is clamoring for her to be in. For the second time in two days, he's breaking his father's rule: heed your head, not your heart.

He knocks on the door, takes a step back, and waits.

I can still go away, he thinks, but an elderly maid in a gray uniform opens the door.

"Is Madame Clermont at home?" Ignazio asks, removing his hat.

A female voice travels from the upper floor. Cheerful, like the sound of laughter in her throat. Then footsteps on the stairs.

"Que se passe-t-il, Agnès?"

Camille appears on the bottom steps. She's wearing a housedress, hair partly down on her shoulders, a sign that she was finishing combing her hair.

Her smile freezes as soon as she sees him, then slowly fades.

He lowers his eyes to the doorstep, where a dog carved in marble looks about to bite his ankles. *"Pardonne-moi d'être venu sans te prévenir,"* he says.

His voice is soft, almost fearful. She shakes her head and puts a hand to her lips.

The maid looks at them both, puzzled.

Ignazio takes a step back. "Forgive me," he stammers, embarrassed. "I see you're busy. I wish you a good day." He turns and puts his hat back on.

But Camille runs and stops him. "Wait!" She puts a hand on his arm and holds him back. "You took me by surprise . . . Come in—please."

The maid stands aside to let him in. Camille says something softly and the woman quickly leaves.

"Come. Let's go into the drawing room."

It's a bright room, furnished with dark velvet couches and prints with still lifes and seascapes. There are also exotic objects, evidently brought back by the master of the house from his trips: a chiseled ivory fang, an Egyptian statuette, Arab-made wooden and mother-of-pearl and wrought-brass boxes. Ignazio pauses to look at them.

The maid comes in carrying a tray with two cups of coffee and a plate of biscuits, which she puts down on a mahogany table.

"Merci, Agnès," Camille says. "Now do go home to your daughter. I'll expect you back later."

The woman takes her leave with a bow. Camille turns to Ignazio. "Her daughter had a baby last night and she must go to help her. It sounds like it was a difficult labor." A shadow falls over her face, a veil of grayness and bitterness. "The poor young woman is on her own. Her husband is at sea and heaven knows when he'll be back." She pauses. "He's with my husband aboard the *Algésiras . . .*" She sits down, pours the coffee, and takes a spoonful of sugar from the bowl for herself. She looks up. "Two, right?"

Standing by the window, Ignazio nods.

Finally, he sits down opposite her and looks at her. In the light filtering through the curtains, Camille's hair fills with flecks of red.

They drink in silence, not looking at each other.

Camille puts her cup back on the saucer and looks up. "Why have you come?"

Ignazio is thrown by the unfamiliar harshness in her tone. A sharpness that alarms him. *She's defending herself,* he thinks. *From me? From the past?*

"So that I could talk to you," he admits. It's easy to be honest with Camille, since it was she who introduced him to that side of himself. And there was a time when he would also have been able to read into her soul without difficulty because she was always clear and sincere toward him.

And now?

They said farewell after Ignazio had confessed to her that he lacked the courage to change the course of his life because he had to measure up to his father's expectations. He was the heir of Casa

Florio and nobody could alter his fate. A "socially appropriate" marriage would be the simple, inevitable consequence of that choice.
Heed your head, not your heart.

After that farewell, Ignazio refused for a long time to open her
letters or ask after her. Like invisible weights, success in business,
power, and wealth had dragged to the depths of his soul his sorrow, his shame at misleading the woman he loved, his regret for
a different life. Every now and then, his memories would surface,
and he was almost grateful for the pain they caused. It would bring
together the sweetness of a never quite deadened feeling and the
subtle delight of keeping a secret: those memories—that life never
lived—were his alone.

But what about Camille? What happened to her?

He knows nothing. He's chosen to know nothing. She's carried on in spite of everything, but has she been happy? Has she
lived or only let herself live? He's had his work—both burden and
blessing—but what about her?

"I know perfectly well that I shouldn't have come, and that I'm
exposing you to gossip. But today—"

"What about today?" She puts her cup and saucer on the tray,
then looks into his eyes. "What do you *want* from me, Ignazio?"

The picture of Camille weeping as he walked away is erased by
this fierce expression and sharp tone. Words trip on his tongue.
Behind the recrimination, there's something that puts Ignazio's
instinct on the alert. Resentment, yes. *But maybe also desire?* He
suddenly realizes that he can no longer read her, that the woman
before him is very different than the one who begged him not to
leave. A change that isn't solely the result of time passing.

Some errors cannot be forgiven. Doors of the past are closed and
walled up.

Ignazio finally struggles to speak, because only now does he realize his true motive in coming to see her. "I came today because I'd like . . . I'd like to apologize for what happened because of me . . . years ago."

"Through your *fault*," she says, correcting him. The blue of her eyes grows darker. "The cause lies elsewhere. The *fault* is yours."

Ignazio puts his cup and saucer on the tray and a drop of coffee spills over, staining the saucer.

"A fault or a cause—what's the difference?" he hisses, stung to the quick. "I could have chosen differently, that's true, but I had, and have, responsibilities. Toward my father back then, toward my family now."

Camille stands up and goes to the window. She crosses her hands over her chest. "You know, last night I understood something." She speaks in fits and starts, her syllables sliding over one another. "Power is what you've wanted above anything else, Ignazio. Power and social recognition. You didn't choose between your family's happiness and ours: you chose yourself." Her voice cracks, and she brushes a lock of hair from her forehead. "I watched you: the confidence of your gestures, the way you spoke . . . And I understood: the young man from back then corresponds exactly to the man you've become. Silly me for having thought the opposite. For having believed, then, that you needed me, in order to be loved for what you were and not for what you represented. You've never needed anything except Casa Florio."

Ignazio feels a twinge, the echo of a loss, under his breastbone. *Not her*, he thinks. *She can't tell me this.*

He shakes his head, slowly at first, then angrily. "Damn it, it's not true. No!" He leaps to his feet and seizes her arms. He wants to shake her but restrains himself because she looks frightened now.

He lets go of her and starts pacing around the room, running his fingers through his hair. "I had to act the way I did because I didn't have a choice. I couldn't do otherwise. Do you know what I am? What I represent in Sicily, in Italy, and for my people? Do you know what the Florio name means? My father created our Casa Florio, but I made it great."

She allows him his outburst, then goes up to him, lifts his hand, and places it on her cheek. There is sorrow in her face, such deep regret that Ignazio's fury is instantly quashed. "You decided not to choose. But at what cost, *mon aimé*?"

At what cost.

All of a sudden, as though he were drowning, his life flashes before him.

His father taking him to the office. The Oretea workers listening to him. The first time he saw Giovanna: not beautiful, not wealthy, but intelligent, willing, and, above all, aristocratic, exactly as he and his father wanted. His children, growing up in a house worthy of a king. His political influence, the ministers boasting about being his friends, the painters and artists who gravitate around the Olivuzza.

Ships. Money. Power.

But right now, there's darkness around him. Beyond the light of the crystal chandeliers and the gleam of silver, Ignazio sees nothing except his deformed image, as though the solitude penetrating him has come from outside. He knows he possesses nothing except money, objects, and people.

Possessing. Without anything truly belonging to him. Except for her memory.

Camille grabs his hands and interlaces her fingers with his. "There's nothing else to say, Ignazio. I'm glad you're in good health.

Rich and powerful, as you always wanted. But there's nothing left of us now."

Ignazio looks down at their joined hands. "No, there is. The thought of you." His voice is hoarse. "I've been able to carry on partly thanks to you . . . and the memory of you. The memory of us." He lifts his head and searches for her eyes. He's defenseless now. "I thought it would be enough for a lifetime, but that's not the case. Forgive me for having caused you so much pain. Last night, you saw the man I've become. Now, I see the woman you are and have always been: strong and brave. Capable of forgiving me."

"I can't forgive you."

"Why not?"

She gives him a frosty look. "You know very well why it's not possible."

Ignazio stares at her, unable to respond. He's sentenced both of them to solitude. He has cloaked his own in gold and prestige. But she? Again, that anguish-filled question, that sense of guilt that for the time being encounters no ties or barriers.

"You . . ." he finally manages to say. "How did you manage to continue?"

Camille seizes his hands again and smiles bitterly. "Like a survivor. After what happened, after months of convalescence, I no longer had the possibility of recovering fully. When I met Maurice, my husband, two years later, I was already only half a woman."

Ignazio takes a step back. *Convalescence?*

He asks her, softly, his hands refusing to leave hers. He's trembling inside because he doesn't know and doesn't understand. It's an unfamiliar state of mind.

Camille cocks her head, and all the years that have gone by appear on her face. "After I lost the child," she says in one breath.

"The—the child?" Ignazio drops his hands. It's as if he's been slapped. "You were . . ."

Camille sits back down. She's turned pale and covers her face with her hands. "I wrote to you, told you everything. You never replied to me. At first, I thought you didn't want to, then I wondered if someone, perhaps your father, had intercepted my letters."

The letters.

The letters, damn it, the ones he didn't have the courage to open because he didn't want to feel any more sorrow, because he didn't want to hear her accusations, because it was over so what was the point of crying about it? It was rebelling against something one couldn't change, right?

His legs fail him. He must sit. The memory of them together, of their bodies in an embrace, of her loving smile, is turned to ashes by this piece of news. He could have had a child with her, he could have . . .

"I realized I was pregnant a few days before I lost it. I'd barely had time to register it before it was all over. I don't know why it happened. Maybe it was the grief, maybe destiny, who knows? When the bleeding started, I was in Provence, a long way from the city, so I could do nothing to stop it. Far from it . . ." She speaks softly, without looking at him. Her mouth lifts in a grimace that is like a bitter smile. "I was lucky to survive." She stands up and goes to him. "Later, I was told that another pregnancy would be fatal to me. That's what you've done to me, Ignazio."

Ignazio doesn't have the courage to look up.

She lifts his face, two fingers under his chin, the way she used to, before she would lean down to kiss him. "You've taken everything from me."

"I didn't know . . . I couldn't have. I . . ." He gasps for air, struggling to breathe. He vaguely smells the coffee, turned cold in the cups, and her perfume. He suddenly finds both smells nauseating. "I didn't want to think about what had happened between us, and I never opened your letters. I kept them, of course, but never opened them. For me, too, leaving you was painful." *But my pain is so insignificant, so tiny, now. My apologies are so pointless . . .*

She shakes her head. A veil of indulgence seems to soften her features, but immediately afterward Ignazio realizes it's bitterness. Disappointment.

"It doesn't matter anymore. Even if you'd known what had happened, I doubt you would have come back. Your confession confirms what I realized a long time ago." She takes a step back. "You're a coward."

Ignazio is stunned. He buries his head in his hands.

Nothing. Nothing exists of what he's preserved in his memory. His secret life, imagined, dreamed, longed for, is a heap of charred bones, ruins on which quicklime has been thrown.

Powerless, defeated, devastated by a sense of guilt. That's how he feels when he lifts his head and stands up, his stomach tight with nausea, pain in his chest. The room seems to have lost light and color, and even Camille seems to have suddenly aged.

He wants to tell her that he's loved her the way you can love impossible dreams. He wants to salvage something of his illusion.

"Forgive me. I didn't—"

She stops him, puts a finger on his lips, then strokes his face with a gentleness that's at once intimate and fierce. "You. That's right. It's always and only you." She pulls her hand away, retreats, and shows him the door. "Get out, Ignazio."

Ignazio can't say how long he walks after leaving Camille's house. He knows only that, all of a sudden, he finds himself faced with a forest of masts and funnels, gathered sails, carts laden with goods.

It's the old port.

He looks around, as though he's just woken up. He searches for his father's beaten-gold ring under his wedding band and thinks about all it represents and what it's meant to him. He feels the impulse to get rid of it, to throw it into the sea, far away, not to feel that weight on his finger anymore. To give up everything.

But he remains motionless. It's a piece of his family's history. Like the wedding band, it's a mark of his choice.

He heads to François and Giuseppina's house. Enough. He must leave and go back to Palermo.

He is Ignazio Florio, he tells himself, but he cannot change the past or change his own destiny. Not even gods have that power. He made a mistake, he was defeated, and now he's paying it back with interest.

He doesn't think about Giovanna or his children.

He could have had another child, another life, another destiny.

And with these thoughts he reaches the Merles' home.

He climbs the stairs two at a time and knocks on the door. Giuseppina opens it, kisses him, then frowns. "You're back late. Is everything all right on Place de la Bourse?"

The events of a few hours ago seem far away. "Yes, yes," he replies laconically. "Is François back home? I know he had a spot of bother . . ."

His sister shakes her head as if to say: Nothing of importance, then looks at him. Ignazio is deeply troubled. She wants to ask him why but doesn't. She asks him to follow her and hopes he'll take the initiative and tell her. Ignazio goes with her into the small drawing room. She looks through some letters lying on the table, and hands him a few. "These arrived from Palermo today, along with a telegram from Laganà."

Ignazio takes them.

There are two letters in particular: one from Giovanna, the other from Giulia.

He lets himself sink into the armchair and opens them.

His wife has written to him about the home and their children. She says Ignazziddu is behaving well, has become more responsible, and that they've spent some time in Villa ai Colli, where the air is cooler, and had Antonino Leto staying with them. Almeyda and his wife also came to visit them. It's a quiet period, but the house feels empty without him. *I hope you come back soon*, Giovanna concludes. She uses her usual modesty, that form of detachment that conceals her feelings and the love she still offers him without expecting anything in return.

Ignazio feels a tightness in his throat.

Then comes the letter from Giulia. His *stidduzza*.

In tentative, tender handwriting, his daughter writes that she wanted to show him how good she's become at drawing; on the back of the page, there's a pencil sketch of one of the Olivuzza poodles. She adds that her mother and Donna Ciccia are trying to teach her embroidery, but without much success. She prefers to watch Antonino Leto and follows him when he paints in the gardens. Then she says that her mother misses him. *And I can't wait for you to be back.*

It's the letter from a little girl to a father she adores and hasn't seen for weeks.

There's a silent cataclysm inside him.

He senses the weight of his sister's eyes on him. "Good news from Palermo?" she asks.

He swallows air and nods. Then he shakes his head, as though waking from a dream. "Next week, I'll take the steamer home," he announces. "I've been away too long. My family needs me."

Giuseppina sighs, her lips tight. "And so it must be."

PART THREE

The Olive Tree

December 1883 to November 1891

Cu di cori ama, di luntano vidi.
Whoever truly loves, looks far into the distance.
—SICILIAN PROVERB

FOR THE EGYPTIANS, IT WAS a gift from the goddess Isis. For the Hebrews, a symbol of rebirth. For the Greeks, it was sacred to Athena, the goddess of wisdom. For the Romans, the tree under which Romulus and Remus were born.

The olive tree has a gnarled trunk, silver-green leaves that gleam in the sun, and a strong scent. Its warm, golden wood is parasite-proof and suitable for inlays and carving: wood for furniture destined to last, to be bequeathed as trousseaux and memories.

And not only that.

Try setting fire to an olive tree or cutting its trunk. It will take a long time—sometimes years—but, sooner or later, a determined, angry offshoot will spring from the ground and bring the injured tree back to life.

To destroy an olive tree, you need to uproot it, dig the soil until there is nothing left of the roots.

That is why the olive tree is also a symbol of immortality.

Together with citrus trees, olive trees are the most common trees in the Sicilian countryside. There's no garden or vegetable patch without one. Some specimens were little more than bushes in 827, when the Arabs conquered Sicily; they were still there when the Normans arrived, in the summer of 1083; and in 1282, when the Sicilian Vespers revolt against the Angevins broke out; and in 1516, when the Spanish arrived; and they were still standing in 1860, when Garibaldi disembarked on the island . . .

Ancient, humble, monumental, sacred creatures.

There is still a single olive tree outside one of the entrances to

Villa Florio all'Olivuzza. It seems left to its own devices, trapped in a basin of concrete that humiliates it, with wild branches pushing toward a residents' parking garage.

The last, silent witness of a wonderful, terrible story.

࿇

In December 1883, Ignazio meets with Abele Damiani in the corridors of the Senate. Originally from Marsala, an ex-Garibaldi supporter and now a deputy, Damiani is a man of his time in every way, from his large handlebar mustache to his bushy eyebrows.

"Senator! Can I call you that?"

Ignazio opens his arms and bursts out laughing. "You have the ability to."

The marble floor mirrors their embrace, and the wall tapestries trap their laughter.

"You can call me whatever you like, Damiani."

"In that case, Don Ignazio. Even though we're on the mainland," Damiani replies, opening his hands. "In the heart of the Kingdom of Italy, in fact," he adds, laughing again.

Palazzo Madama once belonged to the Medici family, and since 1871 has been the home of the kingdom's Upper Chamber, despite Crispi's numerous requests to bring the two branches of the Parliament under the same roof in order to cut costs. The decision was taken by a commission, which, after exhaustive discussions, agreed on a building with the same name as the one that hosted it in Turin, the first home of the kingdom's Senate. Nothing else has changed since then, however: it's not senators elected by the people who sit in the high-backed chairs of Palazzo Madama, but princes of the House of Savoy as soon as they turn twenty-one, as well as men appointed for life by the king once they have reached the age of forty and belong to one of the twenty categories listed in Article 33 of the *Statuto Albertino*: ministers and ambassadors, "land and sea" officers, government lawyers and magistrates. And not just them, but also "persons who for the past three years have paid three thousand lire in direct tax owing to their property or industry."

Like Ignazio Florio.

Damiani takes a step back, looks at him, and opens his arms. "Seriously, Don Ignazio, felicitations. At last, a man who knows about this country's economy."

Ignazio is about to turn forty-five. As usual, his expression oozes a calm apparently impossible to dent.

"Where are you going? If I may ask, that is . . ." Damiani drops his voice and toys with the gold chain of his watch.

Employees and errand boys who pay little attention to them parade past. By now, the Sicilian contingent at Palazzo Madama is substantial, and no one is surprised to hear them speak in their rounded dialect any longer.

Ignazio lifts his chin toward the rooms at the end of the corridor. "To see Crispi."

"I've just been there and will gladly walk with you." They speak in hushed tones and take measured steps. "He's infuriated by this Magliani issue and is angry with Depretis for choosing him as finance minister. He looks like he has a stick up his ass. Trust me, Magliani won't even send the papers to Parliament, let alone explain the accounts."

"Depretis didn't choose him at random," Ignazio whispers. "The man's dangerous."

Damiani stops outside a door and knocks. "They're all sharks here, Don Ignazio."

"Enter!" intones an irritable, stentorian voice. Ignazio goes in, followed by Damiani.

Crispi is behind the desk, engrossed in a document, and doesn't look up. In the cold December light, his mustache seems grayer and sparser than Ignazio remembers it. He is surrounded by open portfolios and dossiers, a chaos of pencils, pens dripping with ink, and drafts of letters, some scrunched up. In front of him, a skinny young man with a curly goatee and metal-framed glasses is hunched over, listening and taking notes.

"We don't want these people to get any strange ideas," Crispi grumbles. "They must present the financial reports before coming to the chamber. The last thing we need is—"

"*Avvocato* Crispi! It's always a pleasure to see you so combative."

Startled, Crispi abruptly stands up. "Don Ignazio! Here already?"

Ignazio approaches as the secretary respectfully withdraws. There are handshakes and softly uttered sentences. Ignazio learned this very early on: that even here the walls have ears and hear what they want to hear.

Damiani lingers next to the two men, observing the unraveling of niceties. He understands. "Very well. Now I've said hello to you both, I'll take my leave," he says with a little smile. "Don Ignazio, I'm always at your disposal." He exits but leaves the door behind him open. A tacit invitation, which the secretary doesn't appear to pick up on, or perhaps he's expecting a sign from Crispi. The latter darts him an angry look.

"We'll continue later, Fabrizio," Crispi says, standing aside to let him through.

The young man puts his notes into a leather portfolio. "Would you like a liqueur, Senator?"

"No, thank you."

Now the door is closed and Francesco Crispi and Ignazio Florio are alone. For a moment, Ignazio sees the man he knew in Palermo, shortly after Garibaldi's supporters arrived in Sicily, and doesn't find him very altered. And yet he's come a very long way since then: a deputy, president of the chamber, minister of the interior, a familiar and respected figure in London, Paris, and Berlin . . . And, for all that, still Casa Florio's lawyer.

He met him when he was a fighter. Now he's a statesman.

Maybe he's always been both.

Crispi motions Ignazio to a seat, sits down in the leather chair opposite him, and silently offers him a cigar. "So, *Senator*?" he asks, a faint smile in his eyes.

Ignazio lets the cigar smoke spread in his throat, then blows it out. He replies in the same tone, only looking down slightly. "You were the one to make sure this happened. Thank you."

Crispi takes a puff, then crosses his hands on his lap. "Apart from the fact that it was your wish, it was crazy that a man like yourself hadn't been made a senator. With all the enterprises you have and the taxes you pay—"

"I'm not the kind of industrialist Depretis likes, you know that. Just read *La Perseveranza* and you'll see."

"That's the Lombard industrialists' paper, Don Ignazio. It's understandably against financial support for seafaring and southern enterprises. You must take into account what your friends do for you."

"Oh, but I do." Ignazio remembers articles in Roman papers such as *L'Opinione* and *La Riforma*. The latter in particular, which is close to Crispi, supported his requests for subsidies for new shipping lines to the Far East. "But the situation is still difficult." He pauses and pinches his lips with his fingers. "Nowadays, more politics is done in the pages of newspapers than here. All it takes is a tiny rustle for cats and dogs to flock."

This time it's Crispi who looks at him sideways. "Although there's a reason for this particular rustle. In other words, there are good reasons for these complaints."

Ignazio's fingers stop. His mouth spreads in a sarcastic smile. "You as well, *avvocato*? Is it about the ships being old or the charters too expensive? Which is it?"

"Both. Because of my respect for you and your family, I can be direct: some of your Navigazione Generale Italiana ships are real pieces of junk, and the tariffs are too high. You have to make changes."

Ignazio softly beats his fist on the armrest. "Then hurry up and bring the bill for shipyard subsidies into the chamber, so that we can build brand-new ships in the Livorno yards. NGI can't make it on its own. You know what happened at the partners' assembly this year. Laganà gave you the details, didn't he?"

"Of course."

"So then you know why I'm asking this."

Navigazione Generale Italiana's—or NGI's—board of directors is going through a difficult period. The number of charters has dropped drastically, since other foreign companies cover the same routes at lower prices or with sturdier, more comfortable, and better-equipped ships. The coal for the furnaces cuts heavily into the cost of transportation, and duty on the goods does the rest.

Crispi smooths his mustache and looks at Ignazio, waiting for him to finish what he's saying.

"This year, the only dividends will be those linked to interest, and the company can't afford it. We'll be lucky if we don't experience a collapse in shares. But in order to build new ships, we need money that NGI doesn't currently have." The furrows on Ignazio's forehead grow even deeper.

"Funerals are for the dead. Let's think about what can be done today." Crispi points his cigar at him. "You're here now, Don Ignazio, and that means you'll have the possibility of speaking directly to whoever may turn out to be useful to you."

"I was already doing that earlier."

"It's not the same thing. Now they must listen to you because you're here and you're like them. You don't need intermediaries anymore."

"That's why I asked you to take an interest in my nomination." Ignazio stands up and starts pacing around the room. He abandons his cigar in the ashtray. "Casa Florio has many friends. I have many friends. But what's here goes beyond friendship."

Crispi knows that; he nods.

Power. Connections. Relationships.

"You've reached a place your father never even thought of getting to."

Ignazio knows that his father would have been more brutal, more direct. He's had to learn on his own how to be diplomatic, how to take advantage of subtle opportunities by granting favors and forming alliances without displeasing anyone. And he's learned it well. "I know." He shifts his attention to Crispi, who's sitting cross-legged, watching him. "But the world has changed since then. One has to be much more wary now."

In the timber- and leather-clad room, Crispi's voice is a murmur. "Nowadays, politics belongs to those willing to change, those who pay attention . . . and are flexible. Never mind if that means betraying your friends and changing political allegiances." His expression turns sharp. "You know Depretis, right?"

"'If someone wants to join your ranks, change, and become progressive, who am I to turn them away?' It's his obsession. He's been saying it for years. And he acted as soon as he found a favorable opportunity." Ignazio gives a crooked smile. "One certainly can't accuse him of inconstancy. Or pragmatism."

"No." Crispi stands up with an impatient sigh and smooths his waistcoat. "I must hand it to him: he behaves like a scoundrel but knows what he's doing. He's a rogue and a bastard, let's tell it like it is. First, he schemed so that the industrialists from the north would enter the Senate, then he realized that, in order to do what he wanted, he had to get the largest possible majority and started looking around. With that argument, he dismantled all of Parliament's formations. And now anyone who wants to change flag can do so and feels justified."

Ignazio leans against the wall, beneath a large print of Italy. "You admire him," he says with a hint of wonder, crossing his arms.

"I admire his political acumen, not him. That's different." Crispi looks at the curtained window. "He legitimized a practice that had been going on for years and took away the stigma. In a way, he put an end to the hypocrisy that reigns in this building. There's no more right or left; there's buccaneering and power games." His expression is like iron striking on stone. "And you, Don Ignazio, must be wary and know who you bond with."

Ignazio glances at the papers cluttering the desk. "I will bond with only one party. Mine." When he looks up, his eyes are like dark mirrors. "Besides, Sicily is a world apart, *Avvocato* Crispi. Here in Rome politicians can do as they please, but Sicilians will always make up their own minds and often do foolish things because they seem incapable of seeing who can do good for them. And nothing and no one can force them to do anything . . . until they choose to."

"And you are between Sicily and the world."

"That's right." Ignazio gives a strange, faint smile, a mixture of resignation and amusement. "My Oretea men know nothing about America, and yet they repair boilers for steamships that will shuttle their relatives or perhaps even their brothers there. The foundry doesn't have a specialized product, like the factories in the north; it makes all sorts of things. I send goods and allow people to travel from Jakarta to New York, my ships land in at least seventy different ports, I sell sulfur to the French, present my marsala wine at international exhibitions . . . but my residence is in Palermo."

"And in Palermo you will stay." Crispi sits back down at his desk and casually closes a few portfolios that have drawn Ignazio's attention. "I've heard your daughter, Giulia, has become engaged to Prince Pietro Lanza di Trabia. Congratulations. The Lanza di Trabias are one of the oldest and most illustrious families in the whole of Italy."

It's the furrow on Ignazio's brow, rather than his silence, that betrays his anxiety. Crispi notices but says nothing. He waits.

"That's another reason I came to see you." Ignazio sits back down and crosses his legs. "I'd like you to handle my daughter's marriage agreements. In total secrecy and informally, of course."

It's Crispi's turn to be puzzled. "What do you mean?"

"I mean she'll have an appropriate dowry, but that the marriage won't take place for another couple of years, since Giulia is only thirteen and my wife, Giovanna, is preparing her to be the wife of a prince. I want to use this time to give her economic security that would be hers alone. I wish her to manage money and property." He searches for the right words. "There's nothing sadder than being imprisoned in an unhappy marriage."

Ignazio hesitates, then decides to stop. Touching on this subject with Crispi is tactless, even though many years have passed since the scandal that swept over him. Yes, even the feared Francesco Crispi was once the object of a scandal, an embarrassing business involving a woman, which forced him to defend himself in court and caused him quite a few humiliations. True, the trial on the charge of bigamy concluded with his acquittal: his first marriage, to Rose Montmasson, was declared null and void because the priest had been suspended *a divinis*, so Crispi's subsequent marriage to the Lecce-born Lina Barbagallo—with whom Crispi had already had a daughter—was perfectly valid. But the memory of forced resignation, the uproar in Parliament, the gossip, the newspaper headlines, Queen Margherita refusing to shake his hand, cannot be erased, and Ignazio knows that. This is partly because, as far as his numerous opponents were concerned, that ridiculous affair revealed the truth: that Crispi was an unscrupulous man. In his private as well as his public life.

Crispi bites his lower lip and swears under his breath. "Of all the traps a man can fall into, marriage is the worst."

Ignazio responds with an expressionless look. His impulse is to reply, *I also know this only too well*, but he restrains himself. In the eyes of the world, he is an exemplary father and husband, and such he must remain. Moreover, he is a happy and proud father and husband. He chose to wear this mask many years ago, and now it's fused to his identity, something he can't and won't give up.

He hasn't had any news of Camille for two years. Her memory has sunk even deeper and throbs painfully. Regret drowning in a lake of bitterness. There are many ways to survive sorrow, and he's tried them all while searching for some peace. In the end, he's discovered that the hardest, but also most effective, thing is to forget having loved.

He clears his voice and resumes: "You know, I don't want my daughter to encounter difficulties if she were to decide to live away from her husband, as happens with many couples. The prestige of her marriage is not enough to shield her from potential . . . unpleasantness that may occur after a few years, and I don't want her to be forced to be beholden to anyone. Above all, you're well aware of the reputation of the Lanza di Trabias' matriarch."

Crispi nods. It's no mystery that Sofia Galeotti, the princess, is a woman with a forked tongue who will not hesitate to set her son against his wife if Giulia is not careful. "But are you sure you want Giulia to marry Pietro? She'll be only fifteen and he twenty-three . . ."

Ignazio's reply comes with a shrug. "The Trabias need the Florios to fix their family finances, and it's the best possible marriage for Giulia. She's young, but she's aware of her responsibilities." He raises his eyebrows. "So? Will you handle this?"

"I'll draft the marriage agreement and show it to you. Little Giulia will have every protection the law can afford her." He stands up and walks to the door.

Ignazio follows him and proffers his hand on the threshold.

"So, are you going back to Palermo soon?" Crispi asks.

"Hopefully, next week. I can look after NGI from here in Rome, but the winery and the *tonnara* require my presence. It's true that I have excellent colleagues, but I don't want to stay far from my enterprises."

"Or your family." Crispi's mouth crinkles into a smile slightly obscured by his mustache. "What does Donna Giovanna say? Has she recovered after the birth? It must have been hard."

"She's still a strong woman." Ignazio mellows and almost smiles. "The little one is growing well. It'll be an honor to introduce him to you when you come to Palermo."

"Definitely." Crispi pauses. "So, Casa Florio has an Ignazio and a Vincenzo once again."

"Yes. As it has been from the start and as it must be."

⌒

An Ignazio and a Vincenzo . . .

Giovanna nuzzles the baby's neck. He smells of milk, of cologne, of good things. Vincenzo gurgles and giggles. He reaches out with his arms, and she picks him up, holds him to her chest, and kisses him. They're alone in the room: she wants to look after this child herself. It's her last opportunity to be a mother, and she doesn't want to waste it.

Figghi nichi, guai nichi; figghi ranni, guai ranni. Small children, small worries; grown children . . .

Giovanna sighs. Ignazziddu is fifteen years old, plays silly games with girls older than him, and his temper is too fiery. Thirteen-year-old Giulia has been promised to Pietro Lanza di Trabia and is getting ready to become a princess. Vincenzo's arrival was a surprise to them both: depending on their mood, they see their little brother as a doll to play with or an annoying visitor.

And that's only right, after all, Giovanna thinks: both are now looking ahead, no longer want their mother as often, perhaps no longer need her, and that's in the natural order of things. She has seen them grow and change, but her almost desperate effort to appear perfect in Ignazio's eyes and get him to love her has taken up a great deal of her energy. Her children were the umpteenth demonstration of her ability to measure up to her husband's expectations. But now she has no intention of making the same mistake. Now she wants this child to be, first and foremost, *her* child.

Giovanna prayed a lot. While her eyes grew sadder at her husband's calm indifference, her face altered, her body withered, and she begged God to grant her something for the years to come, which seemed so empty.

Then Vincenzo came and she lavished on him all the love she was capable of.

At first, she thought that the absence of her monthly cycle was the first sign of a by now aging body. But then her breasts grew sore and her belly unusually hard. After a few weeks, her confusion turned to consternation.

She called the midwife, and when the latter said, "Yes, Donna Giovanna, you're at least two months gone," she remained motionless, her skirts up over her hips, her hand on her mouth.

Pregnant. Her. It was truly a big surprise to her. And even more so to Ignazio.

My miracle is what Giovanna calls Vincenzo.

A miracle because she conceived him when she was almost forty, an age when women no longer have children but look after grandchildren.

A miracle because it's a boy and, although he came out before his time, he did so screaming. He's strong and healthy. And he's always laughing.

A miracle because Ignazio has returned to her.

And perhaps that's what fills her most with joy. Holding the baby in her arms, Giovanna leaves the room. A nanny is waiting for her outside the door.

"Do you wish me to carry him, Donna Giovanna?"

"No, thank you." Vincenzo gurgles and tries to reach out to his mother's coral earrings. She laughs. He's almost nine months old: he was born on March 18 of this same year, 1883, and soon he'll start to walk: she can tell by the way he points to his feet when he's being carried and tries to get up by himself. "Where are Giulia and Ignazziddu?" Giovanna asks with a vague feeling of guilt.

"The young master is having a lesson with the French tutor. And the young mistress has already had German lessons and is now with Donna Ciccia, waiting for you."

"Has she brought the work we're doing?" she asks as she walks down the stairs, one hand on the banister, the other holding her son.

"The needlework? Yes, signora."

At the bottom of the stairs, Giovanna sternly observes the servant women polishing the furniture with beeswax. Then her attention shifts to the Christmas decorations in the corridor. She looks at the candles, the flower arrangements with their red and white ribbons, the wreaths of fir branches from the Madonie decorated in the English fashion. In silver vases on the tables and dressers, shoots of holly and laurel, tied with velvet ribbons, alternate with gold paper decorations.

In the middle of the ballroom, on the Aubusson rug with its pink, blue, and ivory flower patterns and cream edge, bought in Paris a few years ago, a huge fir tree is on display, dressed in crystal, as well as satin and taffeta garlands: it's a trend started by the wealthy Anglo-Saxon families who've been living in Palermo for a long time, and the local aristocracy has followed their example. The dark green of the branches is mirrored and multiplied in the mirrors on the walls, giving the impression of a forest. The room is filled with the fragrance of resin and conjures up images of open spaces and snowy mountains.

Ignazio doesn't know anything about this. It will be a surprise for when he returns from Rome.

Deciding to welcome him back in this way is the most evident sign of Giovanna's joy, and of her awareness that, after all the darkness, life is lighting up this house again.

She now truly feels like a Florio, and not only because she has given the family another heir. She feels it because Ignazio is very attentive toward her. He even performs some acts of tenderness; for example, he never fails to bring her back a gift from his many trips to the mainland.

Vincenzo reaches out to the Christmas tree and giggles, while Giovanna reminisces.

Everything has changed since he returned from Marseille two years ago. She welcomed him back at the door, her hands clasped over her belly and an awkward smile on her face. Giulia rushed to hug him, while Ignazziddu shook his hand.

Then Ignazio finally looked at her, came a little closer, took her hand, and kissed it. There was an unusual light in his calm eyes: a blend of regret, solitude, and perhaps pain. An expression Giovanna, even now, cannot explain.

Then, that night, he came into her bedroom and loved her with the same ardor as during their early months of marriage. It was a night of passion, made up of suppressed sighs and hands exploring each other's body without shame.

Giovanna puts Vincenzo on the floor and lets him crawl on the rug.

Something must have happened there, in Marseille, where *she* was. What, Giovanna had no way of knowing. But she couldn't explain the alteration in Ignazio any other way: he'd become more affectionate toward her, more tender, and even more respectful, if that were possible. She was certain of just one thing: during that trip, perhaps actually in Marseille, something had wounded him deeply. She could sense it with all the insight of a woman in love: an echo that rang halfway between her stomach and her heart, an intuition born of the feeling she'd harbored alone for too many years and confirmed by what she read daily in his eyes, his gestures, and even in his newly regained passion. It was as though the part of himself that Ignazio had always kept concealed from the eyes of the world had become definitively inaccessible. As though an earthquake had taken place in his soul and the rubble had blocked all openings for ever. It was a sorrow of which Giovanna didn't know and didn't wish to know anything. She'd even found herself thinking, to her surprise, that because he'd made her suffer for so many years, it was now only right that he should pay with the same currency.

Yes, something in Ignazio's soul had disintegrated. But she could build something else over these ruins. Something new that would be hers and hers alone. Besides, it was what she'd learned to do best: make do with the little he granted her and make it go a long way.

For her, the most important thing was to have him back.

And so she welcomed him without any questions.

Then, out of the blue, Vincenzino arrived. When she told Ignazio she was pregnant, she noticed he lit up with renewed interest in the family; then a boy was born, and he was hugely, evidently happy. He named him after his father, the father who'd taught him about responsibility and honor, and also after their firstborn. Vincenzino had been dead four years; it was time for a new Vincenzo at the Olivuzza. That was exactly what he told the Oretea workers, when he went to the foundry to impart the good news personally.

In his own way, Ignazio became serene again. Sometimes, though, when Giovanna watched him as he spoke to the children or a guest, she would glimpse that sense of grief, of loss, on his face. It was as though a solid shadow would fall over him, which no one could dispel.

Giovanna couldn't have known that a part of Ignazio had died in that earthquake. And that he would carry the stigma of that bodiless grief all his life.

～

Giulia is looking for ivory-colored thread in the basket. She finds it, cuts off a segment, moistens the tip with saliva, and, squinting, threads it through the eye of a needle.

Between her and Donna Ciccia lies a linen cloth that is laboriously taking the shape of a tablecloth for tea.

Giulia repeatedly makes mistakes. She shakes her head, shaking the bun into which her black hair is gathered. Then she scoffs. "Why does my mother have to inflict this torture on me?"

Donna Ciccia raises a hand to adjust her own hair, now streaked with white, then lowers it onto Giulia's arm. "Because it's something you must be able to do as a good married woman." She slides a length of thread through a needle in a single, quick motion.

Giulia's delicate face takes on a haughty sulk that almost makes Ciccia laugh. There are times when she looks so much like her mother . . .

"I'll have scores of servants," Giulia replies. "My father promised me: I don't need to learn to embroider. I'd rather draw."

"But embroidery is also beautiful."

Giulia rolls her eyes. "My future husband is a prince. I'll be the mistress of the house."

Giovanna comes in, followed by the nanny with the little one. She sits down opposite her daughter and Donna Ciccia and studies them both.

Giulia barely looks up. For a moment, she wonders if her mother has heard her last words, then shrugs. *She can think what she likes, I've no intention of staying cooped up in the house, like her.*

"How far have you gotten with the border of the tablecloth?" Giovanna asks, picking up a section of the work.

Giulia smooths the fabric and shows it to her mother, who takes it, turns it around, and examines it with a critical eye. "The workmanship isn't neat enough," she says, indicating stitches with tangled threads. "It's work that requires neatness and precision. There are little girls at the school who produce wonderful things."

Giulia wants to reply that she can keep her schoolgirls, wretches who would otherwise have no other means of rubbing two pennies together. The only reason she doesn't is because her mother would then chide her, and she doesn't want a pointless argument. God knows why that embroidery school is so important to her.

Donna Ciccia looks at them both and sighs. "They do it for love and pleasure. Giulia isn't like that."

"Not everything one does is for pleasure, Donna Ciccia. You know that better than I. And now that she's a woman about to marry, she needs to learn that fast." Then she turns to her daughter. She must learn quickly that she can't always do what she likes best, because she's going to have responsibilities and, above all, a social role to play. There's a blend of care and warning in her tone. "When you receive guests, you must always have a piece of embroidery in your hands. These are the habits of a good lady of the house. If you want to read, then read when you're alone. Remember, men are afraid of women who are too clever, so don't go scaring off your husband."

"That was once upon a time, Mamma. It's not like that anymore." Giulia's lips quiver and her fists clench the linen. "Besides, I'm me, I like reading, drawing, and traveling. I'm not like you, you prefer to stay at home."

Giovanna squints. "What do you mean?"

Giulia burns with the desire to wound her. She wants to tell her about everything she's gathered over years of seeing her mother and father go their separate ways. On the one hand, her mother's stifling, invasive love, made up of anxious, pleading, almost pathetic looks. On the other, her father's detachment, that coldness that can turn to rancor in just a few seconds. She: placid, stubborn, patient to the point of seeming obtuse. He: cold, dissatisfied, irritable.

How sorry she used to feel for her father! He was her point of reference, her certainty. And she felt such contempt for her mother, a woman who should have been her role model but, instead, had managed only to annihilate herself, begging for affection and attention. She'd never had an ounce of pride. Never really been capable of taking what belonged to her.

She'd sacrificed herself on the family altar, humiliating herself and letting herself be humiliated.

Giulia's judgment is ruthless, it cuts through flesh and blood, the judgment of a daughter who doesn't know what her parents have experienced, and one that can be summarized in a single, arrogant thought: *I will not end up like her.*

"I mean that things change," she replies, in a know-it-all tone. "You and *mon père* have found me a husband, but I'm no rag doll."

"Listen to her! How did these modern ideas get into your head? What—do you want to start studying to become a lawyer, like that northern woman Lidia Poët? Did you see what happened to her? She got sent back home."

Giulia puffs out her cheeks and tosses the cloth aside.

Donna Ciccia intervenes to calm them down. "Don't say that, Donna Giovanna. For heaven's sake, what are you doing?" She puts a hand on her arm. "When you do that, you're like your mother, who would always shout in order to be heard."

Giovanna turns white. Her lips quiver, and she looks about to scream. But she doesn't; she restrains her anger and shakes her head energetically. She looks at Donna Ciccia, then indicates Giulia. "She wasn't born to be an ordinary woman. She has to look to the name she carries and the blood in her veins."

Giulia looks up at her mother but says nothing.

In that look, Giovanna sees her own longing to find her place in the world, the longing that made her damn her own soul to obtain a little love and respect from Ignazio.

But Giulia has neither the humility nor the patience she had.

She's so different, a mystery she has been unable to solve. For her, for this daughter who's as beautiful as she is determined, she feels at the same time tenderness and anger. For the past few months, she's been preparing her to be the perfect lady of the house, a princess worthy of the title, but Giulia doesn't seem to realize that. On the contrary, she practically makes light of her concerns.

But she also feels sorry for her because she's young. She doesn't know that she'll have to defend herself against everything and everyone, she doesn't think about what she'll have to give up just because other people expect her to. She can't begin to imagine what it will cost her to protect her soul in a world where money, titles, and appearances are the only possible truth.

Things that every woman must discover for herself.

Giovanna sighs and stands up. "I'm going to Ignazziddu," she says, without looking at her, and leaves, followed by the nanny.

There's a moment of absolute silence in the room.

Donna Ciccia brings her face closer to Giulia's and murmurs, "Your mother-in-law is going to watch out for any silliness on your part, so that she can then tell your husband, Pietro. That's how it works." She gives her a stern look. "Your mother hasn't told you this yet, so I'm telling you. Be careful. The prince is tied to his mother, and she's a powerful woman." She speaks softly, fearfully, because she knows, feels that Giulia will have some very difficult times in that household. It's more than a gut feeling: it's something that grabs her by the throat, telling her that her little girl will suffer, and quite a lot at that.

"If she's a horrible woman, I'll give as good as I get." Giulia lifts her chin. "I know my place."

Donna Ciccia shakes her head and resumes unthreading the cloth. She saw Giulia being born, followed her throughout her childhood, and now the girl is almost a woman, too self-assured, like all adolescents . . . and all Florios. She has no doubts: she'll learn to her cost what it means to be a bride, a stranger, in one of the most important households in Italy. With that kind of temper, any offense will lead to an argument. But she also knows that no one in the family is her equal in determination and pride, and this reassures her. She doesn't let anything or anyone knock her down, just like the grandmother whose name she bears. She has inherited from her grandmother Giulia the courage and ability to tolerate pain; from her grandfather Vincenzo, she's inherited impatience, haughtiness, and the intolerance of any attempt to diminish her.

But what Donna Ciccia cannot imagine is how fate will put her *picciridda* to the test.

◦⌒

The summer of 1884 is sweltering, saturated with humidity. The sirocco blows into the NGI offices the heavy smell of seaweed and coal fumes from the steamships, filling the furniture with sand and blurring the outlines of the buildings and the distant mountains.

Ignazio shuts the file with the words CERAMICS COMPANY in front of him. He was thinking about it for a while and has finally managed to open here in Palermo a ceramics factory to manufacture, among other things, the crockery for the NGI ships. No more buying dishes, cups, and soup tureens from England or from Ginori: he'll make them now and they'll carry the Florio mark. *I might even produce a few sets for Favignana*, he thinks. *Yes, I'll ask Ernesto Basile to design them.*

He goes to the door, calls an errand boy, and tells him to get the carriage ready so that he can go back to the Olivuzza, then sits back down at his desk and allows himself to loosen his *plastron*. He rubs his eyes. They've been irritated for some time, and the daily compresses of witch hazel and chamomile soothe the burning only for a while. *Just a few more days*, he thinks, relieved, keeping his eyes closed. A smile forms on his lips: this year, he's decided to escape the mugginess by going first to Naples, then to Tuscany. But it's not so much the prospect of a vacation that cheers him up. Some time ago, he purchased a railroad coach and had it furnished like a true "mobile house," as is the fashion among the European aristocracy: he and his family will travel surrounded by their own furniture, assisted by their servants, and will even have an entire car for their baggage. Luxury, comfort, privacy. Another way of pushing away worries and showing your prestige.

He opens his eyes, determined to put an end to this exhausting day. He has one more task to complete: to take care of the personal correspondence that arrived in Palermo with the steamers early in the afternoon.

He takes the paper knife and opens the envelopes. The first is a request on the part of the workforce in Naples, asking him to look into paying them more equitable salaries. *You're like a father to your workers*, they say. He'll reply to them tomorrow.

Then there's a missive from Damiani, who updates him on the latest sessions in the Senate and goes into an extensive account of chatter, gossip, and anecdotes. Those are important, too, as they both know. Ignazio scans it and puts it aside.

Finally, an envelope trimmed in black, for mourning.

He turns it in his fingers, examining it like a dangerous item. Sometimes the heart sees bad news before the eyes.

A Marseille postmark.

He doesn't recognize the handwriting, but he certainly remembers the sender's address. No, it's not his sister's or the Merles'.

His mouth grows dry, and his breath refuses to emerge from his lips.

It's not his hands that open the envelope, those trembling fingers don't belong to him, nor do the eyes that cloud over with tears as he reads the words.

June . . . Illness . . . Cholera . . . Nothing could be done . . .

His hand screws up the paper and closes in a fist. He strikes his desk once, twice, three times. A sob escapes his lips, while another gets stuck under his breastbone and is pushed back.

He mustn't cry.

He takes the card again, smooths it, and reads it once more.

Words composed by a widower, sentences that, behind the veil of formality, reveal acute grief. She was loved by this man, Ignazio knows it now.

His wife, the man writes, made a specific request a few hours before she died, and he has obeyed, imparting the news *to a dear old friend.*

For a second, Ignazio wonders what Admiral Clermont may have felt in writing this note. Could Camille—*God, how painful it is to think of her name!*—have ever told him what had happened between them? Or did she keep quiet, leaving nothing but a suspicion in her wake? Or had she mentioned it as though it had been something of little importance, which now belonged to the past?

She would have had every right to reveal their relationship to him, just as that man now has a right to experience his grief.

He, on the other hand, retains no rights.

He rests his forehead on the desk. He can think of nothing except her perfume, that fragrance of fresh, vital, spring carnations.

That is what he has left. Her scent on him; not on his body, but in his soul. Her smile. The sorrow she left inside him after those reproaches that still burn him, oh, how they burn . . .

Outside, Palermo is getting ready for the evening. Distant sounds drift in from the square: the clatter of carts and carriages heading for the seafront, the puffing of steamships, the shouts of errand boys selling the afternoon papers, the angry voices of mothers calling their children home. The streetlamps are fighting their battle against the shadows taking over the Cassaro, as the first lights appear at the windows. A smell of sea, food, and braziers wafts in.

Around him, everything is alive. Inside him, there's only silence.

༄

It's October 3, 1885, and Giulia, on her father's arm, is walking up the wide marble staircase to Palermo's city hall. There's an almost unbelievable resemblance between them: the same calm, focused eyes, the same prominent nose, the same fleshy lips. The same detachment.

But this closeness also highlights the contrast between Ignazio's black morning coat and Giulia's elegant cream outfit, with its two whalebone corsets outlining her small waist, one without sleeves, the other with three-quarter-length sleeves, hemmed with lace. The skirt, sumptuous and heavy, is made up of eight layers of fabric and ends in a train. Her dark hair is done up in large waves, held with diamond clips.

Donna Sofia Galeotti, Princess of Trabia and Queen Margherita's lady-in-waiting, looks at the young bride, turns her face away abruptly, but immediately composes herself, with a false smile that conceals her wounded pride—wounded by this display of wealth. For her, this marriage isn't the union of two families, but a lifeline: the Trabia estate has gone through a series of hereditary divisions that have severely compromised it, and even the family's houses, including their principal residence, Palazzo Butera, are badly in need of restoration. *And now they finally will be restored*, Donna Sofia seems to think, as she purses her lips and nods.

A few steps away from Ignazio and Giulia is Donna Ciccia. She is visibly moved, but also worried about the dress getting creased. *And this is just the civil ceremony!* she thinks. *I still have to fix those two loose pearls on the collar of the church wedding dress, check the hem of the petticoat, sew up that little tear in the lace of the veil . . .* She feels a pang of anxiety and doesn't think she has enough time. A gut feeling travels through her, making her shudder.

Eyes downcast, Giovanna follows the trio, holding Ignazziddu's arm, while he looks around, head high, impudent. He's flaunting a mustache and a curly little beard, in an attempt to dispel that boyish look that, at seventeen, is now cramping his style.

Suddenly, Giulia slips. Perhaps the sole of one of her satin shoes has lost its grip on the marble, or perhaps she took a wrong step—who knows? Giovanna is startled; Donna Ciccia rushes to catch her, invoking the Madonna. But Giulia grips her father's arm and gives an amused giggle. "That's all we need," she whispers, and he responds by squeezing her hand. Finally, she straightens up, lifts her chin, and resumes her climb.

Despite his unemotional expression, Ignazio is proud and relieved: Giulia's reaction to this small incident is a sign that his *stidduzza* can take care of herself and will never lose heart. Although it was only a few years ago, the time when she would greet him at the foot of the olive tree next to the carriage entrance when he came home is now distant. Ignazio can no longer rely on their chats at dawn or over breakfast, or on the comfort he drew from their understanding, made up only of looks.

He's going to miss it very much.

It was Giovanna who negotiated with the Princess of Trabia: two aristocrats who spoke the same language and practiced on an equal footing the fine art of stinging without hurting each other. And she came out victorious, proving to have admirable skill and an Olympian indifference toward her future fellow mother-in-law's condescending and at times even unpleasant attitude. But it was Ignazio who laid down the property conditions, drawn up by Crispi, intended to protect his daughter, and he, too, who ordered fine furniture for the palazzo and acquired items that would add splendor to the family's art collection, like Giacomo Serpotta's cupids from the church of San Francesco delle Stimmate. The Lanza di Trabias had to accept and keep quiet.

A prudent investment, since with this marriage Giulia will be assuming a prominent role in Italian high society. It's also a way to heal an old wound. Ignazio married Giovanna, the daughter of the Count d'Ondes Trigona, minor nobility. The Lanza di Trabias, however, are princes of old lineage, and the true protagonists of Sicilian history. And now they're forging links with the Florios, whose nobility lies in money and work.

For a moment, Ignazio's thoughts wander to his father. He touches the ring that used to be his, as if he can thereby call on him. He pictures him standing there, surly and frowning. *See this, Papà? At last they'll stop seeing us as laborers. Giulia's going to be the Princess of Trabia.*

And yet . . .

As they're about to walk into the building, he turns to look for his wife and catches Donna Sofia's eyes. She's smiling, but the hardness in those eyes doesn't escape Ignazio and even irritates him.

I did well, he tells himself, smiling back with an expression that's as amiable as it is cold. *Whether you like it or not, you will show my daughter the respect she deserves.*

That very morning, in fact, he explained everything to Giulia, and she, his *stidduzza*, grasped everything perfectly well. He can't give her peace of mind, but he'll help her defend herself in such a way that her role will be acknowledged both in public and in private. He's given her the appropriate weapons.

Leaving the Olivuzza, flanked by two rows of servants in livery, Giulia climbed into the carriage, followed by her father. Her features stiff with tension, she glanced over the city without seeing it, ignoring the outlines of the new buildings along the road from the villa to the center of Palermo, focusing only on the fragrance of her bouquet.

However, once they'd ridden past the construction site of the Teatro Massimo and the carriage had driven onto Via Maqueda, Giulia's eyes opened wide. Beneath the Baroque balconies, on the basalt sidewalks, and outside the front doors of aristocratic homes, a crowd of commoners and petits bourgeois had gathered, craning their necks to peer inside the vehicle and catch even just a fleeting image of the bride, the daughter of the master of Palermo and the future Princess Lanza di Trabia.

Annoyed, Ignazio pulled the curtain shut to shield the window. She turned to look at the indistinct figures that cheered as they passed.

"Are they here to . . . see me?" she asked, her voice down to a breath, her fingers clutching the bouquet. She suddenly appeared to him as what she was: a fifteen-year-old girl about to take a step that would change her life.

"They're here because of what we stand for." Ignazio leaned forward. "The Florios are Palermo. Pietro, your future husband, has the rank of a viceroy, but always remember that first my father, then I, bought our lands, the mills, and the people who work there, and that you're my daughter, in other words, the master's daughter. We're rich because we've built this city brick by brick."

Giulia listened to him, her eyes staring. It wasn't the first time her father had spoken to her like this, as if to an adult, but he'd never done it so frankly.

He ignored her astonishment. "Listen to me. Your dowry is conditional. Do you know why? Did your mother explain anything?"

"My mother told me . . . something else," she mumbled, blushing with embarrassment.

The furrow on Ignazio's forehead deepened, then suddenly relaxed, and he smiled. "Ah, I see." He clasped his daughter's cold, tense hand in his. "Forget that stuff and listen to me. It means that you have a dowry of four million lire, a huge sum, but since your husband's family has no businesses and I don't want to support extravagant aristocrats, I've laid down a condition—in agreement with your husband—that you can choose which businesses to invest it in. Crispi has fine-tuned the marriage clauses."

She looked at him intently, more puzzled than surprised. "What does that mean?"

"It means I don't want the Lanza di Trabias to deprive you of what's yours, because you never know what can happen in life. Pietro will let me know which houses and lands he wants, and I'll buy them in both your names, drawing on the funds from the dowry." He moved closer and brushed her face with his fingers. "You'll have to be alert, my *stidduzza*. You've nothing to fear for as long as I'm around. But you'll have to learn to protect yourself in that house and not let anybody get the better of you, whether it's your husband or, worse still, your mother-in-law, who—let's face it—is a viper. Pietro is twenty-three years old, but he depends on her in every way. Whereas you're an intelligent woman, and you'll know how to defend yourself, just like the grandmother you're named after, who was a wise and determined woman. Remember: only money will give you the independence and the power to choose, and you must never give it up. Do you understand?"

Giulia nodded, her eyes glistening. A few seconds later, she shook her head and murmured, "I don't want to disappoint you."

He hugged her, his beard tickling her neck and scratching her face. "Our family has never been afraid of anything or anyone. We've survived a revolution and a civil war. True, our history isn't as long as that of the Lanza di Trabias, but you are a Florio, and where intelligence and courage are concerned, you're second to nobody, let alone those pedantic aristocrats. Always remember: those who have the money have the power."

It's with this thought that Giulia now climbs the final steps leading her into the presence of Duke Giulio Benso della Verdura, who's been asked to celebrate the marriage in place of the mayor of Palermo.

The thin, gaunt-faced man is waiting for her across the table, with a benevolent smile. Nearby stands Pietro Lanza di Trabia: a burly young man with a dark mustache and a receding hairline that threatens to recede even more.

He's courted her with elegance, as befits a nobleman, given her a precious ring, and escorted her to the parties of Palermo's nobility. He's treated her like a princess.

Does he make her heart beat faster? No. He's pleasant company, but certainly not a man over whom you lose your head. She doesn't know if he'll make a good husband. In any case, she knows her task: to bear strong, healthy children and be a princess worthy of the title she bears.

Marriage is a contract, Giulia thinks, taking her hand away from her father's warm hand and placing it on Pietro's cold and slightly trembling one. A contract between families, with her and her dowry as its object.

And when it comes to business, nobody is more skillful than the Florios.

⌒

"You can't begin to imagine what Queen Victoria's Jubilee was like!"

Ignazziddu stretches his legs before him, a glass of champagne in one hand, a small cigar in the other, and regards his friends: his cousin Francesco d'Ondes, known as Ciccio; Romualdo Trigona, another cousin, but more distant; and Giuseppe Monroy. The three young men have eagerly accepted Ignazziddu's invitation to spend a few days in Villa ai Colli, just outside Palermo, with him. Actually, the entire family is here but is about to leave for Favignana.

The young people are on the terrace overlooking the citrus grove, sprawled on willow armchairs the servants laid out for their arrival. It's late evening, and the night chill is finally tempering the heat of the summer's day. The trees give off the fragrance of orange blossoms, mingled with the pungent scent of wild mint in the vases lined up on the stone balustrade.

"When we arrived in London, it was raining heavily: I can't tell you how hellish it was, getting the suitcases and trunks off the train. My mother and my brother had been sick on the whole trip from Calais to Dover, so they went straight to their rooms to rest. But my father decided to take a tour around the city, and I went with him. Luckily, it had stopped raining. What a sight! Flowers, flags, festoons, and portraits of the queen everywhere, even on the most hidden little street. And that's not all: I saw a house outside which they'd built a large platform filled with palms surrounded by Japanese umbrellas and, in the middle, a huge marble bust of the queen with garlands of flowers all around it; another house with a façade completely covered in flags, and another one with flowers cascading from the windows, forming a number fifty. And then the parade the next day! It was sunny and the swords and helmets were shining so brightly, they looked like a river of silver. What struck me most, however, was what happened outside Buckingham Palace before the parade. As you can imagine, there was a huge crowd. But there was also a great silence."

"What do you mean, silence?" Giuseppe asks.

"Unbelievable, right? Here, there would have been shouts,

hoorays . . . But there, nothing! Then, when the cream-colored horses of the royal carriage appeared, the crowd exploded. They started shouting even louder than the trumpets announcing the queen's arrival. Handkerchiefs waving, hats thrown in the air . . . I was told that as the queen drove by, a man yelled, 'There she is! I saw her! She's alive!' and made everyone laugh. Basically, Queen Victoria's subjects really worship her, unlike us with the Savoys!"

His friends laugh, looking at Ignazziddu with a blend of fascination and envy.

He resumes his story. Only the Florios, the Trabias, and just a few other Italians were invited, he says. He repeats this several times, driving the point home. "All the royal families of Europe were there, not to mention aristocrats and bankers and politicians. My father greeted everybody, circulating from one to the other, with my mother always behind him. You should have seen how they were looking at us. There wasn't one who didn't know us or wasn't asking to be introduced to my father, the owner of Navigazione Generale Italiana . . ."

"But then you went to Paris, didn't you?" Romualdo says.

"Yes, we stayed with the Rothschilds." Ignazziddu smiles and leans forward. "But above all, I spent an unforgettable afternoon at the Chabanais . . ."

Ciccio pours himself a drink and looks at him with a seemingly innocent expression. "Does your mother know you frequent brothels?"

"My mother had the crucifix and kneeler brought to her hotel room," Ignazziddu scoffs. "She adores me, anyway; even if she chides me, she always ends up forgiving me." He drains his glass and sits up in the armchair. "Besides, she was very busy. She had to pick furniture for the Olivuzza, some rugs for the salons . . .

Furthermore, she and my sister spent a whole day at Worth's, trying on clothes. Meanwhile, my father was having his business meetings and practically forced me to attend. I only managed to escape by telling him I was going to visit a museum."

"My dear fellow, your father realizes you're a ladies' man!" Romualdo stands up and gives him a playful slap on the back of his neck. They're good friends who share a passion for women and expensive entertainment.

"If a woman is attractive and wants me, and I want her, where's the harm?" Ignazziddu replies calmly, rolling his eyes. "In the hotel, there was a Russian countess with her husband and, trust me, she turned heads. A real goddess, blond, with green eyes. I looked at her and she at me, and . . ." He laughs, his eyes gleaming at the memory. Then he looks at his cousin. "Hey! Are you listening to me?"

Ciccio and Giuseppe have suddenly stopped laughing, and Romualdo, equally serious, lifts his chin toward something behind Ignazziddu.

Ignazio has appeared in the frame of the French windows. His face is marked with weariness, and he considers the four young men with an expression of reproach. "Gentlemen," he says, his arms crossed over his chest, his voice low. "It's very late. May I suggest you retire to your rooms?"

Romualdo lowers his head. "Of course, Don Ignazio. Do forgive us if we've disturbed you." He gets up, takes Ciccio by the sleeve, and they slip into the villa, followed by Giuseppe, who gives Ignazziddu a worried glance. Ignazziddu's about to do the same, because he's well acquainted with that look on his father's face and knows there's a storm brewing.

And indeed, Ignazio detains him with a hand on his arm. "Of all the ways you could have spoken about your mother and me, you chose the worst. Your mother especially, who always does as you ask and forgives you everything."

His words are like a slap in the face. The young man blushes and tries to walk away. "What did I say?"

"You mustn't talk like that—period. We don't have to prove anything, and you should never boast about what you have or what you are. Leave that bravado to jumped-up lice." He seizes him and draws him closer. "And another thing. The next time you want to go off and enjoy yourself, you just have to tell me. I certainly shan't stop you. But you must realize that there are responsibilities and that they come before pleasure. You've got women too much on your mind. You're a man and you're young, I can understand that. But it's unseemly to show off about certain things. It's a matter of respect, not just for the women you frequent, but for yourself."

"But Papà! It was a brothel, and they were—"

Ignazio closes his eyes, trying to restrain his exasperation. "I don't care what or who they were."

"If it were up to you, I'd live like a monk, all home and work," the son gripes.

"Damn it! Your name is Florio, and you must first and foremost show respect for your family." He raises his hand. "One day, you'll have to be worthy of this ring, which has been passed down, first from my uncle Ignazio, a brave, honest man, to your grandfather Vincenzo, to whom we owe everything, and now to me. You need control and decorum in your life. Otherwise, you won't go far."

He pretends not to notice the grimace on the young man's face as he strolls away and returns to the house. He lets him harbor the illusion of being shrewder, of understanding life better than he—his father—does. He realizes that he needs to keep this son of his close by and teach him to know his place. You don't become an adult if you don't know how to act and when to speak, and—above all—how and when to be silent.

◦⌒◦

The sea in the harbor of Favignana is so clear that you can see the bottom and the fish swimming amid clumps of seaweed. The backwash has a gentle sound: a murmuring of water and wind that caresses the hulls of the boats and stretches to the sandy shore outside the *tonnara* plant.

Ignazio takes a deep breath. There's a salty and vaguely nauseating smell of dried seagrass in the air; in the sky, a few seagulls are supported by the currents, waiting for the fishermen to throw into the sea the fish leftovers stuck in the nets they're mending.

It's always like this in the spring, and this May 1889 is no exception.

Since he arrived for the *mattanza*, it's been a series of bright days, with the sun taking possession of the island, cloaking it in that mellow light he loves.

Ignazio smiles faintly, shields his eyes with his hand, then shifts his gaze to the building Damiani Almeyda erected for him. He makes out the figure of Giovanna in the garden with Donna Ciccia, and that of Vincenzo playing with a ball. His youngest is six years old and shows signs of a sparkling intelligence. A living flame.

Giovanna prefers to stay there with Vincenzo, partly because she needs to manage the house and the servants from Palermo. She's accepted the impossibility of using the islanders as household staff—they're too coarse and sunburned—and has instead consigned them to manual support. All the same, whenever she comes to Favignana, the Olivuzza staff take on a relaxed attitude she finds somewhat annoying, so she feels it's her duty to personally check every room, every dish served at the table, especially when there are guests. She now focuses all her energy on her position as lady of the house.

Ignazio, on the other hand, has chosen to stay on board the *Queen Mary*, the yacht he recently purchased from Louis Pratt in Marseille. The Frenchman had called it the *Reine Marie*, but Ignazio decided to revert to the name by which it had been christened after leaving the Aberdeen shipyard. Thirty-six meters long, with an iron hull and cutter-style sails, it has a compound steam engine and propeller propulsion. It's the largest leisure steamer registered in Italy, and probably the fastest: ten knots. A real treasure. Only his friend Giuseppe Lanza di Mazzarino's *Louise* can compete with his *Queen Mary*.

It was Lanza di Mazzarino who finally prompted him to buy it. Ignazio had long wanted to own a yacht, but had to put business first, then his daughter's dowry, and only then the purchase of new steamships. Of course, he had joined the Italian Yacht Club in Genoa, but that was a step almost all ship owners—from Raffaele Rubattino to Giuseppe Orlando to Erasmo Piaggio, who became the director of the Genoa branch of NGI—had taken.

Then, one day, Lanza di Mazzarino, one of the club's promoters and partners, remarked, "Ignazio, you can't be without a boat of your own. It's unworthy of you. How can the owner of Italy's most important fleet not even have a tub?" And he laughed.

Ignazio didn't appreciate the sarcasm. "I've considered it, but now's not the right time," he retorted, peeved. "I couldn't enjoy it at the moment: I have too much on my mind, what with NGI and the *tonnaras*. I can't afford to go around in a yacht while other people manage my business."

But the other man insisted. "It's a matter of perspective. You make millions with your enterprises, and then you're ashamed to own a boat? Even if you spent just one day a year on it, at least you'd have one and it would be yours."

He realized that Lanza di Mazzarino was right: the yacht would be a symbol—*another* symbol—of the power of the Florios. Like the Olivuzza, like the family railroad coach. Like Giulia's marriage to the Prince of Trabia.

But now, on this yacht, Ignazio knows he made a decision that touches him deeply and has pushed social prestige to the background.

Beneath his feet, past the leather soles, the sea is throbbing, breathing. He can feel it: it's a vibration that rises from his ankles, up to his shoulders, and floods his head and eyes.

Once, right here on Favignana, his father told him, "We Florios have the sea in our veins."

His family's origins surface, his blood sings under his skin.

And then there's Favignana. The only place where he feels complete. The only place where memories don't hurt him, where he can allow himself to observe his ghosts without feeling pain, picture them next to him, albeit concealed in small patches of shadow that escape the invasive light of the island.

His parents. His son. Camille.

"Don Ignazio."

He turns. A sailor in a navy-blue uniform and light-colored cap is waiting to speak to him.

"Yes, Saverio."

"Signor Caruso would like a word with you. He's waiting in the stateroom."

The *Queen Mary*'s stateroom is a functional place, where the demands of sailing are hidden by the luxurious furnishings. There are oil paintings of seascapes on the timber-clad walls, the couch that stands against the wall is made of velvet, and the Persian rug, a purple-red Senneh, has been fixed to the floor to avoid accidents.

"Don Ignazio, what a pleasure to see you." Gaetano Caruso removes his straw hat and gets up. Deep wrinkles run through his thin face and his goatee has turned white.

First, it was his father with my father, and now it's him and me . . . Another family story, Ignazio thinks, shaking hands and looking him in the eyes. There are few people he can trust in the world the way he trusts this man.

Caruso has a portfolio filled with letters. "I've brought you the mail. The ship from Trapani arrived just as I was on my way to you."

Ignazio thanks him with a nod and invites him to sit back down, while he quickly scans the correspondence. There's nothing that can't wait.

"So," he murmurs, sitting down on the couch. "Do tell."

Caruso crosses his hands on his lap. His eyes, dark and alert, are now cautious. But his words are swift. "There's another rumor that they want to replace the prison warden. We don't know who'll come next or whether he'll allow us to have prisoners work at the plant. This rumor's been going around for a while, as you know. But now it seems like a matter of days."

"*Arrè?* Again? Don't they have anything better to do?" Annoyed, Ignazio hisses through his teeth. "We can't be forever wondering what these ministry pen pushers want. And during the *mattanza* at that!" Exasperation wipes away his sense of well-being. The line between his eyebrows grows deeper. "I'll write to Rome right away; Abele Damiani will deal with this matter. I've had to trouble him with something like this before." He pauses and shakes his head. "If I didn't know that employing prisoners saves us a great deal of money, I'd happily do without them. Because, aside from the *mattanza*, we're running at a constant loss."

Dispirited, Caruso opens his hands. "Are you telling me, Don Ignazio? What with the wages for the *tonnaroti* and the workers at the canning factory, and the repair expenses for the plant's boilers and those for the vineyard, here on Favignana we have a loss that . . ." He indicates the village with a vague gesture. "Not to mention the money for the godfathers and the sacristans."

Caruso's surly look makes Ignazio laugh. "I know you think two sacristans are too many for a small island like Favignana, but they also take care of the maintenance of the church, and taking care of Mother Church is one of the duties of the island's owner, since the sea eats away at everything, the buildings first and foremost. Besides, I promised my wife. You know she's a devout woman. As for the vineyard . . ." He rests his elbow on the arm of the couch and taps his fist on his chin. "The fragrance of the wine from the vineyard is one of the few pleasures left to me. I can smell the sea in it."

Caruso is unable to conceal astonishment behind his deferential mask. Sometimes, in the behavior of *u' principale*—he, too, calls him that, like the workers—cracks appear that make him more human. But they quickly close again.

"Don Gaetano, when you're rich you have two choices. Either enjoy life and not give a damn, or else ensure everything goes as best it can for you and those who work with you. I don't need to tell you which I chose."

"I know, Don Ignazio. Even though you're here, on board this ship, looking as if you're resting, I know you're working." He touches his temple. "You work in here. You never stop thinking about NGI, the foundry, the winery . . ."

"Because it's my duty. Casa Florio is my family, and you can't neglect your family." Ignazio stands up and motions Caruso to follow him outside. "But that doesn't mean I can't enjoy the good things I have." Once on deck, Ignazio looks at the plant. "We'll soon have the *tonnara* talked about, even more than now."

Caruso squints. "What do you mean?"

"Crispi and I are discussing a plan. Something very important." He drops his voice and smiles faintly. "A national exhibition."

The other man gives a start. "Really?"

"The time has come for an exhibition in the south. And where else if not Palermo? We have the necessary space, between the city's suburbs and the Favorita, plus . . ." Raising an eyebrow, he indicates himself. "We have the funds and the right people to plan this kind of event."

"That would be wonderful." Caruso spreads his hands wide. "An exhibition in Palermo would mean thousands of visitors and the possibility of displaying our products. It would be a way to show Rome and the north that we're not just goatherds and fishermen."

"Oh, the people in Rome know that very well. That's why there's been resistance." Ignazio indicates the sea behind him. "If we succeed in our intention, who do you think will be in charge of transporting the goods? And who, if not to the person who's organizing the event, to whom do you think prospective companies that wish to exhibit will need to turn?" He moves his head closer to Caruso and squeezes his arm. "But I'm not the only one who wants this. Crispi himself accepts it, and the fact that he's now prime minister, the first southerner to get that honor, may demolish many obstacles. He knows he would have the support of all the Sicilian politicians. All I would do is put in the required money . . ." He rubs his index finger and thumb together. "So that they give me the spaces I want." He straightens up and half closes his eyes. The sunlight is worsening his eye problem, which he's had for a couple of years. "But right now, everything's up in the air. Keep this quiet and *quartiatevi*, be discreet, because an idea like this is a big thing. Once the news spreads, we'll design a pavilion for our business, and tuna, *our* tuna, will be the protagonist of the fair, along with the marsala."

"My lips are sealed, Don Ignazio." Caruso adds nothing else. His surprise is too great, and there could be many consequences if this exhibition became a reality.

Ignazio nods, then escorts him to the boarding ladder. "I'm waiting for news from the foundry regarding some improvements in timing and methods that we need to agree on with the staff of the new shipping line to Bombay."

"I'll bring it to you personally as soon as it arrives."

Ignazio notices his son. Ignazziddu is holding his hat in one hand and a stick with a silver pommel, true to fashion, in the other, but is scrambling like a harebrain, raising clouds of dust. At last, he reaches the foot of the ladder and stops to catch his breath.

Ignazio sighs. There are days when he despairs of making his son his right hand in the management of Casa Florio, and not just because he doesn't have the slightest interest in the negotiations his father always tries to involve him in. It's something deeper, as if Ignazziddu only wants to see the world's beautiful things, which, strangely enough, are always the most expensive.

Caruso toys with the brim of his straw hat. "So, shall I expect you later, Don Ignazio? To take a tour of the plant, you know . . ."

"I'll be there. Meanwhile, I'll send Damiani a telegram."

Caruso and Ignazziddu pass each other on the ladder. Caruso tips his hat and mutters a greeting. Ignazziddu raises his hand in a lazy gesture. Then he goes up to his father, who gives him a dark look. "One would think we didn't teach you manners. Is that a way to behave?"

His son shrugs. "It's Signor Caruso, Papà. He's known me since I was a child. Do I have to stand on ceremony with him?"

"Courtesy has no age limitation. You're nearly twenty-one, so you should know that. It's manners that make a man a gentleman." His eyes drift down to the Tuscan-made leather shoes. "You're covered in dust. Why did you have to run like that?"

The young man waves a piece of paper. "There's something Giulia and I have talked about, and today she's sent me a telegram to confirm it."

Ignazio feels his heart swell in his chest. Three years after her wedding, Giulia, his *stidduzza*, is finally about to make him a grandfather. Last time he saw her, a few weeks ago, he thought she looked peaceful, even if very overweight from her pregnancy. "What do you mean?"

Ignazziddu suddenly hesitates and searches for words. He goes down the deck, partly walking backwards and partly preceding him. "Giulia would like to rest after the birth, but her husband doesn't want to take her out, especially with a baby. You know what it's like . . ." He drops his voice and gives a complicit smirk. "As it is, she's been forced to spend her entire pregnancy glued to her mother-in-law. Afterward, she'd like to have a little peace and quiet."

Ignazio looks at him, stony-faced. "So? Will you get to the point? What are you trying to tell me?"

"Giulia and I wanted to know if you'd let us use the *Queen Mary* to go to Naples for a few days this summer." He says it all in one breath, his mustache quivering under his lips, which curl into a crooked smile. Then his eyes suddenly turn imploring.

That's when Ignazio's annoyance explodes. He swears under his breath and resumes walking, his hands behind his back, his coattails fluttering in the wind. "*You* asked your sister if she wanted to go away, and I'm sure she jumped at the opportunity to remove herself from her mother-in-law, who does nothing but criticize her and speak ill of her with Pietro." He stops and glares at his son. "And I'll bet you've already spoken to your brother-in-law and suggested it would be a way to allow Giulia some rest. Am I wrong?"

The young man bites his lip, as though holding back an embarrassed giggle, like that of a little boy caught stealing from the larder. An attitude capable of overcoming any opposition from Giovanna, who's always allowed her son too much, if not everything. But Ignazio is not Giovanna, and Ignazziddu must learn to ask for things and earn them, not just take them.

Ignazio stops and points a finger at his son's chest. "You can't manipulate people as you please, let alone me. I hate it, and you know that. You've gone and done everything behind my back. Now I can't say no to Pietro and Giulia without appearing a despot."

The young man purses his lips. "One can never ask you anything without specifying why, how, and when. What does it cost you to let Giulia and me spend a little time with our friends? It's not as if you and *Maman* will be using the yacht, and if you did want to go away, you'd still have our train."

"Friends?" Ignazio's tone becomes shriller. A cabin boy polishing the handrail looks up with curiosity. He glares at him, and the boy resumes his work, his head firmly wedged between his shoulders. "How many people have you invited? Are you thinking of telling me everything right away, or else in installments, like those novels Donna Ciccia reads?"

Ignazziddu runs his fingers through his hair, ruffling it. Then he seems to realize he's only doing that out of nervousness and re-arranges his hair. "This yacht can house half of Palermo, Papà, and you know it." He rolls his eyes. "Besides, it's not just about denying *me* something . . ."

The little creep, Ignazio thinks. *No, not little. The big bastard!* He knows perfectly well that his father has a soft spot for Giulia and would do nothing to displease her. Ignazziddu is really good at ma-nipulating people. A skill Ignazio himself developed over time, but which comes naturally to his son.

A talent worth developing.

The young man moves closer and drops his voice. "Please, Papà." His eyes are pleading, submissive even. Despite himself, Ignazio smiles slightly. If he does have to give in, he'll do it on his terms.

"I'll let you know in the next few days, but I'll tell you one thing here and now."

Ignazziddu looks at him, hope and a vague fear in his eyes. "Tell me. Anything."

"From this fall, you'll come to the office with me."

On Mount Bonifato, the September sun forms long shadows, like large waves that descend from the peak to the valley, following the lines of the terraces.

Ignazio clambers out of the dusty carriage and takes deep breaths of the sickly-sweet, steam-charged air that cloaks the coun-tryside. Ignazziddu gets out right after him, sulking. This is rich country, where the recently plowed brown fields alternate with the gray-dusted green of olive groves and the darker green of vineyards. Ignazio looks down at the metal plaque next to the railroad tracks:

a junction just a few meters away from the station. In the center, on the keystone, there's an inscription:

ORETEA FOUNDRY
1889
Palermo

In 1885, he acquired this property just outside Alcamo, where many of their suppliers of grapes and must for marsala live. Ignazio planned it carefully. He had a complex with a square courtyard built: a plant for wine production, with large basins outside for the pressing and ovens for baking the must. He got the idea from a conversation with Abele Damiani, having met him in Rome during a parliamentary session. As often happened, they were discussing what could be done to strengthen the Sicilian economy, and Damiani extolled the potential of a farm near Alcamo. "You could process your must there, then send it to Palermo," he said. "It would be very convenient, Don Ignazio."

"From Alcamo to Marsala, with the roads as they are? And by cart?" Ignazio retorted, slightly irritated. But then he had a flash of inspiration.

A revolution.

No, not by cart. With much larger wagons.

He senses the arrival of the goods train from Palermo even before he sees it. He can feel it in the vibration that travels from the ground to his skin, then in the light hissing borne on the wind. He turns his back to the railroad tracks, walks with his son through the monumental gates with the half-moon that carries the family's crest, the lion drinking under the cinchona tree, and heads over to the plant manager and Abele Damiani, who are waiting for him. They greet one another with warm handshakes. If Damiani is surprised that Ignazziddu is there, he doesn't show it. "I told you it was a good thing to build this edifice," he exclaims, smiling.

Ignazio nods. "That's true, and I wanted to be here today to see the first shipment of barrels from Palermo, which we'll use for the refining of the wine. With the railroad tracks coming as far as here, there'll be no more need to unload the goods outside."

That's right, because this is his masterstroke: asking for permission—and obtaining it—for the railroad line, the national line, to deviate in order to bring the tracks all the way into the plant. An extraordinary thing for Sicily, and practically incredible for this small agricultural center.

He spent a long time conferring with Vincenzo Giachery, learning from his long-standing management experience. In fact, over the past year, since the death of the Oretea's director, he's very much missed the man's great intelligence and sensitivity. But he hasn't stopped: no sooner did he present his idea to Damiani than the sly-looking petty politician moved heaven and earth for the project to succeed; that way, he could boast of having been the one who persuaded the Florios to create work in these remote country areas. Because creating work meant accumulating prestige. And obtaining votes.

But Ignazio doesn't care about all that. He has achieved his goals: to improve marsala production and reduce costs. Or at least so it seems. The moment has come to verify this. He turns to the plant manager. "Have the harvest forecasts all come in?"

"To the last bunch. And a good harvest it was, too, Don Ignazio. Come, I'll show you around the offices."

At that moment, the locomotive enters the courtyard, accompanied by a trail of black steam that soils the sky. The train stops with a hiss, amid the astonished looks of the workmen ready on the benches and at the entrance to the warehouses. For a few seconds, everything comes to a halt. Then there's an explosion of cheers and cries of jubilation. Ignazio, watching the scene with pride, squeezes his son's arm and says, "Remember this moment. It's we Florios who've made it possible."

As the staff gets down to work, the group of men climbs to the upper floor of the building and comes to a wooden double door leading to the administration offices.

There are two bronze letters on the door, as large as a hand: an interlaced I and F; around them, a cogged wheel, also made of bronze, on which a motto is inscribed:

INDUSTRY DOMINATES FORCE

This phrase was Ignazio's idea. Ingenuity, research, and work will defeat ignorance, brute force, and underdevelopment.

His plan for a large exhibition in Palermo is slowly taking shape. He has spoken to many politicians in Rome, and to other large entrepreneurs throughout Italy. He has found in the architect Ernesto Basile the ideal person to handle the projected pavilion. Ernesto has an architectural vision Ignazio likes very much, more refined but also more modern than that of his father, Giovan Battista, who designed the Teatro Massimo. Of course, it'll take money, time, energy . . .

But that motto already contains the ultimate purpose of his project. What does he care about all the obstacles he'll encounter on the way? He'll overcome them all.

Progress cannot be stopped.

◠

Shortly before Christmas 1890, Ignazio starts to feel a strange fatigue that makes it difficult for him to get up in the morning and forces him to rest in the afternoon, abandoning his office on Piazza Marina and giving up on his regular visits to Banco Florio. Giovanna doesn't appear to notice her husband's malaise: one of her dearest friends, Giovanna Nicoletta Filangeri, Princess of Cutò, is ill. She goes to visit her almost every day and takes loving care of her. Every day, she sees her wasting away from an illness that puzzles all the physicians.

"You know something? Apparently, it's connected to a hernia that was poorly treated," she explains to Ignazio over dinner, a few days after the feast of the Immacolata. They're alone in the large dining hall at the Olivuzza. Ignazziddu is out at a party with Giuseppe Monroy and Romualdo Trigona. Vincenzo is in his room, where he has had dinner with his nanny.

Ignazio doesn't reply.

Giovanna looks up and stares at him.

He is motionless, eyes closed, pale.

"What's the matter? Are you unwell?"

Ignazio waves a hand, as though to dismiss that thought. Then he opens his eyes, picks up his spoon, plunges it into the fish soup, and looks at Giovanna with a smile that's more like a grimace. For some time now, he's felt a little nauseated when eating, he says, giving her a look that's meant to be reassuring but only makes her even more agitated.

She realizes that Ignazio has hardly touched his food, and not for the first time. The discomfort he feels and has obstinately ignored now becomes concrete, tangible, practically sliding from him to her and slipping under her skin, alarming her.

Giovanna is suddenly afraid.

She's afraid because her husband has never before had those dark rings under his eyes. Afraid because his face is gaunt and even his hair, usually thick and glossy, seems dull. Afraid because there's a strange, unpleasant smell about him.

"You've grown thin," she mutters.

"Yes, it's true, I've lost some weight. It's been a tiring time, and I don't sleep much."

"Is that all you've eaten?" she asks, taking his hand and indicating his plate.

He shrugs. "I'll think I'll get our doctor to examine me tomorrow," he says, pushing his plate away.

She's surprised by this unexpected decision. She doesn't know how to interpret it, all she knows is that it frightens her. "Yes, of course, I won't go to see Giovanna tomorrow. I'll stay with you. You'll get yourself examined. Maybe all you need is a supplement, or a syrup for sleeping."

Without replying, Ignazio stands up and kisses her on the forehead. "Perhaps. But now I'm going to bed." He walks away. He looks more hunched, and his step is less elastic, less confident.

Giovanna listens to him walk up the stairs. Once silence is restored, she joins her hands in prayer.

The doctor arrives late in the morning. To distract herself, Giovanna has given the order to start decorating the villa for Christmas and to prepare the salon for the arrival of the big fir tree.

But anxiety follows her from room to room, climbs up her skirts, twists around her throat like a small, evil grass snake, then slithers down into her stomach and settles there. Donna Ciccia sees her often put her hands on her belly, clutch the silver and coral rosary beads, then put them back in her pocket. She looks at her and shakes her head without saying anything, because she doesn't like what she senses in the air, and wonders if this time it truly might be appropriate to ask the souls in Purgatory what's going on.

Exhausted, Ignazio has stayed in bed, in the dim light coming in through the half-closed shutters.

Giovanna gives instructions, moves vases and candles, and sharply chides the servant women, who she thinks are too slow. In the end, she tells off Vincenzo, who is bothering the servants with his jokes as they arrange the decorations. She sends him to practice his violin, then regrets it and begs him to cease "that torture."

The doctor arrives, speaks to Ignazio, and examines him with the help of the valet. Giovanna quickly realizes that something's wrong. She sees it in Ignazio's face when he describes how he feels, and this is confirmed when he strips, revealing how almost startlingly thin he is.

She leaves the room, her head down. Inside her, it's as though something is shifting from vapor to solid. Anxiety is turning to terror.

Donna Ciccia is waiting for her. She reaches out and holds her tight. After all, she's been the mother Giovanna never had, the comfort she's always needed. "Come now, calm down. The doctor hasn't said anything yet."

"But he's not himself anymore," she replies, closing her eyes and putting a hand over her lips, as though trying to put up a barrier to stop her anguish from surfacing.

Shortly afterward, the doctor calls her in. Donna Ciccia practically pushes her forward, shuts the door behind her, and joins her hands in prayer.

"Your husband is very run down, signora. I'll take a urine sample and do some tests, and also draw a little blood. Meanwhile, he needs a light but nourishing diet to help him build up his strength and get better. And he needs rest, a lot of rest." The doctor is a tall man with dark hair graying at the temples and a nose blotched by clusters of purple veins. He turns to Ignazio and warns him sternly, "No traveling or excess, Senator. Now is not the time."

Ignazio nods from the bed. He doesn't look at Giovanna; he doesn't want her to worry any more than she already does.

That's why he conceals what the doctor has just told him: that the pungent smell of his sweat, his taut skin, brittle as paper, the discomfort in his eyes, his tiredness, ongoing weight loss, and insomnia all suggest that his kidneys are exhausted and struggling to clean his blood.

Ignazio lets his wife and the doctor agree on the treatment. He hears them mention steam baths, digitalis, iron to strengthen the blood, milk . . . Then he turns to Nanài and asks him to go into his study and fetch pen and paper. Giovanna shakes her head, intending to rebuke him, but he explains, almost gently, "Just a few letters. I can't abandon the business entirely."

Once he's alone, he writes to his friend Abele Damiani, advising him to pay great attention to the matter of the mail concessions. It's true that at the moment they're managed by NGI, but they will expire in a year's time and Casa Florio needs them to be renewed; then he prepares a memorandum for Caruso, requesting news of the modernization of the tuna conservation plant on Favignana.

All at once, a voice through the door.

"Papà!"

His features drawn, anxiety in his voice, incredulity in his eyes, Ignazziddu comes in, props his stick against the door frame, and throws his hat on an armchair, while Nanài catches his coat in mid-air as it's about to fall on the floor.

He stops, facing Ignazio, and is about to sit down on the bed, then hesitates. "May I?"

Ignazio allows himself a smile and pats the blanket with his hand. "Of course! Come. I'm just a little tired."

Ignazziddu obeys.

"Well? What's happening on Piazza Marina?"

For the past year, his son has been working with him, and Ignazio has even given him power of attorney for the affairs of Casa Florio. But he himself has always remained in overall control—discreetly, gently, but firmly—and it's this that has reassured both of them.

"Nothing unusual. Laganà keeps saying that, in order to support the new charter contracts, we have to improve the service, modernize the passenger quarters, and increase the staff wages. But he knows perfectly well that we're working on a tight budget, given that the state subsidies are pretty meager and we're unable to cover all the expenses. True, the steamers are being repaired at the Oretea."

"What about the winery? Any news?"

Ignazziddu bows his head and fiddles with the sheet. "Good news, Papà, don't worry. I had a letter from Mr. Gordon just today. He says they've had excellent results with Antonio Corradi's seal, the one we adopted to avoid any thefts of wine during transit: putting a metal clasp over the cork tops of the casks means they can't be opened without it being obvious that they've been forced."

Ignazio sits up. He's already feeling better. Perhaps the doctor is right: he has to reduce his commitments and get more rest. In a word: delegate. "Excellent," he says. "It takes twice a stubborn man to stand up to a stubborn one."

Ignazziddu laughs.

Ignazio motions him to stand and asks him to pass the cashmere dressing gown. "Let's go for a stroll in the garden."

"Are you sure? It's getting dark."

"As long as your mother doesn't see me. Where is she, by the way?"

Ignazziddu shrugs. "In the green salon, reciting the novena of the Immacolata with Donna Ciccia and the maids, I imagine. Is there anything else my mother does besides praying and sewing?"

"Ignazziddu . . ." his father admonishes him. "That's how your mother is."

"My mother should have been a nun."

Ignazio laughs, then looks out the window: evening is falling after a day that has been unusually mild for December. The grounds—bare, silent, put to rest by the gardeners—are bathed in half-light and only the noise of the wind weaving its currents through the branches suggests that it's winter. He can already imagine the peace he will feel, walking along the avenues that lead to the aviary with the parrots, the parakeets, the blackbirds, and the big golden eagle.

He glances at the bed behind him and leans on his son. "It's not healthy to love one's bed." As he says this, however, he recalls his father's allusions to the illness of his grandfather Paolo. Vincenzo never talked much about it and the little he knew came from his grandmother Giuseppina, peace be with her. All that remains of him are a few words that have been recounted and his tomb in Santa Maria di Gesù.

But there is one memory that's still vivid and indelible: many years ago, his father took him to see a ruined building with, beside it, a lemon tree that had grown wild. It was the house in which Paolo Florio had died of consumption. Vincenzo, his father, was eight at the time. That was when *Zio* Ignazio had started to take care of him.

He shudders.

His own Vincenzo is almost eight.

The Christmas holidays pass in a semblance of calm. Every night, the Olivuzza, warm and welcoming, gleams in the middle of the grounds: the light spreads from the windows, caresses the trees, reveals the outlines of the hedges, and chisels the line of palm trees that rise into the sky. But the light seems also to flood all the rooms, even the most remote, as if Giovanna has ordered the servants to light all the lamps and beat back the darkness. The guests gather around the fir tree, which is laden with red candles. Giulia and Pietro are here, together with young Giuseppe, who's a year and a half old, and his little brother, born on August 22. Ignazio's sister Angelina and her husband, Luigi De Pace, are also present. On the other hand, as often happens, the Merle family has remained in Marseille: since the death of Augusto, Giuseppina's father-in-law, they haven't been back to Sicily even once. Giuseppina, François, and Louis Auguste, who is a grown man now, have, however, sent a chest full of gifts.

Giovanna is doing everything she can to keep her mind and her hands occupied. She has organized the traditional distribution of gifts to the local poor and supplies for the newborn babies of the neediest families, asking everyone to pray for her and her family. She has taken a close interest in the girls of the embroidery school, who have been busy finishing trousseaux for the weddings due in spring, after Lent. She has entertained the guests every hour of the day, except when she joined the ladies of the house in prayer.

All this, just so as not to leave any room for apprehension.

For his part, Ignazio has been alternating mornings of rest with those on which he goes to his office on Piazza Marina. He's trying not to appear weak: that wouldn't be in the best interests of Casa Florio. In the afternoon, he makes no attempt to avoid chattering with the guests. Nevertheless, he hardly moves, pecks at his food, and often sits in his armchair by the fire, reading or writing letters on the portable walnut-and-brass desk.

During the festivities, Giulia has noticed that her father is more tired than usual but hasn't had the courage to ask a straight question. There have been whispers, glances, allusions. Ignazziddu has struck her as very tense, almost ill-tempered, and her mother has hinted at something, but then immediately changed the subject. In the rush of things needing to be done—for the children, for the receptions at Palazzo Butera, for their charity visits—she's had no time at all to speak directly to her father, to find out if there really is something wrong.

It's therefore with a mixture of anxiety and guilt that Giulia presents herself at the Olivuzza one cold, clear afternoon bathed in sunlight that doesn't warm, soon after New Year's Day. Giovanna isn't there: she's at the sickbed of the dying Princess of Cutò.

Without having herself announced, she goes straight into the study. But there's nobody at the desk. "Where's my father?" she asks brusquely of a butler who's dusting the registers kept on the bookshelves. The man looks at her uncertainly: the senator isn't well, and everyone in the house knows it. But it's not something to be mentioned out loud.

"Where is he?" Giulia insists.

The butler has no time to reply. Vincenzino appears in the doorway, hair disheveled and a sketchbook under his arm. He comes in and pulls her by her dress.

"Giulia! I'm going to him. Come with me."

He holds out his hand to her and she shakes it. They haven't spent much time together, she and this little dark-eyed devil, but then, there's a good thirteen years between them. When she married, he was only two: he's closer in age to her children than to her.

"How's Papà?" Giulia asks in a low voice.

Vincenzino shrugs and clutches her hand. "So-so." And in saying this, he opens his other hand in front of himself and moves it, imitating a wave. Ups and downs.

They come to the door of their father's room. Giulia knocks.

"Come in," a voice answers.

She hesitates, her hand motionless on the elaborate brass door handle, a bitter twist to her mouth. Her father's voice has always been deep and firm. This voice, though, is faint and hesitant.

She finds him in his armchair, wearing a smoking jacket.

"Have you got that, Nanài?" he's saying to the servant. "I want the carriage at nine on the dot. And remind Ignazziddu that he has to come, too. Laganà is waiting for us on Piazza Marina and . . ." At that moment he turns his eyes away and sees Giulia. His face spreads in a smile and he stands up and goes to her.

She clasps him in an embrace.

And understands.

She hides her face in his velvet collar, quickly building a dam inside her to stop her anxiety from overflowing. She's felt how thin and frail his strong, solid body has become. She's smelled an odor that the familiar aroma of Eau de Cologne des Princes, bought from Paver in Paris, can't overcome. She's seen how little his arms have risen, as if lifting them is too much effort.

Giulia moves away and looks at him, her eyes filling with tears. "Papà . . ."

Vincenzo is watching the scene, a pencil between his lips, his narrow eyes shifting from his father to his sister.

With a look, Ignazio implores Giulia to say nothing, then says to the boy, who has settled in the armchair where he himself was sitting, "Why don't you go down to the kitchens and ask them to bring us up something to eat, Vincenzo?"

Vincenzo opens his eyes wide. "I know there are fresh taralli. I smelled them earlier," he exclaims and jumps out of the armchair. "Milk for you, Papà?"

"Yes, thank you."

"Taralli?" Giulia interrupts him. "But you eat them on All Souls' Day."

Vincenzino shrugs. "It's all the same to me," he retorts, an amused gleam in his eyes. And he goes out, hopping on one foot.

"You're spoiling that boy too much," Giulia remarks, while Nanài moves a chair closer for her to sit down on.

"It's your mother. She can't say no to him."

Nanài exchanges glances with his master, then closes the door behind him.

"So, what's happening?" Giulia asks as her father sits down again. She can no longer hide the panic in her voice. She leans toward him and takes his hands.

"Nothing, nothing. I've been sick, some kind of poisoning of the kidneys." He puts a finger on her lips to silence her. "I'm better now. They've given me tonics and made me drink water and various concoctions I'd rather not talk about . . . and then they gave me milk, as if I were a baby. The diet they put me on seems to be having an effect. I haven't yet gotten all my strength back, but I know I'm on the right path."

Giulia brushes a lock of hair from his forehead, searching

frantically for some sign on his face, some trace of truth in what he's saying. But she can't find one. So she searches some more. She takes his face in her hands, looks into his eyes, and sees there what's hidden beneath the lie he's trying to tell himself and others.

Fear. Depression. Resignation.

She feels a chill come over her, like a rivulet of spring water. She dismisses it. "What does *Maman* say?"

He shrugs. "She's scared. But I'm not the kind of person to let myself be knocked down."

The image of a tall, sturdy olive tree materializes in front of Giulia's eyes. A tree that—as her father has always said to her—cannot die even if cut off at the root. But now *this olive tree* is collapsing before her very eyes, as if its sap is drying up, as if its roots are no longer able to draw nourishment from the earth.

"What about the doctors?"

"They say I'm getting better. But I'm the one who should speak before they do and say how I am. And I feel better." Almost as if to reinforce this assertion, he beats his chest with one hand. Then he continues, trying to maintain a cheerful tone, "I have to get back on my feet as soon as possible. As you know, Casa Florio is sponsoring the National Exhibition in November, here in Palermo . . ." And he adds with a smile, "Palermo like Milan and Paris, can you imagine? You should see the projects Basile is bringing to fruition for us. They're wonderful. The entrance pavilion is a reproduction of Moorish architecture, and there'll even be a panoramic viewpoint from where people will be able to admire the city."

"The architect Giovan Battista Basile? Isn't he too old for a commission like that?" Giulia asks. She knows what his answer will be, but she likes to see how her father changes whenever he's able to talk business with her. His eyes light up, his back seems straighter, and his voice has its old intensity.

"Not him. Ernesto, his son. Apparently, the father's not well. He's designed pavilions in an Arab-Norman style with little cupolas over the doors and a grand entrance that overlooks the new theater, the Vittorio Emanuele."

Giulia lets go of her father's hands and crosses her arms over her chest. "I've heard something about the National Exhibition. The other day the prefect came to my house and had a conversation with Pietro. He told him the Prince of Radalì is very pleased with the deal he made. He's already counting out the money coming his way."

Ignazio gives her a sideways look and almost smiles. With that calm, reserved air of hers, Giulia has always been good at catching the really important points in a conversation. For a long, dizzying moment, he imagines her running Casa Florio and making it prosper thanks to the intuition and acumen she's shown over the years. *Not like Ignazziddu, with his head in the air . . .* But then he shakes his head, as if to free himself of that absurd idea. "Radalì was clever, my girl," he replies. "He granted us the use of the terroir of Villafranca, where he has his citrus groves, for free, because, as he well knows, once the exhibition is over, he'll be able to sell the land at the price he wants. He'll make a ton of money."

Giulia nods, pleased that her father's ill health is no longer the focus of the conversation. "He's no fool. On one side he has the theater, on the other Via della Libertà, and then, at the far end of his lands, the hotels and the new gardens, with the road that'll reach all the way to the Parco della Favorita. He'll be able to do whatever he wants there."

"Indeed." Ignazio stretches. "Once again, Palermo should thank us. It's because of the Florios and their saints in heaven that certain things are getting done. You know, in Rome, nobody wanted the exhibition to be held here. Sicily would be too far away, they said, and it would cost too much to transport everything by ship . . . in other words, our ships, and that's what some call gobbling up success." He pauses and asks for a glass of water. The anxiety that receded for a moment surfaces again. "Everything will be organized by the Florios. The ships that'll bring the exhibitors and their goods will be Florio ships. The biggest pavilions will be the Florio pavilions, with their tuna, their marsala, their machines from the Oretea." He smiles and looks into the now empty glass, seeing through it the patterns on his dressing gown. His is a distant, oblique smile. "And we in our turn must give thanks to *Avvocato* Crispi," he concludes.

Giulia raises her eyebrows, then nods slowly. Francesco Crispi is the protective deity of Casa Florio in general, but also her personal one; she realized that on the day of her wedding, when her father told her that it was Crispi who had drawn up the matrimonial articles that secured her dowry. "True. But he couldn't have done anything without you." She is laconic and direct. That politician could have done nothing without the Florios' money.

Ignazio is about to reply when Vincenzino arrives, followed by a maid with a tray on which are milk and biscuits.

Giulia thanks her and takes a tarallo: a soft biscuit, covered with lemon icing, that's usually made for All Souls' Day. But everyone in the house knows that Vincenzino is greedy for them, and they gladly make an exception for him . . . *Perhaps they make a few too many exceptions*, she thinks, with a frown. But as soon as the other dish appears, she bursts out laughing. "*A' pignuccata!* Much better!" She takes one of the honey-covered dough sticks and puts it in her mouth. Then she licks her fingers, immediately imitated by her brother.

Watching them, Ignazio feels his heart swell. He sees again Giulia when she was a child and, beside her, for the first time in so long, his Vincenzino, that child who was denied an adulthood. He remembers their games in the grounds, their laughter, the sound of their breathing as they slept, their mischievous pranks that were the despair of Giovanna.

Nothing is left of all that.

As for *this* Vincenzino, he can only watch him from a distance. He's too lively, always on the move, and Ignazio can't keep up with him, occupied as he is in recovering his strength. He takes a sip of milk and stops again. He looks at Giulia, who's spoon-feeding her brother and telling him about those nephews that for him are more like cousins, given their closeness in age. He listens to their laughter and wonders how much of their lives he has missed. What has happened to the years when his children were still little? He was busy growing his business, reaching those heights of wealth and power of which his father had only been able to get a taste. His mother had told him, much earlier: *Of the things we can miss out on, the childhoods of our children are among the most painful.* It's only now that Ignazio has understood this.

Now that he can do nothing about it.

And this pain blends into another, that nameless pain that speaks of a time that might have been and wasn't, of a joy he turned his back on and which has become crystallized in the realm of things that are lost and, for that very reason, perfect.

For a moment, the aroma of the taralli is replaced by that of carnations, the aroma of the summer in Marseille.

Then it fades.

～

The weeks go by, winter is coming to an end. Ignazio gets back on his feet and tries once again to take full control of his business. He even plans to go to Rome and writes to his friend Senator Abele Damiani.

But his body doesn't agree.

He realizes this one morning, after a sleepless night in which he suddenly experienced severe pain in his back, along with retching. When he tries to get out of bed, he feels dizzy, and his legs won't support him. He looks at his hands and sees that they're shaking. He staggers to the dresser, supporting himself first on the edge of the bed, then on the armchair, and looks for himself in the mirror.

And doesn't find himself.

Because that hollow-cheeked ghost can't be him, he thinks with terror. That gaunt face, that body that seems lost inside the nightshirt, that dull, yellowish skin. None of it belongs to him.

He calls for Nanài, once, twice. The third time, the man arrives and, when Ignazio sees his own eyes reflected in his, he realizes. He realizes there's no more time, that this thing that's poisoning him is determined to carry him off in a hurry.

"Call my wife," he murmurs. "And the doctor, too."

A few moments later, the door between Ignazio's room and Giovanna's is flung open. In her dressing gown, her hair disheveled, Giovanna crosses the room, stumbling in her slippers.

She sees him and lifts a hand to her lips. "You weren't like this yesterday," she says.

Ignazio stands there motionless, saying nothing. It would be too much effort.

She returns his gaze. She's a strong woman. But she's also scared. "Something . . . Something must have happened last night."

When the two doctors arrive, they examine him and again take blood and urine samples, in the hope that tests will give some indication. That'll take time, though. If they were somewhere else, in a northern city, for example, they would have other instruments entirely, but here . . .

As soon as they've finished their visit, they join Giovanna in the grounds, far from prying ears. The two men look at each other, embarrassed, searching for the right words, the most delicate, the least cruel. But they hesitate.

She needs only a glance to understand.

And she has one realization: she doesn't want to know.

She turns abruptly and runs off to look for Ignazziddu. She finds him in his father's study, looking through papers. She asks him, begs him, to talk to the doctors, because it can't be true that . . .

Meanwhile, the two doctors are waiting in the grounds, looking at each other in dismay, not knowing what to do. Ignazio's son arrives, and they talk to him.

He listens with bowed head. He feels as if the sky is trying to crush him, as if the trees around him are about to fall on him, as if the earth is shaking. He says he'll place two rooms at their disposal, here in the Olivuzza. There's no point in their leaving, not with their patient in that state.

He goes back inside the house, gives instructions to the servants, dismisses the doctors with a handshake, then again takes shelter in the grounds.

Nobody stops him.

He walks unsteadily, wandering along the avenues with his arms open, as if searching for the consolation of an embrace.

He weeps.

He has already lost a brother, and he remembers him well. He knows what it means to bury a piece of life and doesn't want to do it again. The smell of that torture is still in his nostrils, the smell of the white lilies around Vincenzo's coffin. His father is not much more than fifty, he can't go like this.

It's too soon, *much* too soon.

What will I do? he asks himself. He weeps with angry sobs, for a long time, while, in her room, his mother weeps in the arms of Donna Ciccia.

But he can only think of the pain exploding inside him.

As spring takes its first timid steps, Ignazio feels the life unlatch itself from his skin and bones, like a garment one is obliged to discard. He remains in his room, buried in the armchair by the window. The air is just a little warm, scented with hay and flowers. The hum of insects is broken by the cries of the birds in the aviary and the yells of Vincenzino playing with the velocipede in the grounds.

It's March, and he can smell the scent of the earth warmed by the sun. Oh, there will still be cold days, as always happens. But the reign of winter is over and very soon buds will open on the trees, the rose hedges will blossom, the pomelia will be covered in white flowers, and in his beloved orange grove in Villa ai Colli the trees will give up their last fruit.

He doesn't have much time left.

Such a brutal thought, such an honest thought, that despair wells up in him.

Everything. He is about to lose everything.

His sons, whom he won't see grow, won't be able to advise or support: Vincenzino, who's so small, but also Ignazziddu, who still has so much to learn and doesn't have the humility to do so. His wife, Giovanna, for whom he feels, if not love, a deep tenderness for the generous devotion she has always shown. But also Favignana, with the rough profile of Marettimo and the soft profile of Levanzo, which emerge as soon as you sail around the island. The boats lowered for the *mattanza*, their black hulls cutting through the blue of the waves as it turns red with blood. The dusty white of the tuff quarries. The smell of the sea mingling with that of the tuna. And then again, the Marsala winery, with its walls of tuff eroded by the sea, the iron worked in the Oretea, the funnels of the NGI ships . . .

He will lose all this, and he can't do anything about it, because he knows that death wants us as naked and pure as when we come into this life. Because his will can do nothing against fate.

In his mouth there is the acrid taste of bile, which seems to mingle with the taste of tears. Lately he has been weeping a lot, more than he would have liked, but how can he stop himself? He weeps in silence, feeling the despair that invades his veins and bones and leaves him exhausted, a wreck tossed on light waves.

Of course, he will continue to pretend, telling everyone that he'll rise again, that the doctors will find a new treatment. Of course, he will fight to the end, but he can't lie to himself.

He is dying.

And this idea—or rather, this certainty—is destroying him.

His has been a life of work, just like his father's. An entire existence spent at the service of an idea: that the Florios should be richer, more powerful, more important than anyone else. And that's how it has been. He has succeeded.

And now?

Now that he has demonstrated it?

Now that he no longer has a project, an office, a deal he can devote time and energy to?

My hands are full of things, but my heart is empty. I still have ideas and desires, and I would like to live and be with my family and see my grandchildren and follow life as it goes forward.

But instead . . .

Despair pierces his throat and takes his breath away.

Now that I'm going, what remains?

⌒

The weeks go by, and May arrives.

Now Ignazio can't even stay seated in his armchair anymore.

From the doorway, Giovanna watches Nanài and another manservant washing him. She looks at her husband's motionless face, sees in it his shame at being taken care of like a baby, an embarrassment even stronger than the physical pain he must be feeling.

Close by stands Ignazziddu. He squeezes his mother's shoulder, trying to hide the unease he feels at seeing his father handled like that by strangers. He looks away, then stammers something. He says he's going to the offices on Piazza Marina to see what's happening, and then he'll drop by Banco Florio to reassure everyone.

He's running away, running from this pain he can't bear.

Ignazio has seen him.

He shakes his head slightly, trying to withstand the waves of pain. He prays that his son will shake off his fear and become a good administrator. And it's this thought that makes him turn his face toward his wife.

"Giovannina . . . call the notary."

She merely nods.

The notary, Francesco Cammarata, arrives at dusk to record Ignazio's wishes: his inheritance is to be divided between the two male heirs, Ignazziddu and Vincenzo. He knows that Ignazziddu isn't ready yet, that it'll take sharp teeth not to be eaten up, and that his son, who has become the eldest through no fault of his own, may not have the necessary shrewdness to run Casa Florio. But he can't do otherwise. He bequeaths a regular income to Giovanna and a share of the estate to Giulia. He also makes bequests to the house servants and a few of the workers.

Giovanna is sitting behind the door, next to Donna Ciccia. She's holding her rosary of coral and silver, praying almost without moving her lips. She doesn't even know what she's praying for. Perhaps for a miracle. Perhaps to ask forgiveness for sins she doesn't even know she committed. Perhaps to find relief. Perhaps so that her husband will find peace.

When the notary comes out, it's Donna Ciccia who walks him to the door. Giovanna remains on the threshold of the bedroom, one hand on the door frame and the other clutching the rosary to her heart.

Ignazio turns his head on the pillow and sees her. He gestures to her to come closer.

"I've been thinking of you," he says, trying to smile. His lips are cracked, and his beard is now almost completely gray.

"And I've been thinking of you," she replies, lifting the rosary.

"You must get better. You will get better. The Lord God must grant me this."

He clasps her hand and indicates the door with a motion of his chin. "*U' sacciu.* I know. Now let me sleep for a little while. Then, when Ignazziddu comes back, tell him to come and let me know what's happening at NGI. We must also write to Crispi and remind him about the renewal of the mail concessions. Even when the procession has stopped, the candle can still burn out . . ."

She nods, swallowing a lump of tears. Annoyance and bitterness mingle, together with the feeling of having, for the umpteenth time, lost first place in her husband's life.

Casa Florio before God, before the family, before the children. Casa Florio, always, before everything.

Ignazio is alone now. He dozes off, drifting into a torpor caused by his exhaustion and by the laudanum they've started to administer to ease his pain.

In the semidarkness of the room, the gleam of the little electric wall light covers everything in a yellow patina.

He's awakened by a whisper of fabric. A rustling of skirts coming from the darkest corner of the room, an old, familiar sound that makes his heart beat faster.

He opens his eyes and peers into the gloom. He even raises his head to get a better look.

Then he sees her and lets his head fall back on the pillow.

It could only be her.

The figure advances toward the bed with small, silent steps.

Curly blond hair with reddish hints. Very light skin. A smile that can't quite blossom fully on the thin lips.

He can smell her scent: fresh and clean. Carnation.

Camille.

She looks twenty years old. She's wearing the same dress she wore the day they met, in Marseille, in the summer of 1856.

She sits down on the edge of the bed and reaches out a hand toward him. The mattress doesn't bend beneath her weight, nor does her hand wrinkle the material. But her touch is warm, and her gaze—that gaze—is full of understanding and love. Her blue eyes are no longer reddened by tears or resentment, but seem illuminated by a light of forgiveness that, for a moment, Ignazio doesn't think he deserves. Then he understands, and now he closes his own eyes. He understands that love, true love, love that never dies, can exist only if accompanied by forgiveness. That in each one of us there is remorse searching for absolution.

He savors that touch, breathes in that scent of flowers that staves off the stink of illness.

He can't say if Camille is really there or if she's a ghost imprisoned between sleep and waking. He knows, though, that he has stopped being afraid, and that the wound he's been carrying inside him for years, that lack of forgiveness for the pain he inflicted, that emptiness dictated by an absence he forced on himself, well, that emptiness is no longer there. And even his guilty feelings toward Giovanna are fading, because now he knows, he has understood that you can love different people at the same time, and that you only need to accept what you feel and what you receive, like a gift. That he may have been wrong, but that there is no more time to make things right. Now he has only to forgive and be forgiven.

Now she is talking to him.

He closes his eyes. He surrenders to the sound of her voice, which is the sound of memory, those whispered words of French that caress his heart and allow a few sparse tears to wash his soul before sliding down from his eyes. He allows himself, at last, to be at peace.

At the Olivuzza, time seems to slow down and occasionally it's as if it has folded in on itself, waiting.

Vincenzino has broken off his violin lesson. He tiptoes to his father's room, accompanied by the governess, who stops him going in because "he mustn't be disturbed." Vincenzino, who's only eight years old, is living with a nameless terror, a fear that is reflected in his mother's frantic gestures. His mother is increasingly grim and distant, always with her rosary in her hand, absorbed in prayer, followed by Donna Ciccia begging her to eat something or at least to rest a little.

The only one taking care of him is Ignazziddu, and even he sets off in the morning for the Oretea or Piazza Marina, or God knows where, and often goes to the club in the evening, coming back late, very late. But his face, too, has hardened, and Vincenzino notices.

He would like to ask, to know, to understand, but he's not sure which questions to pose. He knows that something serious is happening, but he's still a child and can't put the pieces together.

He only knows that his brother is always running away from home as soon as he can.

Then, one evening, the governess comes to fetch him from his room. He's in bed, numb with exhaustion.

The governess's bloodshot eyes are the final piece of the mosaic he has assembled in his mind.

Because, at that moment, Vincenzo understands.

His father is dying.

As far as he's concerned, death belongs to the tombstones in the chapel of the Santa Maria di Gesù cemetery, behind which, he's been told, are his grandparents and that brother who shared his name and whose place he knows—in the terrible, unintentional way typical of childhood—that he took. To him, that other Vincenzo is an image, a photograph his mother keeps on her dressing table and looks at every day. And that's how he imagines him: pale, asleep, covered in powder amid garlands of silk flowers, like a china doll.

The governess helps him put on his dressing gown and takes him to his father's room. He goes in. He's assailed by the smell of mustiness, sweat, and fear. Beside the bed is his mother, holding his father's hand and clutching a handkerchief in her other hand. A priest in a purple stole is putting away the holy oil and the missal.

Ignazio is little more than an outline beneath the sheets. Made transparent by illness, his skin is marked with a network of bluish veins. On the night table, a cup of milk and a spoon.

Vincenzino lets go of the governess's hand and approaches the bed. He takes one of his father's hands and lifts it to his face, hoping for a caress, even though his father has always been sparing with them.

The hand is warm, almost hot.

"Papà." He's scared. He has to gasp for air and, in doing so, he pushes back the tears burning his throat.

"Vincenzo . . ." Ignazio murmurs. "My son." His voice is a thread, a hoarse winnow of air grazing his windpipe. His face lights up and a smile of tenderness appears. He strokes his cheek and ruffles his hair. On the other side of the bed, Giovanna lets out a sob.

"You'll be like my father. Just like him."

Then he looks behind his son's back, and his smile broadens. The boy feels his brother's fingers come to rest on his shoulder, squeezing it so hard it almost hurts.

"An Ignazio and a Vincenzo." Ignazio's words are a breath. His last. "As it was from the start, so must it be."

&

When, on May 17, 1891, news of Ignazio Florio's death reaches the Oretea Foundry, the workers hug one another in disbelief and burst into tears, as though it's not the master who's died, but one of them. NGI's seamen disembark from their ships and gather outside the foundry, while a crowd of men and women, their eyes red, their breathing uneven, pours down the streets toward the villa, and stops, silent, at the garden gates, observing the parade of carriages: the most prominent families in Palermo, and then of the whole of Sicily, are arriving to pay homage to Senator Florio—but it is they, the workers and the seamen, who are his people.

Inside the villa, the maids are bustling, retrieving black crepe outfits from trunks, covering mirrors, and shutting windows. Only one stays open, on Donna Ciccia's instructions: that of Ignazio's bedroom, so that his soul may fly away. She remained at his bedside for a long time, like a statue made of flesh, as though she could still speak to the man her *protegée* had loved and, she knows, will continue to love for the rest of her days.

Ignazio's body has already been dressed in a very elegant black suit—made by Henry Poole, Savile Row's most prestigious tailor—once reserved for special social occasions. Only, the suit is so loose on him, it doesn't look like it's his.

At the foot of the bed, a priest is muttering prayers, accompanied by a small group of orphan girls and novices from the nearby convent. The air is suffused with frankincense, flowers, and candle wax. It's so overpowering, it takes your breath away.

After the body is blessed, Donna Ciccia escorts the priest and his small procession to the door, while Vincenzo returns to his room. He has a fit of crying and his governess chooses to stay and comfort him.

Looking even slimmer in her black silk faille dress, Giovanna roams about the house, her bony fingers spasmodically clutching her skirt, her feet tripping over the rugs. There is a lost look in her eyes. She follows the maids around, ordering them to keep the parquet and the black-and-white checkered floors polished, and to dust everything; she asks the butler to keep a record of those who come to express their condolences. It won't be said that the Florios don't say thank you.

Ignazziddu, on the other hand, is still in a corner of his father's bedroom, with his sister, Giulia. She's wearing a black crepe dress and has lifted the mourning veil over her hair. She looks at Ignazziddu. "I can't believe he's gone."

Her brother shakes his head. "Now I have to take care of the family," he murmurs. "Me. Do you realize?"

Giulia turns just slightly and stares at him with her pale eyes, the same as her grandmother's. She can neither indulge her brother's fear nor justify it. She swallows a lump of tears, straightens, and replies confidently, "Yes, you. You're Ignazio Florio now."

He looks at her and opens his mouth to say something, but Giovanna walks into the room, searching for them with her eyes, coming to them. "The first visitors are here, the d'Ondes cousins are already in the salon," she says, then looks at Giulia, "with your relatives."

She nods. "I'll go and welcome them."

Ignazziddu follows her with his eyes. He knows Giulia has always been stronger than him, and watching her leave increases his fear.

He's afraid of everything now.

He hates funerals, he hates the pain eating away at him, bringing back to the surface the sense of abandonment he felt when his brother died. He wishes he could hide, vanish, become invisible to everything and everyone.

So, when his mother grabs him by the sleeve, he instinctively hugs her in a desperate embrace. But she wriggles free, places her hands on his shoulders, and pushes him away. Then she looks at him with her dark eyes and hisses, "Now you mustn't leave me alone."

At these words, all of a sudden, Ignazio ceases to be Ignazziddu. It's his future he hears in that angry, unhappy voice.

Giovanna turns to look at her husband, the man she loved so much, and whom only death was able to take from her. She approaches and touches his sleeve. Then she kneels, rests her head on the bed for a moment, and takes his cold, stiff hand.

She removes his wedding band, kisses it, and presses it to her heart. Then she slips off the family ring, the one his father, Vincenzo, gave him on their wedding day, the one that had belonged to another Ignazio, and before him to his great-grandmother Rosa Bellantoni.

It belongs to another era: when the Florios were mere shopkeepers, *putiàri*.

Giovanna has no way of knowing this. Nobody, not even Ignazio, has ever told her about this distant, humble past, except through embarrassed hints. She only knows that her husband never parted with this ring.

She replaces the wedding band on his finger and rests her hand on his motionless chest, like a caress. Never again will she touch this man she accepted inside her, with whom she had four children, and who gave her so little love and so much sorrow.

She will never touch him again, but she will never stop loving him. Nobody can take him away from her now.

Giovanna straightens her back and stands up.

She goes to her son, takes his hand, and practically forces it open. She puts his father's ring on his finger.

"You're the head of the family now."

Ignazio has no time to object, to say that this old-fashioned ring is loose on him, that he doesn't want it, that it's too heavy. All at once, the room is filled with people crossing themselves, muttering prayers, then coming to him to express their condolences.

Giovanna sees the Trigona cousins and bursts into floods of tears, her mouth open in a silent cry of grief, when one of them hugs her.

Ignazio stands there, next to his mother, as she cries her eyes out. He feels people's eyes on him, hears their whispers, fragments of sentences.

And he doesn't know what to do.

On November 15, 1891, a large cavalcade of coaches advances across Palermo and stops outside the Salone delle Feste of the entrance pavilion to the National Exhibition, next to the Teatro Politeama Garibaldi—renamed in 1882—which has at last been given the final touches for the occasion.

From the largest coach, emblazoned with the coat of arms of the House of Savoy, King Umberto I and Queen Margherita step out. Then follows the coach of the prime minister—Antonio

Starabba, Marquis of Rudinì—who's from Palermo. He took Crispi's place a few months ago, but he, too, is a southerner, the former mayor and former prefect of Palermo. After inaugurating the exhibition, the king and his entourage cross the semicircular square, leaving the two towers with Moorish domes flanking the entrance behind them. That's where the statues of Industry and Work are, forged in bronze by another man from Palermo: Benedetto Civiletti.

The cavalcade passes between the pavilions. They're imposing, full of light, with large arabesque-patterned arches. In the center of the exhibition there's a Moorish garden with, in the middle, a fountain enlivened by tricks of light. Farther on, another green holds the Arab Café, set up under a tent, next to the straw huts of the Abyssinian village that dominates the Eritrean exhibition, in homage to the colony that the Kingdom of Italy has succeeded in conquering with great difficulty and much blood, like that shed at the Battle of Dogali.

Meanwhile, Palermo waits, ever more restless. Outside the gates, tickets in hand, gather workers and barons, schoolmistresses and lawyers, merchants and seamstresses, united by the same excitement and enthusiasm. In the eight months it took Ernesto Basile to complete this ephemeral village of marvels, a string of rumors and indiscretions, often exaggerated and nearly always contradictory, spread. There's even been idle talk of a café with scantily clad Arab dancers and huge fountains spewing wine.

And so, as soon as the gates are opened, the crowd pours into the pavilions with all the impetuousness of a flow of lava. Mouths agape, necks craning, eyes filled with wonder, people enthuse over the Belvedere, which towers more than fifty meters high, and ascend to it on the hydraulic lift manufactured in the Oretea Foundry.

They stroll through the pavilions devoted to the mechanical and chemical industries, and to goldsmithing. Small groups of women admire the goods of the textile and furniture companies; the wealthier ones explore the arts pavilion, which exhibits more than seven hundred paintings and three hundred sculptures, while the lazier visitors head for the Café Chantant, which stands behind the pavilion dedicated to ceramics and glass.

Ignazio has barely glimpsed any of this, however. He first had to welcome the king and queen, with his mother—a patch of black wool crepe in a crowd of elegant colors and clothes—calmly accepting their condolences. Then he was caught in the celebratory whirlwind, shaking hands, greeting friends and acquaintances, paying homage to court dignitaries, and exchanging comments with politicians of varying ranks, who have come from all over Italy. He's been rooted to the spot.

And so, in the middle of this crowd that could trample him, disoriented by the chatter and sounds emanating from the pavilions, bothered by the cloying scent of sweets baked for the children, Ignazio has looked around, able only to see his father, who wanted this exhibition so much but was unable to view it completed. For as long as he was able to oversee the business, it always occupied the center of his thoughts: ensuring the building works were carried out on schedule, that the constructions were luxurious, that the Florio businesses had the right amount of visibility. As for Ignazio himself, he insisted that the cafés and entertainments have an appropriate place and be characterized by that accent of exoticism and sensuality that was so fashionable. The rest was managed by the engineers and, of course, the indefatigable architect Basile.

Everybody has congratulated him and his family, because the

government, of course, played its part, but the initial impulse and the funds . . . those were provided by the Florios. Everyone in Palermo knows: you can see it in the looks they give him, a mix of surprise, deference, and, above all, envy.

"Let them look," his father would have said. "Let them look. The rest of us have work to do."

Except that Ignazio wants to understand. He wants to see what other people have seen.

So, one morning, he gets his landau ready. With the hood up so that he can go unnoticed, he rides down Corso Olivuzza, full of new bourgeois villas punctuated by small gardens, and reaches the building site for the Teatro Vittorio Emanuele, where work resumed a while ago, also under the guidance of Ernesto Basile.

The fellow's a genius, he realizes when he takes in the tall pillars standing in relief against the sky. Admittedly, Basile's father, Giovan Battista, had a hand in it (he died in June of that year) but Ernesto unearthed a few structural flaws, and so partly redrew the plans. The building has been awaiting completion for longer than fifteen years. *If Basile doesn't manage to finish the theater*, Ignazio thinks bitterly, *then we'll be stuck with this stump forever.*

It's not far from there to the exhibition gates. Ignazio gets out of the carriage and steps in swiftly, trying to avoid the eyes of those in attendance, who remove their hats before him, begging for a greeting or even just a glance. He rushes through the goldsmithing pavilion and reaches that devoted to the mechanical industries, with windows overlooking the garden, currently crowded with visitors. He lowers his head and covers his face with one hand, not wishing to be recognized.

Slowing down, he walks gingerly to the center of the space, where the boilers from the Oretea Foundry are on display. Metal monsters, maws of glistening black iron with massive forms. Cylinders so large that a man standing up with his arms outspread couldn't touch the walls. They're the heart of the ships that transport goods and people around the world. *Their* ships.

All around, there are various hydraulic presses and, on smaller displays, cutlery, saucepans, and various items for the home. The products of other foundries seem to pale in comparison with those from the Oretea; they may be more evolved from the technical point of view, lighter and more attractive, but they're not as large or as powerful. *Besides, who cares?* he thinks. *Our items have the most visibility. This is what Palermo and all Italy have come to see. The power of the Florios.*

He proceeds in a leisurely fashion, looking around, and finds himself in the Labor Gallery, a huge corridor with a sloping roof from which a cascade of light falls, and where dozens of voices resound in a cavernous hum.

It's impossible not to see the tall pillars built with tuna cans from his *tonnaras.* Aluminum cans of every size, from the huge red ones supplied to the army, to those for everyday use, on which the sun glimmers, intensifying the colors of the enamel. Then there are fishing nets, papier mâché tuna and olive branches, arranged artistically to suggest the inside of the *tonnara.* There's even a *muciara,* one of the small boats used during the *mattanza.*

He continues to the wine section. He hides his smile with his fist, because he could find it with his eyes shut by following the sweet, intense smell of wine and liqueurs.

But he's not prepared for what he finds before him.

A tower almost scraping the roof, constructed of marsala bottles and surrounded by barrels. On the top, on a Corinthian capitol, stands a statue of Apollo, the god of the medical arts, symbolizing the healing properties of wine. Around the pillar, there are pyramids of bottles representing the different varieties of marsala, from vintage to reserve.

An employee comes up to him. "Don Ignazio, what a surprise! How—"

"No."

Abrupt and almost rude, Ignazio lifts a finger to silence him, his eyes fixed on the tower of bottles, the pyramids of barrels, the shelves filled with liqueurs. The man steps back, disconcerted.

Here it is. The Florio cognac in prime position.

It was launched a few years ago, employing techniques of the Charente region, encouraged to the very last by his father, and now managed by Ignazio personally, with the help of French experts. The result is a mellow, warm, delicate spirit, with the sweetness of honey, the colors of sunset, and a sumptuous wealth of flavors.

It's currently their most successful product.

He goes closer and throws his head back to have a better look.

He can see it now. Now that he's forced to look at this tower of bottles reaching up to the ceiling, he understands what his winery can produce.

My winery.

It belongs to the Florios, and therefore to him, because he is Don Ignazio Florio now. It's not his father's anymore, or his brother's. It's *his.*

Like his *tonnaras.* Like his Oretea. And all the rest.

How did he not realize it till now? Why didn't he understand this earlier?

Because they kept it hidden from him. That's why. His father to start with, always sheltering him, always allocating him provisional tasks. He never *really* trusted him.

As soon as his father died, they drowned him in problems, in legal commitments, in paperwork, in bills to pay. Then that pain in the neck Laganà started annoying him: all he can do is complain that there's no money. And then there's his mother, who keeps urging him to be cautious and, amid tears and sighs, exalting his father's exceptional qualities.

It doesn't matter anymore, Ignazio thinks. *He's dead and I'm alive. I'm here. And I'll show everybody that I can be just as great as him.*

He takes a deep breath and looks around. There's pride and wonder in his eyes, as well as something new that makes him dizzy and clouds his eyesight.

He will never be the prisoner of a name.

He will not be like his father.

He will not be like the others.

PART FOUR

Pearls

February 1893 to November 1893

Malidittu u'mummuriaturi,
ma chiossai cu' si fa mummuriare.
Damned is he who dishonors,
but even more so he who lets himself be dishonored.
—SICILIAN PROVERB

THEY'RE SPLENDID THINGS, PEARLS. AND strange. They're not inert, but neither are they alive.

Pearls hide in oysters, which resemble the rocks to which they cling, but inside are welcoming, vibrant with the luminescence of mother-of-pearl. And pearls are born from pain. Their origin is linked to an alien body that enters the oyster, forcing it to respond by forming a concretion of mother-of-pearl around the element that wounds its flesh.

From suffering, beauty is born, as is the case with many rare and precious things.

Pearls occupy "the first place, and the most eminent place, among all things of value," declares Pliny the Elder in his *Naturalis historia* (first century AD). And he goes on: "Pearls [are] of various types depending on the quality of the dew that they have received. If it has flowed pure, what strikes the eye is the whiteness of the pearl; the same pearl is pale if it is conceived when the sky is threatening." Pliny also tells how Cleopatra wagered with Antony that she could eat, in a single dinner, ten million sesterces. She then asked for vinegar, in which she melted one of the two pearls she wore on her ears and drank it. During the reign of Caesar Octavian Augustus, the passion for pearls, which by law could be worn only by patricians, leads some merchants to specialize in them. A passion that doesn't fade over the centuries: Elizabeth I is always portrayed in clothes adorned with pearls, a symbol of purity and virginity as well as economic power; apart from Vermeer's famous *Girl with a Pearl Earring* (1665–1666), there are many paintings by Dutch artists of the seventeenth century in which pearl earrings, necklaces, and bracelets feature; in the 1859 portrait attributed to Franz Xaver Winterhalter, Queen Victoria, then in her forties, is shown wearing a 161-carat diamond necklace and a pearl bracelet adorned with a cameo depicting her husband, Prince Albert, the same bracelet that Victoria has on her wrist in the portrait done in 1900 by Bertha Müller and which can be seen at the National Portrait Gallery in London: an elderly, tired, sad queen dressed in mourning (although Albert has been dead for almost forty years), with that bracelet as a mark of fidelity.

But all these pearls are still natural. It is only toward the end of the nineteenth century that a Japanese researcher, Kokichi Mikimoto, develops a method for "creating" pearls. It makes him immensely rich and, as the marketing genius that he is, he declares, "I want to live to see the day when there will be so many pearls that every woman will be able to buy a necklace and we will be able to give one to those women who cannot afford it."

Prophetic words: today, cultured pearls are within everyone's reach. They are popular, sometimes even banal jewels.

Natural pearls, born of the sea and of a hidden wound, remain a possession of the few.

It's a cold, bright day, swept by an angry wind. The gusts draw curses from the guests scrambling into the Church of San Jacopo in Acquaviva to avoid being splashed by the waves that beat on the jetty.

San Jacopo has simple, austere lines. It's quite different from the opulent baroque churches of Palermo, the city of the future bride and groom. But it faces the seafront in Livorno, just as if it were a safe haven for them.

Along the nave, a profusion of roses and white lilies in baskets adorned with cascades of ivy. In the air, the smell of incense mingles with the perfume of the flowers. Beyond the walls, the rumble of the sea serves as a counterpoint to the music of the organ.

Through the half-open door of the sacristy, the parish priest glances out at those who have already taken their places in the pews. He rubs his hands on his cassock, then raises them to his face and shakes his head. Never in his life would he have expected to have such an important wedding to celebrate. And in February, too!

Soon afterward, a man opens the front door of the church and peers in. He vanishes, only to reappear immediately afterward; on his arm is a woman dressed in black.

Mother and son.

Ignazio and Giovanna.

Behind them, Giulia Lanza di Trabia and Emma di Villarosa, holding Vincenzino by the hand. He's restless and excited. They walk down the nave, heads held high, handsome, haughty, elegant. While Ignazio places himself to the side of the altar, the three women and the boy sit down in the pew in front of him, immediately joined by Romualdo Trigona and Giuseppe Monroy, the bridegroom's witnesses; smiling, the two of them kiss the women's hands and ruffle Vincenzino's hair. Then they approach Ignazio and they all laugh together.

Who would ever have predicted that he would be the first to capitulate?

After a few moments Pietro Lanza di Trabia arrives, looking grim. He signals to Giulia and she gets to her feet, while Giovanna watches anxiously.

The two of them move a few paces away.

Giulia raises her hand to her chest, as if to calm her agitation. She doesn't have the courage to speak, to ask any questions. Her youngest child, Blasco, who's only two, is very ill and until the last moment she has been unsure whether or not she would attend her brother's wedding. She puts a hand on her husband's arm in a silent request.

"Nothing new after what they told us by telegram last night," Pietro murmurs with a shrug. "He's still weak with fever, still coughing." He holds back a sigh and squeezes her wrist. "Be brave. We're here now."

Giulia blinks and looks away. She won't cry, not today.

She looks at Giovanna and merely shakes her head. *Nothing new*, she seems to be telling her, and her mother collapses in on herself, clutching her coral-and-silver rosary. Then Giulia raises her eyes and looks at Ignazio. Her brother is twenty-four years old, and still so immature . . . And yet he's very much in love. He's ready to change his ways.

Despite the pain, Giulia smiles. No, she couldn't have missed his wedding.

 ᘒ

"So here we are!" Romualdo Trigona exclaims, slapping Ignazio on the back.

Ignazio steps aside but laughs. "Hey, easy does it!"

He's perhaps the happiest he's ever been. Certainly the happiest since his father's death.

That thought is a shadow, a drop of ink that's finding it hard to dissolve in this limpid ocean of happiness.

He's about to marry the most beautiful woman in Palermo. He had already started courting her when the illness that would kill Ignazio Florio revealed itself, but he had been doing so in a joking, lighthearted manner.

And then everything had changed. A tender feeling had been born, which had stayed with him, gently, through the weeks preceding his father's death. Hers had been the only true words of comfort; hers the caresses that had eased the pain of that loss.

Romualdo looks up at the ceiling of the nave. "Of course, this church is really bare, but all the same . . ." Then he looks again at his friend and, for a moment, his gaze, usually so sardonic, turns curiously grave. "Did you imagine, when you met her, that you would end up marrying her?"

Ignazio leans his head toward his friend. He frowns, then a smile relaxes his features and fills his eyes with pride. "No. But I realized right away that she was a special woman."

And so she is, he tells himself.

It all started on a bright spring afternoon, during a stroll with Romualdo, as it happened, in the public gardens of Villa Giulia, held fast between the sea of the Foro Italico and the Botanical Gardens. There, amid the avenues of palms and the cheesewood hedges, they saw three girls dressed in white, escorted by a governess with a strong German accent. As shameless as ever, they followed them. The girls noticed and started laughing and talking among themselves. Then he and Romualdo began whistling and exchanging humorous remarks in overloud voices.

There was a gust of wind and a straw hat blew away, ending up in the dust and drawing shrieks from the three girls. That was when Ignazio recognized Emma and Francesca, the Notarbartolo di Villarosa sisters, a family linked to the Florios by a long-lasting friendship. They were considered two of the most beautiful young women in Palermo.

But what of the other one? Who is she?

Tall and statuesque, with amber skin. She had started running along the path after the hat, which the wind was still pushing away. Everything about her gave off a spontaneous, irresistible grace: from her light, flexible step to the hand holding tight to the white skirt that kept lifting, revealing two shapely calves; from her other hand, held in front of her eyes to shield them from the sun, to her vague smile in which there wasn't a trace of malice.

Ignazio was faster than her: he had run after the hat and now he caught hold of it, carried it to her, and introduced himself, as charming and brash as only he could be.

The girl took the hat in her hands and then, looking up for a moment, said her name, her cheeks blushing a delightful red.

Franca Jacona di San Giuliano.

Yes, Ignazio had heard about her at the Casina dei Nobili in the Foro Italico. During one of those idle conversations punctuated by wreaths of cigar smoke and the clink of glasses of cognac, someone had told him that this girl had blossomed all of a sudden, just like that, and become a real beauty. Then this person had winked.

Ignazio had smiled, a brief, predatory smile, and said that he would judge for himself when he got the chance.

Nobody had mentioned that long, willowy neck, enhanced by the lace collar; those full breasts rising and falling beneath the ruffles of her blouse; those elegant calves exposed as she ran to recover her hat. Those large green eyes, clear and filled with embarrassment, that were now staring at him.

It was those eyes that made Ignazio lose his senses. No woman had ever looked at him in such a direct, sincere way, not even the most uninhibited. In those eyes there was a promise of wonders that seemed addressed only to him.

They didn't frequent the same circles of friends or attend the same social gatherings, but, after that encounter, he searched for her ceaselessly. He started going back and forth in his landau beneath the balconies of Palazzo Villarosa, where she lived; he would gaze at her from a distance; he made sure their paths crossed at Villa Giulia, where she loved to stroll; and he sent her passionate letters. Innocently bashful at the start, Franca accepted this courtship, first with vague incredulity, then with such abandon that Ignazio was shaken by it. But in the few moments in which they managed to be alone together, their hearts missed a beat with the fear of being discovered, given that the Jacona di San Giulianos would never agree to their daughter being courted by someone like Ignazio, the most shameless lady-killer in all Palermo.

Ignazio knew that from the start, nor could he say they were wrong. He had never been a saint, and he liked women.

He liked them a lot.

But she's different. She's Franca. And he—he knows it, he feels it—will love her all his life.

Giulia goes to her mother and brings her up to date on Blasco's condition. Giovanna mutters a weary "May God's will be done," then advises her to go and wait for the bride. Giulia nods and sets off with Emma. Vincenzino takes advantage of the distraction to slip away and join Ignazio.

Giovanna turns to Donna Ciccia, who's sitting much farther

back, and shakes her head. Donna Ciccia crosses herself. The two women no longer need many words.

Giovanna's husband died less than two years ago, and she's wearing an elegant, tight-fitting mourning dress made of satin and velvet, with a row of small pearls at her wrists. A patch of darkness among the flowers Ignazio has gathered from the hothouses of half of Italy. She feels despondent and out of place, as though life has escaped her control and she can do nothing to keep the pieces from slipping away. She's very embittered: this marriage is so different from what she had hoped for her son—and not only because the ceremony is about to take place in an unfamiliar city, far away from Palermo and their friends, and in a church so bare. She felt a pang in her heart when she walked in. She shifts uneasily on the pew. *It's as if they've eloped*, she thinks, and in a way, that is the case.

In Palermo, there's never a shortage of prying, judging eyes, whispers, words dropped at the right moment and with ease, which is what makes them heavier than boulders. It's an illusion to think that some things go unobserved; imagining that no one has noticed you is a form of naïveté for which you're likely to pay dearly. Gossip is a succulent morsel that fattens the emaciated ego of whoever spreads it and fuels it.

So it was inevitable that the rumors of Ignazio and Franca's courtship should reach Giovanna, even penetrating the thick curtain of grief over her beloved husband's death. These rumors worried her so much that she asked Donna Ciccia to find out if this flirtation was about to turn into something more serious.

The speed with which Donna Ciccia gathered gossip and conjecture about Franca's virtue left Giovanna speechless. They had in fact been seen on several occasions, and in positions unbecoming to a young woman from a good family. And what was even more disconcerting was how calmly Ignazio admitted to being in love with Franca. They'd been seeing each other for months, even though her parents were against it.

He stated this with determination in his voice and a feverishness in his eyes that troubled his mother deeply, bringing home to her, once again, the fact that her son was a grown man and wouldn't heed her anymore.

He swore to her that Franca was the right person—"I can feel it, Mamma: there's no one else like her"—and that he wanted to marry her, that with her he at last felt happy and light. That he was tired of living in that house, which had turned so gloomy since his father's death; that he wanted to enjoy himself, and love, and not think only about work and the dead who, like ghosts, kept hovering around him.

That was too much for Giovanna. How dare he throw her grief in her face? She protested, reminding him of his flings all over Europe, all the money—too much money—squandered on parties and trips, his less-than-worthy acquaintances, his lack of respect for his father's memory, and his ungratefulness toward both him and herself. She even went so far as to imply that the Jaconas were taking advantage of him, since although they had a title, they were riddled with debts. Everyone knew that Franca's father's business was going badly, that her family couldn't pay its suppliers. Ignazio shrugged at this—"Everyone has debts in Palermo, *Maman*"—then continued to claim that Franca was the ideal woman for him. There was nothing else to discuss.

And so Giovanna reacted as best she knew, or rather as social practice dictated. She took her time and waited for this infatuation to blow over, denying everything and spreading the rumor that Ignazio had been beyond reproach and that if anyone was to blame, it was that young woman, because she'd shown herself to be, if not easy, then at the very least careless, to become so intimate with her son who, as everybody knew, was a hot-blooded young man.

It was all in vain. Palermo had continued weaving stories; the names of Franca and Ignazio circulated on the streets, took shelter in salons, behind fans and hats raised over the faces of those who, between a nudge of the elbow and a smirk, even talked of secret rendezvous that turned into brazen encounters.

But then something unexpected suddenly happened: Franca's family was forced to move to Livorno for a while, probably owing to increasingly insistent creditors. At least that was what everyone said.

Giovanna heaved a sigh of relief. She hoped it would all fizzle out, like a fire deprived of wood, and that Ignazio would find someone else to have fun with.

But no.

"Of course, I would have preferred this wedding to be celebrated in Palermo, but this is fine. As long as my Franca is happy."

Costanza Jacona Notarbartolo di Villarosa, Baroness of San Giuliano, squeezes the hand of her niece, Francesca di Villarosa, who's sitting next to her in the carriage. The younger woman nods. "That's right," she mutters, pursing her thin lips and lowering her face, which seems to merge with the half-light.

She's wearing a black dress. A mourning dress.

She was widowed before she was twenty. She had married Amerigo Gondi, a Tuscan aristocrat, but a terrible illness snatched him away after they'd been married only three months; all the treatments and the healthy air of the Palermo countryside, where they'd moved in the hope that he would get better, were in vain. Sensing his approaching demise, Amerigo asked to die in Viareggio, where he'd been taken on one of the Florios' steamships, on the orders of Ignazio, who was aware of the deep affection between Francesca and Franca. And it's because Franca is like a sister to Francesca that the latter has agreed to attend the wedding: her cousin's marriage is the only glimmer of light in the clinging darkness in which she spends her days.

She hastily dries her tears. She doesn't want her aunt to see her cry or feel sorry for her. She doesn't want to bring sadness to a joyful day.

But Costanza has noticed and, embarrassed, bites her lip. Then she turns to her son, Franz, and adjusts the collar on his jacket. The boy makes a grimace that's meant to be a smile. Costanza sighs and turns to her lady-in-waiting. "Dry his mouth, he's slobbering," she mutters, a hint of sorrow in her voice.

There's sorrow in Francesca's eyes, too, as she silently watches these gestures. She knows what her aunt feels for this child, who was born sick, and knows what she's suffered: Costanza lost five very young children, and only Franca and Franz survived. But now a little joy is finally coming to her and her family: she has protected Franca with loving ferocity and prayed that she at least would be happy.

This marriage is the answer to her prayers.

⌒

When the coach stops outside San Jacopo in Acquaviva, Franca gives a start. She looks at her father, Pietro Jacona, then lowers her eyes. She shouldn't be nervous: she's beautiful and she knows it. She saw it when she looked at herself in the mirror shortly before setting off for the church. In the gilded wood mirror, she saw her regular features, her large green eyes, her long black hair styled in big waves, her slender figure. She's nineteen years old, possesses grace and elegance, and is wearing a splendid dress made of ivory silk, with a long silk tulle veil. It doesn't matter if she's pale or that she's feeling very chilly. She's about to marry the man she loves, she who's never loved anyone before.

Her fingers are trembling, her heart pumping blood into her veins at high speed: she can hear it thundering in her ears, so loud that it drowns out the sound of the waves crashing on the pier, a hollow sound that silences her thoughts. She feels like a romantic heroine, but this, she believes, is not a happy ending. It's the start of a wonderful life. Hers.

Then come the memories, the painful ones, of moments when she suffered, when she thought she'd lost everything, when she and Ignazio were forced to part. When she first met him, it was as though a violent light had torn through the gloom in which she'd lived for almost twenty years. Until that time, few people had taken notice of the *Baronessina* Jacona di San Giuliano, who lived in a barely respectable apartment in Palazzo Villarosa, *u' palazzo cornutu*, the cuckold's palace, as it was called, maybe because of the two chimneys that dominated the entrance, or perhaps because of the many extraconjugal affairs of the man who'd had it built, Francesco Notarbartolo, Duke of Villarosa. Then came Ignazio Florio, with his attentions and his courtship, and the whole city sat up and noticed her. She ended up on everyone's lips. Unable to attack her indisputable beauty, the critics, fierce at times, picked first and foremost on her way of walking, talking, and dressing. But their criticisms hadn't lasted long: although the Jacona di San Giulianos were now in financial straits, they had never spared expense when it came to their daughter. Not only had they given her an impeccable education, entrusting her to a German female tutor, but they had also raised her to love beauty and elegance. So, riding the crest of accusations aimed at Ignazio—a heartbreaker, a dissolute womanizer—the gossips fixated on tales that labeled her as "compromised." Spoiled goods, a woman who'd been too careless to be considered respectable: a shameless sinner.

At this point, Franca had to face her father's wrath: first, he shut her in at home, then dragged her away to Livorno with her mother and brother. All her protestations about being truly in love with Ignazio Florio were futile: like a wave of sewage pouring out from Palermo, gossip and malice also soiled Livorno, in addition to the cruel comments about her father and his unpaid debts.

Franca looks at the church doors. Her anxiety is like a layer of ice. Will she measure up to her new family? The Florios own the largest naval fleet in Italy, her mother-in-law knows half the crowned heads of Europe, and her sister-in-law is a princess. She will become one of them, not the wife of a provincial baron or a low-rank marquis.

A Florio.

She realizes now that everything is about to change, and the thought of it makes her head spin. Her corset is suddenly squeezing her breath out of her.

What about Ignazio? Will he really love her forever, as he keeps saying, or will he tire of her?

She's afraid.

But why now?

Her father is watching her with furrowed brow and seems to read in her face that fear, that insecurity that's making her close her eyes. Surrounded by his beard, his lips form a harsh line. He's been opposed to this marriage from the start. He tried in every capacity to dissuade his daughter, first with rational argument, then with anger, and finally with cruel declarations: Ignazio is unreliable; he has no backbone; he's too spoiled to assume responsibility for a family; he's incapable of being faithful; he's devoted to nothing but the pursuit of pleasure.

Every accusation came up against, on the one side, Franca's tears, and on the other, Ignazio's determination: he gave proof of unexpected perseverance and followed them all the way to Tuscany. After a while, Pietro had to capitulate. But he didn't resign himself completely, and in his heart of hearts dreaded the day his daughter would realize that there were sound reasons for his initial refusal. Now, though, he can only hope that the scars left by that struggle will heal.

"Are you all right?" he asks her.

She tries to reply but can't. Then she clears her throat and murmurs, "Yes . . ."

He squeezes her hand. "Always be careful, Checchina. The fellow's a womanizer, and even though he says he loves you, keep your eyes open."

She suddenly raises her head and looks at her father. All trace of fear has gone. "He won't need to look for other women, he has me," she says in a determined, almost angry voice. "He's promised, he'll want only me."

Without waiting for the driver to open the door of the coach, Pietro leans forward and flings it open. "I know he says he loves you, my dear Franca, and I don't doubt it's true," he retorts, helping her to her feet, then adds in a low voice, "but man is a hunter . . ."

The wind carries his words away.

Francesca and Emma help her out of the coach, supporting the dress to stop it getting dirty. Costanza tries in vain to hold back the veil as it waves in the wind. A few more steps and they are on the threshold of the church.

Emma and Francesca bustle about her, laughing, kissing her, smoothing the folds of her dress. A few paces behind, Costanza, trying to hold back her tears, covers her face with her fingers, but then exclaims, "Child, you're so beautiful!" and embraces her, laughing and crying at the same time, drawing protests from Emma and Francesca: no, you don't cry at a wedding, it's bad luck.

Costanza takes her daughter's face in her hands, kisses her on the forehead, and murmurs, "You're marrying a man who moved heaven and earth to have you, you know that, don't you?" But she's unable to wait for her daughter's reply: Emma and Francesca almost push her inside. They go in, leaving Franca alone with her father.

He goes closer to her, takes her hand, and places it on his arm, which she squeezes. In silence. Between them, in a flash, is the memory of the words spoken, the words yelled, the words unsaid. But they are now merely the echo of a distant past, giving way to affection and hope.

The door is flung open. The strains of the wedding march reach Franca and envelop her, almost as if sucking her in to the flower-strewn nave. Her first steps are unsteady, making Pietro give her a puzzled glance. But as soon as she spots Ignazio at the altar, Franca is transformed: she loosens her grip on her father's arm, straightens her back, and advances resolutely, head held high.

She barely notices Giovanna, who's all in black, stiff, her face full of grief, or Vincenzino, who's staring at her, stunned, craning his neck to get a better view of her, or Giulia, who's smiling at her sweetly. Her mother and cousins have watery eyes and are clutching their handkerchiefs. There's almost nobody else there.

It's a very different wedding than the one Franca imagined in her adolescent dreams. An overcast sky, an icy wind, an unknown church, no pageboy, few guests.

But she wouldn't have wanted it any other way, and she doesn't need anyone except her Ignazio.

Everything she desires now is here before her.

Pietro places Franca's hand on Ignazio's, and Ignazio raises it to his lips. "You're beautiful," he whispers, almost unable to breathe.

She would like to laugh and cry out for joy. She can feel life dancing in her chest. She's the luckiest and most loved of women, she tells herself, and she thanks heaven for this.

And she manages to say a word, just one, that wipes out the waiting, the suffering, the gossip, the nasty rumors, the doubts, the separations, the quarrels. She looks at the man who's about to become her husband and exclaims, "Finally!"

The atmosphere at the wedding luncheon is calm and relaxed. Franca and Ignazio hold hands and laugh. They're in their own world, immersed in a happiness that's hard to imagine: it's almost as though the air all around is filled with light. Ignazio's sister, Giulia, looks at them and bows her head over her porcelain plate, which is still full of food she's barely touched. She was never given the option of whom to love, given that hers was an arranged marriage. She lets her gaze wander over the guests and reflects on how her life, apparently so enviable, is quite different than the way it seems: she has a son who's seriously ill, perhaps in danger of dying, a mother-in-law who hates her, and a husband who treats her with respect but no more than that. She's never felt that passion she now glimpses on Franca's face.

A short distance away, Pietro is watching her. Giulia is beautiful, intelligent, and sophisticated, it's true; but as the years pass, she's coming to resemble far too closely her mother, Baroness Giovanna d'Ondes. She has her mother's hard, stern lips, the same crease between her permanently furrowed brows, and her character, too . . . At that moment, Pietro's gaze actually falls on Giovanna, who's smoothing a nonexistent crease in the tablecloth, her eyes staring into space. Pietro is unable to suppress a shudder of anxiety: Will his wife become *that*?

"*Amunì*, come now: Why the sad face?"

Romualdo Trigona doesn't wait for the servant to bring him a chair. He grabs one and sits down next to Pietro, crossing his legs with the arrogance that distinguishes him. Then he indicates the bride and groom with his chin and folds his hands on his knees.

"Ignazziddu still doesn't know what's in store for him," Pietro murmurs, and gives a sarcastic little laugh.

Romualdo does the same. "He's in love . . ."

"I know. That's the only thing on his mind, but it won't last. Apart from anything else because the clouds are gathering . . ."

Romualdo frowns. He orders a waiter to bring him a glass of champagne, then asks his friend, "What do you mean?"

Pietro moves closer and lowers his voice. "You know, since the arrest of Bernardo Tanlongo, governor of the Banca Romana, and of Cesare Lazzaroni, the head cashier . . . I mean, since the dirty tricks they got up to . . ."

Romualdo nods. "But even back in December it was obvious something nasty was going on, with that row caused in the Chamber of Deputies, when Colajanni asked why the government hadn't made public the investigation of the parliamentary commission into the banks."

"An investigation that was launched when Crispi was prime minister." Pietro pauses and nods his head in the direction of Ignazio. "The Florios weren't too bothered about that, partly because our Ignazio had, and still has, his mind elsewhere. But the fact that even Crispi is involved is quite serious. The truth is that, unfortunately, nobody's exempt from blame in this matter." He beats his hand on Romualdo's arm and assumes a tense expression. "I can understand why Crispi didn't denounce the situation: too many people were involved, too many banks. Do you remember the Bank of Naples and the trial of its director? Cuciniello had been making loans left, right, and center to people who weren't eligible for them." He leans forward. "And now they've found a real mess in the offices of the Banca Romana. Fake documents, plates for printing, and papers signed by important people, who right now are feeling scared. Tanlongo was running the bank's coffers as if they belonged to him."

Romualdo nods, sips at his champagne, then puts his hand in front of his mouth and whispers, "That's right. I heard he and Lazzaroni kept the plates of the banknotes that should have been destroyed and printed them again, falsifying the date and the signature of the former cashier. Banknotes on new paper, but with old serial numbers, in other words, which they granted to whoever asked for a loan without needing a guarantee: friends and relatives, or simply people whose names they didn't want appearing on the bank's registers . . . or that weren't meant to appear."

Pietro opens his mouth to speak, closes it again for an instant, then murmurs, "In Parliament, they're now saying the whole system is rotten. All of it. There are even rumors the king is involved."

Romualdo raises a hand to stop him and looks away. "People say all kinds of things, you know how it works. With all these rumors around, the truth must be hidden somewhere."

Pietro merely nods but makes no comment. He's a Sicilian and respects the golden rule that everyone soon learns in Sicily: *a' megghiu parola è chidda ch'un si dice*—the best word is the unspoken one. Then he looks up, and his serious expression quickly vanishes, wiped away by a laugh. Ignazio is approaching, arm in arm with Giuseppe Monroy. "Here's the groom!"

Romualdo stops a waiter and orders more champagne. There's a peal of laughter: nearby, Franca is chatting merrily with her cousins and sister-in-law; even Giulia is smiling, as though her anguish has abandoned her, at least for a moment.

Ignazio takes the bottle of champagne from the waiter's hand, saying that he wants to uncork it himself, but he's nervous and part of the contents splashes over him and his friends. They laugh.

As they drink, Ignazio puts his arm around Romualdo. "So? What were you all talking about? From your faces, it looked as if someone had died."

"We were talking about what happened in Rome," Pietro replies, "and the fact that people like Crispi have gotten caught up in that disaster. Being a deputy of the kingdom has opened his eyes to all kinds of murky happenings and, even though he can't go into details, he's determined to warn his friends."

"But that's because Rome has given free rein to Tanlongo and his sort," Ignazio says. "How is it possible that in all these years no one carried out checks on his bank? Opportunity makes the thief . . . and the forger, in this case." He gives Romualdo a slap to get him to shift in his seat. They share the chair, precariously balanced, like two little boys.

"I don't know, but I'd be careful if I were you." Pietro's expression is serious now. Ignoring a new burst of laughter behind them, he looks at Ignazio with a mixture of reproach and concern. "I wouldn't have allowed Credito Mobiliare to open a branch in the same building as Banco Florio. They're not above suspicion either. It would have been wise to exercise more caution."

Pietro isn't many years Ignazio's senior, and yet he acts much older. He's sometimes so wary and quiet, Ignazio wonders how his sister hasn't already died of boredom. He shrugs. "They may have their troubles, and things to hide, but Banco Florio is robust, with nothing to hide. My father worked with Credito Mobiliare from the time of the merger with Rubattino. It's a large bank, run by respectable people. In addition, they've appointed me vice president of their Palermo branch and I'm on their board of directors. If anything were amiss, I'd already be aware of it, don't you think? They've offered me ample guarantees. In any case, people in Palermo know we're separate companies."

"Possibly . . ." Pietro mutters.

Giuseppe turns and shakes Ignazio by the shoulder. "Your wife's looking for you. Forget about business, it's unfair to neglect such a beautiful bride by talking about this boring stuff."

Ignazio turns and meets Franca's adoring gaze. He blows her a kiss, then turns back to his friends. "I'm taking her to Florence and Venice, you know, then we're going to Paris. I want to show her the most beautiful places. She deserves it, we both deserve it, really, especially after what we've been through in order to get married, all the gossip people spread about us. Anything, as long as I can get away from Palermo."

Romualdo stands up and adjusts his cravat. "Very well. Off you go, have fun, and come back with a brat, preferably a boy. We need fresh blood in the family."

Ignazio and Giuseppe laugh, while Pietro scoffs. Franca stands up and comes over to them. She takes her husband's hand, squeezes it, and kisses it in front of everybody.

Outside the windows, the wind is still blowing.

⌒

It was in Paris, during the honeymoon, that Franca *truly* understood.

She read it in the eyes of the clerk at Cartier's, who stepped forward with a bow, making himself available. She saw it in Ignazio's abrupt, almost rude rejection, followed by the command, "*Appelez-moi le directeur, s'il vous plaît.*" She heard it in the obsequious, anxious tone of the manager, who apologized ad nauseam for not having personally welcomed them, then launched into many congratulations, good wishes, and compliments on the young bride's elegance and her young husband's good fortune.

Franca understood that Ignazio speaks a universal language that opens all doors: the language of money.

They were led into a room with mirrors and velvet couches, where they were served champagne—she sipped it, happy to savor this wine that had been completely unknown to her until a few days earlier—and then the parade of jewelry began: a serial opening of large cases that revealed wonder after wonder. Franca made a few comments in her hesitant French. Ignazio listened to her, smiling, corrected her pronunciation, and caressed her neck in a way that made her sigh more than once.

"Choose whatever you like," he whispered in her ear. With trembling fingers, she touched a string of pearls that glowed on red velvet. She adored pearls, but until then had been able to afford only a thin string of them.

Franca was dizzy, and not because of the champagne. It was that succession of diamonds, emeralds, rubies, and pearls that stirred her. Because they were the unarguable, overwhelming sign of a new-found awareness: that the Florio family was hugely wealthy. And now the Florios were *her* family.

Ignazio purchased a pair of splendid pearl earrings, and above all a necklace worthy of a princess: thirteen strings of "angel skin" coral from Japan, faintly pink beads that stood out against Franca's honey-colored complexion. He also ordered a bespoke *collier de chien* neck-lace for his wife's swan neck, made up of pearls linked by diamond bars and a layer of larger pearls at the base.

There were similar scenes at Houbigant's, the perfumier of Queen Victoria and the tsar; in the huge store on Rue du Faubourg Saint-Honoré, Franca discovered the name of Ignazio's perfume—Fougère—and was able to choose her own cologne. At Worth's, the designer of Empress Eugenie's and Elizabeth of Austria's clothes, where she was welcomed like a queen and shown styles that best highlighted her statuesque figure. At Lanvin's, where she bought dozens of scarves for herself and her mother. At Mademoiselle Re-bours's, where she was shown the most splendid fans, including one made of ostrich feathers, created for Marie of Romania, the crown prince's new bride.

"For me?" she would ask, her large green eyes brimming with astonishment. And Ignazio, feeling his heart swell, would stroke her face or hand, nod, and encourage her to choose.

This is a dream, Franca thought, touching the jewels her husband had given her. And then there was Paris itself, with its lights, its bou-levards, its buildings, its elegant women and shiny carriages. Every single thing was a source of wonder, filling her heart and her eyes with such beauty that at times she felt herself bursting with joy. And so it was also for Ignazio, who, thanks to Franca, was seeing the city with new eyes, moved by his wife's innocence, surprise, and enthusiasm.

Another dream is her arrival at Villa dell'Olivuzza. When they returned to Palermo, the newlyweds moved into Villa ai Colli, but only for as long as work on the Olivuzza wasn't yet complete. Ignazio said very little about what the workmen were doing, explaining only that he'd always found the house too dark, that it was time to enlarge it and let more light into the rooms. But he always added, with a smile, "You'll see, you'll see."

And now the moment has finally come.

The carriage stops a few meters outside the main building of the Olivuzza, in front of a large wrought-iron gate that leads to the wing Ignazio has reserved for the two of them.

He helps Franca out, then takes her by the hand and leads her up a red marble staircase. They walk through a winter garden full of lush plants and bathed in warm light pouring down through the glass ceiling, followed by a multitude of servants and Giovanna, who smiles indulgently, holding Vincenzo by the hand. Franca looks around, more intimidated than surprised, her face filled with awe.

At the end of a corridor, Ignazio stops outside a door. "Wait here," he orders the servants. Giovanna stands aside, and an expression of sadness akin to regret softens her pale face for a moment.

Franca turns to look at them: smiling faces, knowing looks . . . and is almost annoyed by the fact that everybody knows what awaits her, everybody except her. But Ignazio stands behind her, his hands over her eyes. "Don't look. Keep your eyes closed," he whispers, as he opens the door and leads her into the room.

Giggling and stumbling, Franca obeys and takes a couple of steps forward.

When she opens her eyes again, she feels as though she's suspended between heaven and earth.

Above her, a blue sky, and on the cornice of the ceiling, cupids holding up garlands of roses. Before her, an ivory-colored canopy over a large bed, and feather mahogany furniture with gold inlays. At her feet, ivory-colored tiles covered in rose petals, as though the petals thrown by the cupids on the ceiling are strewn on the floor.

It's her own personal corner of paradise.

"For my rose," Ignazio whispers in her ear. "All for you."

Franca turns and looks at him, too filled with happiness to be able to speak.

They kiss in front of everybody.

The first sirocco of spring in Palermo is a slap in the face. Intolerable heat and closeness. You can feel it from early morning, when you feel crushed by your blankets and a coating of sweat on your back makes you throw everything off and fan yourself with the sheet. Then, once the windows are flung open, you feel a new, warm atmosphere. The sky is hazy, the air still.

In the coach driving him to Piazza Marina, Ignazio feels the heat and pants. He fans himself with his handkerchief, then wipes the sweat away. He hates the heat.

A day like this, with this wind and this temperature, should be spent at sea, on the *Fieramosca*, the yacht he bought shortly before his father died. It cost him quite a bit—"An irresponsible expenditure," his mother called it—but it was worth it. True, they already had a yacht, the *Sultana*—huge, with a white hull—on board which he took his beautiful wife, who was thrilled. Ignazio bought the *Fieramosca* to replace the *Queen Mary*, which he considered *passé* and had sold to a Tuscan marquess.

Actually, he also built the *Aretusa,* a steam launch, all in steel: but above all, he bought the *Valkyrie*, a regatta yacht with a streamlined bow and a narrow hull. It was sold to him by the cousin of Emperor Franz Joseph, Archduke Charles Stephen of Austria, and he intended to use it to take part in the most important sailing contests in the Mediterranean. He cannot live on business alone, but that's something neither his mother nor Giovanni Laganà nor Domenico Gallotti seems to understand.

The two men who, as it happens, have summoned him "urgently" to the office.

They really are a nuisance!

Laganà and Gallotti didn't even leave him in peace when he was traveling around Europe on his honeymoon: letters, notes, telegrams . . . Don't they realize he needs something else, that he can't always be shut up in that office? He wants to feel free. He wants to live. He doesn't want to end up like his father, who died in his fifties after a lifetime of work, he tells himself with a touch of irritation.

He sometimes feels a dull anger toward his father: he shouldn't have fallen ill so soon, he shouldn't have forced his son to assume this role, to take on these responsibilities, thus preventing him from really living. That's something he can't bear.

Restlessly, he moves aside the curtain over the coach window: he's in the side streets of the Borgo Vecchio, and workingmen greet him deferentially. "*Assabbinirìca*, Don Ignazio" echoes through the alleyways and beyond the doors of the hovels. Poor, hollow faces, women prematurely faded, children with large, hungry eyes playing on the streets. The stench of rotten fish assaults the nostrils and mingles with the odor of the garbage fermenting on street corners and in the drainage channels, where there's an accumulation of mud, rags, and scraps of food.

These people, though, don't seem to notice. Some of them work for the Florios, Ignazio tells himself, and yet he wouldn't be able to recognize them. His father, on the other hand, knew all of them, one by one, and was respected and admired by them.

But to what benefit? he wonders, responding with a listless wave of the hand. He doesn't like this neighborhood, with its poverty and its despair. He doesn't like Palermo, this Palermo, to be honest. He likes the elegant villas that are springing up on the outskirts of the city, the ballrooms of the aristocratic palaces, the lobbies of the theaters. He loves London and Paris, the Côte d'Azur, the peace and quiet of the Austrian mountains.

He loves to feel the wind on his face as he walks the deck on his yachts.

Not this stale air that stinks of rottenness.

He doesn't remember—or maybe he doesn't want to remember—that, only a little less than a century ago, his grandfather Vincenzo lived in a place like this, and that before him, the uncle whose name and ring he, Ignazio, bears had arrived here from Calabria to escape a life of poverty and bitterness. Both men struggled to stand out in this hostile, unpleasant city. And they succeeded because they gained the respect of the common folk, the people.

But his parents made sure any memory of this was almost wiped out, that it was mentioned in the house as little as possible. Because, if you don't speak about the past, it ends up disappearing. And if it disappears, it's as though it never existed.

It's the present that awaits him today. And it's going to be a difficult day, Ignazio can feel it.

He climbs the stairs, greets the clerks he encounters, and reaches the office on the second floor. Domenico Gallotti, director of NGI, has a round face, thick side whiskers, a squat body, and a belly that betrays his love of good food. He's been waiting for twenty minutes, pacing the room, his hands joined behind his back.

"Sorry to have kept you waiting," Ignazio says as he enters.

"And I'm sorry if I made you hurry, but there are things that can't wait any longer." No preamble, no polite formulas. Gallotti does nothing to hide his impatience. On the contrary: he remains on his feet and drums his fingers on a small portfolio he has placed on the desk.

"You wrote me a number of troubling letters during my honeymoon," Ignazio replies, sitting down at his father's desk. He stops and looks at the large number of papers spread across the worktop, awaiting his signature. Then, after a few moments' silence, he motions Gallotti to take a seat.

Gallotti sits down and looks at him through half-closed eyelids. "I realize I must have seemed somewhat insistent, but this is a difficult period. The Banca Romana affair is bringing to light a lot of problems in our banking system . . . and I assure you, 'problems' is a euphemism. In addition, there are some tricky matters concerning Casa Florio specifically, starting with the renewal of the maritime concessions. Your father, may God rest his soul, agreed to a ten-year concession, and very soon the renewal will be settled. We have to make sure this renewal is to our advantage. Don't forget, Don Ignazio, that state subventions are a major—I would go so far as to say essential—factor in NGI, because they allow us to navigate routes that otherwise would be uneconomical, thus maintaining our financial health."

Ignazio shifts uneasily in his chair. He's annoyed at being treated like a child. "I know perfectly well how important they are, Signor Gallotti. Tell me rather how things are proceeding in Parliament."

Gallotti opens the portfolio and takes out a memorandum. "Obstacles, Don Ignazio. Obstacles above all in Parliament, because Giolitti and the industrialists close to him don't look kindly on a renewal in our favor. They'll ask for a report on the company's state of health, starting with the condition of the fleet, which, as you know better than I, hasn't been modernized for many years."

"We can remedy that," Ignazio replies with a dismissive gesture of the hand. "We'll do the most urgent repairs and leave the rest for later. The Florio name guarantees the robustness of NGI. There's nothing to fear from any inspection they might choose to do."

"That's true. But people hear things, and they get worked up. The uncertainty connected with the renewal doesn't help. A few days ago, the representatives of the workers in the shipyard in Palermo, through the Workers' Consulate of which they're a part, told the *Giornale di Sicilia* that four thousand families would be out of work if the concessions weren't renewed. There's already been a demonstration outside Palazzo Villarosa, and there's a risk that riots could break out. Or worse still, that strikes could be called. It's good to bear that in mind."

"The workers in the haulage yard and the Oretea have always been hotheads. Yes, I know they'd like to strike, but they won't. My father could always talk to them; I'll do the same. Strikes are pointless, especially when we're having to deal with what's going on in Rome."

"That's precisely it." Gallotti takes a bundle of papers from the portfolio and holds them out to Ignazio.

What else now? Ignazio thinks as he leans forward and takes the bundle. It's a parliamentary report drawn up by a deputy from northern Italy, Maggiorino Ferraris. "'It is more than one person's opinion that the day Navigazione Generale Italiana ceases, of its own accord, to exist might not be a bad day for the country,'" he reads aloud. "*E che minchia*—what the hell does this Ferraris want?" he exclaims angrily. "Does he think Italian maritime trade would be so much better if we weren't around? Does he have any idea what he's saying?"

Gallotti curls his lips in a grimace. "The parliamentarians who are friends of ours, those close to Crispi, have protested. This is an argument that has little to do with the economy and a lot to do with the political friendships of Ferraris and especially of the prime minister."

"With all the dirt coming out about the Banca Romana, I'd be surprised if Giolitti lasted much longer. Crispi told me about him in a letter. He's an inexperienced bureaucrat who knows nothing about governing. Someone who was nice and safe, studying in Turin, while people like Crispi were fighting for the unity of Italy."

"That may be so, but today he's prime minister, and it's obvious his main task is to protect businesses in the north, because they're the ones who voted for him, just as it's in the interest of Crispi and his people to defend our voters. What Ferraris says here reflects what a lot of people are thinking, Don Ignazio. That's how it works for these northerners: the yokels who work the land, south of Rome, don't bring them votes. As for the nobles who own the land, they're not interested in working with industry or bothering with trade."

The air suddenly seems to become motionless. Ignazio looks at Gallotti, mouth half-open, waiting.

"Read on," Gallotti says, indicating a passage in the report.

"Ferraris complains about the fact that our steamers are built abroad and suggests favoring those companies that use ships built in Italian shipyards—obviously Tuscan and Ligurian ones. In addition, he asks for the single mail and transportation lines to be put out to tender, abolishing the concessions your father was so enthusiastic about."

Ignazio can feel anger rising from his belly to his throat. "They want to cut us off at the knees. If they take the concessions from us, we can shut up shop." He breathes out through his thin lips. Then he looks out the window, wondering what his father would have done, how he would have reacted, who he would have turned to. "Let's go to Rome," he finally decides. "You, me, and Laganà. Nobody's going to get the better of us. Nobody." He passes his hand across his forehead. "And now we need to tell the workers not to get so upset . . . *'sti capuzzelli*, these blowhards have nothing better to do than spread propaganda."

Ignazio gets to his feet, puts his hands in his pockets, and walks over to the window. His sporadic use of dialect—Gallotti knows this at least—is an unmistakable sign of irritation.

"My father guaranteed them everything they need, and so have I: treatment if they get hurt, wages that other workers in Palermo can only dream of, houses for rent near the foundry or the haulage yard. My father even suggested helping their children to study after they'd finished work, but they didn't want that. Yet they've kept yelling that they want rights, rights, rights! Now they've even set up that association, the Sicilian Fasci of Workers . . ." He utters the words as if he has something rotten in his mouth. "The papers are shouting that we have to reduce working hours and increase the wages. What are they talking about? The fact is that abundance never caused famine. They've forgotten what it meant to look for day work on Piazza Vigliena and left, right, and center."

Gallotti nods. "You're right, Don Ignazio, the Fasci could be a problem, because they've gathered a lot of worker's associations and mutual-aid groups under one banner, saying, 'Anyone can break a stick, but who can break a bundle of sticks?' You know their chief, Rosario Garibaldi Bosco, was even involved in the founding of the Italian Workers' Party, don't you? Not to mention those thirteen peasants from Caltavuturo who tried to occupy the land and were killed by soldiers of the kingdom, drawing the attention of the whole of Italy to us. There's unrest, no doubt about it. However . . ." Lowering his voice, Gallotti moves closer to Ignazio. "I feel I should advise you to set the matter aside for now. Few of our workers have joined the Fasci, thank God. Most know how lucky they are and that they wouldn't find other steady work just like that. Trust me, they remember what it's like to wait on Piazza Vigliena to be hired for the day. Right now, let's think about the concessions, otherwise there'll be no work left for anyone."

"All right. But I'd also like to talk with Laganà. He assured me there wouldn't be any problems in the Senate." Ignazio says this hastily, accompanying his words with a shrug.

What he doesn't see—or doesn't want to see—is the skeptical look Gallotti has given him. And indeed, Gallotti immediately goes on to say, in a caustic tone, "There are other things Laganà ought to assure you about."

Ignazio frowns. "What do you mean?"

Gallotti pauses and bites his lips. He doesn't quite know how to act. He would have had no qualms talking to the father, but the son is so arrogant, so impatient, that he hesitates. Finally, though, it's his respect for the memory of the father that makes up his mind for him, his loyalty to that man who died much too soon. "The thing is, Don Ignazio, if I may be so bold . . . Let's just say that he should have been less cooperative toward our rivals."

Ignazio stares at him, dumbfounded. His bewilderment turns to suspicion. He vaguely remembers a few remarks he heard in Livorno just after his wedding, remarks he filed away in a compartment of his memory, thinking they weren't important. With a shudder of anxiety that furrows the skin on his arms, he ventures, "Yes, I've heard some very unflattering rumors about him . . ." He would like to understand, to ask questions, but there are too many things he doesn't know, or that he's neglected, and he's afraid of seeming superficial or, worse still, not very bright.

With a grimace, Gallotti emits a sigh that's almost an angry snort. "They're much more than rumors, Don Ignazio. Were you told that Laganà is very close to Erasmo Piaggio, in whose interest it would be to move much of NGI's activity to Genoa?"

Ignazio doesn't move. Laganà? The Laganà his father liked and respected to the extent of making him general manager of NGI? Is he behaving that way now? True, he's always been demanding, occasionally annoying, but to actually raise suspicions as to his conduct . . .

Gallotti seems to understand his hesitation. "Don't get me wrong; I acknowledge his good points. But I assure you he's behaving in a way that's devious at the very least. And he's no novice at these little games, Don Ignazio. You were too young, but anyone who has white hair like me can remember what he did when he was administrator of Trinacria. In fact, your father, who knew him well, treated him as he would have treated a particularly aggressive guard dog; in other words, he kept him on a leash."

Slowly, Ignazio says yes, he also remembers something. When

Trinacria went bust, his father waited for Laganà to make a move before he acquired it. Then, as the insolvency administrator, it was always Laganà who allowed him to buy equipment and steamers at ridiculous prices. *He made him his spy and promised him a position in our company*, he realizes in a burst of intuition.

And now . . . is he playing the same game now, at their expense?

"I'll speak to Laganà," he says, indignantly. "He owes me an explanation, if only because of all that this family has given him."

Gallotti makes a gesture that seems to mean: *I expected nothing less*. Then he opens the portfolio and takes out a few sheets that he passes to Ignazio to sign. Finally, he stands up and takes his leave. "I'll come to Rome with you, but first speak to Laganà. Make sure he's loyal."

Gusts of wind bring the scent of orange blossom and tilled earth into the villa, stirring the white curtains at the French windows that overlook the grounds.

In a corner of the green salon, which is flooded with the pink light of spring, Franca is sitting on a high-backed chair in a flowing white dress and with the Cartier *collier de chien* around her neck, posing for a portrait.

"Please keep still, signora," the painter admonishes with a sigh when she shifts on her chair. Ettore De Maria Bergler has sparse black hair, an imposing nose, and a face like a pirate's above a slender body. He has a cigarette in his mouth and an absorbed expression, with a few outbursts of impatience due to his model's lack of discipline.

"True, your husband asked me to portray you as naturally as

possible, but if I do that, I might depict a grimace on your face. Destiny grants only goddesses and a few lucky women a beauty such as yours. So you mustn't move, or I shan't be able to capture that beauty."

Having said this, he again concentrates on drawing with his carbon pencil.

"I'll be as still as a Greek statue," she promises, with a childlike smile.

"I find that hard to believe," the painter mutters, sweat pouring from his receding hairline. "*Vous êtes si pleine d'esprit et d'élégance!* It's a challenge to get you down on canvas."

She throws him a grateful glance, then moistens her lips. They taste sweet, and she quivers with pleasure. Every morning, the *monsù* bakes croissants. She and Ignazio wolf them down, laughing, and the kisses they exchange after breakfast taste of desire and icing sugar.

"Donna Franca, good morning. I'm sorry to disturb you, but Donna Giovanna has asked for you."

Franca turns to look at Rosa, who's in charge of the embroidery school with Giovanna d'Ondes. She thanks her, then glances apologetically at the painter.

"I'll never finish!" De Maria Bergler is irritated. "And now your husband will be angry with me."

"I'll tell him it's all his mother's fault." Franca stands up and abruptly lifts her hand to her neck. "Would you be so kind, master, as to help me take this off?"

The painter goes to her, unclasps the necklace, and hands it to her. Franca strokes it with a kind of tenderness, then slips it into her pocket. She loves touching it, feeling it on her: it reminds her of her honeymoon.

"Doesn't your mother-in-law like jewelry?" the painter asks, putting his sketch away in a large portfolio.

"My mother-in-law is in mourning and doesn't appreciate any kind of display. I try to respect her grief. I should also change my dress, but I don't have time."

De Maria Bergler nods. What he doesn't know is that, ever since her first encounter with Giovanna, Franca has been very careful about the jewelry she wears in her mother-in-law's presence.

It happened in the Hotel Excelsior in Abetone, a small town closer to Siena than to Livorno, chosen by the Jaconas because it was quiet and discreet. Giovanna arrived by coach with her son, and the two families sat down to tea in a small lounge. Franca remained silent, with her eyes down, intimidated and respectful, aware of the fact that, without his mother's consent, Ignazio would never marry her. She listened to the exchange of pleasantries, the trivial chatter—"How was the weather in Livorno? Ah, cool even there?" "And what about the little one, Blasco, how is he?"—registering the silent war the two mothers were waging: Costanza armed with age-old nobility, but buried in debt; Giovanna with imposing wealth, but with a name that, despite everything—despite her—was still that of a merchant family.

The conversation carried on for so long, time seeming to her to stretch to infinity. Then, abruptly, Giovanna motioned her to come closer. She obeyed, hesitantly, while Ignazio shifted on his chair and Costanza held her breath.

Giovanna looked her up and down. For a long time. It seemed to Franca as if those eyes were rooting about in her soul, in search of the qualities that might make her a true Florio, and she was terrified that none would be found. Instinctively, she lifted her hand to the thin gold chain she had around her neck, from which hung an elegant cameo.

Donna Giovanna noticed the gesture and gave an almost imperceptible start. On Franca's neck, half hidden by the cameo, was her husband's ring. The one she had given her son the day Ignazio had died, and which had been in the Florio family for generations.

Franca realized that. In her mind, her fear of having offended Donna Giovanna in some way was superimposed on her embarrassment at having put on that ring without the other woman knowing. Then, however, she remembered when Ignazio had given it to her: he had told her how important it was to him and his family, and that it represented the genuineness of his commitment to her. It was the tangible sign of his love, much more precious than any other jewel.

At that point she looked straight at Giovanna with her large green eyes. Self-confident, proud, in love.

Into Giovanna's eyes there came a hint of infinite sadness: the sadness of a woman who had lost her husband and was now seeing a beloved son stolen from her.

Giovanna's hands, which she had been holding tight over her stomach, now relaxed, and with a gesture she invited Franca to sit down beside her. The sadness hadn't gone, but it had been joined by a subtle threat: *I'll let you have him, but beware if you aren't worthy of him and the name of the Florios.*

Remembering that look, Franca feels troubled. Giovanna has never stopped looking at her that way. Will her mother-in-law's suspicion of her ever end? she wonders. Ah, if only Ignazio hadn't left, especially now that . . .

Ignazio is in Rome, dealing with the maritime concessions. He told her he couldn't postpone that journey and that, given that it was a business matter, it was better for her to stay behind in Palermo. Franca nodded, resigned, trying to figure out why her beloved, good-natured husband was suddenly so upset.

Walking toward her mother-in-law's apartments, which are in the oldest part of the Olivuzza, she looks around, wondering if she will ever manage to accustom herself to these rooms that seem endless, filled with luxury furniture—from the walnut Louis XVI chests to the French Empire-style dressers with their marble tops, from the carved and gilded wooden tables to the ebony coin boxes with plates of hard stone and ivory—with porcelain Capodimonte statues; engraved silverware; antique bronze and marble objects; precious Persian, Indian, and Chinese carpets; and paintings of every size, from little seascapes to seventeenth-century portraits with just a hint of light, from mythical subjects to Sicilian landscapes so luminous as to seem like windows open on the world. Everything, to her, is incredible.

The doors open before her as if by magic, revealing multitudes of servants who bow to her as she passes and then seem to vanish into the twists and turns of the house.

Occasionally, though, she feels an unease that worries her: she can't even tell them what to do, given that they all know their particular tasks and carry them out perfectly; she doesn't have to dress herself, or brush her own hair, because she has Diodata, her personal maid, a shy, silent girl with large dark eyes, always waiting for a sign from her; she doesn't have to put away her own clothes because there's a wardrobe mistress to take care of it; she doesn't have to think about how to arrange the flowers because there's a servant just for that, whose job it is to change the arrangement every day. She doesn't even have to choose the menu for receptions, because the *monsù* knows the tastes of the guests and panders to them completely. So she prefers to keep silent, because she's afraid of getting things wrong, of being the odd one out, thus demonstrating to everybody—especially to her mother-in-law—that she can't measure up to the name she bears.

Sometimes she has the feeling she's a guest in her own home.

"Oh, you're here."

Giovanna raises her head from the loom that occupies the center of the sitting room where she spends her days, embroidering and praying. Franca remains in the doorway for a moment, then advances into that semidarkness suffused with the scent of flowers. Beyond the door, there's a huge house, full of light and activity. Here, on the other hand, everything is motionless. Even the large French windows are closed.

From a corner of the room, almost invisible, Donna Ciccia nods to her. Franca knows the woman has taken a liking to her, and yet somehow she doesn't feel entirely at ease in her presence.

She goes to her mother-in-law and kisses her on the cheek.

Seeing that Franca is wearing a white dress, Giovanna curls her lips. Then she takes a coral bead, slips it on the length of thread, and makes a stitch. "This evening we'll have a Mass said for the holy soul of Giulia's boy Blasco. You'll come, won't you?"

Franca holds her breath. She knows perfectly well that no woman from Casa Florio would dare miss a Mass of intercession for a relative, especially not the third child of Giulia, who died just after her and Ignazio's wedding. She's being put to the test again.

"Of course," she murmurs. "Poor little thing. He didn't have time to grow up."

Giovanna's hands stop above the loom. "I know what it is to watch a son die," she says. "It's like having your bones torn out. Your heart feels as though it's about to burst and you wish you could give your own life. And now my wretched daughter is going through this."

"Don't think about it," Donna Ciccia intervenes with a sigh. "They're two angels now."

Giovanna nods. She wipes away a tear and falls silent.

Franca takes a step back and a shiver runs down her back. Furtively, she puts her hand on her belly, then looks around. Everywhere there are framed images of her father-in-law. On the wall is an oil portrait of him, next to an even larger one of Vincenzino, her husband's brother, who died years ago.

This is not so much a room, she thinks, *as a temple to memory.* She retreats toward the door almost without realizing it. She feels defenseless against such great anguish, she's afraid that Giovanna's suffering might attach itself to her like a shadow or, worse still, like a *magarìa*. A curse. *When someone's this unhappy, they probably can't even imagine that other people could be content; it's even possible they see other people's joy as an injustice.* She tells herself this as she reaches the door, her stomach clenched with the sense of oppression that hit her as soon as she entered the room. She vaguely senses that all this happens when suffering goes beyond limits and makes it impossible to bear even a flicker of hope.

Why isn't Ignazio here to protect me from all this?

Franca.

Ignazio is distracted by the thought of her—her half-open mouth, eyes aflame with passion, her lithe body—but only for a moment, like a sunbeam that vanishes immediately. Here in Rome, there's nothing but gray clouds, stern men, and white government buildings.

At the desk, opposite him, sits Camillo Finocchiaro Aprile, the minister for mail and telegraph, a calm-looking man with a thin mustache and a golden pince-nez that makes his pale eyes look even smaller than they are. Originally from Palermo, he and the now former prime minister Crispi share a past as followers of Garibaldi, as well as, obviously, special consideration for those who represent Sicily and its interests—Ignazio Florio first and foremost.

The room—austere, with red wallpaper and bulky mahogany furniture—is saturated with the smell of men's cologne. Next to Ignazio are the heads of NGI: Director Gallotti and General Manager Laganà. Despite Gallotti's advice, Ignazio hasn't found the right time for a private talk with Laganà, and the rumors he's heard about him are contradictory: on the one hand, he truly seems to have "a very friendly rapport" with various Ligurian ship owners; on the other, no one denies that he's worked hard at opening Credito Mobiliare branches within Banco Florio, thereby adding luster to the company. In other words, he undoubtedly knows how to go about things. In the end, Ignazio feels that he himself is a better judge of character than those who, like Gallotti, try to treat him like a child, so he's brought Laganà to Rome with him. But there's palpable tension between the two men, partly because of the extremely delicate situation.

There's no guarantee that NGI's concessions will be renewed. Too many people are against the idea, starting with the Ligurian navigation companies that want a share of the generous state subsidies and are supported by a unanimous political bloc.

How on earth do they imagine they can compete with NGI? Ignazio wonders, running his fingers through his hair. They have the largest fleet in Italy, with almost a hundred steamers.

"Your fleet is one of the oldest and most run-down in the Mediterranean," Finocchiaro Aprile says, arching his eyebrows. "Some of your vessels date back to your grandfather's days—may God rest his soul. You must admit that."

Ignazio makes a gesture of annoyance. Domenico Gallotti clears his throat and protests. "That's a trifle—nothing that can't be fixed with a few repairs or by purchasing new steamships, especially once we've obtained the subsidies. But refusing to renew because of that . . . what nonsense!"

"You think so?" the minister replies. There's a hint of provocation in his voice. "Then why haven't you already taken care of it?"

Laganà shakes his head and is about to speak, but Ignazio stops him. "Because it involves cost, as you well know. NGI keeps going thanks to subsidies, but they're only enough to keep up with the French and Austrian fleets, certainly not to make a profit. That's why I applied for help to set up a shipyard: so that we could *build* our own steamers, since we already have a haulage yard where the men from the Oretea Foundry work. Only, the municipality couldn't spare a penny, and not a peep from Rome—nothing. Whatever happened to that project? There's certainly been no lack of goodwill on my part."

The minister pulls a face, his eyes fixed on the edge of his desk.

"Help us," Ignazio insists. "Give us the money and we'll modernize everything." There's almost a note of pleading in his voice now, contrasting with the fiery look in his eyes and the hands clenched on his lap.

"Yes, but we can't do anything like that," Finocchiaro Aprile mutters. "Our majority is too narrow to approve the renewal." He stands up and opens the window. The bustle of the Roman streets bursts into the room. Shouting, wheels rolling on cobblestones, even an accordion. Annoyed, he pulls the shutters to, then turns and asks softly, "Have you spoken to Crispi?"

That's right. Crispi.

The three men exchange tense looks.

When Crispi received Ignazio in his office, he studied him for a long time, superimposing the father's image on that of the son, perhaps hoping to have before him an interlocutor as attentive and sharp as the father had been. Or perhaps because he had to come to terms with the passing of time, because this was the third member of the Florio family who'd turned to him. They'd all come: the coarse, fearsome Vincenzo, then Ignazio, who'd been both refined and ruthless. And now this one, little older than a boy, whom Crispi couldn't quite make out yet.

As for Ignazio, he was seeing someone very different from the energetic, astute man with a rebellious twinkle in his eye whom he'd met in Rome many years earlier. They were in the imposing lobby of the Hotel d'Angleterre then, immersed in the padded luxury of this hotel full of foreign travelers. He remembered *Avvocato* Crispi kissing his mother's hand, then his father taking his arm and striding away with him to an isolated couch. They sat there talking while he went for a carriage ride with his mother and sister.

Ignazio couldn't help thinking that this pale, weary seventy-year-old no longer had the energy to be steering the ship of politics through all these heavy storms.

Maybe he no longer even had sufficient influence for that.

Crispi motioned him to take a seat and himself sat down with difficulty. "There's too much chaos about, Don Ignazio," he said between puffs from his cigar, his voice hoarse from the smoke. "My enemies scream and protest that times are hard. But one thing I can tell you: it's true that Giolitti and his northern friends are currently leading the game, but that won't last long. He seems quite responsible, but in truth he's plotting in the shadows. He's basically acting the decent person, but he's worse scum than the others, and he's clouding the issue because he's in trouble. The whole mess with the

Banca Romana proves that no one is innocent. He covered up for people at all levels, and sooner or later the rot will surface. But for now, as things stand, he's here and there's little I can do. Speak to Finocchiaro Aprile. He's from Palermo. He's expecting you."

"I've already thought of him," Ignazio replied. "But I wanted your opinion first. You've been Casa Florio's lawyer for many years, and you know my family well."

Francesco Crispi squinted, with the expression of a veteran blood-hound and a glint of smugness in his eyes. "*Caciettu chi a' canuscio*, Don Ignazio. Of course I know it. That's why what Ferraris said didn't cause much damage. If it hadn't been for me, other people would have spoken after him, and the consequences would have been far worse. Let's just say that I made sure his words were . . . well, forgotten."

"And for that I'm grateful."

Crispi waved a hand covered in liver spots. "I did what I could, but now it's up to Finocchiaro Aprile."

And these are the words Ignazio repeats now to the minister. "Crispi did all he could to limit the damage. You know better than I do that, at present, he can't be asked for more."

"We can't wait," Domenico Gallotti says, barely controlling his frustration. "No one has any way of knowing when this government will fall. Political alliances are dictated by the convenience of the moment. You know that, too."

Laganà nods, still saying nothing.

"I'm afraid my hands are tied," the minister says. "There are too many protests against the management of the NGI routes and . . ."

Ignazio gets to his feet and paces up and down the room. "Damn it, we need those concessions, don't you see? There's an entire city that makes a living from the money NGI brings in. What would happen if the concessions weren't renewed?" He's almost shouting, unable to conceal his anger.

Finocchiaro Aprile sighs. He can't hide any longer—not from the sharp eyes of these three men. He crosses his arms. "I know. But there's very little I can do at the moment. The northern deputies close to Giolitti are more numerous than we are, and more unanimous." He gives him an eloquent look. "It's up to you, Don Ignazio, to play the right card with the people of Palermo. To scare them. You know only too well that there's nothing more . . . persuasive than fear."

Ignazio understands. Finocchiaro Aprile is asking him to take a difficult reality and paint it in even darker hues, by evoking the specter of a treacherous enemy, a devastating economic crisis, in order to move public opinion.

He likes the idea. The smile that appears on his lips is both light and sharp.

Finocchiaro Aprile relaxes slightly in his chair. Gallotti blinks, then says, "Do you mean protests?"

The minister opens his arms. "Protests, demonstrations . . . Your Oretea workers are among the most active, and there's a strong presence in Palermo of the Sicilian Fasci, those petty politicians who claim to defend workers' rights . . ."

"Agitators who refuse to work," Laganà grumbles.

Gallotti gives him a dirty look.

"They're workers who care about their jobs. If they're scared, they'll make ripples." Ignazio stares at Finocchiaro Aprile, who nods and adds, "You know the right people to talk to or who can talk on your behalf. Make sure they get scared, and let the entire island know, because if the port of Palermo stops working, the whole economy of Sicily will collapse."

Ignazio remembers what his father did when it came to rippling the waters so as to encourage the merger with Rubattino. That was a very successful maneuver. *And some things don't change*, he thinks. *Fear is always fear.*

There's a knock at the door and a round face appears. "May I come in?"

An embarrassed silence falls over the room. Ignazio looks away. The minister motions the man to enter. "We weren't expecting you, Don Raffaele," he says as soon as the door is closed. "This is a private meeting."

"So I imagined," Raffaele Palizzolo says in an obsequious tone. "That's why I waited outside. I wished to show no disrespect. I'm here as an honest Sicilian, but also as a relative of Don Ignazio's. His wife, Donna Franca, is the niece by marriage of my sister, the Duchess of Villarosa, as I'm sure you know." He holds out his hand, which Ignazio shakes with some hesitation, then, uninvited, takes a seat next to him. "Besides, I'm here to give my contribution, because Palermo cannot lose the concessions."

In the room, the unease is almost tangible. For years, Raffaele Palizzolo has been known in Palermo as someone who likes to play God. He listens to everything, observes everything, and then is always able to use the information to his own advantage. It's a skill that has clearly proved useful to him here in Rome, too, at least since he became a deputy. For some time, though, a long, menacing shadow has been hanging over him, connected to a crime that shook the city to its core: on February 1 this year, Emanuele Notarbartolo, former director of the Banco di Sicilia, a man of great integrity, respected by everyone, was murdered, stabbed twenty-seven times, on the train from Termini Imerese to Palermo. Since then, rumors have persisted that Palizzolo was involved in the killing, given that he had skeletons in his closet. Like many others—more than many others—he had made a mess of the bank's finances, and Notarbartolo—according to the well-informed—had discovered it. Although these are only rumors—obviously, there were no witnesses to the murder—it's hard for those present to shrug off the feeling that they're in the same room as a criminal.

The silence that follows Palizzolo's statement is finally broken by Laganà. "Of course we all agree about that. The problem is how to intervene without causing damage."

"Listen to me," Palizzolo says, leaning toward the minister's desk with uncalled-for familiarity. "We need to give them a fright. As you well know, minister, people listen to me in the Chamber of Deputies. I just need to make a speech."

The minister raises his head and strokes his chin. He looks at him and Palizzolo bows his head. He's implicitly asking for permission to act because, before being politicians, these men are Sicilians and make their move only after the right person has been informed of their intentions and given his approval.

Now the minister is listening to him. "What do you want to do?"

"There's unrest in Palermo right now. We just need to show them what could happen." Palizzolo's face clouds over. Then he looks at Laganà and Gallotti. "Can you imagine what would happen if the news arrived that the concessions haven't been renewed? At the very least, there'd be barricades on the streets. And what government could allow a popular uprising? Definitely not this government, with all the disasters it's already having to face."

Ignazio exchanges glances with Gallotti, who raises his eyes to the sky: yes, Palizzolo must have been eavesdropping on their conversation.

Laganà moves, leaning on the minister's desk. He speaks without concealing his irritation. "We were talking about this very thing just before you came in, the idea that we could urge the workers of the Oretea and the haulage yard to protest, but I imagine you've already grasped that."

Palizzolo shakes his head. If he's upset by this scarcely veiled reprimand, he doesn't show it. "We need to threaten a strike. We need something that gives everybody a fright." He turns toward Finocchiaro Aprile, ignoring the minister's bewildered expression, and continues, leaning forward, his hands on his thighs: "You're from Palermo, so you know what I mean: Giolitti doesn't want this bother, but we're going to give it to him anyway."

Ignazio examines his fingertips. "Basically, you'd like to scare him and put him under such pressure that he'll ignore the demands of his own people."

By way of confirmation, Palizzolo spreads his hands. "One thing they still haven't understood here in Rome is that the guts of Italy are in Palermo. Anything decided in Rome first has to go through there."

Gallotti nods and turns to Finocchiaro Aprile. "What do you think, minister?"

Aprile shrugs. "Of course, it's riskier than I'd thought, but it may work. You'll have to be careful not to lose control of the situation in Sicily; I'll do what I can from here. Any help we can get will be useful, from wherever it comes," he concludes, eloquently. His voice is like the chiming of a grandfather clock in an empty room.

Ignazio nods, satisfied. He gets to his feet and holds out his hand to the minister. "NGI and Palermo will be grateful to you for whatever you're able to do." He looks at him intensely. "The Florio family will be grateful to you personally."

Camillo Finocchiaro Aprile understands. He gives a slight smile.

◌

Hesitantly, Franca raises her hand to her lips. The dark green satin dress emphasizes the line of her breasts. She can almost see in the mirror her mother-in-law looking at her disapprovingly. She can even hear her voice. "Too much décolleté, *figghia mia*, especially in your condition."

In her condition.

She runs her bejeweled hand over her belly, which is starting to swell. She's almost four months pregnant. She smiles. Of course, now that the June heat has arrived, it's become harder to bear her pregnancy, but the joy she feels helps her to overcome any discomfort. And on top of that, Ignazio is so happy, he smothers her with his attentions, showers her with magnificent gifts, like the emerald-and-diamond earrings that appeared as if by magic on her dressing table the day after she told him she was expecting a baby.

She puts them on, slips a few bracelets on her wrists, then calls Diodata and points to a shawl in the wardrobe. It's an ivory silk shawl by Lanvin: she asks for it to be draped over her shoulders, thus at least partly covering the décolleté.

Ignazio is waiting for her at the carriage entrance, next to the great olive tree. With him are Giovanna and Donna Ciccia. Giovanna kisses her son and runs her hand over his chest. "Don't come back late," she says. "You mustn't tire yourself."

"*Maman*, Franca is becoming the greatest expert on the best couches in Palermo. Ever since it became known that she's expecting a child, the mistresses of all the houses have been competing for the honor of not letting her get too tired. And Donna Adele de Seta is the most solicitous of them all."

Giovanna ignores her son's witticisms and looks Franca up and down. Franca really can't get used to that stern, sad look, and instinctively lowers her eyes. But as if in response, her mother-in-law comes to her and adjusts her shawl. "Of course, it's hot, but you must keep covered."

She's covered. And not only because of the cold.

"Ne vous inquiétez pas, Maman," she replies, leaning over and kissing her on the cheek.

Ignazio helps her into the coach, one hand behind her back, a hand that slides imperceptibly downwards. Once inside, he pulls her to him and kisses her. "My God, you're magnificent. Pregnancy is making you even more beautiful." He lets his hand run over her slim, no longer corseted hips.

Franca blushes in the dark and returns his embrace. Everyone told her that, once she was pregnant, Ignazio would stop coming to her bed "in order not to hurt the child." That hasn't happened . . . But not even that ardor has made her forget that, during the receptions to which they've been invited, her husband has often behaved in a somewhat too casual manner toward some of the female guests. That's why, even though she's tired, she prefers to go with him: because she wants to remind everyone—first and foremost, him—that Ignazio Florio is no longer a bachelor in search of amusement.

By the time they get to the De Setas' palace, the reception rooms are already full to bursting. In between whispered gossip and inquiring glances, the women of Palermo are on display in a whirl of silks and jewels, while the men of Palermo—with greater discretion—are forging new relations or consolidating old alliances. A play in which Ignazio and Franca are now protagonists. Apparently, all the old malicious rumors about them have been swept away by their obvious happiness and by the news of Franca's pregnancy. Ever since they got back from their honeymoon, they've gone from one party to another, but have had to put off holding a reception at the Olivuzza because of Franca's condition. The season is now almost over, and the De Setas' party is one of the last social events. Very soon, the families will leave their residences in the city and set off for French seaside resorts or Alpine villages in Austria or Switzerland; others will withdraw to their villas in the country. As for Ignazio and Franca, their favorite yacht, the *Sultana*, is awaiting them for a Mediterranean cruise.

That's what Ignazio is talking about with Giuseppe Monroy. "There's no reason not to go," he's saying. "The *Sultana* is very solid and the doctor on board will have everything he needs to treat Franca."

Giuseppe nods and raises his glass in a toast. "Don't forget, you're expecting the family heir. It's only right to be cautious."

"You don't need to tell me that. Even if my mother objects and—" Ignazio breaks off, distracted by a girl in a light pink dress passing in front of them in the company of an elderly lady, probably her mother.

"Who's that? I'd like to know where they're keeping her hidden," Giuseppe says with a laugh.

"Well, the important thing is that they come out . . . when the time is right," Ignazio concludes.

He leaps to his feet and starts walking behind the girl, while Giuseppe, amused, watches him and shakes his head. After a few steps, the woman stops to chat to a friend and the girl turns and looks at Ignazio. It isn't a casual glance, far from it. He has time to notice her dark, narrow eyes, her generous mouth, and the milky breasts that seem to be trying to escape her corset. He wonders if they're firm, or else soft and a little droopy. Too many times he's been deceived by a dress "held up" in the right places . . .

The girl is still looking at him, now in an almost brazen way. A quiver runs through him, but he hesitates. *First I should find out who she is*, he tells himself. *Heaven forbid she's a relative of the Marchesa de Seta, a niece perhaps . . .*

Just then, someone comes up to him, taps him on the shoulder, and whispers, "Your wife's looking for you, Ignazio."

He spins around. Franca is coming toward him, with her luminous smile and her easy gait. She takes him by the arm and entwines her fingers with his. "Darling, help me get away from Donna Alliata. She wants to tell me what happened during her labor, and her daughters', and I'm already scared enough about my own. Please ask me to dance: I'm pregnant, not ill, and I can permit myself a little waltz with my husband."

Ignazio takes her hand and leads her into the center of the room just as the orchestra is starting to play. He puts his arm around her waist, and she laughs, she laughs loudly, just as she has been taught *not* to do.

But she does it. *Let them get a good look at me*, Franca thinks, aiming her gaze at that hussy in the pink dress, because she noticed how the girl was looking at her husband, oh, yes, she noticed all right, and it upset her more than a little.

The girl turns her back on her and walks away.

Franca shifts her gaze to the matrons sitting around the room and, as if in response to their silent disapproval, smiles. She knows what they're thinking: a woman in her condition shouldn't even come to a party, let alone dance. But she doesn't care. She keeps spinning around, throwing defiant glances at the others, the women who are still beautiful and desirable, and imagining their thoughts: they're convinced that soon enough Ignazio will find someone else with whom to satisfy his urges. Because that's what a husband does when his wife is pregnant.

I have everything you can no longer have and perhaps never had, she says, looking at the matrons. Then she leans on Ignazio and strokes his neck in a silent declaration of possession. And inside herself, she says: *Your husbands behave like that. Not Ignazio. He's mine and he loves me. And I'm enough for him.*

∾

July in Palermo is like a mischievous child. Clear days alternate with others laden with a dampness that attaches itself to the skin and makes breathing difficult. Then the sirocco arrives, bringing with it sand from the desert and transforming the mountaintops into dark patches against an ivory sky.

Today, though, July has decided to behave: the day is clear and airy, making you want to be in the open air. So Franca has given orders for tea to be laid out in the grounds of the Olivuzza, beneath the palms next to the aviary.

She's waiting for the arrival of Francesca and Emma di Villarosa, who are coming to spend the afternoon with her and keep her company. She's sitting in the boudoir next to her bedroom, reading Annie Vivanti's *Marion artista di caffè-concerto*, a novel that her sister-in-law, Giulia, lent her—telling her not to let her mother-in-law see it because "there are things in it that are a little . . . improper." Her pregnancy is quite visible now, she feels tired constantly, and, above all, she's alone. *Ignazio has been unfair,* she thinks, nervously leafing through the pages. First, he promised her that cruise on the *Sultana,* then, with the excuse that she should take care of herself, he informed her that they would remain together in Palermo. In the end, he changed his mind and left for a trip to Africa, maintaining that he really needed rest after the exhausting wait for the renewal of the concessions.

A renewal that was finally approved: for another fifteen years, in other words, until 1908, NGI will keep the monopoly of the subsidized services. A result obtained thanks to an inflamed speech by Raffaele Palizzolo in the Chamber of Deputies—"In one day there'll be six thousand families without bread . . . it would be a national disaster"—to the solid grouping of Sicilian parliamentarians around Crispi, who thus demonstrated that he was still a valuable ally, and to the social pressure generated by articles in the *Giornale di Sicilia*, which had depicted in the blackest colors the fate of not only Palermo, but the whole of Sicily if the concessions were not renewed. Terrified at the prospect of losing their jobs, people poured out onto the streets and there were rowdy daily demonstrations, which turned into genuine celebrations when the good news was announced. At the haulage yard and the Oretea Foundry, such was the joy, it was as if rain had arrived after months of drought. Of course, there was a price to pay: NGI would have to modernize its old steamers and buy three new ones, but these weren't insoluble problems.

At the Olivuzza, Ignazio insisted on toasting with the best champagne, while he told Franca how things had gone, imitating now Crispi's voice, now Palizzolo's. And Franca laughed when he told her that now Finocchiaro Aprile would finally be able to buy that farmhouse he'd had his eyes on for a while. At which Giovanna shook her head, asking for more discretion.

But the euphoria soon faded after Ignazio's departure, and Franca and the Olivuzza fell into a silent torpor that had little to do with the heat.

When the maid tells her that her cousins have arrived, Franca gets up and goes to meet them.

"Franca, darling, you're more beautiful than ever." Emma, in a white cotton dress and a straw hat, kisses her on the cheeks.

Behind her, composed and serious, Francesca nods hello. She was always the liveliest of the three, envied by everyone for her beauty. Now, though, she is . . . lifeless. Her premature widowhood has relegated her to a limbo from which she finds it hard to emerge, partly because many people treat her as if she were the most unfortunate of women.

Trying to dismiss that thought, Franca opens the French windows. "Come, let's go into the garden. I've had tea laid out next to the aviary," she says, her cheerfulness a little forced.

The two sisters exchange puzzled glances. "But . . . aren't we saying hello to your mother-in-law?" Francesca asks.

"No, let's not disturb her!" Franca exclaims impatiently. "She's probably embroidering in her boudoir. We'll go to her later."

She seizes Emma by the hand and almost drags her along the garden path. In the last few days, apart from pining for Ignazio, she's been feeling restless, in the grip of unpleasant thoughts, and needs to move.

When they reach the aviary, they find Vincenzino playing with a hoop, while his governess watches him idly. The boy greets the three women, kissing the sisters' hands with a seriousness that draws a smile even from Francesca, then skips away.

Just as used to happen in the old days, Franca sits down between her two cousins.

"How are you?" Emma asks, taking her hand.

"The baby's started moving. I'm forced to sleep on my side at night. What about you? How are you, my sweet?" she asks Francesca.

"I'm quite well," Francesca replies, a vague hint of a Tuscan accent in her voice.

Franca takes her hand, enclosed in its black silk glove, and receives a squeeze in return. "To tell the truth, I'd like to get out and about more, but what with the heat and Ignazio being away, I don't have many opportunities to leave the house. As far as my mother-in-law's concerned, leaving the house just means going to church, so I'm bored, that's it."

Emma gives a slight smile and reaches her hand out toward Franca's belly, then hesitates. "May I?" she asks.

Franca nods, takes Francesca's hand, too, and puts both women's hands on her belly.

"The other evening, I was at the house of Robert and Sofia Whitaker," Emma resumes. "There was a little group talking about you and Ignazio."

Francesca glares at her, but Franca smiles. "What did they make up this time? That Ignazio has a new mistress? Some time ago, I heard a rumor that there was a Spanish woman on the *Sultana*, a singer . . ." She raises her eyes to heaven. "Incredible! Is it so difficult to believe that he loves me and that he's started to behave himself now that he's about to become a father?"

Francesca purses her lips. "Actually, what Robert said was that Ignazio was very skillful in the way he obtained the renewal of the concessions, and Giuseppe Monroy was also full of praise for him. Obviously, there was a bit of gossip, too. It's the thing that adds spice to these evenings that otherwise would be exceedingly boring. But you know better than I that there's nothing in such stories."

Franca nods, suddenly serious. "Yes, and in fact I don't usually take any notice of them. All the same . . ." She lowers her voice. "Sometimes I have the feeling I must justify everything I do, not only to my husband and my mother-in-law, but to the whole city."

"It's inevitable that everyone's watching you, given your position," Francesca replies. "The important thing is that you have nothing to feel guilty about. You've always behaved in an exemplary fashion."

"But if you're pregnant and you want to dance a waltz with your husband, you end up on trial," Franca murmurs.

"As my tutor used to say, 'As rust consumes iron, envy consumes the envious,'" Emma remarks.

Franca throws her head back and stares at the aviary. "And yes, with the two of you, I can admit it: I was upset that Ignazio left without me. On the other hand, I have to take care of myself. I don't want to tempt fate."

Emma waves a hand to dismiss that thought, while Francesca squeezes Franca's shoulders and gives her a kiss. "There are some things we shouldn't even say, *ma chère*. And always remember, men need their freedom. Or at the very least, the illusion that they're free. That way they come back happier than before." She gives her a wicked smile, the first in many months.

Franca smiles back and tells her she's right. She leans forward, pours cold tea for her cousins, and offers them biscuits. They laugh and joke as if they were still adolescents.

And yet the thought, *that* thought, is a malign seed, a seed that keeps growing. *Why did Ignazio leave anyway?* Franca thinks. Even his mother tried to dissuade him: now was not the time to leave a wife in that condition. And even though the question of the concessions was now settled, it was hardly wise to neglect the business.

Why?

Giovanna watches her daughter-in-law walk away with her cousins along the garden paths, having first heard the noise of the coach wheels on the cobbles, then the voices becoming gradually fainter.

She would have liked them to come say hello to her, instead

of which her daughter-in-law dragged them away. *Sperta idda*, she thinks. She's a sly one. If Franca had brought them straight to her, she wouldn't have allowed her to go into the garden, not in this heat.

She drums her fingers on the window frame and Donna Ciccia raises an eyebrow. "Who was that?" she asks, inserting a length of thread.

"My son shouldn't have left," Giovanna murmurs. "It wasn't the right time to go away, not with what's happening. The workers are still too agitated." Admittedly, she doesn't understand much about politics or business—that's all men's stuff—and Ignazio did tell her many times not to worry because there were no hotheads among their workforce, and even those Workers' Fasci that held a congress in Palermo a couple of months ago—a congress! As if they were deputies!—wouldn't last long. But Giovanna, just as she did when her Ignazio was alive, reads the *Giornale di Sicilia*, and she hasn't found any reassuring news in it. On the contrary, for some time now there's been this complicated story of banks going bust because they ran out of money . . . or at least that's what she's understood. She tried to talk to Ignazio about it, but he just laughed and told her that Credito Mobiliare and Banco Florio were as sound as could be and nothing and nobody could touch them.

And the situation in Palermo isn't the only thing that's worrying her.

She turns her gaze to the garden again; she hears the voices of the three women, borne on a gust of wind, and spots Vincenzino running and laughing. Reluctantly, she's forced to admit that Franca is conducting herself like a good wife, she's eating and resting. Whereas Ignazio . . .

Anxiety climbs up her thin legs like a grass snake and wraps itself around her waist. She rubs her face with her hands, massaging the lines, which have become deeper since her husband died.

Suddenly, Donna Ciccia is beside her. The woman's grown old, her hair is completely white, and her face, which has always been stern, now actually seems carved in stone. "Don't be afraid, God will take care of him. Remember, I know certain things. They love each other, and Ignazio must be careful he doesn't do anything foolish."

Donna Ciccia doesn't need to specify what stupid things she's referring to: Ignazio's passion for chasing skirts is well known, and he's never hidden it. True, he's married now and seems genuinely in love with Franca. But has he really changed? Or was it just the euphoria of those first months of marriage?

Giovanna shakes her head; Donna Ciccia sighs and spreads her hands as if to say: *That's where we are.*

She, too, loves Ignazio; she saw him born, she saw him grow up and become an adult. Spoiled, protected, and defended by his mother, he grew like a plant ready to turn wild if neglected. But how could one blame Giovanna? Vincenzino's death was a blow from which she never fully recovered. She was left alone with her grief, and she reacted by attaching herself to Ignazziddu. She lavished all her love on that son, who, with the years, became an elegant, haughty—and also, after his father's death, immensely rich—young man.

Ignazio is used to being top in everything. In life, in business, with women. *But what will happen now that he's about to become a father?* Donna Ciccia wonders, sitting back down at the loom.

When Giovanna told her that Ignazio wanted her to meet the Jaconas at Abetone, to discuss the engagement, Donna Ciccia had felt a shudder of uncertainty. As far as she was concerned, Ignazio was an irresponsible boy and still too young to enter into a marriage.

After giving it some thought, she decided to ask the souls in Purgatory what would be the fate of such a marriage. She knew that, if asked with purity of heart and simplicity, they always replied, for good or ill, and couldn't lie. And never mind if Giovanna didn't like her to do "those things."

So, one summer night, she went out by one of the garden doors and headed to the crossroads at the entrance to the villa, because there, as at all crossroads, good and evil, life and death, God and the devil meet. She passed a watchman, but he merely acknowledged her with a nod of the head. There was a bothersome, slanting wind, and she pulled her shawl up over her head to stop the leaves and sand from getting in her hair. When she got to the crossroads, she crossed herself and said an Our Father, a Hail Mary, and a Gloria, because she didn't want the Lord to be angry at the souls of the dead being called on to answer a question from the living.

"Armuzzi di li corpi decullati, tri 'mpisi, tri ocisi, tri annigati . . ." she murmured, then continued in a whisper, because she knew that these were things that not everyone ought to hear. *You souls of beheaded bodies, three hanged, three murdered, three drowned . . .*

Then she waited. And the answer came.

First of all, she seemed to hear the tolling of a bell, although she couldn't have said where it came from. Then, from one of the roads, three cats appeared. She-cats, judging by their colors. They passed the crossroads, then stopped to look at her with that air of defiant indifference that only wild she-cats have.

That was when Donna Ciccia understood: yes, there would be a marriage, but with lots of women involved. She returned to the house, head bowed, indifferent now to the wind ruffling her hair. She wasn't sure what to do, but in the end decided not to say anything to Giovanna.

Later, she was tempted to question the souls in Purgatory again to ask what would become of that child who was about to come into the world, but something stopped her.

She looks at Giovanna. She loves her as if she were her own child, which, in a way, she is. She wasn't even twenty when she started taking care of her. Now Giovanna is in her forties and she herself is in her sixties. And the fact that she's almost reached the end of the road of life scares her, not for herself, but because she senses that, when she's no longer there, other storms will come, and Giovanna won't be able to weather them without suffering perhaps more than she has already suffered.

Ignazio's homecoming throws everything into confusion. The Olivuzza is overrun with suitcases, crates, and trunks, but also with animal skins that will end up on some wall or other, or else be turned into rugs, like the tiger skin that will flaunt itself in the stateroom of the *Sultana*. In the late July heat, the pungent odor of the animal skins makes Franca, who's now in her sixth month, feel extremely nauseated, and Giovanna immediately gives orders for them to be taken away.

Ignazio has come back from his journey filled with energy: he's constantly coming in and out of the house, running up and down the stairs, singing. He moves between the rooms followed by his manservant Saro, who's replaced Nanài, giving instructions, indicating where to put the crates and suitcases; every now and again he stops by Franca, who's sitting in the boudoir next to her bedroom, and gives her a kiss on the forehead. From the baggage there emerge statuettes of bone, carved stones, strange engraved wooden boxes. He shows these things to her, telling her where he bought them, or what he was doing at that particular time. Franca listens to him, joy dancing in her eyes: she's happy to have him by her side again and admires these strange objects, turning them over and over in her hands, smelling the fragrance of the wood or the spiced aroma of the oils.

It's late in the morning when Ignazio takes his straw hat and says with a sigh, "I have to go to the office."

She nods. "Come back soon, my love. You must continue telling me about your journey," she murmurs, giving him a kiss.

At the front door, though, Giovanna is waiting for him, hands folded in front of her, a stern look on her face. Having seen Romualdo Trigona's coach stop in front of the house, she's guessed her son's true intentions.

"You're not going to the NGI offices," she says reprovingly, following him.

Without slowing down, Ignazio waves his hand dismissively. "Of course I'm going there, *Maman*. Tomorrow, when I'm calmer. What difference does a day make? Right now, I'm going to the club with Romualdo: they're expecting me." He walks away, eager to tell his friends about his African adventures and to be brought up to date on what happened in Palermo while he was away.

Giovanna stops and shakes her head in bewilderment. Her husband would have rushed to Piazza Marina and wouldn't have returned home until he had checked every register, every transaction. Whereas her son . . . But what can she do about it? *That's the way Ignazziddu is.* Head bowed, she goes back inside the house and heads to her apartments. Just then, however, from the upper floor comes a noise of trunks being shifted and hurried footsteps. Giovanna raises her eyes to the ceiling and sighs. Leaving your wife to run and see your friends is never a good sign.

∽

It's almost impossible to move in Ignazio's bedroom, with all the trunks and suitcases. On one side, clothes and shoes, on the other, English shirts and cravats, all scrunched up. Saro is throwing the dirty linen into a large basket, which is so full by now that Diodata begs him to stop, or she won't be able to carry it to the laundry room. Saro takes a step back and Diodata lifts the basket, arching her back with a moan, and makes for the door, but slips on a fold in the rug and ends up on the floor.

"Heavens, what a tumble! Did you hurt yourself?" Franca goes to her, followed by Saro. While Diodata apologizes profusely, her face red with embarrassment, Saro picks up the shirts strewn all around.

And it's there, in the middle of all that white, that a red patch appears.

Franca sees it, as does Saro. He tries to cover it with his foot, but in vain: the edge of it is still visible beneath his shoe.

Lace.

Franca doesn't immediately understand. She feels a strange sensation, a stab of pain to the stomach that takes her breath away. "Move," she orders.

Saro is forced to stand aside.

Franca bends and picks up the garment.

Red. Silky. A transparent petticoat. Material that reveals more than it conceals. A showy thing, the kind worn by a woman who wants to display her merchandise. And the scent . . . Tuberose. It revolts her, makes her nauseated.

She sways.

Behind her, Diodata puts a hand over her mouth. Saro grabs a chair and makes Franca sit down. She's shaking uncontrollably.

"It must have happened at customs, Donna Franca," Saro hastens to explain. He tries to take the heap of silk from her, but she's clutching it in her hands and looking at him, speechless. "At customs they opened all the baggage, *li misiru ri sutta n'capo*—they turned everything inside out. They must have mixed up Don Ignazio's linen with some woman's." Saro reaches out his hand again.

Franca raises her eyes, look at him, and shakes her head.

She would like to clutch at that idea, but something makes it crumble in her chest.

A premonition.

Words crowd into her head and turn into demons. The words of her father, who's always been hostile to Ignazio. The discreet but clear words of Francesca and Emma. The words of her mother-in-law, punctuated with exasperated sighs. And then the whole chorus of Palermo: the whispers of the gossips hiding behind their fans, the hints dropped by the matrons as they throw her pitying glances and by the younger women with their arrogant looks, the murmured insinuations of the men, who smile as she passes and nudge one another. Shrill, discordant voices, which all tell the same story.

Franca looks at the petticoat she's still clutching in her hands and raises it in front of her. She herself has never owned anything like it: the kind of thing that might be worn by a *cocotte*, a hussy, as her mother would say. She's always thought that her beauty and her love were enough for Ignazio. And yet . . .

She lowers her eyes to her belly, which looks huge to her now. Her hands are swollen, her face has grown round. She feels monstrous, deformed. All the wonderful things her pregnancy has brought her now seem to her marks of an irreversible transformation.

Maybe even Ignazio sees me like that, and so . . .

She lifts her hands to her face and bursts into tears, without shame.

"Get out. Out!" she cries in a voice so shrill it doesn't even seem to be hers. Saro and Diodata silently leave the room, and Franca weeps for a long time, shaken to the core by the violence of her emotions. It takes her several minutes to calm down. Then she angrily wipes away the tears. Hands clasped around that little heap of red silk, she sits down, straightens her back, stiffens her jaw, and waits. She *has* to know. She's entitled.

∽

And that's how Ignazio finds her when he returns at dusk. Singing to himself, he walks into the bedroom, which is shrouded in long, soft shadows, notices that it's still untidy, and vaguely wonders why. When he sees his wife, he smiles and goes to her.

"Franca, darling, what are you doing here? Don't you feel well? And why is there still all this mess? I asked Saro to—"

She simply holds out the hand in which she's clutching the petticoat. "Whose is *this*?"

Ignazio turns pale. "I don't know . . . What is it?"

"Women's things!" Franca cries, her voice shaking. Then she gets to her feet and stands before him. "It was rolled up among the shirts! What was it doing in your linen, can you tell me that?"

"There must have been some misunderstanding. Calm down," Ignazio says, taking a step back. "Someone at the hotel must have gotten confused, or maybe the maids mixed up my linen and yours."

"What? I've never owned this kind of . . . of . . ." Franca's voice gets louder, and as if in response to a call, Saro rushes out of the dressing room and into the bedroom.

"Signora, I beg you!" he exclaims. "I told you, it was a mix-up at customs."

"But of course, that's what it was!" Ignazio says, echoing him. "They opened everyone's baggage, it was a real mess."

"I don't believe you," Franca says, her voice cracking. She's about to start crying again. "You . . . You . . ." she stammers, and again she displays that little heap of red silk, but her hand is shaking now.

Then she sees it.

The look Saro and Ignazio just exchanged. A complicit look, the look of men united in deceit.

She understands.

She drops the petticoat to the floor, turns, grabs the bottle of Fougère from the dressing table, and hurls it at Ignazio. "You disgusting liar! You traitor!"

He bends to the side to avoid it; the bottle falls to the floor and shatters, releasing into the room an overwhelming scent, a mixture of lavender and spices. No sooner has Ignazio straightened up than he's hit on the arm by a silver hairbrush; then it's the turn of a jar of hair oil, which smashes at his feet. "What are you doing, my love? Calm down! Is this any way to behave?" He tries to grab hold of her arms, but she dodges him and lands a punch on his chest.

"You swine! How could you?"

"You'll harm the child, Franca, calm down!"

"You wretch!"

She's yelling now. Anger and the hormones of pregnancy have taken possession of her mind, and fear and shame have done the rest. He's been unfaithful to her, it's true, and everyone knows it. They've always known that he would be unfaithful. The humiliation of it is like a terrible poison, and it smothers everything, even her love, even the joy of motherhood.

Footsteps in the corridor. Giovanna appears in the doorway; beside her, Vincenzino, in his nightshirt, watching the scene with a mischievous look in his eyes. "What is it, are they quarreling?" he asks, laughing. Giovanna stops him from entering, then enters herself and goes to Franca.

"Who was it?" she asks in a low, stern voice.

"Him!" Franca cries, pointing to Ignazio. "He was unfaithful to me! Me, pregnant with his child!" Her sobs grow louder, and her face is almost distorted with rage.

Giovanna spins around to look at her son. Ignazio tries to speak, opening his hands as if to apologize, but she silences him with a glance that's like a slap in the face, a glance that says: *Be quiet, if you don't want to cause more damage.* Then she turns to Saro, who's been hiding in a corner of the room. "Come here, you. Take Signorino Vincenzo to his room and stay with him until I return."

As the boy is dragged away, Franca collapses onto the chair, in tears. *She's crying so much, it hurts to hear her*, Giovanna thinks, locking the door. Then she heaves a long sigh, her hand propped on the door frame. She's always known this moment would come.

Ignazio is standing motionless in the middle of the room, arms dangling by his sides, looking in turn at his mother and his wife with the air of someone who knows he's condemned, but doesn't yet know what sentence he will have to serve.

Giovanna turns, crosses her hands in front of her, and looks at Ignazio and Franca. Ever since the early days of their marriage, she has sensed that they would never have the inner strength they would need to be truly united. Because those two married without ever having had to exercise patience, without realizing what the spirit of sacrifice entailed. They believed that "forever" meant traveling throughout their lives along a broad, placid river. Instead of which, it meant dodging rocks, avoiding whirlpools and eddies, trying never to run aground. You could do that only if both of you rowed in the same direction and had your eyes fixed on the same horizon.

She herself had wanted it with all her heart, and she had sacrificed everything to that ideal of love. But in the end, she'd had to resign herself to the fact that, in a couple, it isn't unusual for one to love for both. Because there are those who don't want to love or, quite simply, aren't able to. And so she had learned that love can be kept alive even when the other person forgets to nourish it. She had learned that, in order not to fall into despair, you can even agree to pay the price of a lie every day. She had learned that being content with crumbs is better than starving to death.

Now it's their turn to learn. To figure out how to make what little they had in common suffice.

Ignazio comes to her. "Mamma, you tell her there must have been a mistake. I swear I would never have done anything like that."

"Oh, do shut up!"

Startled, Ignazio takes a step back. His mother has never before spoken to him in that tone. She's always been on his side, always defended him. And now what's happening?

Giovanna bends down, takes the petticoat between her thumb and index finger, then drops it and walks over it. "I always thought the two of you married without realizing what you were doing. Now I'm sure of it."

"I knew perfectly well, *Maman*," Franca retorts, irritably. "But he—"

"She's making a scene over nothing," Ignazio almost shrieks. "It's nothing but a—"

"Quiet. Both of you." Giovanna looks at her daughter-in-law and lifts her face with two fingers. "Look at me, my girl. Now is when you realize that it's always up to women to bear the heaviest burden."

She says this in a calm, almost gentle tone. "It's a law of nature, at least until the world is turned upside down and we women get to wear the trousers at home. You have to keep silent and, if necessary, pretend not to see. Whatever happens, you're his wife now and that's the way it is. No matter if your heart's bleeding: there are more important things than your pride, and one of these is the family name. The other is your child."

Franca puts her hand on her belly, as if wanting to protect her baby from what's happening. Turn the other cheek? Accept everything? Suffer in silence? Not even her mother would dare say anything like that to her. She would like to rebel, to say that she has her dignity, but then she looks up and sees something in Giovanna's eyes.

The woman isn't simply defending appearances, she's telling her how she managed to survive the pain of being cast aside, of not mattering as much as a man matters, the humiliation of not really being taken into consideration. It's an old pain, and yet it's still alive and immediate. And Franca feels it, understands it. Recognizes it.

"I married him because I love him, *Maman*, not for the name, you know that," she murmurs, wiping her tears with the back of her hand. She straightens up. "I want the respect I deserve."

"He can't give it to you," Giovanna replies curtly. "My son needs to show everyone that women fall at his feet. I don't know how many times his father reprimanded him, and how much money he made us spend. He loves you, that's obvious, or else he would have left the house and run away to the club. Because he's someone who runs away," she continues, while Ignazio stares at her, dumbfounded, open-mouthed. "The reason he's here, trying to convince you that he wasn't unfaithful to you, is because you're his wife. But don't think he'll stop chasing skirts just because he's married. That's who he is. You can't change his nature."

Ignazio can't believe his ears. Of course, it's a good thing that his mother should be reminding Franca how to behave, but at the same time, he would never have thought she had so little respect for him, or that she could expose his weaknesses with such ease. "No, it's not true!" he protests, walking about the room. "Mamma, you're talking about lies people tell and yet you believe them? You don't know what I feel. But then, how could you know? You and my father never loved each other. Do you think I don't know that? That I didn't see how you walked behind him and he hardly looked at you?"

Giovanna seems to be holding her breath; her pale cheeks are spotted with red. "What do you know about me and your father?" Her voice has become scratchy. She's bitter, filled with rancor. She puts a hand on her son's chest, as if wanting to push him away. Silence falls in the room. "Neither of you knows what it's like to be with someone your whole life," Giovanna resumes. "You're still just a couple of children with milk staining your mouths. Love!" She laughs, but it's a laugh made up of stones and glass. "You fill your mouths with that word and you don't even know what it means. You"—she points a finger at her son—"have always had everything and have never done anything to deserve it. And this one"—now indicating Franca—"is a *picciridda* who lived under a glass bell, protected from everything and everyone. Love is fine for the stories of Orlando and Angelica, because that's what it is: a story, a fairy tale. You two don't know what repentance and sacrifice are. You're not capable of forgoing anything, Ignazio, and nor is your wife, from what she's saying." She lowers her voice, as if talking to herself. "That was our mistake: we didn't teach you that first one has to earn things, and then one has to keep them."

She walks over to Franca. "You married him. He's the way he is, and you can't do anything about it," she says, close to her face. "You can bring scandal into this house, and then you'll have me as an enemy and I won't give you any peace. Or else you can be strong and tolerant, because Ignazio loves you in his way." Her voice becomes a breath. "Only one thing counts. Take this on board as if I were your mother: he must always come back to you. It doesn't matter how, or after how long. If you want to keep him, get it into your head that you will always forgive him. Keep your eyes and ears shut, and when he comes back, keep quiet."

"With all the hurt he's given me?" Franca's voice is also a whisper now. Her tears are falling again. "After seeing . . . that?" she adds, pointing to the little heap of red silk on the floor.

Giovanna bends down, picks it up, and hides it in her hands. "Now it's gone," she murmurs, with a hint almost of complicity in her voice. Then, unexpectedly, she strokes her: the first real gesture of affection since Franca came into this house. "*Figghia mia* . . . You still don't know what it means to be married to a Florio. When you realize, you'll remember everything I've said to you, and you'll understand." She straightens up. "I'm going to throw this filth away," she says, waving the petticoat. "Don't give the servants any more reason to talk. And you"—turning to her son—"don't cause any more damage than you already have."

Ignazio nods and mutters a yes.

Giovanna opens the door and leaves the room. She feels exhausted, as if that premonition of unhappiness has turned into something tangible. The pain, her pain, is once again mortifying her flesh.

She walks along the corridor. The silk feels burning hot in her hands. She can't wait to get rid of it, hoping that with it, certain memories will go away.

She loved Ignazio, her Ignazio, blindly, like a dog that returns to its master even when it's been beaten. And after many years, when that other woman had perhaps vanished from his thoughts, he too loved her, in his way: simple affection, of course, made up of familiarity and understanding. Affection, not real love, but it was enough for her because she had realized it was all she could have, that Ignazio couldn't give her more. It had taken time and tears, but she had realized.

And now she can only hope that these two will also realize what their fate is. And accept it.

That evening, Ignazio, alone in his father's study, glances at the papers that have accumulated while he was away.

From the cellars in Marseille there are reports of a decrease in the production of grapes due to a number of outbreaks of phylloxera. He shrugs, thinking there hasn't yet been any news of contagion in the Trapani area, but they'll have to keep their eyes open, because that would be a really bad blow. Then he reads the protests from the owners of the sulfur mines: they're asking him to intervene and obtain a further reduction in the excise duty. In the end, his skin crawling with anxiety and nerves, he snaps. "Damn paperwork!" he cries, standing up and starting to pace about the room. His father created a company to bring together the sulfur producers and helped them to obtain more favorable taxation, but it now appears this isn't enough for them. They keep complaining about that and about their excessive costs compared with the revenue from sales of their product. And yet . . .

Ignazio sits back down and rereads the papers more calmly. No, the Italian market isn't large enough to absorb Sicilian sulfur: maybe it would be a good idea to rent out some of the mines, like the one in Rabbione or the one in Bosco. Or else he could look for foreign partners, especially among the French and the British. The British have even developed a faster and cheaper system for producing sulfur. Maybe he could get in touch with Alexander Chance, the industrialist who patented the process in Great Britain. He might even be interested in taking over their production if the price was advantageous.

There are too many things to take into account, too many questions that are asked of him. Yet again, he wonders how his father managed to let nothing escape him. But then he immediately thinks that, when it comes down to it, he himself has nothing to feel guilty about, because he's doing the best he can. And besides, what problems are there anyway? Nothing serious. There's not the slightest sign of a crisis. His business is solid, as sound as the house built on a rock that's mentioned in the Gospels.

Plus, his back is covered by Credito Mobiliare, with which he's forged a very fruitful partnership: Credito Mobiliare has a branch in Banco Florio, as well as shares in the company, and is willing to guarantee to the government that the company will modernize its ships and buy new steamers. In short, the money is there.

Of course, the banks are still being shaken by constant earthquakes. The trial of the directors of the Banca Romana has just started and the charges are serious: from embezzlement to corruption, from dealing in fake currency to misappropriation of funds. It's even rumored that IOUs signed by the king, who needed money to satisfy the whims of his mistresses, were found in Bernardo Tanlongo's house. It's inevitable that such a scandal will have consequences, but as for worrying about the future of Casa Florio . . .

Ignazio stands up again. First, he goes to the window, pulls back the curtains, and stands for a while looking down at the deserted piazza. Then he turns abruptly and goes to the cabinet where, on a silver tray, bottles of cognac, Armagnac, and brandy are lined up, some of them his own products. He pours himself a finger of cognac and sips it.

But the true reason for this restlessness won't go away.

Fool, he says to himself, softly beating his palm on the wall.

He should have been more careful with the baggage. How the hell had that woman's petticoat ended up among his shirts?

That woman.

He can still see her in the lobby of the hotel in Tunis. A simple memory that gives him a quiver of pleasure: blond hair, very clear skin, two cold blue eyes that fixed themselves on him, filled with promises abundantly kept.

He spent two mad, carefree days with her, having lunch and dinner brought to his room and drinking champagne. He left the room only once, to visit the bazaar, where the jewelers were and where he bought, for Franca, a necklace made up of a row of gold hearts on a thread, and for the other woman, a bracelet, also of gold, with an emerald mounted in the middle.

Ah, that's probably when she changed her clothes and the petticoat ended up among my shirts. I was in such a hurry the day I left, I just threw everything in the trunks, not even getting Saro to help me. But what does it matter? Why should I feel guilty over an unimportant fling? I don't even remember her name.

He takes another sip of cognac. As if his business responsibilities weren't enough, now his wife has to start behaving unreasonably. She ought to understand, damn it, that he has needs. *Pregnant women are always so delicate, as if they were all Madonnas*, he reflects,

347

with a curl of the lips. He needs to feel free. Free to do what he wants, to enjoy himself, to feel lightheaded.

She's still his wife, isn't she? She's his home. The queen of his heart. The mother of his children. When it comes down to it, he'll always go back to her. And she'll have to forgive him.

Ignazio has put on the Meyer & Mortimer suit and the silk cravat with the diamond pin, and now he's having a breakfast of coffee and croissants in the dining room on the second floor of the Olivuzza, which looks out on the winter garden. It rained during the night and the balustrade glitters with raindrops, whose gray light seems to be trying to mold actions and thoughts. November has shaken off the gold of autumn and hidden it under a milky blanket.

Giovanna comes in, wrapped in a black shawl. She orders the servant to stoke the fire in the hearth, then asks for breakfast: tea with a little crumbled bread in it. Franca isn't here. *She may still be asleep*, Giovanna thinks. *That's a good thing, given that it might happen any day now.* She's been keeping a close eye on her lately. Or rather, she's been keeping an eye on her and her husband, to see what the consequences of their quarrel are. Ignazio has been lavishing gifts and attention on Franca: bunches of flowers, little items of jewelry, a whole afternoon spent together . . . Franca has often been in a good mood, but Giovanna has noticed some of her glances at Ignazio, sometimes sad glances, sometimes stern, almost reproachful. *Give her time*, she's told herself.

While a servant brings a pot with the tea, Nino, the butler, approaches Ignazio with a tray on which there's a visiting card. Engrossed in reading the newspaper, he doesn't notice it at first. Then all at once, he sees the cream-colored card. He picks it up and frowns. "Gallotti? At this hour?" he exclaims. "Yes, let him in."

Giovanna looks up at her son, then returns to her tea.

Domenico Gallotti appears in the doorway: his hair is disheveled, his cravat knotted sloppily, and he seems upset. Ignazio looks at him in amazement: Gallotti has never before been neglectful in his dress, and his conduct has always been distinguished by composure and refinement.

"What's going on, Signor Gallotti? Take a seat. Would you like coffee?"

Gallotti shakes his head nervously. It's as if a dark fog has crept in with him and has gone to ground in the corners, filling the room with shadows. "Don Ignazio, forgive me, but I have very urgent news and . . ." He turns, as if only now noticing that Giovanna is here. He seems uncertain suddenly, then bows his head in greeting. "Donna Giovanna, I didn't see you. Good morning," he murmurs, throwing a hesitant glance at Ignazio.

But Ignazio waves his hand, as if to say: *She's my mother, she can stay.*

"Sit down, Gallotti, and tell me what's happened. Has a steamer sunk? Has there been an earthquake, or a fire?" He gives an ironic smile, while the servant shifts the chair to seat the director of NGI.

A cup of coffee is put down in front of Gallotti and he stares at it as if it were something revolting. Then he passes his hand over his forehead. They aren't raindrops, they're beads of sweat. "No, Don Ignazio. And if I may say so, that would have been better."

Ignazio grabs a croissant, tears off a tip, and dips it in the coffee. "Really?"

"Yes." A pause, long and heavy.

Ignazio is now looking at him with great attention.

"Yesterday evening I met Francesco La Lumia. You know, one of the cashiers at Credito Mobiliare, an excellent young man. I saw him grow up. I found him that job myself after the death of his father, a very honest man I had the honor to know since he was a child. Francesco's a highly reliable person, someone who knows what he's talking about . . ."

Ignazio glares at him. The man's nervousness is infecting him and turning to anxiety. "Get to the point, Gallotti. What happened?"

"Let me tell you. Late yesterday afternoon, he came up to me as I was leaving NGI on Piazza Marina and told me he had something urgent he needed to talk to me about. I was quite surprised at his tone because he's a very calm person. I assumed he'd gotten into some trouble, so I agreed. I went back inside and told the watchman I would lock up myself, and Francesco came in with me. The look on his face was frightening, believe me. As soon as we got into my office, he burst into floods of tears. And he told me that . . . that . . ." He passes his hand over his forehead again. His fingers are shaking.

"Holy Mother of God, you seem to be telling me a serial novel. What happened?" Angrily, Ignazio pushes the cup away. The crumbs spread all around, while Giovanna, who up to now has remained motionless, lifts her head and stares at Gallotti.

The man swallows and raises his hands to his face. "By the end of the month Credito Mobiliare will close all its branches. In the next few days, it's going to declare bankruptcy."

Ignazio lifts his hands to his mouth, as if to stifle a scream. "What? Bankruptcy?" he says, in an almost plaintive tone.

Giovanna, startled, looks first at her son, then at Gallotti. Bankruptcy? What does that have to do with them?

"It's all the fault of that megalomaniac Giacinto Frascara!" Gallotti almost yells, leaping to his feet. "Who right now, in fact, wants to hand in his resignation as managing director because he's scared. And what will he say to the poor people he's ruining? It was he who wanted to expand operations, because he decided to make Credito Mobiliare the biggest bank of them all. Francesco told me there's a rumor that's been going around for a while that they'd started to turn down loans because they lacked liquidity, but nobody ever imagined that the crisis was as serious as that. Frascara has gone and talked to everyone, from Giolitti to Gagliardo, the minister of finance, and even tried to convince the National Bank . . . But the problem is, there's no more money. If it goes well, he'll obtain a moratorium, but nothing more."

Ignazio also gets to his feet, but slowly, almost as if fearing that his legs won't support him, and looks around. Suddenly, this room with its heavy mahogany furniture, in neo-Renaissance style, which he's known since his childhood, seems to him an unknown place. He goes to his mother, who's now staring at him in fright, and strokes her cheek. Then he goes to the window. "The branch . . . I had them put their offices next to mine . . ." he murmurs, and his voice quivers and breaks. "Right next door, literally. People deposited their money there because, even though the sign said Credito Mobiliare, they were our offices. I did hear some worrying rumors, with all the dirty tricks people were getting up to in Rome. But I never imagined they were so exposed. I always told myself we weren't particularly involved. And now . . ." He passes a hand over his face. "People trusted our name, because we're the Florios. Except that we've also been had. And I even invested in Credito Mobiliare, thinking it was sound."

The silence that follows is as icy as a winter wind. *And that's what it is*, Ignazio thinks.

Almost as if in response to this thought, there's a sudden violent downpour of rain. The shutters creak, the doors slam. The servants hasten to close the shutters, but it's too late, the cold has entered the room.

Everything seems to creak around him.

Giovanna turns and gestures to the servants. Nino nods, orders them all out, and closes the door behind him. "So now people will think it's the Florios who are stealing money and will withdraw their deposits from our bank, too, even though we've had nothing to do with this." Giovanna's voice is sharp and clear. She strokes the table-cloth, which she herself embroidered years ago. "That's how it is."

Gallotti sits down again slowly, looking at her in surprise. He nods. He would never have imagined that Donna Giovanna Florio would know quite so much about how business works.

Ignazio, meanwhile, is pacing up and down the room, staring into space. "I can't allow our name to be dragged through the mud because of these people who had to eat even the nails off their walls. Why should the just pay for the sinner?" He rubs his eyes, as if trying to wake from a bad dream. He goes back to his chair and hits the table with his open hand. The silverware and the Limoges porcelain bounce. "Those wretches! I was told not to give them too much rope, that I was making a mistake, but how could I know? Who could have known?"

Gallotti looks at him and shakes his head. *Apparently, everyone knew*, he would like to reply. But he can't. There would be no point, not now.

Ignazio covers his face with his hands. "What now?" he asks. "What should I do?"

The sole response he gets is silence, broken only by the sounds of the firewood crackling in the hearth and the rain beating on the windows.

Giovanna is breathing rapidly, Ignazio almost panting.

Gallotti gets to his feet with a squeak of his chair on the floor. Then he runs his hand through his hair. "Don Ignazio, if you'll allow me, I'd like to pay a visit to a couple of friends who might know something more," he says, embarrassed. "That way, we might be able to figure out how much time we have."

Ignazio looks up and nods: yes, he can go. He doesn't have the strength to speak. Gallotti opens his hands, resigned, then bows briefly to Giovanna.

She thanks him and asks him to get any news to them as soon as possible, but she remains motionless until the door has closed behind him. Then she leaps to her feet, seizes her son by the arm, and shakes him.

"Enough now. Don't be afraid," she says in a peremptory tone. "Go to Banco Florio right away. Speak with the staff, calculate the damage. These are their accounts, not ours; see if we have any debts with them, and for how much. See everything for yourself, with your own eyes." She pauses and leans toward him. "This is what your father would have done," she concludes. It isn't a reproach, it's a plea, an appeal to his pride. "Get rid of that beaten-dog expression. We're Florios, and that's all that matters."

Ignazio takes a deep breath. Leaning on the table for support, he gets to his feet. Giovanna lets go of him when she sees that the panic has finally faded and he's regained his self-control. Only then does she allow herself a slight smile. "All right, Mamma," he replies. "But if Franca . . ."

Giovanna nods and gives him an encouraging look. "I'll send for you, yes. Don't worry."

When the door closes behind her son, Giovanna slumps back onto her chair. She thinks about *her* Ignazio. With him, none of this would have happened, she's sure of it. Her eyes fill with tears, because now more than ever she misses his strong embrace, his calm, cold gaze.

"What are we going to do, *cori meo?*" she asks, turning her face to the window. "What are we going to do?"

౨

Credito Mobiliare closes its branches on November 29, 1893.

A few days earlier, Franca gives birth.

To Giovannuzza.

A girl.

Part One: Sea

(September 1868 to June 1874)

It has been seven years since, on March 17, 1861, the birth of the Kingdom of Italy, with Victor Emmanuel II as its sovereign, was proclaimed in Parliament. The elections of the first united parliament were held in January (only around four hundred thousand out of the twenty-two million inhabitants were entitled to vote) and witnessed the triumph of the Historical Right, chiefly made up of landowners and industrialists and inclined toward heavy taxation, considered necessary to repay the debts accumulated by Italy's unification. What is especially resented is the so-called grinding tax (January 1, 1869) on bread and cereals, which directly affects the poor and triggers protests, some very violent. Although some politicians consider it a "medieval-style levy, a Bourbon and feudal era tax," it will remain in force until 1884. Moreover, in 1870, determined to impose "economies to the very bone," Finance Minister Quintino Sella puts forward another series of harsh measures.

The end of the Second French Empire (1852–1870) and the beginning of the Third French Republic (1870–1940) have important consequences for Italian history. Having lost the support of France, the Papal States fall on September 20, 1870. After brief shelling, to cries of "Savoy!" Italian troops enter Rome through a breach in Porta Pia, a gate in the Aurelian Walls. On February 3, 1871, Rome becomes the official capital of Italy after Turin (1861–1865) and Florence (1865–1871). On April 21, 1871, the Italian government approves the so-called Law of Guarantees, which ensures the pope's personal sovereignty and his freedom to carry out his spiritual ministry. But Pius IX, who considers himself a "prisoner of the Italian government," rejects this in his encyclical Ubi Nos (May 15, 1871). Furthermore, on September 10, 1874, the Holy See decrees the so-called non expedit, which prohibits Catholics from taking part in Italian politics, a prohibition that is frequently circumvented until it ends in 1919.

The reduction of the deficit, the completion of many important projects in Italy (from the Moncenisio railroad, inaugurated on June 15, 1868, to the Fréjus tunnel, opened on September 17, 1871) and around the world (the Suez Canal is inaugurated on November 17, 1869), as well as the influx of foreign funds, make 1871–1873 a "sizzling triennium" that plays a crucial part in the birth of Italian industry. This leap forward is interrupted in 1873, however, following the financial crisis that affects Europe and the United States; the "great depression," caused by a series of speculations and risky investments, will continue, with its ups and downs, until 1896 and do nothing to help bridge the deep gap between northern and southern Italy—the latter partly disadvantaged by the fact that the large investments in the railroad network in the north are not matched in the south, where the government focuses on developing seafaring.

Part Two: Tonnara
(June 1877 to September 1881)

On March 18, 1876, just two days after the announcement of the balanced budget amendment, the Historical Left comes to power—

Agostino Depretis becomes prime minister on March 25, 1876—formed of middle-class men, inclined toward lower taxes than the Historical Right and firmly determined to modernize Italy. It will rule Italy continuously for twenty years until 1896, with various governments headed by Agostino Depretis, Francesco Crispi, Benedetto Cairoli, and Giovanni Giolitti.

The Historical Left also asserts itself in many Sicilian colleges, but, contrary to electoral promises, the difficult situation in the south remains unchanged. On July 3, 1876, Member of Parliament Romualdo Bonfadini presents the government with a report based on an investigation into conditions in Sicily, which also addresses the Mafia question, described as "the development and perfecting of high-handedness directed to every evil purpose; it is the instinctive, brutal, and self-interested solidarity that, to the detriment of the country and official institutions, unites all those individuals and social tiers that like to make a living not by means of labor, but by violence, deceit, and intimidation." But the report is not divulged in full; in 1877, two young representatives of the Historical Right, Leopoldo Franchetti and Sidney Sonnino, publish an independent inquiry carried out "in the field," entitled "Sicily in 1876," which will highlight in all their seriousness the problems affecting southern Italy, including corruption, influence peddling, the lack of efficient agricultural reform, and, above all, the absence of "a feeling of a superior law for everybody." In 1877, an investigation into agriculture and the conditions of the farming classes is undertaken by a council headed by Senator Stefano Jacini: it is published in fifteen volumes between 1881 and 1886, and highlights the worrying situation of Italian agriculture, its overall underdevelopment, and the poverty of the farmers. But its results are generally ignored by the government.

Victor Emmanuel II dies on January 9, 1878. He is succeeded

by his son, Umberto I, who in 1868 married his cousin, Margherita of Savoy. Deeply conservative in spirit (as is his wife), he nevertheless immediately tries to obtain the favor of the people: as soon as he accedes to the throne, together with his wife and nine-year-old son, Victor Emmanuel, he visits many Italian regions (in Naples, on November 17, 1878, he escapes an assassination attempt by the anarchist Giovanni Passannante) and often travels to locations struck by natural disasters (the 1882 flood in the Veneto, the 1884 cholera epidemic in Naples).

On February 7, 1878, Pope Pius IX dies. Although the new pope, Leo XIII, shows himself to be more open to dialogue, the rift with the Italian state continues to mark the country for a long time.

Part Three: The Olive Tree
(December 1883 to November 1891)

On October 18, 1882, at a banquet hosted by his Stradella constituents, Prime Minister Agostino Depretis gives a speech that relaunches the Trasformismo policy he outlined eight years earlier in another speech, also in Stradella. The dividing line between the right and the left consequently becomes blurred, in favor of what the historian Arturo Colombo describes as "a prudent as well as skillful absorption of men and ideas that belonged to the oppositions." The success of this stance is already evident in the "extended suffrage" (two million out of twenty-nine million people are entitled to vote) that takes place on October 29: Depretis's left doesn't win, and 173 "ministerial" deputies—in other words, deputies not formally attached to a party—are elected to the Chamber. It's the start of a period during which Italian politics is no longer expressed through ideology, but constantly seeks a compromise, based on necessities, favors, and concessions.

In order to overcome her isolation on the international front, and in response to the so-called Slap of Tunis (the French occupation of Tunisia, toward which Italy had colonial intentions), Italy seals a defense pact with Germany and Austria (the Triple Alliance) on May 20, 1882. This expansionist impetus then focuses on Eritrea, first with the acquisition of the Bay of Assab (1882), and second with the occupation of Massawa, but then stops abruptly with the defeat at Dogali (January 26, 1887). After Agostino Depretis dies (July 29, 1887), the new head of state, Francesco Crispi, makes no secret of his imperialistic aims. In the spring of 1889, the Italian army resumes its advance toward Asmara. The Negus, Menelik II, signs the Treaty of Wuchale (May 2, 1889), in which Italy sets herself up as a protector of Abyssinia. Eritrea is declared an "Italian colony" on January 1, 1889, but in October of the same year Menelik contests the interpretation of the Treaty of Wuchale in a letter to King Umberto I. An international scandal ensues, and Crispi is forced to resign.

The entry into the Triple Alliance further aggravates Italy's relationship with France, her principal trading partner. Still in the midst of a "great depression," the Italian government abandons the free trade policy adopted since the days of the Historical Right and, in 1887, raises custom charges on imported goods, in this way intending to protect its budding industry (textiles and steel above all, but also shipping). A true tariff war breaks out, chiefly at the expense of southern Italy, whose constant flow of wine, citrus, and oil exports to France is suddenly interrupted.

On May 15, 1891, Pope Leo XIII issues the encyclical Rerum Novarum, which tackles the "worker question," given that it is "essential to assist the workers without delay and with appropriate measures, since most of them live in dire poverty, unworthy of a human being." By criticizing both liberalism and socialism, the encyclical highlights the charitable spirit of the Church and her right to intervene on the social front.

Part Four: Pearls
(February 1893 to November 1893)

After Prime Minister Crispi resigns (January 31, 1891), he is succeeded first by Antonio Starabba di Rudinì (from Palermo), then, on May 15, 1892, by the Piedmontese Giovanni Giolitti, who will be in power for more than ten years, on and off, between 1892 and 1921. But the Giolitti government is fated to fall on December 15, 1893, following the greatest financial scandal in Italian history.

At the end of the nineteenth century, the Banca Romana is one of six Italian institutions legally authorized to issue banknotes and to extend this issue, within certain limits, beyond what is guaranteed in gold. In 1889, on Crispi's orders, the minister for industry, Francesco Miceli, launches an investigation into the bank's activities and unearths some very serious accounting irregularities, including an excess issue of twenty-five million lire, the irregular printing of banknotes to the value of nine million lire, as well as substantial unofficial financing of entrepreneurs, politicians, and even the king. But the findings of this inquiry aren't made public until December 20, 1892, when they fall into the hands of the Sicilian deputy Napoleone Colajanni, who reads them out during a boisterous session in the Chamber. On January 19, 1893, the governor of the Banca Romana, Bernardo Tanlongo, is arrested, along with the head cashier, Cesare Lazzaroni, charged with embezzlement and falsifying public documents; the two inquiries (parliamentary and judicial) are, however, characterized by gaps and omissions—a flurry of compromising documents mysteriously "disappears"—and accusations that bounce from Giolitti to Crispi. On November 23, a report is read out, drafted by the "Committee of Seven," the Parliament's investigating committee, which brings to light the responsibility of former ministers, deputies, administrators, and journalists. Giolitti is forced to resign, and Francesco Crispi becomes head of state for the third time (December 15, 1893). The trial of Tanlongo and Lazzaroni, however, concludes on July 28, 1894, with a "political" sentence: both men are acquitted.

But the Banca Romana scandal (which will lead to the creation of the Bank of Italy on August 10, 1893) is not the only thing that throws the country into turmoil. In 1891, in a Sicily going through serious difficulties thanks to the economic crisis, and still a hostage to large landowners, the Sicilian Workers' Fasci are created, associations whose aim is to obtain greater social justice. A predominantly urban phenomenon—and therefore considered harmless because similar to mutual aid societies—the Fasci movement acquires national fame when the peasant masses join it: on January 20, 1893, in Caltavuturo (near Palermo), five hundred men and women "occupy" lands that are communal property, "wishing in this way to show that they are collective assets" (*Corriere della Sera*, January 21, 1893), and the carabinieri open fire, killing thirteen people. Demonstrations continue throughout the year, especially from August onward, with strikes and protests in the regions of Palermo, Agrigento, Caltanissetta, and Trapani.

Although very distant, the Banca Romana affair and the question of the Sicilian Fasci play a crucial role in Italian history, as illustrated by this speech by Napoleone Colajanni in the Chamber of Deputies (January 30, 1893): "Over the past few days, I have spoken to you of the banking matter, and I must now briefly speak to you about the painful events in Caltavuturo. Although this isn't immediately evident, the two matters are intimately connected, because the first shows a social struggle taking place high up, among the ruling classes, in order to obtain maximum entitlement, whereas in the events at Caltavuturo, on the contrary, you witness the struggle of the poor to obtain the bare essentials."

A NOTE FROM THE TRANSLATORS

A translator of our acquaintance likes to tell the story of how a client once asked her to translate a short text with the words: "Can you just type this into English for me?" Most readers, we would hope, realize that translation involves more than just "typing" from one language to another. But what they may not be aware of is how much of a translator's work consists of more than finding the best way to express in one language what was originally written in another—how much, in fact, involves *research*.

This is especially true when it comes to historical novels or novels set in particular regions with their own traditional customs and dialects (the issue of dialect was mentioned in the translator's note to the first volume, *The Florios of Sicily*). We need to fully understand what it is that's being described before we can render it in English, and this occasionally requires a certain amount of background reading.

When particular events or people or places are mentioned, we need to find out if there is a widely recognized English name for them. And where technical terms are included (some of which might not be found in standard dictionaries), we need to do a fair amount of research to discover the English equivalents. This saga of the Florios contains a good deal of information about activities as varied as shipping, winemaking, and sulfur mining—each with its own specialized vocabulary and all needing to be researched.

Take tuna fishing, another of the Florios' businesses that features frequently in the books. What is a *tonnara*? What is the *mattanza*? These are just a few of the terms related to this topic that appear in the books. Not only do we have to make sure we grasp the specific processes to which they refer, we then have to decide, in the (frequent) cases where there is no exact English equivalent, whether to find a vague equivalent or use the original Italian and modify the text to make the meaning clear. If we have managed to make the author's work comprehensible, while at the same time conveying her tone and style, then we have done our job as translators—which is a lot more than just "typing"!

Katherine Gregor and Howard Curtis

Here ends Stefania Auci's
The Triumph of the Lions.

The first edition of this book was printed
and bound at LSC Communications in
Harrisonburg, Virginia, March 2024.

A NOTE ON THE TYPE

The text of this novel was set in Adobe Garamond Pro, a typeface designed in 1989 by Robert Slimbach. It's based on two distinctive examples of the French Renaissance style, a Roman type by Claude Garamond (1499–1561) and an italic type by Robert Granjon (1513–1590), and was developed after Slimbach studied the fifteenth-century equipment at the Plantin-Moretus Museum in Antwerp, Belgium. Adobe Garamond Pro is considered to faithfully capture the original Garamond's grace and clarity, and is used extensively in books for its elegance and readability.

HarperVia

An imprint dedicated to publishing international voices,
offering readers a chance to encounter other lives and other
points of view via the language of the imagination.